Last chance for freedom

"You are right to say that we have known difficult times before. We have kept our cause alive when others have predicted its doom. We have given our troops, our stalwarts, reason to keep up the fight, even when men of good reason have declared that it should cease, that they could never defeat the mightiest military power in the world."

He paused, glancing at his coat where it hung from the central tent pole. The coat was blue, with a buff lining and facings. The colours had originated with the Whig party in England, the party that opposed the coercive policies of the king and his government under Lord North. The coat seemed the physical sum of Washington's life.

As a young man he had wanted nothing more than to acquire a commission in the regular army, to wear the red coat of a British officer. He had long since divorced himself from that ancient dream. It no longer seemed to matter, just as he no longer cared that his elder brothers had attended fine English schools and he had not. The embarrassment over his poor colonial education had faded, just as his red coat had become blue.

"We must have a victory this summer," he murmured.

Also by Harold R. Thompson

Empire and Honor

Dudley's Fusiliers

Guns of Sevastopol

Sword of the Mogul

The
End
of the
Tether
A Novel of the Battle of Yorktown

Harold R. Thompson

ZUMAYA YESTERDAYS   AUSTIN TX

2017

THE END OF THE TETHER

© 2017 by Harold R. Thompson

ISBN 978-1-61271-288-8

Cover art and design © April Martinez

"Zumaya Yesterdays" and the phoenix colophon are trademarks of Zumaya Publications LLC, Austin TX. Look for us online at http://www.zumayapublications.com

Library of Congress Cataloging-in-Publication Data

Names: Thompson, Harold (Harold R.) author.
Title: End of the tether : a novel of the battle of Yorktown / Harold R.
    Thompson.
Description: Austin TX : Zumaya Yesterdays, 2017.
Identifiers: LCCN 2016003064 | ISBN 9781612712888 (trade pbk. : alk.
paper)
Subjects: LCSH: Yorktown (Va.)--History--Siege, 1781--Fiction. | United
    States--History--Revolution, 1775-1783--Fiction. | GSAFD: War stories. |
    Historical fiction.
Classification: LCC PR9199.3.T4668 E53 2016 | DDC 813/.54--dc23
LC record available at http://lccn.loc.gov/2016003064

To L, B, & M

[W]e must abandon New York and bring our whole force into Virginia; we then have a stake to fight for and a successful battle may give us America.

— Lord Charles Cornwallis, April 1781

We are at the end of our tether, and now or never our deliverance must come.

— George Washington, April 1781

Part One

MANEUVERS

Chapter 1

The Continental

*J*t was well past three o'clock, and the steamy heat of the Virginia Tidewater country was at its oppressive peak. Sweat pooled under Lieutenant Daniel Brattle's neck stock and heavy wool frock coat. His feet were in swollen agony, threatening to burst through the sides of his shoes; but he kept up with his battalion as it marched in a column of fours, the pounding of wooden field drums and the squealing of fifes driving it forward. He gave himself to the music, to the drums, denying the churning in his guts. Muskets were popping away far in his front, evidence that their advance troops had finally caught the enemy after two days of pursuit.

Success is within our grasp, he thought. *It is certain, unless we throw it away, as we have done before, so many times.*

He took a deep breath to steady himself. His commanding officer, the Marquis de Lafayette, had declared the English general, Lord Charles Cornwallis, was running from them, turning his back on the American rebels in a desperate bid to avoid combat. Daniel knew that was nonsense; but if they pushed Cornwallis up against the James River, they could destroy part of his army. Perhaps all of it.

Daniel's brother Joshua, marching five paces ahead, turned with a grin.

"Still with us, little brother? You look a touch pale."

Daniel shook his head.

"I'm fine. It's these damned shoes of mine."

Joshua nodded. "Push on, then. We have the earl's army just where we want it, and maybe you'll find new shoes soon."

"I am aware of the situation," Daniel snapped. "Please remember that I have served a full day longer in this army than you have."

Joshua stared, then gave him a curt nod.

"True enough." He turned to the soldiers marching closest to him, raising his voice to call, "Push on, boys! We're about to catch half the lobsters still this side of the river, with the other half unable to cross back to help 'em."

"It's lobsters for supper," someone shouted in reply, and a dozen other voices joined in with cries of agreement.

Daniel fought to steady his anger. Joshua had no right to treat him like a child, a boy under his wing who needed encouragement. And in front of the men!

Yet that was how it had been since the beginning, since Daniel's mad rush to enlist in the new Continental Army following the spark of battle at Lexington and Concord, when the Massachusetts militia had exchanged shots with British regulars. Joshua had joined a day later, following their father's advice to "look after your brother." So, Joshua considered himself Daniel's protector, even when Daniel knew he had no need of protection.

He had proven himself time and again, had risen in the ranks until now he marched as an officer in his Massachusetts company of light infantry. It was true Joshua had earned his promotion first, and was senior lieutenant; but that was because he was older. Daniel was as much a seasoned veteran, part of the small core of Washington's army that had served since the New York campaign six years ago.

He adjusted his cap—a black leather dome with a small turned-up brim in the front—and examined the marching company beside him. These were *his* men to train as much as Joshua's, a collection of veterans and new recruits. In appearance, they were typical, the officers and sergeants wearing the new uniform coat of blue-and-buff, the enlisted men marching in fringed hunting shirts of gray linen, some with matching breeches and stockings, others with overalls, still others with buckskin leggings. Most were armed with new smoothbore muskets and bayonets from France, although a few still carried the long-barreled, slow-to-load rifles favoured by the frontiersman.

They will do well, Daniel thought. *They will do well today.*

The column neared the battle front, the crackle of musketry growing louder with every step. Each echoing shot sent a thrill through Daniel's chest, a vibration that traveled outward through his long limbs. Somewhere ahead through the pines, the advance force of Lafayette's second-in-command, Brigadier-General Anthony Wayne, had been battling the delaying tactics of Lord Cornwallis for hours, hoping to force the British to halt, to turn and face them in the open. Daniel's battalion had been sent forward as reinforcement while Lafayette remained behind with a rearguard at Green Spring Farm, where he had made his temporary headquarters.

Daniel trod on a stone, a lance of pain stabbing through the sole of his foot. He stifled a groan but didn't stumble. The forced march had been grueling, the column leaving a wake of stragglers, exhausted men, victims of the heat, broken-down men with bruised, lacerated and bleeding feet. Daniel had endured, although his legs felt like India rubber, a numb contrast to the twin spikes of pain contained in his binding shoes.

The pain is nothing, he told himself. *Ignore it. Keep up. Do not allow the men to see your discomfort. Do not allow your brother to see your weakness.*

The battalion came to a narrow causeway that crossed a swamp, the road made of new corduroy, the split logs still green. Daniel removed his cap and wiped his brow. The swamp lay wide and flat on either side, a mire fed by meandering streams, impassable by either infantry or cavalry. Undulating grass glistened in the high afternoon sun, the intermittent pools shining like polished steel. At the far side of the swamp stood a belt of dark and scrubby pine trees. Within the pines, the fight raged.

Daniel gripped his sword hilt, the wire wrapping slippery under his palm. His father had sent him the sword upon his promotion to officer rank, and he seemed to draw strength from its reassuring presence as another fierce wave of anxiety shook him. He could not abide the slowness of the march, did not want to wait any longer. The enemy was there!

The army had been dodging and chasing Cornwallis for weeks, ever since the English earl had first entered Virginia. Now, here was their chance, the best opportunity for success they had yet encountered. Perhaps this day, July 6, 1781, would be remembered as a great turning point by future generations of independent Americans.

Once past the swamp, the battalion passed through the fragrant pines. The men ducked to avoid low branches that dripped pine tar down over their caps and shoulders. Farther on lay another clearing, a grassy meadow. In its center stood a long line of dark infantry, and Daniel realized he was looking at General Wayne's division. He counted half-a-dozen infantry regiments, a Massachusetts artillery battery in the center, some light cavalry moving about on the far left. He could see no sign of the enemy, no source for the continued musket fire; and for a moment, he worried the British had escaped after all, that this desperate drive would come to nothing.

The battalion wheeled right, stepping off the log road to take up position in the line. The fifes and drums became discordant as they mingled and conflicted with the music from the other regiments. At last, Daniel spied the enemy—a few flashes of red among some bushes, British infantry in extended order. Skirmishers, most likely crack shots selected for the task of rearguard. These were the fellows who had resisted Wayne's advance. Behind them lay another belt of pines, even thicker than the first. That was all.

The battalion halted, changing formation from fours to a line of two ranks. The companies shuffled together to form at intervals on either side of the colour party. The heat seemed to have increased, for within the confines of the meadow there was no refreshing breath of wind. The Congressional and regimental flags hung limp in the still air.

Sweat ran into Daniel's eyes, and he wiped at it with a grimy knuckle, sighing as he took his position in the rear of his company, joining a dispersed third rank of sergeants and officers. He glanced to the right flank, found Joshua, who stood with Captain Putnam, then turned at last to face his front.

The last of the redcoat skirmishers vanished into the dense woods, and the firing died away. The men in front of Daniel grumbled in anger.

"Silence, there!" he barked, and realized at once that he had put too much force into his words. The men were frustrated. They knew that beyond the trees lay the James River, and probably a small enemy detachment still attempting to cross. This is what they had come for, why they had marched all day.

"We should make a general advance," he said, turning to Joshua. "There's not much time. It must be nearly five o'clock."

"Even so, we won't go away empty-handed," Joshua called back. He pointed ahead and a bit to the left. "Look! The lobsters have seen fit to leave us with a little present."

A hundred yards distant, just in front of the tree line, stood a bronze cannon, a six-pounder. It teetered on the edge of the corduroy road, abandoned with its black muzzle facing the Americans.

"There's an easy prize of war, boys!" Daniel cried, hoping to ease some of the tension, the sense of an opportunity gone.

As they watched, American skirmishers, men who had been fighting hard all day, rose from their positions in the long grass and sprinted toward the gun. Others spread out on either side of the road, facing the forest. Daniel gritted his teeth, wanting to go forward with them. There seemed no point in waiting here, standing in this field. The capture of one gun was not the victory he had anticipated.

"Well, we have chased Cornwallis across the James," he murmured. "That is success in itself."

He watched as the skirmishers surrounded the gun, taking hold of its wheels, lifting the heavy oak trail. They began rolling it backward.

There were sudden flashes of movement among the pines, and Daniel caught another glimpse of red. He froze, staring. A company of British infantry suddenly emerged from the woods, marching at quick-step along the corduroy road.

"It seems they haven't all departed," he remarked.

Perhaps the enemy rearguard had reformed for an attempt to rescue the gun. In that case, there would be a fight after all, although it would be a small one, and one-sided. He suddenly chuckled, some of his anger and frustration giving way to excitement. Let them try to take the gun back! Let them try it!

There was more movement within the trees as another British company appeared, then another, then another until an entire battalion had come onto the field. Daniel's laughter died, and he stared in wonder and alarm as a second battalion appeared behind the first.

The American skirmishers had already dropped the trail of the gun and snatched up their muskets as the redcoat skirmishers reappeared, dashing for shelter among the few bushes the meadow provided. A musket cracked, and an American fell.

The two British regiments wheeled left, turning from file into line. Faster than Daniel could have imagined, more battalions were emerging from the pine woods, drums beating and fifes squealing to announce their terrifying presence.

The American skirmishers began to run back toward their main line. Others dropped to the ground to fire at the unexpected threat facing them. Daniel spied the silent figure of General Wayne high on his horse behind the division.

The British line was growing and spreading, becoming a wall of red coats, white crossbelts, and black cocked hats. Daniel swallowed, his throat thick. Within minutes, the British force had grown so wide that it overlapped the Americans on both flanks. It was obvious that here was Lord Cornwallis's entire command. He had not crossed the river at all.

"It was a trap," he muttered, and his heart sank. Cornwallis had led them on a chase, and they had taken the bait.

"Steady, lads," he heard Joshua say.

The British regiment in their immediate front was a unit of Highlanders, men in diced Kilmarnock bonnets and dark belted plaids. The Scottish Highland battalions were the fiercest in the British Army.

Shouted commands at last rose in the close summer air, the voice of Colonel Wyllys, the battalion commander, crying, "Prime and load!" Daniel's men pulled open their cartridge boxes, fumbling for the paper cartridges that could mean life or death, all the while keeping their eyes pinned on the enemy.

Then the drill training took over, each man biting a cartridge open, pouring a pinch of gunpowder into his musket pan, dropping his musket butt to the ground, drawing his ramrod, and thrusting the cartridge and ball home. For one fleeting moment, Daniel felt a burst of admiration that his men would stand and load and not run in the face of such a cunning and dangerous enemy.

The British were still dressing their lines, the battalions in front forming two ranks at open order, with eighteen-inch intervals between every man. The battalions in the second line assumed a denser formation, packing together so that every man touched the elbow of his neighbor.

The American fifes and drums struck up again in a fierce challenge. Daniel listened, realizing with astonishment that the fifes were playing the signal to attack. General Wayne would not run. Perhaps that was why his men called him "Mad Anthony."

A few seconds later they advanced, shortening the distance to bring the enemy within close musket range. The British line drew closer, every man in its ranks staring straight to his front like a statue. Success seemed impossible. Nothing could ever break that wall.

The American line halted less than seventy yards from the enemy. Only a few minutes had passed since the skirmishers had discovered the cannon in the road. Daniel peered into the faces of the Highlanders opposite, saw the sharp tips of their bayonets stab toward him as they raised their muskets, aiming directly into his men.

A white cloud of smoke burst along the enemy front. The sound of a thunderclap followed, and a ball hummed past Daniel's ear. The air filled with the sharp crack of lead balls striking flesh. Daniel glanced quickly toward Joshua, just in time to witness the spray of blood and teeth from Captain Putnam's jaw. The captain's hand came up to the wound as his body pitched to the grass. His sword spun away from him.

Daniel looked down as the captain writhed on the ground, blood pouring from his mouth. Time seemed to stand still, the men around him moving slowly, as if in a dream. He could smell the grass, the swamp to their rear, the sharpness of the pines...

Joshua's raised voice broke the spell, bringing him back to his duty.

"Make ready!" Joshua shouted.

There followed a metallic rattling as his men cocked their muskets.

Joshua cried, "Take aim!"

The men aimed.

Joshua paused, then shouted, "Fire!"

A volley blasted from the company, smoke jetting outward. At once, the men reloaded, not waiting to see the effect of their fire; and now other companies had joined the fight, trading volleys with their opponents in the meadow. Sulfurous smoke began to settle in the space between the combatants, a white haze that turned the British into pale apparitions.

"We will fight," Daniel muttered as he drew his sword.

They had been surprised, but General Wayne believed in his men enough to send them against superior numbers of trained troops. Daniel listened to the commands of the colonel, and those of his brother, as the volleys thundered. The churning in his stomach and the pain in his feet were both forgotten. In front of him, men fell, bleeding and wounded.

His hopes for victory had been dispersed, blasted away, but they would fight, for there was no alternative. They would fight as they had fought for so many years, in situations just as desperate. They would fight as they always did, although Daniel knew in his heart they would lose this day.

Chapter 2

The Redcoat

Smoke roiled in dense clouds, the air shattered by flying missiles, but Sergeant Tom Martin paid no mind to the chaos of battle. He marched with his regiment, the 1st Light Infantry Battalion, as they left the concealment of the woods, and kept his eye on the men in his company, ensuring they did their duty.

I was born for this, he thought, as he had thought so many times since taking the King's shilling.

The approach of battle always produced in him a strange calm. He had stood without fidgeting as they waited within the trees, preparing to spring their trap; and he had only smiled when he saw the army of Lafayette standing in stupefaction, pinned with its back to the swamp. When, in their panic, the enemy had attacked rather than withdrawn, Tom had felt no shock, no surprise. Perhaps to attack was the best course open to the rebels; he neither knew nor cared.

He moved to the right of his company and dressed the line, shouting, "Dress to the right at open order! Dress!" The men reacted as on the parade ground, just as they should. They were professionals, British regulars. Tom felt they could withstand anything, and this mad enemy charge would not raise even a single hair on a single man's neck.

He faced his front. A volley thundered on his left, then another as, one by one, the British regiments opened fire; his left ear went numb from the concussion. Through a hollow ringing, as if from a long distance, he heard men and horses screaming in pain. It was a chilling sound, but one he had grown accustomed to long ago; and he maintained his steadiness, his example to the others.

His regiment was positioned on the extreme right of the British line, and they faced nothing but empty meadow. With no one to fight, they stood still, a wall of men with shouldered arms. It was their duty to wait as the volley fire merged into a single unending crackle of musketry, now and then punctuated by the deeper-toned thump of a field gun.

The wait was not a long one.

"Battalion will advance," the Regimental Sergeant-Major suddenly cried, his high-pitched voice clear above the din. Tom gripped his beloved fusil, his short light-infantry musket, preparing himself for the next command in the sequence. It soon came, the sergeant-major bellowing, "Quick...*march!*"

The battalion stepped off, moving at the new quick-step of one hundred-and-eight beats per minute. Under the sergeant-major's directions, their line wheeled slightly left toward the enemy's left flank. Tom caught a glimpse of horsemen—American dragoons, by the look of them—looming from the smoke then turning and withdrawing into the next belt of pine trees. He gritted his teeth, stifling a small cheer that burst from his lips as a grunt. The American dragoons had run without firing a shot, leaving the entire rebel flank exposed.

"Battalion," the sergeant-major shouted, "charge...bayonets!"

The men in the front rank swept their muskets down, the golden light of late afternoon rippling along the ridge of steel. Tom held his own weapon at the charge and cried, "Steady, lads! Steady!" He would not have anyone rush forward, breaking the alignment.

The distance compressed to fifty yards, then forty. A few American muskets jetted smoke in their direction, a scattering of rebels firing from their line at an oblique angle. A single rebel broke ranks, turning and running. Another followed, then another. The rest held their ground, edging back, trying to refuse their line to meet the new threat.

"Steady, lads!" Tom repeated. "Wait for the word!"

It was then the word came, from Colonel Abercrombie himself, leaning forward in his saddle and pointing with his sword. Tom heard the long-drawn-out cry to charge, a cry that let loose the fury and tension of battle. As one, the 1st Light Infantry leapt forward with their sister regiment, the 2nd Light Infantry, in close support on their left.

Tom ran on the right of his company, screaming with the rest as his feet pounded the grassy turf. He leapt a stunted pine then dodged the body of a wounded man in a hunting shirt. Nothing could stop him. He was a sergeant in the British Army. He was a redcoat. His enemies derided him as a Bloody-back, a lobster; but his company had served in the battles in the north and in the south, and they were unbeaten in the field from Brooklyn Heights to

Brandywine, Camden to Guildford. They would remain unbeaten after today.

Tom had lost friends and comrades in those battles. He had lost them at the hands of the rebels. He was determined to see that they had not died in vain, to be buried here in this increasingly foreign continent without anything to show for their ultimate sacrifice. He screamed and charged on behalf of those dead men, and for the comrades who charged with him.

The enemy did not wait to meet the charge. The American ranks disintegrated. A few brave souls lingered, making their individual stands for pride or patriotism; but most fled back through the trees. The British light infantry stormed after them.

Tom darted between the thick pine trunks. His shirt was soaked with sweat under his short wool jacket, but his breathing came in long even draughts. The battalion had lost its coherence, but they were light infantry and accustomed to a looser formation. Ahead loomed the open ground of the swamp. Americans in gray hunting shirts and blue coats were struggling to cross in ones and twos. Some had sunk in the bog, shrieking in terror as they tried to swim, their legs entangled in weeds or encased in quicksand. A few British muskets boomed as the redcoats chose specific targets.

Tom halted on the edge of the swamp. His comrades milled around, some firing but most just staring, unable to continue the pursuit through the mire and stagnant pools.

From behind them rose the piercing music of the fifes, shaping the call for the battalion to reform and rejoin the fight. The battle still raged. Some of the rebel units were holding, their volleys ringing through the piney woods.

"Right, lads," Tom said, although he was a mere lad himself. "Form up and get ready. We've crushed their flank. Now we'll roll up their line."

Chapter 3

The Continental

*T*he broken regiments intermingled as they made their way through the trees to the causeway. The exchange of musketry had lasted barely fifteen minutes. Daniel's company had fought, men falling with every British volley. Then the Highlanders had advanced. Daniel was certain his men would have stood to meet the kilted soldiers had the company on his left, a company of fresh levees, not turned and fled. Through the smoke, he had sensed the gap, the emptiness, the lack of support. So, they had broken.

At least we are walking, he thought. *Walking and not flying in terror. This is no rout.*

He stared at the burning sky. Powder smoke still drifted in batches, and his sword hung limp in his hand. He stumbled but quickly recovered. Pain seared his right heel, but it seemed meaningless now.

He glanced over his shoulder but did not see the British, just the powder-stained and vacant faces of his fellow patriots, their hats at odd angles, their muskets carried in a variety of poses. Exhausted men.

There was no sign of Joshua.

He halted on the edge of the corduroy road, standing aside to allow the straggling column to move past him, searching the faces of all those who wore regulation blue coats. He recognized several from his regiment, and others from his brigade, still others from more distant units. He was shocked to see General Wayne himself limping along on foot.

A few paces behind the general, his features indistinguishable in the fading light, was a familiar figure, his gait unmistakable.

"Joshua!" Daniel called, raising his sword like a standard, a rallying point.

Joshua glanced in his direction then moved toward him. A slight smile played about his grimy features, but Daniel saw pain there as well. He held his right arm bent against his chest; and when he came to a staggering halt, he reached out to grasp Daniel's shoulder with his left hand, steadying himself.

"Our day has not ended well, eh, little brother?" he said, chuckling. His fingers clutched at Daniel's coat, and beads of sweat stood out on his pale forehead. "We thought we would capture their gun, but we left three six-pounders on the field."

Daniel glanced at his brother's crooked right arm, at the bright blood soaking the blue sleeve.

"You're wounded."

Joshua's face twitched. "I met the service end of a Highland bayonet."

"How bad is it?"

Joshua shook his head, then nodded toward the north, at the line of retreat.

"It doesn't matter. Help me along the causeway."

His left arm slid over Daniel's shoulder, his legs almost buckling. Daniel held him, supporting him until he regained his balance. They began walking in step, picking their way slowly along the edge of the swamp.

"Where is the wound?" Daniel asked. "Don't let the surgeons take your arm, Joshua! You have a right to refuse!"

Joshua was slow to respond, finally murmuring, "It is not my arm. My arm is holding the wound. It is in my chest. I think the bastard missed my vitals, but I feel my strength ebbing. Get me to the farm."

"I will. I'll carry you if I have to!"

They wound between the fugitives and stragglers, past the swamp and into the farmland beyond. When Joshua began to drag his feet, Daniel held him up, pausing for a moment to rest. At last, they reached the shelter of Green Spring Farm, which had once been the home of one of Virginia's first governors and was now a rallying point for the defeated army.

Daniel eased his brother down, placing him on the ground with his back against a stone wall. Joshua closed his eyes. The shadows were long, and Daniel realized the sun had already set. His brother's skin glistened in the light of a few standing torches, and strands of blond hair were plastered to his forehead with sweat. His arm had dropped to his side, and Daniel saw the wound, an ugly wet rent four inches below the collarbone.

Daniel stared about him. Injured already filled the yard, lying in rows on the soft ground. The surgeons and their mates were moving from one supine figure to another. Daniel waited, wanting to insist on immediate help but understanding that other men were as bad or worse. All had to wait their turn.

When a surgeon finally reached Joshua, Daniel showed him the wound. The man examined it in the light of a candle lantern.

"His chest has been punctured with a bayonet," the surgeon declared, as if revealing some great medical secret. He probed the wound with a blood-stained finger, and Joshua stiffened and moaned. "It runs deep, but his heart is obviously safe, and he has not coughed blood, so I do not think the lung was injured, either. I see no foreign matter, no bits of shirt or coat. I can stitch and bind the injury, but only time and God may heal him. Or they may not."

"Do what you can, sir," Daniel said. "I will look after him from then onward."

The surgeon performed his task, fumbling with his needle and gut. It did not take long. When he had finished, he simply nodded and moved on to the next patient.

Daniel slid down beside his brother. His feet still throbbed. A few spoke in quiet conversation, and he recognized the voices of men from his battalion. They had gathered in this corner of the yard as if drawn together by some unseen force. He met the eye of one of his senior officers, Major Stephen Osborne. The major approached, then knelt at Daniel's side.

"We have nearly a hundred wounded," Osborne announced. "We must leave the worst cases here, under a guard. Wagons have been procured for the others. You must place your brother in one. The army moves in thirty minutes."

"Thirty minutes, sir?" Daniel echoed.

"Aye." Osborne's long face resembled the caricature of a melancholy hound. "We'll be moving on to Bird's Tavern to join General von Steuben's division. There has been no indication that Cornwallis means to pursue, but he may still send Tarleton to harry our retreat."

Daniel nodded at the mention of Tarleton, the hated Tory dragoon commander. He would not be caught by the likes of him, and would never allow his wounded brother to fall into the hands of such an enemy. He pushed to his feet.

The army was formed and ready even before thirty minutes had elapsed. With the help of two lads from his company, Daniel lifted Joshua into a rough wagon that already held about a dozen wounded men. Joshua lay in his blood-soaked shirt and waistcoat, his coat draped over him like a blanket. The wagon jerked as it started rumbling behind its team of oxen toward the road.

Daniel hobbled close behind. The darkness was now complete, and he kept his eyes on the blurred forms that marched in front, the backs of the men in his regiment. Major Osborne's horse was close by, a dark outrider.

Lafayette's army was moving north, back the way it had come.

Daniel reached out to grasp the tailgate, steadying himself. The wagon bucked and jolted with every imperfection in the road. With every jolt, Joshua groaned.

Hours seemed to pass. Daniel shuffled along, dozing, his bruised feet moving of their own volition. Then the wagon lurched, its wheels dropping into a pothole, and through his sleep he again heard Joshua cry out. The sound jarred him awake.

He coughed, rubbing his eyes. To the right of the road, he spied the dim glow of candlelit windows. A house.

"Stop," he told the driver, but his voice was a croak and the man did not hear him. The wagon carried on.

"Stop!" he shouted. "I command you to stop!"

The driver turned, but his face was lost in darkness. Daniel shouted again, and the driver at last tugged the reins and brought his team to a halt.

Daniel pulled the pins to open the tailgate.

"I'm taking you to a house," he said to his brother, uncertain whether Joshua could hear or understand. "I would not have you suffer any longer."

Joshua's eyes opened, and he rolled his head from side to side, gasping, "Every movement is like a knife tearing my chest and shoulder apart."

Daniel turned to the file of soldiers passing the stalled wagon and snapped, "You there! Help me take a wounded man to that farmhouse."

The stern tone of an officer was enough to compel three soldiers to break ranks. As the wagon driver watched in silence, two of the men lifted Joshua, then set him on his feet, his arms draped over their shoulders.

"Mind his injury," Daniel barked. He spied Major Osborne sitting on horseback, watching from the far side of the road, staring over the top of the moving ranks. The major made no move to interfere.

The third man grasped Joshua's ankles, lifting his legs. Together, the soldiers carried him like a large sack of meal, crossing a field toward the glowing lights.

The farmhouse stood within the dark shelter of a grove of elms, a solid structure of fieldstone and mortar. The lower windows were shuttered, the candles glowing from the upper story. As the three men set the wounded officer down, Daniel advanced to the door and beat on it with his fist. Behind him, the army continued to pass with a shuffling of many feet on the darkened highway.

Daniel beat on the door again, this time shouting, "Open up in the name of the Congress! Open up!" His voice had risen to a shriek, and he stood gasping, fist still raised. At last he heard movement, a dull thump, and the door opened a crack. A golden spear of light fell across his sleeve. He saw blood on the cloth. His brother's blood.

He looked away, to the space in the doorway. A woman's face stared out at him. The woman glanced at his sleeve, then turned to where Joshua leaned, ashen, in the arms of the three soldiers.

"My brother is wounded," Daniel said, fighting to keep the edge of hysteria from his voice. "There was a battle...he needs a place to rest."

"Bring him in," the woman said without hesitation.

"Thank you, madam," Daniel said, then almost sobbed as he repeated, "Thank you."

The door opened wide. In the hall stood two women, both young, each wearing only a chemise, shawls over their shoulders, their hair down. The taller one had answered the door, and she held a cocked pistol in her hand. Behind her stood a Negro with a fowling gun. The black man eyed the soldiers with open suspicion as they brought in the wounded officer. Daniel had left his brother's coat in the wagon, and the blood on Joshua's waistcoat and shirt was dark and brown like rust, with a fresh patch of scarlet at its center.

"We heard the army passing in the road," the taller woman said. "You can take him to the study..." She shook her head. "No. There is nowhere to place him. Take him upstairs, if you are able. I'll show you." She turned to the other woman, a wide-eyed girl with golden hair. "Abigail, light a fire in the kitchen, then draw some water."

"I'll fetch the water, Missus," said the man with the gun. "Miss Abigail can get some bandages."

"Very well, Adam." She turned away, took a candle from a sconce on the wall. "Follow me."

Daniel's shoes were loud on the floorboards as he trailed behind the others. They struggled up the stairs, Joshua complaining with every step, then to a room on the left side of the landing. In the room stood a low poster bed with no canopy. On the bed lay two bright quilts and a feather bolster. The woman set her candle in another sconce, placed her pistol on the mantel, then pulled back the quilts. Bits of straw fluttered on the edge of the mattress. The soldiers set Joshua down on the bed. They were not gentle, and he cried out again.

"Be careful, damn you!" Daniel barked. One of the men glared at him with indignation, but another, whom Daniel suddenly noticed was a sergeant, said, "Our apologies, loo-tenant."

Daniel snatched off his cap and ran his fingers through his hair.

"It's all right, Sergeant. You may go. Thank you."

The men nodded to their unknown hostess, then tramped out of the room. Daniel knelt at his brother's side. He sensed the woman standing next to him, felt her warmth.

"Has a doctor seen to the wound?" she asked.

"Yes. It has been stitched and bandaged."

She pointed to the bright fresh blood on Joshua's torn shirt. "Perhaps the stitching has broken. I can see to it. I have some knowledge of these matters."

The younger woman, Abigail, and the Negro, Adam, had returned with a basin of water and a tray. On the tray were scissors and some strips of linen. Daniel found a stool, pulled it toward the bed and sat. He reached for his brother's hand. It was clammy in his grip.

Joshua had said nothing during the journey from the wagon. Now, he turned to look at Daniel and gasped, "The pain is inside, Daniel. In my chest, and my neck."

"The muscles have stiffened," Daniel insisted. "That's all, from the pain."

"No. My nerves are on fire."

The older woman was now cutting away Joshua's waistcoat and shirt, revealing the loosened bandage, the protruding bit of bloody stitch. Joshua ignored her as she worked.

"I fear that bayonet went deep, and I'm done for this time, Daniel."

"Don't say that! Conserve your strength."

"I'll say what I like." Joshua released Daniel's hand and snatched at his sleeve. Trembling, he pulled himself up to stare into his brother's eyes. The woman stepped away, watching but not interfering. "Promise me, Daniel! My life may not be worth a Continental dollar compared with our cause. Promise me that, if I should die, you will not give up the fight! Promise me!"

"I promise!" Daniel insisted. "I promise! But you won't die! The wound isn't serious."

Joshua held his brother's arm for a few more heartbeats, then nodded. He slumped back in the bed.

The woman took the scissors from the tray and said, "I can replace the stitch with ordinary thread, clean the old blood away and dress the wound. Abigail, did you boil the water?"

"There wasn't time!" the girl squeaked.

"It doesn't matter. You and Adam must hold him as I work."

Daniel kept his eyes fixed on the wall as the woman pulled out the torn stitch, then dabbed at the wound with a bit of wet linen. Joshua stiffened, and she said, "There is something here. A piece of cloth."

Joshua grunted, but Adam pressed him down to the bed, saying, "Don't you move one bit." The woman held up a dark scrap of bloody cloth, turning it in the dim light.

"A shred of his coat, perhaps," she said. "Or his shirt."

Daniel clutched at his forehead. The surgeon had missed that.

The woman tossed the scrap on the tray, continued cleaning the wound. Abigail had fetched a sewing box with spools of thread, needles and beeswax as the older woman worked. There was blood on the sheets. Joshua's breathing was heavy, his neck and jaw stiff.

When the wound was stitched and dressed, the woman said, "Our concern now is fever. We will see how he fares tomorrow."

"He will not die," Daniel insisted. "Listen to me, Joshua! If the fever comes, you must hold on!"

There was another stamping of heavy boots on the stairs, then on the floor outside. The door creaked open, and a deep voice said, "Lieutenant Brattle."

Daniel turned at the sound. Major Osborne stood in the doorway. With him was the sergeant who had helped carry Joshua from the wagon. The major's expression was grim as he repeated, "Lieutenant Brattle. Daniel. The army is withdrawing, and you must see to your duty. You must leave your brother here and return to the regiment."

"Leave my brother?" Daniel echoed. "I will not leave him! He is the only brother I have left to me!"

The major bristled, his eyes blazing wide, but then his stance softened just as quickly.

"Daniel, Tarleton's men may come."

"If they were coming they would have been here already. You said there was no pursuit." Daniel was shaking his head. "I cannot leave him. I cannot."

"You must think of your country, sir, and put it above all things."

Daniel rounded on him.

"No, sir! We have done our share, and more. We will come back."

He saw the war of emotions on the major's face, outrage mixed with disappointment, sorrow with sympathy. For a moment, Daniel was ashamed, and wondered if at last he had lost faith in the cause, that this newest defeat, coming so close after high hopes of victory, had been too much, and that something inside him had broken.

He again rubbed his forehead.

"Forgive me, sir. I spoke out of turn. Forgive me."

Osborne cleared his throat. "Perhaps I may obtain permission to allow you to remain for a short spell, to catch the army later."

Daniel just nodded, suddenly unable to speak. He had been a good officer, until now. Had he not?

"Lieutenant, I know that Joshua is the only brother left to you," Major Osborne continued. "I will speak to Colonel Wyllys on your behalf, but you must take care. Though the enemy has crossed over the James, they may return. I would not wish to lose you and Joshua both." He clamped his cap down on his head, nodded to the older woman, who did not look at him, and said, "Madam."

He and the sergeant left the room.

Daniel perched on his stool as Joshua began muttering something unintelligible. The wound was free of the debris the surgeon had somehow missed and bandaged anew. Abigail was stroking Joshua's forehead like a loving sister. His eyes were closed.

Daniel turned to the older woman, who was cleaning her hands with a bit of rag.

"What regiment are you with?" she asked, some wariness in her voice.

"We are with Gimat's Light Infantry Battalion," Daniel said. "With Lafayette's division of the Continental Army."

"The Continental Army," she repeated.

"Yes. Forgive me, ma'am. We have taken advantage of your hospitality, and without introductions. My name is Daniel Brattle, of Boston." He rose to his feet and bowed. "The patient is my brother, Joshua Brattle."

"I am Catherine Seawell," she replied. "That is...Catherine Seawell. This is my younger sister Abigail, and this is Adam..." She nodded to the black man, who stood in the corner, both hands clasped about the muzzle of his gun. "...the retainer of this property. He serves the owner."

"I had assumed that you were the owner. Or your husband."

"My husband is dead, and my cousin is the master of this place, but he is not here." She paused, then added, "My mother was a Virginian by birth, though my sister and I are also come from Boston."

"You astonish me, Miss Seawell." Daniel tried to laugh, but it came out as more of a gasping cough. He took a breath. "How strange that four Bostonians should meet in the Virginia countryside," he added, "and under such strange circumstances."

"Strange, indeed." Catherine turned to her sister and the retainer. "Abigail, you may go and get some sleep. Adam, if you would, watch the door. There may be others about. Perhaps redcoat stragglers. I will stay with our patient."

They left without protest. Daniel kept to his stool. He studied Joshua's pale face, the beads of sweat now glowing orange and yellow in the candlelight. Catherine pulled a wheat-sheave chair to the opposite side of the bed and sat. Joshua clutched his wound and grimaced but kept his eyes firmly shut. His breathing was now even and unlaboured.

"I must extend my thanks again," Daniel said at length. Weariness, stiffness, and pain had begun to flood his limbs. His dark hair had come loose from its ribbon, and stubble covered his chin. He felt wretched and unkempt. "You have shown us great hospitality, great sympathy."

"I could never refuse to help someone in need, Mister Brattle. We will know if your brother is safe in a day or two."

Her voice was soft. He looked at her. So concerned was he for his brother that he had not actually seen her, and now he noticed her smooth skin, her perfect teeth. She had a long English face, a noble nose. She was not much older than he, perhaps younger. The shawl had fallen away to reveal her long smooth neck. Her hair seemed to have an auburn sheen, although in the light from the candle he could not be certain of any colour. He thought that she was beautiful, and for some reason that filled him with sadness. At once, grief and worry overcame him, and he held his head with one hand and began to repeat in an anguished murmur, "Oh, God, oh, God, my brother..."

She came to kneel beside him, cradling his head. He did not know her, but she let him weep into her breast like a child.

Chapter 4

The General

General George Washington stood under the tent awning, a gold locket clutched in one hand. He had removed his coat and waistcoat, but found no relief from the summer heat. His personal headquarters colour, his flag as Commander-in-Chief, hung limp against the linen canvas wall to his left. The flag was a field of deep blue with thirteen white stars, each with six slender points, now obscured within the silk folds: hidden, the general realized, like the thirteen states they represented. Unrevealed to the world.

Behind him, inside the shade of the large oval marquee tent, his chief aide and military secretary, Lieutenant Colonel Tench Tilghman, cleared his throat for the second time, perhaps impatient for Washington to continue his dictation. The general had been composing a letter to the youthful Marquis de Lafayette, his commander in the south; but Washington was in no rush. He fingered the gold locket, stroking its smooth surface. Inside was a tiny likeness of Martha, his wife. The locket was a memento of home, of Mount Vernon. Home was never far from his thoughts.

"General?" Tilghman said. "Are you well, sir?"

Washington turned.

"Forgive me, I was lost in thought. I find a forked path lies before us."

Tilghman sat at the general's camp desk, a quill poised in his right hand. A faint smile touched his lips.

"We are well versed in choosing our paths, sir," he said.

"And so, we must choose again." Washington entered the tent and folded his hands behind his back. "Write this. 'You must follow Cornwallis closely, but do not allow him to bring you to open battle. Watch his movements and report them to me.' That is all."

The aide's quill scratched across the page. When he was done, he passed it to Washington. The general hung the locket to its usual place around his neck, then took the quill and signed the bottom of the paper with his customary scrawl.

"I have great faith in our Lafayette," he stated. "It is men such as he who will see that we succeed in our struggle."

"His constancy reflects your own, sir," Tilghman said.

"And yours." Washington did not take his aide's comment for idle flattery, for Tilghman was bound to the cause of independence. His father had sided with the Tories, and two of his brothers were serving with the redcoats. He had given much, had lost family and friends, and the cause was all he had left.

His fate is my hands, the general thought. *My failure, or my success, will be his as well.*

He glanced up as Billy Lee, his mulatto manservant, entered with a silver tray bearing a coffee pot and two china cups with saucers. Hot coffee in this heat seemed an odd choice, but sometimes it helped. Washington knew to trust Billy in these things, for he was a servant but also a friend.

"Thank you, Billy," Washington said as Billy placed the tray on a scissor-legged camp table. Billy nodded, smiling one of his enigmatic smiles then bowing and ducking out of the tent. The general watched him go. Billy *was* a friend, yes, but also a slave. Slavery was another enigma, a problem so huge it seemed a mountain to climb, a mountain that would have to wait until after the war, after they had achieved success.

Washington turned back to Tilghman, but for a moment he could not speak. All he could see now were many such mountains—his problems and his failures, military and otherwise. He was the Commander-In-Chief, and thus responsible for this stalemate in the north, and for two years of British victories in the Carolinas and Georgia. Lord Charles Cornwallis's destruction of the American army of General Gates at Camden. Savannah and Charleston both in enemy hands, all attempts to reclaim them disasters.

Meanwhile, morale in the ranks had plummeted, although he had done all he could to sustain it. In January, a group of Pennsylvania regiments had mutinied, demanding better rations and back pay. Desertions, each a small betrayal, had been common. Then there had been the shock of Benedict Arnold's treason last autumn. Arnold had been Washington's favorite general, a fighter, the best tactical leader in the army. And he had been a friend.

"It is important that Lafayette maintain his game of cat-and-mouse," he said. "Cornwallis is waging the only active campaign of the war for the moment."

He touched a finger to his jaw, pressing to thwart a sudden stab of pain. A toothache, a tiny insult in trying times. Such aches had plagued him for years, but he always refused to have the infected tooth pulled. One day he would have nothing left but his gums, but he had no wish to hasten that moment.

"A minor inconvenience," he muttered. The pain was something to accept, something to rise above, just as he knew he must accept and rise above the obstacles he now faced.

He began to pace the floor of the tent.

"You are right to say that we have known difficult times before. We have kept our cause alive when others have predicted its doom. We have given our troops, our stalwarts, reason to keep up the fight, even when men of good reason have declared that it should cease, that they could never defeat the mightiest military power in the world."

He paused, glancing at his coat where it hung from the central tent pole. The coat was blue, with a buff lining and facings. The colours had originated with the Whig party in England, the party that opposed the coercive policies of the king and his government under Lord North. The coat seemed the physical sum of Washington's life.

As a young man he had wanted nothing more than to acquire a commission in the regular army, to wear the red coat of a British officer. He had long since divorced himself from that ancient dream. It no longer seemed to matter, just as he no longer cared that his elder brothers had attended fine English schools and he had not. The embarrassment over his poor colonial education had faded, just as his red coat had become blue.

"We must have a victory this summer," he murmured.

"What was that, sir?" Tilghman asked, rising from his seat.

"A victory," the general repeated. "Now more than at any time. If we do not achieve something soon, I do not believe I can hold this army together through another winter."

Tilghman's face was bleak.

"We have a great many wants just now, sir. Meat and flour, arms, horses, wagons, some sort of permanent transport corps. Leather for shoes, broadcloth for new uniforms. Gunpowder...even fresh recruits to make up for losses caused by mutinies and desertions."

"Yes, yes. My desk is littered with letters from officers, demanding all of these things. And others complaining about their lack of promotion. Promotion! When our country itself nears dissolution."

Tilghman nodded. "It is an army, General."

"An army which needs a success, however small."

He moved to the camp desk, shuffled through the stacks of routine orders that waited for his signature. A victory, like his first small triumph at Trenton, would raise the morale of the troops, would give the people another reason to support the war, to justify the presence of the soldiers who pilfered the produce of their farms and slept in their fields. It would give the people a reason to have faith.

"The coming operation will require the support of our allies, the French," he said. "I would make use of their navy."

"You still seek to convince them of your plan to assault New York?"

"That is my intention." He found the paper he sought, a copy of the dispatch he had received more than three years ago when the forces of the British general Johnny Burgoyne had surrendered to the Continentals at Saratoga. That victory had convinced the French to enter the war on the American side, bringing ships, troops, and much needed supplies.

Washington knew the French simply wished to redress their losses in the last war, but he had at once dismissed their motives as irrelevant. And it was true that many of the French officers, men like Lafayette, had also come to grasp and love the American ideals of liberty.

So far, French and American efforts, such as a costly assault on Savannah, had been dismal failures; but the General liked and trusted the new French commander, the Comte de Rochambeau. They had met again last month, at Newport, Rhode Island. Rochambeau had made it clear that he would subordinate himself to American command, that his role would be to offer advice. In that, he had shown respect, a trait Washington believed essential in any useful ally. Without it he would never have agreed to cooperate.

The generals had then discussed plans for an offensive operation. Washington had advanced his notion to assault New York, the scene of his greatest defeat in 1776, but Rochambeau had not agreed. The help of the navy was paramount, the Frenchman had explained, and the navy did not favour New York. The French Admiral de Grasse, would come from the West Indies to aid in an attack, would join his forces with Admiral de Barras's fleet at Newport; but in his letters, he insisted the waters off Sandy Hook were too shallow. Both de Grasse and Rochambeau preferred to stage an operation somewhere in Chesapeake Bay. The bay offered easily navigable waters and a variety of possible campaigns.

Washington had acknowledged the merits of Rochambeau's reasoning, but feared the French would succumb to fever in the heat of the south. His New England troops also hated the region for its climate, poisonous snakes, bothersome mosquitoes. And the main enemy force, under General Clinton, was in New York. It irked him the French could not see that an attack there was more logical.

The Newport meeting had ended without resolution. Rochambeau's only promise had been to move his forces to join the Continentals here at Peekskill.

"When the Comte de Rochambeau arrives," he said now, "there will be no time for further disagreement. The people are weary of the long war, its lack of conclusion. These next few months are crucial. The Emperor and Empress of Russia have offered to mediate a settlement between America and Britain, but any such mediation will only lead to a compromise with which no one will be pleased. It will not allow for American independence."

He knew he must bring the enemy to battle somewhere.

Tilghman had folded and sealed the letter to General Lafayette, then set it aside on the desk. Washington stared at it. If there was to be an operation in the Chesapeake, one option was to strike at Cornwallis in Virginia. For now, Lafayette would watch him, just as Washington would watch General Clinton in New York.

New York or the Chesapeake, the general mused, once again choosing to ignore a stab of pain in his jaw. That was the choice before him now.

Chapter 5

The Continental

$\mathcal{D}$aniel sat on the cool stone steps, stockings off, giving some relief to his blistered feet. Dappled sunlight, filtered through the elms that bordered the carriage lane, played across the chafed flesh, the red welts his shoes had left. He wriggled his toes.

Behind him, the stone farmhouse was solid, a sheltered island. He could not have chosen a better place for his brother to recuperate. There was a milk cow in the barn, chickens and geese in the yard. The foraging armies had not touched this place.

He considered his resentment of his brother's protectiveness just before the battle, but the memory brought only shame. His anger had been petty, frivolous. And to think that, only hours later, he had faced the prospect of Joshua's death.

On the first morning after their arrival, Joshua had risen from his bed and walked about the room, insisting that he was all but recovered. He had even managed to keep down a bit of broth. But as the day stretched into afternoon, fever had flared, alternating bouts of fire and ice rolling over him in waves. At times the symptoms abruptly ceased, the fever seeming to break, and in one of his lucid moments, he declared, "I think I was hasty in my pronouncement. I feel as if I might live after all."

Then the fever would rise again, and he would sink into delirium, his sweat soaking the sheets, quilts, even the straw of the mattress. He had bellowed the words to soldier's songs that made Daniel blush when Catherine was present. He had told amusing stories from start to finish, unaware of his audience. He had conversed with dead comrades. He had muttered, laughed, and cried out at imagined terrors.

Daniel had stayed at his brother's side throughout the night, and Catherine had tended to their every need. She had washed the wound and changed the bandages, had bathed the sweat from Joshua's forehead. Her only regret, she had said, was that she had no salt herring in the larder, for she claimed it was the cure for fever.

In the end, Joshua had not needed any salt herring, for with the first gray of dawn, he became quiet. Catherine had at last announced, "The crisis seems past, the fever broken for good. Now perhaps your brother can rest."

Joshua lay on his back, his features calm as he slept.

"You believe he will live?" Daniel asked, his voice hoarse although he had barely spoken a word for hours.

"He will. The fever was the danger. His wound is in the flesh only and shows no sign of corruption. He must have a strong constitution."

"He always did. A will, has my brother."

Daniel had only then risen from his stool, staggering from the sickroom and downstairs to the front door. He emerged into the sunlight to stare about him, to truly inspect his surroundings.

The sun was well up. He gazed across an untended field, overgrown with tangled weeds and clumps of grass. Still, the field was alive, and beautiful, and his brother would live.

The door swung open, and Catherine was beside him on the step. She was dressed in a simple cream-coloured gown with narrow blue stripes, its bodice without a stomacher and fastened with pins, and a deep-blue petticoat. A white neck handkerchief covered her shoulders, and a white cotton cap with a pleated ruffle around its edge covered her hair.

"I have examined your brother's wound again," she said, "and it still lacks evidence of corruption. Maybe he will wake up soon, though I expect he will not regain his strength for many weeks."

"He's still sleeping?"

"Yes." Her slender fingers lightly brushing his bloodstained sleeve. "There are still some clothes here that belonged to my cousin. They may suit you. Give me your uniform, and I will have Abigail launder and mend it."

He swallowed, his throat thickening with gratitude.

"We came to you as strangers, and you have shown us nothing but kindness. I would have it that more citizens of this country were the same. Soldiers are often not welcome, are not trusted. You did not hesitate to take us in. You are truly God's servants, ma'am."

A smile flashed across her face. She added, in a lower voice, "My late husband was of your size. His clothing would have fit you well."

He grimaced, never comfortable in the presence of a stranger's misfortune.

"Your husband was killed?"

She kept her attention on his sleeve.

"Almost three years ago."

"He was a good patriot." His left hand fidgeted with the tail of his coat. "So many good men have died for their country these last years."

She met his eye. He saw her sorrow, and something else, something more immediate. Fear, he decided. Fear of him. She started to back away.

"Have I said something to offend you?" he asked, confused, mentally retracing his words.

She had backed into the doorway. "My husband did die for his country, sir. I should never have spoken of him." Her skin had become flushed, and she was biting her lip. She hovered in the doorway for a few more seconds, then turned and entered the house.

He grabbed his stockings and shoes and followed, wishing to counter his error, whatever it might have been. She was climbing the stairs, likely returning to Joshua's room. He closed the distance, and they entered together.

Although still a place of sickness, the room seemed almost cheery. Emerald paint covered the upper half of the walls, the lower portion clad in white wainscoting. A pastoral scene in a carved frame hung above the mantel. Sunlight from the east-facing windows cast a golden fan across the bed quilts and a section of floor. Joshua lay with his head to one side.

Catherine paused at the foot of the bed, gazing down at her patient. For the moment at a loss for words, Daniel continued past her to his stool and sat.

"How did you come to be in Virginia, Mrs. Seawell?" he asked at length, deliberately opening a new line of conversation. He spoke in a whisper to avoid waking Joshua.

She did not look at him.

"I suspect the same reason as you, Mister Brattle."

"The war brought me here. Orders brought me here. It was no choice of mine." He sighed and repeated, "I am sorry for your loss. We have all known much tragedy in the pursuit of our great project."

He trailed off, knowing his words must seem empty, the stuff of speeches.

"You should not sleep in this room again," she said. "There is an empty chamber next door. Abigail and I share the third chamber."

"Soldiers are able to sleep most anywhere. Even a hard floor." He narrowed his eyes, a spark of memory suddenly kindling in his brain. "Are you indeed *Mrs.* Seawell? Was that your husband's name? What regiment was he with?"

She smoothed her apron.

"You would not know it, I think."

"I am familiar with the names of many regiments in the Continental Army. Or was he with a state regiment? Or the militia?"

"You are full of questions, Mister Brattle!"

"It's just that I know the name, ma'am." He hesitated. "Edmund Seawell is a well-known Boston lawyer. And a well-known Tory."

She answered him with silence. Daniel waited, but he had already decided she must be a member of this same family. A Tory family.

"Your husband fought in the Provincial Corps," he said. "In a Tory regiment. That is why you are reluctant to tell me."

"You say that like an accusation, sir," she snapped. "Yes, my husband was an officer in a Loyalist regiment. Not *Tory*, sir. *Loyalist*. His name was not Seawell, but Checklee, a name I mistakenly did not give as my own. I shared that name for so short a time, I hardly associate it with myself. Edmund Seawell is my father, and as fine a citizen as any in the land."

Daniel nodded. He realized his statement had, indeed, been an accusation, as she had discerned correctly. But whether she was a Tory herself was another matter. He could not imagine a Tory would flee from Massachusetts to Virginia, nor work so hard to save the life of a patriot soldier.

"I did not mean to insult your family," he ventured, "but I have been fighting Tories for a great while now. We have all been forced to struggle with divisions among friends and relations. All of us."

"I understand," she murmured, her anger abating. She looked away, to the window. "Abigail is preparing a meal," she remarked with forced lightness. "Adam has maintained a kitchen garden, and there are some early vegetables. Shall you have something? All you have eaten is plain broth."

Daniel was reluctant to abandon the conversation, but he suddenly realized he was very hungry—and very tired.

"I appreciate the offer, ma'am."

She nodded. "Very well."

She glided past him too quickly, as if fleeing. She made very little sound as she descended the stairs.

Daniel rested a hand on Joshua's arm, questions flooding his thoughts. He wondered whether Catherine was an exile, perhaps one who had not shared her family's politics. Maybe circumstances and disagreements had forced her to leave Boston and come to Virginia to be with her cousin.

A light footfall sounded behind him. He turned, but it was Abigail who entered the room. She was dressed much like her sister, her gown a plain brown, her petticoat cream with brown stripes. She moved with her thin shoulders hunched, her eyes downcast.

She is a funny little thing, Daniel thought. *Just an odd slip of a girl, still very much a child.*

"I will watch Mister Joshua," she said in a tiny voice, "if you would care to take your meal in the kitchen rather than here."

He nodded at her, knowing he would so prefer, that he would welcome fresh surroundings now that Joshua was out of danger.

"Thank you, Abigail."

He did not bother with his stockings and shoes, but descended the stairs with his lower legs and feet still bare, going the length of the hall to the back door. From there, he followed a flagstone walk, scattering a few pecking hens as he crossed the yard, then paused in the kitchen doorway, one hand pressing the brick wall as he peered into the dim interior. His eyes adjusted slowly.

The kitchen was a single large room with a high ceiling. To his left, the stone fireplace and adjacent bread oven occupied all of one wall. Catherine stood over the hearth fire, tending to a large iron cauldron hanging from the lug pole. She had donned an apron and was stirring the cauldron's contents with an iron spoon.

"You see, Mister Brattle," she said, "despite the modest comfort in which I was raised, we dine in the kitchen like the servants. We have lost much of what we had, but we still have plenty. I would offer you a cured ham, or turtle soup, but this simple stew will have to do."

Her words seemed to confirm his suspicion of exile. He stepped into the room, quickly taking in its contents. Cupboards and shelves stood against the walls between tall windows, and to his right was a wide hutch filled with pewter dishes. Two tables sat in the middle of the room, one parallel to the fireplace, the other branching away from the first at a right angle. Utensils covered the first table—wooden bowls, basins, a jar of long spoons, a tin colander, and a wire sieve.

Catherine had set pewter spoons and napkins on the dark wooden surface of the second table. Daniel found a place on the bench as she ladled out stuff from the cauldron. When she placed a steaming bowl in front of him, the inviting aromas of pork and cabbage rose to his nostrils. There was hard bread on a plate, and cheese. Herbs hung from the ceiling beams, adding their fragrance to that of the food.

"I've eaten plenty of stew of late," he said. "I presume yours compares favourably."

He took his spoon, dipped it in the bowl, raised it to his mouth to test the heat. Catherine sat opposite and did the same. He watched her for a moment, studied the smooth line of her nose, the pout of her lips.

"Perhaps you fear that I may judge you harshly," he said, "and yet we share a similar experience."

"How so?" she asked, her eyes glinting in the dim light.

He paused, for he was still ashamed of what he was to tell her, still baffled by the actions of his eldest brother Benjamin.

"My father is a wool merchant, and prosperous, fully in favour of independence. Yet my eldest brother is an outspoken Tory. Joshua and I rarely mention his name. As if he is…as if he had never been."

Benjamin now lived in New York. Daniel had not seen him since the beginning of the war.

Catherine stopped eating and studied him.

"Thus we have something in common," he added.

"Perhaps," she said. "But your brother has become your enemy. You have made him so. Perhaps in his eyes, you are *his* enemy. I do not believe in making enemies, not within my family, and not within my own country."

He took his napkin and dabbed at his mouth.

"But are you not here because your family and you…disagree?"

"On the matter of independence?" She shook her head. "I do not know if it would be best for America, but my father opposed it, believed a compromise should be reached. He did not agree with the king's policies, but nor did he wish to be ruled by the radicals. To him the Whigs were nothing but a gang of street ruffians, ever ready to cast a brick, or a torch, or to apply a coating of tar and feathers to anyone who raised their voice against them. All in the name of freedom!"

Daniel sighed, for this was a familiar argument.

"These things did occur, true. But my brother and I fight for independence, and *we* are not street ruffians, ma'am. Neither are the men who serve with us, and whom we call comrades. They are merchants, farmers and tradesmen, men devoted to our cause. The ruffians and criminals to which you refer did not last the first year in camp. Such people know no duty beyond that to themselves, while we have suffered for almost six years."

She looked away. "And I, too, have suffered. All of us have, for the radicals—those who called for war—have had their way, and we fight amongst ourselves. Some fight for the king, as did my husband. Some fight against him, as do you. The rest wait to see who shall die next, and who shall come out best." Her voice dropped to almost a whisper. "But it was the radicals who brought this upon us, and it is they whom I despise. Why did reason not prevail? How did we come to this? I have searched for an answer, but I have yet to find it."

She closed her eyes, squeezed them shut, but she could not prevent a single tear from escaping. It rolled halfway down one cheek, and there it hung, suspended. Daniel stared at it in astonishment. He rummaged in his waistcoat pockets, looking for a handkerchief, wishing he had not already used his napkin. He found nothing.

But Catherine used her own napkin, and quickly composed herself.

"It is the war itself that I despise more than anything," she said, her voice soft and even.

Daniel leaned forward on his elbows. They had all lost something. He had lost a brother to politics; he did not think he would ever see Benjamin again, although he would always maintain the hope that one day there could be reconciliation.

"I admit that I am tired of the war," he said, and found truth in the words as he spoke them. He had not understood the depth of his weariness, his frustration with the endless lack of solid gains, the prize that continued to recede from them with every step. He glanced at the herbs hanging from the rafters, at the orderliness of his surroundings. Life continued here, life that was not all marching, camps, sickness, fatigue and death. Was this not what they fought for? To live in comfort and prosperity?

"I could stay here," he added, "leave the war behind me."

He met her eye and held it.

A shadow fell across the open doorway. He turned as Adam entered the kitchen, his stern demeanor unchanged from the first time Daniel had laid eyes on him.

"Missus Catherine," he said, "Mister Joshua awake."

Daniel glanced at Catherine, then put down his spoon. He stood.

"Pray excuse me. I should see to him."

"Of course," Catherine said, nodding. She folded her napkin and placed it on the table.

Daniel left his stew half-finished, brushing past Adam as he fled the kitchen. In the house, he climbed the stairs with a heavy gait. Abigail stood at his appearance when he entered the front bedroom. He ignored her.

Joshua was sitting up, his face pale, his head against the piled bolster. When he saw Daniel, he found his crooked grin.

"Ah, little brother," he murmured, "it's good to see you."

Daniel rushed to the bed and threw his arms around his brother's shoulders.

"Thank God you're safe!"

"No bear hugs," Joshua said. He leaned forward and coughed. "I'm still suffering the result of a Scots bayonet."

Daniel released him, went to his stool and sat.

"But you're safe."

"Maybe I am, if I rest here a while." Joshua coughed again, his hand to his mouth. "You were fortunate to stumble across this house. Or, more truly, *I* was fortunate. I swear I would not have survived in an army hospital tent."

"You remember your ordeal in the wagon?"

"Some of it. But the pain made much of it a blur." He held a hand over the wound. "It still aches, but I can bear it. A dull ache."

Daniel took his brother's hand.

"We will remain here until you regain your strength. We are invited to stay as long as we wish."

"Have you any notion of the army's movements?"

Daniel glanced toward the eastern windows. The imperfect glass distorted the sunlit fields beyond.

"None, save that it is in retreat. Away from here."

The bitterness of his own tone astonished him.

"Maybe they will send someone to inform us," Joshua said. "Or perhaps the enemy will discover us here, a foraging party from Tarleton's dragoons."

"That is the chance we must take. You are not strong enough to move."

"I don't relish being taken prisoner, or being subject to Tarleton's quarter, which is no quarter at all. I will not put you in danger for my sake, Daniel."

Daniel let go of his hand.

"The enemy is gone, Joshua. Crossed the James. This is a haven, a place of peace."

"A place of peace, eh? So, you have become well acquainted with our hostesses?"

"I have." Daniel remembered Abigail, saw that she was busy stitching the hem of some garment, maybe a new apron. "Miss, may I impose upon you to leave me alone with my brother for a moment?"

Her eyes went wide, as if she were horrified with this suggestion, but she said, "Very well, sir."

As she scurried from the room, Daniel remarked casually, "It is the most remarkable thing. They are from Boston."

"From Boston? How did they come to be *here*?"

"I did not ask," Daniel said. He would not tell Joshua the family was Tory, that their father was Edmund Seawell. He stood and moved to the window. He clasped his hands behind him, fingers twisted together.

"Then maybe it *is* providence," Joshua continued, "that we should fall into the care of folks from home so far south. The elder one must be a good woman."

Daniel sighed. "Good? Yes, she is good. A good woman, indeed."

Joshua stirred in his bed, attempting to sit up.

"Something is bothering you. What is it?"

Daniel shook his head. *Maybe this is just simple fatigue*, he thought, *or a whim, a passing fancy. Or maybe I truly have had enough*. He faced his brother.

"I believe our war is over, Joshua."

Joshua smiled and frowned at the same time.

"What do you mean? Surely, there hasn't been a victory somewhere. Something I missed in my stupor?"

"No, Joshua. What I mean to say is that I think we should not go back to the army."

Joshua stared at him, but then his face turned dark, dark as the mouth of a cannon.

"You made a promise to me, little brother. That you would never give up the fight."

"I promised to carry on if you perished, but you did not. Now, it will take you weeks, nay, months to recover fully! There is no point. We have served well—"

"We are not finished!" Joshua cried, pounding the side of his bed, but his anger collapsed into a fit of coughing.

Daniel waited for the fit to subside. When it did, he said, "You do not always know best, Joshua."

Joshua waved one hand, a feeble gesture.

"We will discuss this later. When I am stronger."

⁂

Later in the day, Joshua was able to rise and take a turn in the kitchen yard. He managed to drink a saucer of broth but tired quickly and soon returned to his bed. He and Daniel did not speak.

While Joshua slept, Daniel supped with Catherine and Abigail in the dining room. The meal was simple—leftovers from dinner earlier, corn chowder and a pork pie—but it was superior to what he had grown accustomed to in the army. The room, with its chandelier and wood paneling, the long oak table, was perhaps the finest in which he had even dined.

When they had finished their meal, Abigail cleared the dishware, leaving Daniel and Catherine alone.

"You and your brother have quarreled," she said.

"We have disagreed. We do so often enough. It's a small matter."

"I think perhaps that it is not a small matter."

"You are astute. Or else you have keen ears."

She smiled faintly. "Maybe a bit of both."

He pushed his chair away from the table and crossed his legs.

"It doesn't bother you to play hostess to two rebel soldiers? Two men who may have faced your late husband on the opposite side of the field?"

Her smiled vanished.

"You are my guests, and I would never have turned away a man in need because of the colour of his coat. You have a right to know my opinions. I disagree with the war. *It* is my enemy, not you, sir."

"Then tell me how it is that you came to be here? And why here, a Boston woman in Virginia? Virginia is no Tory province. They would not favour your opinions here."

"I know now that it was a mistake to bring my sister here, but I do not feel unsafe. We have not been here more than a few weeks."

"A few weeks? Then you traveled here alone in time of war?"

"I have long since mourned my husband, Mister Brattle. I am accustomed to being alone."

He studied her flawless skin in the light of the candle flame. This was how he had first seen her, days ago.

"Your husband was a good and honest man?" he asked.

"He was."

"You loved him?"

She almost laughed.

"You are impertinent, sir!"

"I am. I overstep myself. I apologize." He rubbed his hands together, wondering why he had asked such a question.

"I did love him," she said. "I was in my eighteenth year. James Checklee served in my father's practice, an apprentice clerk. We were not married long before our troubles began. We had spoken out against the mob. A neighbor, someone we had supposed was a friend, condemned my father as a Tory.

"First the 'patriots' cast stones through our windows. Then, they returned with torches and an ultimatum. Leave, or they would burn us within our own home. So, like sensible folk, we fled to the safety of General Gage's army. When General Howe took command and evacuated Boston, we went with him to Halifax, Nova Scotia, where we were forced to live in the luxury of a muddy army tent.

"From there, we went to New York, and only slightly better lodgings. Later, we discovered our names on a list of those not friendly to the cause. Our house and property were confiscated. All men are created equal, with an equal right to own property, save for suspected Tories."

He shifted in his chair.

"It is...regrettable that such things happened, in the beginning. Where was your husband killed?"

"At Fort Washington, in New York."

"I was there. On the other side of the river, in Fort Lee."

She did not react to this admission with revulsion, as he had half-feared. Instead, her eyes seemed to lose their focus, as if gazing into the past.

"James had agreed, like my father, that the king's policies in America had to be changed. My father had spoken out against the Stamp Act, and the tea tax. My husband had been opposed to the war, and opposed to fighting the king, but at last he tired of running. He joined a Loyalist regiment in New York, under General Howe. He had been afraid he would die, and he was killed in his first action. We had been married only a few months. We did not have any children, which I believe to have been a blessing."

"I'm sorry," Daniel whispered. "That is regrettable."

She did not appear to hear him. She went on with her story, explaining that a cousin from her mother's side had written to her from Virginia. Her kind and beloved cousin John Chester, who had always been so good to her. A favourite, a Southern curiosity in the family.

He had implored her to come to him, explaining how much he longed for the presence of his kin in these troubled times. She had wanted to go, to leave New York, but her ailing father condemned the notion as absurd.

Then, her father had died, leaving her alone. Remembering the letter, she at last replied to her cousin's request. She received no further letters from him, but had no wish to wait. She bought passage for herself and her sister on a Loyalist privateer bound for the British base at Portsmouth, Virginia.

They had been two women traveling alone. She knew it was dangerous and foolish. Acquaintances in New York had said it was madness, that Virginia was the very seat of the movement for independence. Some whispered that she was "going over to the enemy." She had countered their arguments by stating that Lord Cornwallis and his army would soon be there, and would offer protection.

She had known the location of her cousin's farm. Once landed in Portsmouth, she and Abigail had set out on foot with nothing but the clothes on their backs.

"We each possessed one pair of stays," she said, "one cap apiece, one gown, two petticoats, one pair of shoes, and a few aprons and odds and ends rolled up in a blanket."

The journey had given her a purpose. The people they met along the roads and in the inns had been helpful and courteous, and she had thanked them and moved on. No one had harmed or threatened them in any way. When they at last reached the farm, they found it abandoned to the care of a single retainer, Adam, and his family. Adam claimed not to know where his master had gone.

"So, we are castaways," she concluded, "though it is my sister's welfare that concerns me. I fear I may have ignored her best interests in bringing her with me. We had discussed our plan, of course, and she was as eager to leave New York as was I; but she is young, and would do whatever I wish. My life is my own, and I may endanger it if I choose. But not hers."

"What will you do now?" Daniel asked. "Will you stay here?"

"I admit to not knowing, Mister Brattle. I feel that I have been running for a long time. I wish to rest. No one has molested us here at the farm. No foraging parties have come from either side. You are our first visitors."

"There you have been fortunate." A cough emanated from upstairs, from Joshua's room. Daniel's eyes flickered toward the ceiling. "The cough worries me. It seems to be worsening."

"We will watch him closely. He must not overtax himself."

Daniel grimaced. "I know my brother. He will try—try to wear himself out." He folded his hands before him. "I cannot thank you enough for your help, and here we are, soldiers—and rebels, at that."

She looked at her hands.

"It has been…lonely here. I welcome your company. And I appreciate the fact you have not tried to sway me, Mister Brattle, not attempted to convince me this war is warranted, though you must believe it so."

He stared into the candle flame.

"I am no longer certain what I believe, Mrs. Checklee."

Chapter 6

The Redcoat

Sergeant Tom Martin marched his squad in double file, following a newly worn track in the sandy Virginia turf. Another session of target practice had ended.

"Well done, lads," he remarked as they marched. "Another day well spent, instead of wasted, sitting idle here in Portsmouth."

He had learned to love the art of shooting from his village pastor—his teacher—who had taken him birding in the autumn. Now, he did his best to impart his musketry skills to his men. With Captain Barlow's blessings, he had built a small shooting range just outside the camp. He knew the men enjoyed the training, and the competitions to see who could hit the smallest mark, the most distant, or the most in a row.

They marched into camp, tramping between the rows of wedge-shaped linen-canvas tents. Drying laundry draped the peak of every ridge pole, and wood smoke hung in a perpetual haze, even in the bright sunshine. Tom breathed in the familiar scents—the smoke and the horses and the cooking. *How many camps have I lived in*, he wondered, *since the beginning of this war?* It was impossible to count them. They had all looked, sounded, and smelled the same.

Sometimes he missed his former existence, those placid days when he had gone birding, when he had been studying for the clergy. He remembered his life as a quiet one, his hours filled with the analysis of Greek and Latin. It had been a time of comfort and innocence, a second childhood, without the hardships of long marches, disease, cold, and shortages of food.

But he had grown bored, and something about the beat of a martial drum, the flash of a bright uniform, had stirred his blood. He had always loved to watch the militia on the village green, and had trembled with excitement every year when the recruiting parties had come to the country fair outside Winchester, in Hampshire.

In the spring of 1776, when Tom was seventeen, the recruiting parade had been larger and grander than usual. A squad of soldiers under the command of a sergeant, all with ribbons fluttering from their cocked hats, had accompanied a corps of fifes and drums and a large army band of French horns, clarinets, and bassoons. The musicians had played "God Save the King" and other patriotic airs while a huge draught horse pulled up a wagon loaded with five kegs of beer. Soon, a crowd of country lads had gathered, Tom among them. Two soldiers had served out the beer for free; then the sergeant, a fine robust-looking fellow with a wide grin and ruddy cheeks, had stood upon a bench and made a speech.

"The laurels fought for and obtained in all parts of the globe last war," the sergeant said, "have procured our army a fame so glorious as not to be equaled by any people in any age. Will you, my dear countrymen, permit those laurels to fade or those actions to be forgotten?

"No, heaven forbid! The time to enlist is now, for a more critical period never presented itself than the present. His Majesty's deluded subjects in America are in open rebellion! Like unnatural children, they would destroy their ever-indulgent parent, forgetting the torrents of blood spilt and heaps of treasure extended for their preservation in the last war."

For Tom, disciplining Britain's ungrateful children had been a small factor in his decision. The greatest had been his boredom, and the sight of those vivid uniforms—the cocked hats, the red coats with their blue facings, the white waistcoats and breeches, the fine powdered hair, and the belts, muskets and shining bayonets. These, and the drill, the commands and the bang and crash of the bands, had been enough. To march like that, in that splendid costume, had been Tom's dream, the dream of a lad who had spent too many days at a desk with a quill in his hand.

He had approached the recruiting sergeant, his belly and brain full of beer, and written his name on the roster.

"A man who can write his name, then?" the sergeant said. "You'll come in handy, lad, if you but do your duty."

So, he had taken the King's Shilling, and there had been nothing his mother nor the pastor could do about it, although Mother had chased the column of new recruits as it marched away, crying, "Come back, Tommy! Come back!"

At sight of her, running in her apron and waving a handkerchief, Tom had experienced an acute moment of regret. Some consequences, such as leaving home, a home he had not realized he loved so much, he had not considered. But his fate had been sealed with his signature. All he could do was wave back; and then she was left behind, a spot of white tumbled at the side of the road.

"So, I chose the life of a soldier," he sang to himself as his squad reached their section of camp. It was a hard life, but Tom had vowed he would make his mother proud. And so he had, for he was now a sergeant of light infantry.

A fierce whining and barking greeted the squad as they halted and broke ranks. Their company mascot, a white bulldog named Bone, emerged from the shade of a tent to greet them, wagging his tail and scurrying from man to man, finally halting at the wiry form of Corporal Gibb, the dog's self-appointed keeper.

Gibb ruffled Bone's ears and said, "There, now, my boy, we're back!"

"A fine afternoon's shooting," Tom said, pausing at Gibb's side. "Now, let's carry on."

Gibb straightened and nodded. "Straight away, then, Tom."

Tom insisted the men clean their weapons at once, flushing the barrels three times with hot water then swabbing them clean with scraps of oiled linen. When that part of the task was complete, they sat on the ground in their shirt-sleeves, dismantling and cleaning their flintlocks. They joked and told tales as they worked, while Corporal Gibb amused them all by throwing a stick for Bone, chuckling when the dog returned with the stick in its mouth.

"Give it here, you silly beast," he said. "It ain't yours to keep, you understand. Here, then, I'll throw it again."

Tom cleaned his own weapon—his fusil, the shortened Land Pattern musket issued to sergeants and junior officers. When he was satisfied, he held it before him, admiring the gleam of the polished wood. He had planed away a section of the walnut stock as a cheek rest to make aiming more comfortable, and had fitted a rear sight to the barrel. The weapon had become an object of personal pride.

"I think you're in love, then, Tom," Gibb said, sprawling on the ground next to him. Bone sat between the corporal's feet, his long pink tongue lolling as he panted from the heat and exertion.

"A light infantryman's musket is an extension of his very body," Tom said.

"Aye, well, we all need some extension."

The corporal laughed, for light troops were often the smallest men in the army.

"We make up for our shortcomings in many ways, Corporal," Tom said.

The light infantry were chosen from the most agile and intelligent men in a battalion. They were expected to use their wits and initiative, to fire at picked enemy targets, operating in pairs or alone at wide intervals, using all available cover. Their tactics were those of American Indians, formalized by the British Army. Tom's current battalion was an elite force, an amalgam of the light companies of several separate regiments. It was a force trained to fight, not to parade.

No longer did they powder their hair or worry about how white they could make their belts. Now, they used leather belts of plain black or brown, wore shortened jackets with no decorative lace, small felt caps, and linen gaiter breeches instead of knee breeches. Their simple kit made movement easy and comfortable, while their drab appearance made them less obvious targets to the American riflemen.

"We have a fine set of fellows," he continued. "I'm proud of them."

Gibb frowned. "Aye, most of 'em deserve that. But then we have you-know-who."

He jerked his thumb toward a stout fellow who sat apart from the others, lank brown hair hanging over his flat face. The man had scattered the pieces of his musket lock seemingly at random, and was busy wiping his lock plate with a scrap of filthy cloth.

"Private Hassler," Tom said.

He rose to his feet, moving to stand at Hassler's shoulder. Hassler was a new arrival, and a source of frustration for many.

"I trust you intend to oil the parts of your lock, Private Hassler," he said, "and assemble them correctly."

Hassler squinted up at his sergeant, and his lips pulled back to reveal the remains of crooked teeth.

"It don't need oil every time."

Tom stared down at the man in disgust and disappointment. The war was no longer popular in England, and in desperation, the army had begun to recruit criminals and dullards. That was the only explanation he could conceive for the presence of Hassler.

"I say it does require oiling, and I'll teach you to obey my orders."

Hassler laid his musket across his knees and grumbled, "What do a churchman know of guns anyway?"

"Damn your face, I could have the hide flogged from your back for that remark alone!" Tom snapped. "Do as I say! One man's musket that doesn't spark, or misfires because it's fouled, could mean one man dead. I'll not have the likes of you killing anyone in this company."

Hassler shrank from Tom's words, and his gaze swept the gathering. Some stared at him with amusement, some with contempt.

"I'll do it," he growled.

Tom's anger did not subside with Hassler's compliance.

"You'll do it and more. Corporal Gibb, put Private Hassler on extra drill parade for a fortnight. Maybe that will teach him some respect."

Gibb sprang to his feet. "Ser'nt!"

Some of the men chuckled. Hassler glowered at them but said no more.

"I'll make a light infanteer of you yet, Private Hassler," Tom added.

Hassler was his project. A task to accomplish, and a way to while away the time before the rebels next gathered their courage and attacked anew.

Chapter 7

The Earl

*C*harles, the Earl of Cornwallis, stood on a strip of beach near the mouth of the York River, gazing across the water toward the old Virginia tobacco port of York Town. Accompanying him was a guard of His Majesty's Marines and a group of satellite officers, including his second-in-command, Charles O'Hara. They waited in silence, for no one, the earl knew, would voice an opinion until he had made his own pronouncement.

"An altogether unremarkable place," he said, reaching with his right hand to adjust his gold lace-trimmed cocked hat. Sunlight glinted from the matching lace on the cuff of his finely tailored coat as he turned to O'Hara. "But perhaps it will do."

Perhaps this little collection of houses on the edge of the low bluff *would* serve him. He studied its single street, the prominent houses of brick and wood; then the rough track below on the beach with its warehouses, shacks, and wharves. At the northwest extremity of the town stood a spinning windmill and a large courthouse. Over the courthouse towered a flagpole, although no banner flew from it. Flanking the town were two streams—a narrow defile to the west and a wider sluggish watercourse to the southeast.

The earl pursed his lips. He was tired of waiting, of mulling over his every step. It was time to make a choice.

A chill rose along his spine and neck, although the heat should have been oppressive. He stifled a shiver, a skill he had perfected these last few weeks. The chills had been coming more and more often, and he feared he had fallen victim to the persistent malaria that had struck down so many of his troops here in the Southern colonies. He kept his expression impassive. He could let no one know, lest they think him unfit for duty.

Clearing his throat, he touched O'Hara's arm.

"General," he said, "if you will accompany me?"

O'Hara's ruddy face lit with a quizzical smile, and he raised his eyebrows.

"And where are we going, My Lord?"

"Along the beach, my dear fellow," the earl explained. "Along the beach."

They strolled a few paces, leaving the others behind. Gulls cried overhead, and the lapping waves brought the clean smell of the sea. Cornwallis gazed aloft and spied an osprey soaring out over the bay in search of its slippery prey.

"General Clinton's orders, to say the least, have been rather perplexing," he said—an understatement. Sir Henry Clinton, commander of all British forces in America, seemed incapable of making a firm decision. "One moment he suggests that I establish a naval base on the Chesapeake, next we receive suggestions to attack Philadelphia, then an order to return to New York, then again a suggestion to establish a Chesapeake base. Suggestions, General O'Hara. Suggestions! One after the other!"

"We must interpret as best we can, My Lord. You must do what you think appropriate."

Cornwallis removed his hat, held it in his hands, idly brushed at a speck of lint.

"Then we must establish our base, either here at York or at Old Point Comfort."

"Our engineers have deemed the latter unsuitable, so here it must be. And yet you are still not satisfied?"

Cornwallis did not answer for a moment. In truth, he was far from satisfied. He stifled another chill. Reaching into one of his large coat pockets, he pulled out a handkerchief and mopped his brow.

"No," he agreed. "My thoughts on this matter are well documented, General O'Hara. I consider the establishment of such a small outpost, vulnerable to attack or siege, inadvisable, and I have said so to our superior. Yet he wishes for such a post, and he shall have it."

It is my duty to obey, he thought. *My duty as a soldier to fight the king's enemies, though I have always considered it folly.*

He had been so convinced since the beginning of the war, since the evacuation of Boston, when he had first expressed his belief that the Americans could not be coerced. He understood their cause, their need for more autonomy, and thought it justified. Yet he had volunteered for the American service when so many officers sympathetic to the rebellion had refused. He was a soldier, first and foremost; and with the death of his wife, the army had become his entire life, the place he turned to for solace, for activity. There was nothing else left for him.

"We have had some success, here in the south," he said, replacing his hat.

O'Hara barked a sharp laugh.

"The rebels are teetering on the edge, sir! They simply need one last push."

"Perhaps." Cornwallis was not so certain. He had thought so before, had dealt the rebels several severe blows, but always they had risen to fight again.

He still believed the plan for the southern campaign had been sound. General Clinton's aim had been to establish a chain of coastal bases from which to mount raids into the interior, to pacify the Southern colonies then move northward. In accordance with this plan, a British force had quickly taken Georgia and held Savannah against a French and American attack.

Then, Clinton had captured Charleston, giving him a third stronghold. Advancing from there, Cornwallis had won his battle at Camden, thus delivering another blow to the rebel cause, the crowning achievement in a string of stunning reversals.

But the earl had never seen the military wisdom of mounting raids from coastal strongholds, and still did not. The key to victory, he believed, was to destroy the American armies. It was very simple: keep a large force in the field to attack the rebels wherever and whenever possible. After Camden, he had devised such a plan.

And thus began my greatest frustrations, he reflected.

The campaign had not succeeded. He had fought engagement after engagement, waiting for the Loyalists to flock to him. They existed in numbers at least as great as the rebels, but to his dismay, the majority had remained passive. The few who came to fight had, on many occasions, behaved with such shocking savagery their efforts may have been a detriment to the British cause. And in the end, the rebels had dealt them two devastating defeats, the first at King's Mountain and the second at the Cowpens.

Cornwallis had continued to achieve victories with his regulars, but his last, at Guilford Courthouse, had been costly. Too costly. And he had left the Carolinas still in enemy hands. Since then, he had been pursuing the rebels under Wayne and Lafayette, scurrying about the Virginia countryside in an absurd game of hide-and-seek.

He had won every battle, but his campaign had failed. His strategy had not worked. There was nothing else to do but obey Clinton and establish another coastal stronghold.

"This shall be our naval base, General," he declared, putting as much force into his voice as he could. There was no more time, and he was weary. This would have to do. "We shall begin transporting the army here once all necessary preparations are made."

He watched the lazy operation of the little windmill at the west end of town. He had made a decision. He would come to York, and here he would stay.

Chapter 8

The Loyalist

*A*dam had shot a pair of wild ducks for dinner; and Catherine took her time with their preparation, for the kitchen was still where she felt the most at ease, the place where her darkest fears did not intrude. She had always loved the kitchen in her home as a girl—its warmth in winter, the heady aromas and the activity, but also she felt a power here.

In her father's house she had never needed to cook her own meals, nor make or mend her own clothes. Now, she did all of those things and many more. She tended the garden, prepared the game Adam brought from the forest, the fish from the creeks. Had Adam not been there, she thought she could even have hunted and fished herself. She had learned to live and survive on her own.

She ground some roasted chestnuts in her mortar.

"Why don't you stoke up the fire, Abigail?" she suggested. "And add another log. I'll be ready with this directly."

"May I stuff the ducks with the chestnuts?" Abigail said.

Catherine grinned. "If you like."

Abigail poked at the fire, sending sparks rushing up the chimney. Catherine set the pestle down and fanned her face with one hand. The room was hot, and the air from the facing windows provided little relief. She glanced at Abigail, at the damp strands of blond hair that protruded from her linen cap.

"This is enough to make us mourn for a New England winter," she remarked.

Abigail set down the poker, then dropped onto the bench beside the work table.

"I always disliked the cold at home," she said, resting her head in her hands. Her brow puckered. "But still, it's different here. Do you ever miss our room in Boston, Cathy?"

"Of course I do, but we mustn't think of it. Just remember how much we disliked New York before we complain too much about this southern climate." She began mixing the herbs into the crushed nuts. "It was the people I despised there more than anything."

She wrinkled her nose at the memory of the New York Loyalists and their military benefactors under General Clinton. They had been more concerned with parties and balls than the civil conflict that had torn their country apart. Frivolous, foolish people, behaving as if the war did not exist, that beyond the confines of their comfortable rooms nothing had changed.

Yet the city was filled with the signs—the churches crammed with rebel prisoners, the streets overflowing with loyal refugees and escaped slaves. Some were destitute, living in shanties of scrap lumber and sailcloth while the more fortunate Loyalists, those with means, turned a blind eye to the suffering of their fellows. They had been deluding themselves, Catherine thought, denying their tragedy. Hiding from it.

She and Abigail were better off here, even though Cousin John was nowhere to be found.

"Roast duck," said a voice from the open doorway, and she turned to see Daniel's silhouette against the glare of the day. "I feared it was a rumour."

Catherine's smile was automatic.

"I would never make such a promise, Mister Brattle, if I could not keep it."

"Again you are too good to us," Daniel said. "It's uncommon to find such fare in the army while on the move, even for the officers."

Her smile did not waver.

"Should not the officers and the men eat the same? All men are created equal, I seem to remember reading."

"Alas, that is not how the army functions." He entered the room, his funny little black cap in his hands. The hearth fire cast a ruddy glow across his cleaned and mended coat. "Those who lead are afforded certain privileges. Though I remind you that I began my career as a private man."

"Then you have earned your roast duck. And you are lucky that you do not have to share it with an entire army."

"Like you, I am only lucky in some things." He sat on the bench. "Though I was lucky to find you here, Mrs. Checklee."

"You flatter me, Mister Brattle. And please, I prefer Seawell."

She began tidying the table, stacking the mixing bowls and mortar on a wooden tray as Abigail stuffed the ducks. Daniel watched her from his place on the bench, and she paused to study him in turn, to examine the contours of his features, outlined in shadows. He looked very handsome today, she thought, and said, "And I was lucky in the character of the man who arrived at my doorstep."

"Now you flatter me, Miss Seawell."

She turned away quickly, busied herself with one of the ducks. She placed it in the Dutch oven, then set it on the fire. Behind her, Daniel began drumming his fingers on the rough table.

"I wish you would tell me something about your cousin," he said. "The man who owns this property."

"Cousin John? I could tell you much, but where to begin?"

John was their Southern relation, a delightful curiosity in a typically sober New England family. He was almost old enough to be Catherine's uncle, but they had always addressed each other in their letters as "beloved cousin."

She returned to the table, sat on the bench.

"I can tell you that I fear for his safety, even for his life. He is a peaceful and unadventurous man, and not accustomed to hardships or ill treatment. I cannot imagine him taking up arms for either side in this contest, even though his grandfather, William Chester, was a soldier in the last war with France. A Virginian, though he served in the campaign to capture the French port of Louisbourg.

"It was there he met my father, who at that time was also an officer in a provincial regiment. They became fast friends. Before that war ended, my father had married William Chester's youngest daughter, Mary. My mother. They settled in Boston, and there my father began his law practice. Cousin John is the eldest son of my mother's brother."

"A prosperous man, if this plantation is any indication."

Catherine nodded. "The tobacco trade, Mister Brattle. In his youth, he shipped his products to Europe and the other colonies, but his mild nature finally convinced him that he loved the land more than the sea, and so he purchased this property. Since then, he has lived here as a bachelor, alone with his servants and slaves. His visits to us, his Northern cousins, became fewer and fewer—since becoming a slaveholder, he has not been as welcome in the North as he once was. However, he has never been sparing with his letters."

She sighed and stared at the ceiling beams.

"We don't approve of slavery, but it is the way of things here. I feel that I came to know every inch of this house and its grounds from his descriptions, every petty detail of the weather in Virginia, and the operation of the farm. And I knew his worries about the escalating war, for I shared them."

Daniel leaned on one elbow.

"He never spoke of leaving in his letters?"

"No! I can only imagine his fate."

John had been dismayed by the drive for independence, the radical nature of Virginia's House of Burgesses. He had few friends here, had distanced himself from his neighbors, thanks to his conservative views. It was possible he was in prison. Or worse.

She felt her reserve begin to crack. They had all lost so much...

She covered her mouth with one hand. Daniel hesitated, then leapt to his feet and fumbled in his waistcoat pocket, probably searching for a handkerchief. He found none, and the look of disappointment on his face was enough to staunch her tears. Her sob turned to strangled laughter.

There was a stack of clean and folded linen rags on the table, and at last, he snatched one up and held it out to her. It was an absurd gesture, but she took the offering, nevertheless, and dabbed at her drying eyes.

"I have feared," she continued once she had fully regained her composure, "that our connection to John would become known in the surrounding townships. But as you already know, you are our first visitors, and you are certainly no monster, no savage with a torch in your hand." She passed him the rag, forgetting it was not his to begin with. "You are something else altogether, Mister Brattle."

He cleared his throat. "You must remember to call me Daniel."

He reached for the scrap of cloth, but in grasping it he took hold of her hand. Perhaps it was an accident, but his touch lingered. Her instinct was to pull away, but she did not. Warmth spread through her fingers, along her arm.

"Your hands are rough," he murmured, "from so much work."

Abigail was staring with her mouth open, and Catherine finally made a fist, snatching her hand back.

"Only one of many small changes in my life, Mister Brattle. Daniel."

He dropped the rag, taking his cap from the table and fingering its bill. She noticed his ears had blossomed redder than ever before.

"Perhaps you might come examine Joshua," he stammered. "That was what brought me here to the kitchen. The cough has worsened, and there is a wheezing when he breathes. And his spirits are low. I don't think he has forgiven me since our quarrel."

Catherine nodded. "I have already noted the change, and also find it worrisome, though he seems determined to exhaust himself. His wound is healing well, but he has not allowed his body to rest."

Daniel's eyes were pleading.

"I would not see my brother wither before my eyes, after surviving such a grievous injury."

"My grandmother would advise a poultice of fried or raw onions," Catherine stated. Then she took a deep breath to steady herself. She would not dwell on what had just passed between them. She had to remain practical. "If we apply such a poultice, it may ease his symptoms. And we must wait and pray. You must trust in God. Joshua is strong. A trait he shares with his brother."

"I will do as you say," Daniel replied, nodding. "I will trust in God's mercy, and trust in you, as well."

⚜

When Catherine examined Joshua, she discovered his state had worsened to the point his cough and the wheezing in his chest made it difficult for him to speak. He seemed to find eating a demanding task, as well. His skin was pale and damp, his eyes dark and hooded. The fever had returned.

"I have the poultice," she whispered to Daniel. She carried the chopped raw onions in a wooden bowl. "If you would undo his shirt, I will apply it."

That night both Catherine and Daniel remained in Joshua's room, alternately sleeping and watching his progress. Catherine woke the next morning still sitting in her chair. Everything reeked of the onions.

She could hear Daniel snoring but could not see him. Stiff-necked, she rose and crossed to the bed. She saw at once that Joshua was sleeping normally, and his colour had returned, although his breath still hissed like a tea kettle. When she touched his brow, she could find no sign of the fever.

She cut short any sense of triumph.

"In this lifetime, little is certain," she murmured. Her mother had often said so.

She moved around to the other side of the bed. There she discovered Daniel asleep on the rug, his knees drawn up. She gazed down at him, then knelt by his side. With one hand, she smoothed a few strands away from his brow, and he stirred. He looked so helpless, like a small boy who needed her care; and she felt a certain melancholy at the sight of him.

His eyes opened, stared at nothing for a moment, then focused on her.

"Your brother's fever has passed," she told him.

"The poultice worked, then?" His voice was thick from sleep.

"Perhaps it has helped. But we still must be vigilant."

He struggled to sit.

"We have come this far, there is little sense in stopping now."

"In that we are in agreement."

Vigilant they were, through that day and into the next. Catherine applied a fresh poultice every few hours. By the late afternoon of the second day, Joshua developed a rattle in his throat and began coughing up thick, yellow sputum. He was able to speak in a hoarse croak, but too much effort fatigued him. Between spasms of coughing, he slept.

Catherine brought Daniel a bowl of carrot soup and some brown bread, and he sat eating at Joshua's side. She took her customary chair, turning it to face the west windows. Outside, the descending sun had torn the horizon into strips of amber, scarlet and indigo.

"We had a happy childhood," Daniel said, "the two of us." He set aside his empty bowl, placing it on the floor at his feet. "No, it was the three of us.

Benjamin was there, too, of course. It was he who taught me how to fish in the creek behind Mister Rowntree's grist mill. We spent many a summer's day capturing frogs there, or scouring the woods for honeycombs, or hunting in the autumn."

She searched for soothing words, but all she could think of was, "You will always have those memories." She knew that must sound like cold comfort.

"Memories, yes." He stood and folded his hands behind his back. "At times I despise all that has happened since those simpler days. If Joshua were to die, it would be a cruel injustice. To have come this far, to have shown such devotion, to have made such sacrifice, and all for naught."

She rose from her chair, drawn to stand at his side. Together, they gazed down at their patient.

"It *would* be a cruel thing, though an injustice which is all too common."

After a moment he said, "And I have seen it more often than I care to admit."

"I have no doubt Joshua will recover," she said to encourage him, gripping his sleeve, "and then you will leave, return to your army. I anticipate the first, but do not relish the thought of the latter."

He met her eye, then reached down to clasp her hands. This time she did not resist.

"If Joshua recovers, I am uncertain what I will do, Catherine."

If he kisses me now, she thought, *I will let him.*

But he did not. Instead, he dropped her hands and grasped the footboard of Joshua's bed.

"For now, I must concentrate all my energies on my brother's recovery," he said.

She smoothed her hands on her petticoat. Had she really wanted him to kiss her? She acknowledged the desire. Yes, she had. She had wanted that very much.

She shoved the thought behind her.

"I will continue to help you," she whispered.

Chapter 9

The Redcoat

*T*he battalion fifes and drums were marching through the camp streets, screeching out "The Grenadier's March" for reveille. Tom Martin's company roused, the men stumbling from their tents, pulling on their breeches and coats. Tom was already awake and dressed, waiting as his men formed line. Low voices grunted, complained, joked and chuckled. The sky was still dark, a deep velvet blue.

"Cursed fifes," Tom heard Private Hassler grumble. "Enough to pierce me eardrums."

"To wake the dead," remarked Sam Webb, a member of Hassler's mess and the youngest man in the company.

Tom took the roll, calling out the names one-by-one and checking them against his list. Finding all able men present, he dismissed the company to breakfast.

The company was divided into groups of five men each for sleeping and messing. A designate from each mess, camp kettles in hand, departed for the cooking lines, where the camp stoves were established. They would return with the kettles full of rice gruel and tea. Gruel, bread and tea was the standard menu for breakfast, with a bit of butter, hopefully not too rancid.

Bone snuffled the ground a few feet away. Tom felt faintly sick, as he always did in the morning; but he knew a mug of tea would set him right, and he refused to wait. He started a small bivouac fire at the end of the street where he and Corporal Gibb shared a tent. He would brew up his own tea.

Rubbing his hands together, he watched as a dark form approached from the line of officers' tents. He recognized Captain Barlow, so touched his cap and said, "Good morning, sir."

"Good morning, Sergeant." The captain wore a long-sleeved waistcoat with no markings of rank, and he carried an officer's fusil. The only obvious indication of his position was the slim straight sword dangling at his side. "The men have thirty minutes. Then we will strike camp."

"Yes, sir."

The day before, Barlow had warned him the army would be leaving Portsmouth. They would march the short distance to the docks, and there would board navy transports and sail to some unknown destination.

"Would you like some tea, sir?" he asked, gesturing toward Gibb. Gibb had already produced a dark brew.

"Thank you, Sergeant."

Gibb passed Tom a steaming tin cup, and Tom passed it to the captain. As Barlow took a sip, Gibb passed a second cup to Tom.

"It looks like the beginning of another campaign," the captain said. "I have word we will be establishing a new base of operations."

"A new campaign?" Tom said. "Something to toast, then, sir. New campaigns and new opportunities to thump the rebels."

He raised his cup, and Gibb did likewise with an enthusiastic exclamation of "Frustration to the rebels!"

Barlow stared at them, his mouth a grim line. Then, he, too, raised his tin vessel of tea.

"New opportunities," he said. "Whatever they may be." He sipped from the cup then added, "A detachment will remain in Portsmouth to level the fortifications here."

"We'll be abandoning Portsmouth for good, sir?" Tom asked.

The captain took a final gulp of tea and tossed the rest on the little fire. The liquid splashed into the flames with a hiss.

"Lord Cornwallis does not like to remain in one place for long, Sergeant." He surveyed his company. "Have the men formed and ready. We are to receive fresh rations onboard ship. I will go and shake up Lieutenant Nicholson."

Barlow moved off, and Tom prepared to carry out his orders. He imagined himself as small cog in a massive machine of men and horses, supplies and camp followers. Around him in the darkness, others were making ready, just as he was. Two regiments of elite Foot Guards, the Light Infantry, the Royal Welch Fusiliers, the MacDonald Highlanders, the Loyalist corps, including the Queen's Rangers and Colonel Banastre Tarleton's British Legion. The Royal Artillery. A great machine of war.

He spied Lieutenant Nicholson, the company's other surviving officer, yawning and stretching. The lieutenant was an odd sort for the light infantry. He seemed to be about Tom's age, although in all other ways they differed.

Nicholson was the son of a minor lord, stood to inherit a handsome estate. He even wore his hair powdered, and had retained his long tailcoat.

"Good morning, Mister Nicholson," Tom called, touching his cap with all four fingers.

Nicholson started, then replied, "Good morning, Sergeant."

"Fine day for a march, sir," Tom tried. The morning sky was brightening, wisps of cloud flaring scarlet and gold.

"Yes." Nicholson's face wore a look of disapproval. "Sergeant, it is not in my practice to chat with the men in the ranks. Remember your station."

"Of course, sir." Tom hid his disappointment. Nicholson was nothing like Captain Barlow. "My apologies, sir."

"Of course." Nicholson nodded, then looked away with indifference.

Tom sighed and busied himself with his kit.

"Bloody aristocrats," he muttered.

With their breakfast of tea and thin porridge safe in their bellies, the members of the company struggled back into their jackets and donned their accoutrements. As they were pulling on their cartridge boxes, Sam Webb called, "Where we going, Sarge?"

Tom turned. "Don't know, Sam. Somewhere with comfortable beds, I'll warrant."

"Comfortable beds made of hard ground," someone else quipped. "The best of luxury."

"Sergeant, am I to do extra drill on the deck of the ship?" Hassler demanded as he struggled with his crossbelts.

Tom gave him a level stare.

"Why, that's a fine idea, Private. Thank you for the suggestion."

Laughter bubbled through the company. Hassler shrank from it, muttering to himself.

"You'll learn a few things, Private Hassler," Tom added. "Enough to pull your weight with this company. Now, lads, let's load the wagons. It's time to be off."

Chapter 10

The Continental

$\mathcal{D}$aniel had gone all the way up the lane to the road, taking the air after so many hours in the sickroom. Almost at once he saw the cloud of dust rising in the distance. A rider approaching. He froze, wondering if he should rush back to the house; but then he decided a single rider could pose little or no danger, whoever he may be.

It did not take long for the rider to reach him. The fellow slowed his horse to a walk, calling out and waving one hand. He was covered in dust, but his blue-and-buff uniform was unmistakable. A Continental officer.

"Halloo!" the rider cried again, coming to a halt at the gate, the dust swirling. He swept off his hat, revealing a head of golden curls tied in a loose queue. He laughed.

"Lieutenant Brattle! At last I have found you. I knew you at once."

Daniel squinted at the man; then recognition dawned. Lieutenant Karl Grumman, a Pennsylvania German.

"I have been to three plantations in my search," Grumman continued in his accented English. "Had I not found you here, I had planned to return to Malvern Hill, having failed in my mission. And here you are!"

Daniel nodded. "And a good afternoon to you, Mister Grumman. I trust you bring news from the army."

Grumman's teeth flashed white within his grimy features.

"Indeed, sir." He reached into a saddle bag, taking out a document folded and sealed with wax. "I bring orders from the colonel. Major Osborne has sent me. General Lafayette moved the army to Malvern Hill on the sixteenth of the month. He will be moving on to Richmond soon, then to Williamsburg."

Daniel took the letter. It seemed to weigh heavy in his hands.

Grumman rubbed his chin.

"It is my impression that Major Osborne will have you return to your company as soon as conditions permit. He requires his officers. As I understand, there was some trouble, talk of dissolving your company."

Then dissolve it, Daniel thought but did not say. Instead, he forced a smile. "I thank you for taking the trouble to find me. The mistress of this house will give you refreshment, and the retainer will see to your horse. You must be tired from your journey."

Grumman bowed in his saddle.

"I appreciate the hospitality. I admit it has been a day of some frustration."

Ten minutes later Grumman was in the kitchen with Catherine, and his horse was in the barn with Adam. Daniel returned to the house, to Joshua's room, the sealed letter in his hand.

"A courier has brought orders from Major Osborne," he explained.

Joshua was propped up in bed, although his face retained its pallor.

"That is splendid…news, brother," he croaked, then cleared his throat. "Do you mean to read them…any time soon?"

Daniel could not meet his eye.

"I do."

"And what will you do…when he requests our presence…with the company?"

"*Our* presence? He will not order you to return so soon, Joshua. You're not fit to serve."

"But you are."

"Yes. If I so choose."

Joshua rolled his eyes toward the ceiling.

"By God, Daniel…you were the first of us…to enlist. Now…you want to run."

Daniel's jaw clenched. The letter crumpled in his fingers as his hands balled into fists.

"I shall do what I wish, damn you! I *was* the first to enlist, and I'll be the first to go home, if I so desire!"

Joshua turned his face away.

"So be it, then." He coughed.

Daniel sank onto his stool, his anger slowly evaporating. He smoothed the crumpled letter on his knee. The wax seal had remained intact.

It is my fault, he thought, *that Joshua has not recovered from his wound. My loss of heart brought on this second fever.*

For a moment, shame overwhelmed him. He had failed—failed his brother utterly. The war was not over, however much he might wish it to be. He had given up while Joshua continued the fight, even from what might have been his deathbed.

"I will keep my promise to you, Joshua," he said softly.

"I did not...hear you. My ears—"

"I will keep my promise," Daniel almost shouted. "We will return to the army. When you are well enough."

The brothers glared at each other. After a moment, Joshua grinned.

"I always knew...you would come round."

Daniel said nothing. The war now seemed folly; but he had come this far, and he had promised.

He had promised.

⁂

Within a day, colour had returned to Joshua's complexion. He spoke in a hoarse but fluent voice, and again rose from his bed to walk about the room. For a second time, Daniel knew the respite of having his brother returned to him.

"Damn me," Joshua said, sounding his old cheerful self for the first time in weeks. "I have faced the Devil twice, and twice I have seen him routed. Three times, if you consider the wound itself. A few inches lower, and it would have pierced my heart, or lung. With such luck, it should not be so hard to defeat Lord Cornwallis, eh?"

Daniel managed a smile.

"Then we should send you against him all by yourself."

"You truly have a strong constitution, sir," Catherine remarked from where she stood at the foot of the bed.

"I don't believe the disease went as deep as it seemed," Joshua said. "An uncomfortable malady of my throat, perhaps. Or perhaps it was your fine onion treatment that cured me, ma'am. I don't imagine I will be much use to the army for some time to come, but that is a good thing. The boys won't have me around, smelling as I do."

That afternoon, Daniel remembered his orders. They still lay on the table beside Joshua's bed. He took them and broke the seal.

Joshua was sitting up.

"Read them out loud," he said.

"'You are to report to your company,'" Daniel read, "'in the location of Malvern Hill. If the army is not there, seek them in Richmond. The enemy are no longer active this side of the James, and if you are able to proceed at once, I urge you to do so. If not, I will dispatch a troop of dragoons to your location one week from the issue of this order.'" He held the single sheet of paper at arm's length. "It is signed by both Major Osborne and Colonel Gimat."

"Ah, well." Joshua sighed, leaning back against the headboard, hands behind his head. His wrists looked very small, just skin stretched over bone.

"I think that we are not, as the letter says, able to proceed at once. We must wait until they come to fetch us, some six days hence."

⁂

Daniel joined Catherine in the parlour that evening while Joshua rested. By the light of the candles, he scribbled an account of his time here in Catherine's house. Catherine sat in the corner reading a little book, something from her cousin's library. They did not speak.

Daniel paused in his writing and studied her, just as he had studied her so often since their arrival. The flesh of her long neck seemed to glow in the warm candlelight. He remembered again how she had looked to him on that first night, when she had let him weep into her shoulder.

"I will have to go with them when they come," he said. His voice seemed very loud in the still room. "The dragoons. I am bound to obey my orders."

She kept her eyes on her book.

"You are a free man, Daniel. You are bound by nothing."

He sighed. The truth was there, staring him in the face, a truth stronger than his recent near despair.

"I have made my decision. I cannot abandon my brother, and…I still believe in our cause, however desperate."

"Then you are in fact following your own conscience, not your orders."

"Yes."

She said nothing more. He tried to return to his writing but could not concentrate.

"What will you do when we leave?" he asked at length.

She shrugged. "I am unsure. Were there some way of determining the whereabouts of my cousin John, I would go to him. I must discover his fate somehow. I will not be able to rest until I do.

"And I have Abigail to consider. Perhaps we shall remain here yet for some time. Perhaps John will come back. There is so much uncertainty."

"Yes. That is it exactly, Catherine. There is too much uncertainty."

She studied her page.

"I understand, Daniel. You have no need to explain yourself."

He slumped in his chair, trying to commit every line and curve of her face to memory.

She is beautiful, he thought. *An angel sent from heaven for us to find, to save my brother's life.*

He set down his quill. Standing, he crossed the floor and knelt before her chair. She simply watched him as he reached for her hands, which still clutched the book; and for a moment, she resisted, pulling away from him. Then the tiny volume fell, landing softly on the carpet, pages fluttering like the wings of a dying moth.

He kissed her fingers, and she reached up and ran one hand through his hair, which hung loose about his shoulders.

"Catherine," he breathed, and he stood, pulling her up with him; and now he was looking down on her. Her face was in shadow, but the candle-light made her eyes two bright points. He drew her to him, kissed her. Only after he felt all hope was lost did she respond, her lips warm and moist.

After a moment, they drew apart, but now he was shaking his head.

"This cannot be," he gasped. "When I go, I may never see you again."

"I know," she murmured, and she leaned her head against his chest. "But don't speak of it. It doesn't matter. Not now. I have longed for you these last days, but now there is only the moment. Are not soldiers said to live for the moment? Eat, drink, and be merry, for tomorrow we may die, or some such?"

"Yes. Tomorrow may bring anything. Tomorrow may see me on my way to Richmond."

She reached up and placed one hand behind his neck, the other on his shoulder.

"Then we have until then," she whispered.

⁂

A squadron of cavalry pounded into the yard five days later. Daniel had taken breakfast in Joshua's room, and he went to the window. When he saw that the horsemen wore green coats and breeches, he leapt to one side, behind the drapes, his heart racing.

Tarleton's Legion dressed in green coats.

Then he noticed that the riders also wore leather dragoon helmets wrapped with scraps of scarlet turban. Their coat facings and waistcoats were red. He knew this regiment. This was a squadron from the 4th Continental Light Dragoons.

Joshua was on his feet and beside him at the window, dressed in nothing but shirt and breeches.

"It seems our orders were true to their word. I have no doubt they have come to fetch us."

The dragoons halted in the yard, formed in twos. Daniel counted a dozen troopers, a sergeant, a trumpeter, and an officer. With the squadron were two spare horses, saddled but without riders.

The officer dismounted and approached the front door, holding his sword against his leg as he walked. Both Adam and Catherine were already there to meet him.

The officer saluted Catherine by touching his cap; the man spoke. A moment later, the front door creaked open, and the tread of heavy boots sounded on the stairs.

The dragoon officer came into the room. He had a swarthy complexion, a heavy scar running across his right cheek. Daniel knew him well, a former infantryman who had transferred to the cavalry.

"Lieutenant Daniel Brattle," the dragoon said, his eyes cold, "I am Captain Philip Holyoak, Fourth Dragoons."

"Sir," Daniel said, unnerved by the officer's formality. "You have come to fetch us?"

"Indeed, I am here as your private escort when I should be watching the country for enemy movements. A strange use of my troops, this helping wounded men rejoin the army."

Daniel folded his arms across his chest.

"We left wounded men at Green Spring Farm who will never rejoin the army, sir. I think my brother would be justified in returning home to Boston, but he would rather continue the fight."

"Commendable, I am sure. I will give you an hour to prepare. The army is still in Richmond. A moderate ride of twenty miles." He grimaced. "A march of one or two days, for one or two men unencumbered. Two days at the most."

"I would gladly have done so, Philip," Joshua cried, "but knew you were coming and didn't want you to be disappointed not to find me here."

The dragoon eyed him.

"I have brought extra mounts for you. I trust you can ride?"

"Of course," Joshua insisted.

Holyoak grunted, then repeated, "One hour."

Daniel stared past the dragoon's shoulder. Catherine stood in the hall, listening. He saw her turn away. This was the hour he had dreaded, come too soon.

"One hour, then," he said, his voice very small to his ears.

He took one last look at the room. There was little to do save help Joshua down the stairs. They had only the few things they had brought with them.

"Let's get started," Joshua said. "I am growing sick of these four emerald walls."

Once dressed and downstairs, Daniel helped Joshua ease down to sit on the back step. The cavalry troopers had dismounted and were resting in the shade of the elms, their horses cropping the few long tufts of grass in the yard. They had also built a fire in the fire pit and were stirring something in a camp kettle they had suspended on sticks over the flames.

Daniel found Catherine and Captain Holyoak in the kitchen. Holyoak sat at the table eating a modest meal of bread and cheese. Catherine filled Daniel's canvas haversack.

"Something for your journey," she said, bringing it to him. He took it, and she went back to the table, then returned carrying a folded bundle.

"For Joshua," she explained. The bundle was his uniform coat, still stained with his blood. "I mended and laundered it as best I could."

Daniel slung the haversack over his shoulder and took the coat.

"Thank you. Thank you for all you have done."

"If you are ready, we should leave now," Holyoak announced. He was standing, brushing crumbs from his breeches. "There is no sense in tarrying."

The time had come. Holyoak ordered his troopers to fall in, and they hastily struck their small camp, dousing the fire. Catherine, Abigail, and Adam gathered on the steps while Daniel helped Joshua mount one of the spare horses.

Catherine advanced to Captain Holyoak.

"These are brave men, Captain. You must not judge them harshly, nor think their welfare a waste of your time."

"I do not judge them so harshly as you think, ma'am," Holyoak said. "I am certain you are right about them."

The dragoon captain turned and mounted. Daniel approached Catherine and asked again, "Will you remain here long?"

"I have told you that I do not know, Daniel." Her voice was heavy with regret.

"Come with us," he said fiercely, pulling off his cap and holding it in front of him. "You and your sister."

"Come with you?" she repeated. "But we are safe here, and in your camp, I would be amongst many who would count me among their enemies. Massachusetts men, not strangers. No one would trust me, suspecting me of subterfuge at every turn. I would cause trouble for you."

"No one would dare molest you, if you were my wife."

He was trembling as he spoke. The notion seemed mad, and yet this was what he wanted.

"Your wife?" she whispered. One hand came up to her mouth, and she bit her fingertips. "But our families are unacquainted, and could never be friends." She suddenly balled her fists, and added, "How could you ask me such a thing? Why now, as you are about to leave me?"

"What are you discussing there?" Joshua called.

Daniel ignored the intrusion.

"If not now, when could I have asked you?"

There were sudden tears in her eyes, and she swept them away with the back of her hand. Her breathing had become rapid, almost panicked.

"I don't know, I don't know. I have to learn what has happened to John, and what of Abigail? I can't answer such a question. Not here, not now. Not so suddenly, as you are leaving."

"Not now?" he echoed. "Then perhaps some day you will?"

She closed her eyes and shook her head. He waited, but she did not answer the question.

He stepped toward his horse.

"Then I will come back for you. Even if you leave this house, the war will end some day, and I will find you."

"If I leave here, how will you find me?" she asked.

He jammed his cap onto his head.

"I will find you. Unless you tell me not to try."

She said nothing. She did not look at him, and she did not answer. Abigail had come to her and was holding her hand, concern in her wide eyes.

Captain Holyoak called, "Lieutenant, we must go!"

Daniel placed one foot in the stirrup and swung into the saddle. It felt strange to be sitting on horseback—he had never been a comfortable rider. The trumpeter put his brass instrument to his lips and blew a series of clear notes, the call to begin the march. Holyoak placed himself at the head of the column, and Daniel and Joshua took positions in the rear. The squadron started off, wheeling in twos to the left, back toward the road.

Daniel kept Catherine in his sight. She stood in the yard, holding Abigail close. He could feel a hollowness building inside his breast.

"What if you were killed?" she called after him.

"I will come back!" he shouted.

Then they were in the road and moving at a steady canter toward Richmond.

Chapter 11

The General

$\mathcal{T}$he green hills of the Hudson valley burned in the August heat. Across the land, the joint French and American camp stretched like a series of small mountain ranges, the canvas peaks extending from White Plains to Dobb's Ferry. The camp lay less than twenty miles from the enemy—General Clinton's vast army in New York, where the redcoats lived indoors, having occupied the former American barracks on the grounds of King's College.

General Washington had once again made his headquarters in a large marquee. The tent was well and elegantly furnished with chairs, side tables, and a larger camp table covered with maps of New York and the Chesapeake. Washington had ordered the sides of the tent tied up to allow for the flow of air. He wished to make things as comfortable as possible for his guests, the French General Rochambeau and his sizable staff. The General had even allowed his aides to remove their coats in the heat, although he continued to suffer in his wool broadcloth. As part of his personal code of civility, he would not appear before his ally half-dressed.

Rochambeau must have agreed, for he, too, retained his full uniform. He sat across from Washington, legs crossed, his polished boots gleaming, a faint smile lighting his handsome, amiable face. He was more than fifty years old, a man of vast experience and patience.

"I have full confidence in you and your command, my friend," he said. He had some grasp of English, and when he spoke French, Lieutenant-Colonel Tilghman served as an interpreter. "However, you must agree that a campaign against New York would contain many difficulties for which we have yet to discover satisfactory solutions."

Washington clenched his jaw to stifle another stab of pain. The intensity of his toothaches seemed to rise in correlation with his level of frustration.

"There are difficulties, yes, but we still have not heard from Admiral de Grasse. His presence may provide a solution to many of these problems."

The Comte de Grasse was the French naval commander in the West Indies.

"That may be so," Rochambeau agreed.

"Indeed, we can make no definite decision without knowing the admiral's plans," Washington concluded, although he bit off his words. He did not wish to place too much emphasis on the naval aspect of the campaign. It was beyond his control.

"I believe the Comte de Grasse still favours the Chesapeake," Rochambeau stated. "He has said nothing to disabuse me of that notion."

Washington made no reply, but glanced at the letter lying on the side table at his elbow. The letter had been the object of that morning's conversation. It was another dispatch from Lafayette, explaining that Cornwallis had taken a position on the York River, at York Town. The English earl was fortifying the town as a post and had made his encampment there, although no Royal Navy squadron was yet present. The only sea power in the vicinity was a flotilla of unarmed transports, a few small privateers, and two British men-of-war.

"Cornwallis and his little force are vulnerable," Rochambeau continued. "Vulnerable in a way that General Clinton in New York is not, from both sea and land. You must agree, *mon Generale*, that his situation would seem to offer a clear opportunity."

"Such an operation would also contain difficulties," the General warned, "many of a logistical nature."

Rochambeau nodded, then frowned and looked away. Washington sighed in irritation. He knew Rochambeau had been disappointed when he had marched into camp here at Dobb's Ferry on the ninth of July at the head of almost five thousand well-equipped troops. The Frenchman had expected to find ten thousand equally well-armed Continentals waiting for him, but the American force here on the Hudson had shrunk to just over half that number. Rochambeau had expressed nothing but astonishment and respect for what this rabble, the northern Continental Army, had achieved; but he did not support Washington's greatest ambition—to retake New York.

The General had nurtured that ambition since 1776. Every day, he had sent expeditions to probe General Clinton's defenses, looking for a weakness. His men had behaved well under enemy fire and had fought several skirmishes. They had not discovered any vulnerable points in the British walls, but that did not mean those points did not exist. There was a way in, Washington was certain, but Rochambeau was barely willing to discuss the option.

The General cleared his throat, weighing his words, then realized Rochambeau was watching something outside the tent. A horseman approached at a walk. The General frowned, unhappy at the intrusion. It was a dispatch rider, most likely carrying more complaints from his subordinates, more demands for supplies, or for promotions. He no longer had time to spare for such trivialities. Time was now the enemy. The war for independence would succeed or die based on whatever agreement he could finally reach with Rochambeau, perhaps this day or the next.

"A courier, sir," Tilghman said, rising from his chair. "I will see to it."

"Thank you, Colonel." He snatched up his glass of claret. There would be no further meaningful conversation until Tilghman returned.

Indeed, the officers sat in complete silence, unsure where to look, or what to do with their hands, sweating in the stifling heat. Flies buzzed, and the General waved one away. He watched as the dispatch rider turned his horse and moved off. Tilghman was walking back to the marquee wearing a tentative smile. He carried an ordinary wooden letter box, covered in leather and studded with brass rivets. Upon entering the tent, he set the box on one of the map tables.

"It is from Admiral de Grasse," he said. "Good news, perhaps?"

Washington paused, his glass in his hand, then leapt to his feet. He glanced at Rochambeau, who was leaning forward in his chair. This was not some petty annoyance. It was the very news they had been waiting for.

With mingled excitement and apprehension, he went to the box, opened the latch and lifted the lid. Inside was a single folded sheet. Taking it out, he broke the wax seal and opened it. It was written in a fine hand, in French. He handed it to Tilghman.

"Read it out loud for us," he said, "if you would, Colonel."

Tilghman read carefully, speaking each line as it was written then translating into English. Rochambeau approached the camp table to study the maps. The Frenchman leaned over the chart of Chesapeake Bay.

"Cornwallis," he said, stabbing his finger at the map. He pointed to the mouth of the York River.

Washington folded his arms, still trying to absorb the contents of the letter. The Comte de Grasse reported that his fleet had left the West Indies but would not risk the shoals off New York. He was bound for the Chesapeake. The General's jaw clenched to thwart a stab of pain. The Chesapeake.

Rochambeau spoke again, a flurry of French syllables, and Tilghman at once translated, "The Marquis de Lafayette reports there is as yet no British fleet in the Chesapeake. If de Grasse should arrive before the enemy..."

"We might encircle Cornwallis." The General spoke carefully. "We could cut him off from both sea and land. His army is only seven thousand strong. By acting swiftly, we may bring overbearing force against him."

Like a curtain opening upon a stage, the entire campaign was revealed to him. He did not favour it, but he could see it, and at once understood its possibility of success. It would be a slow crushing, the eventual surrender of a second British army, another Saratoga. It would be a victory to ensure the continuance of their revolution, perhaps a victory decisive enough to make the king and his ministers in the British Parliament give up their claim to the colonies in exasperation.

But to make the attempt would mean to at last turn his back on New York, to never reverse his greatest defeat.

He felt rising anger, fought to contain it. He was trapped. There was no longer any choice, for he could not operate without help from the French navy. His allies had forced this campaign upon him. As of this moment, his ambitions against New York were collapsing like a fortress wall that has been pounded by artillery for months.

The Chesapeake it would be. And now he could see one redeeming feature—after six long years, he would be returning to Virginia.

For a moment, his anger abated.

Home. I will be going home. The line of march would take him past Mount Vernon.

"We will exchange New York for York," he at last declared, doing his best to keep his tone light. "I know the country there. Flat, sandy soil, some forest and open spaces. It is excellent terrain for a siege."

There was much to consider, he thought, turning to gaze outside at the neat camp streets. There was so much that could go wrong. Overbearing force would be a necessity. The troops available to Lafayette and von Steuben in Virginia would not be enough against the disciplined, undefeated, and well-entrenched army of Charles Cornwallis.

The General made a quick calculation. He could leave about four thousand men here to hold the Hudson highlands against General Clinton. His remaining two thousand Continentals would then march with Rochambeau's five thousand to Virginia.

The required logistics were staggering. The march would cover five hundred miles. They would need wagons and naval transports, food caches along the way. They would have to stage diversions to ward off flank attacks. There were several rivers crossing their path, the greatest being the Hudson itself. There was the possibility the enemy would thwart the plan altogether.

If his army was attacked on the march, it could be dispersed. If the British navy arrived in the Chesapeake before de Grasse, or defeated de Grasse at sea, the campaign would fail.

But if the march was a success, and the navy remained in support, Cornwallis could be destroyed. The General suddenly realized, as he turned to look again at the map, this was perhaps the greatest opportunity he had encountered since the beginning of the war.

His heart seemed to pause for a moment in wonder. His toothache had vanished.

Chapter 12

The Redcoat

Tom Martin stood on the parapet of the unfinished redoubt, watching his men as they dug with pick and spade, piling the earth to increase the height of the wall. Many of them had tied their neck stocks around their foreheads to keep the stinging sweat from running into their eyes. Already, their gaiter trousers were stained with the reddish earth; and the perspiration glistened on their pale, bare skin, matting the hair on the chests of the older men, running in rivulets through the dust that clung to them.

He knew they hated to dig, but most took to it as they would to any duty, joking and bantering as they worked. Only Private Hassler grumbled, although he, too, was a source of mirth as he uttered a curse each time his pick struck the turf.

"I never thought I'd be diggin' no holes," he grunted. "Army promised me I'd be out of gaol if I joined as a soldier. Didn't know soldiers dug no holes."

"Never thought you'd dig holes, then?" Corporal Gibb cried, and laughed. "That's half of soldiering, my fine fellow. Every time we move to a new post we got to dig holes to protect ourselves from a siege. Got to dig holes when we're besieging someone else. Got to dig ditches to drain our tents. It's not all marching and glory, you know."

"Plenty of marching," Hassler said. "No glory as I see it."

"You wouldn't know glory if you tripped and fell in it," Sam Webb remarked without mirth.

Tom disliked hearing the men bicker, even if Hassler was the subject. He glanced at Lieutenant Nicholson, who loitered nearby, present only because it was required of him. He waited for Nicholson to speak, to offer an encouraging remark, but the officer was staring at his fingernails.

Tom snorted, then called down into the ditch, "Why doesn't someone give us a song?"

"A fine idea, that, Sergeant," Gibb replied, and at once launched into "Bold General Wolfe." A moment later, a few others joined in.

The song was a bit maudlin, but Tom nodded in satisfaction, cradling his fusil in the crook of his arm. He gazed at the crystal blue of the water. Just off the coast, the transports and a pair of frigates remained at anchor. The men and stores had all landed by now, and the little army was busy erecting a chain of landward defences similar to those they had just destroyed at Portsmouth, albeit on a larger scale.

When completed, the fortifications would consist of two stout lines—two chains of forts and breastworks. The outer line lay well south of the town, covering the mile of land between the heads of both creeks. Already, four outer redoubts were complete, one in the southeast to command the road to Hampton, one on either side of the road to Williamsburg, and another in the northwest beyond Yorktown Creek, a large star-shaped redoubt commanding the river road.

The inner line was barely two hundred yards from the town—a dozen redoubts with a large Hornwork, a fortified gun battery, in its center. Tom could see almost the entire line from his perch, the work parties like scurrying ants on a series of anthills. Every man who was not on the sick list was at work digging trenches, redoubts and batteries. Working alongside the infantry was a large force of black civilians who had come in from the surrounding countryside. Many of the blacks were escaped slaves—men, women, and even children, lured to the British by promises of freedom.

An orderly brought water from Wormley Creek, two wooden pails suspended from a pole across his shoulders. Tom called for a break, and the men drank from a shared tin cup, some dashing part of its contents over their heads. During the brief lull, Bone came snuffling along the parapet, nose to the ground. The fine earth had stained the bulldog's white legs a reddish brown.

Tom greeted the mascot, saying, "You'll find nothing of interest here, Bone. No rabbits in these holes. Just men."

The dog wagged his long tail and carried on, scrambling down the east face of the rampart. He then crossed the ditch and climbed out onto the edge of the bluff, heading toward Wormley Creek southeast of the town.

Tom watched the dog recede into the tall grass and shielded his eyes with his left hand. The ground rolled away from him in a gentle green swell, marred only by the brown lines of the works and a scattering of ragged tree stumps where the army had cleared a field of fire. This was where they would fight, should it come to that. The land was wide and open, so like England with its hedgerows and fields, here and there a copse or a single standing tree. In the far distance ran the dark belt of the pine woods, contrasting with the luminous blue of the sky with its benign, drifting cotton-bale clouds.

In the center of this stage, a single wagon rolled along the Hampton road —a local farmer or merchant coming to do business with the army. Aside from the labourers, no other civilians were present. Those who had not fled mostly kept to themselves.

Though they must play host to our officers, Tom thought, *who are billeted in their homes.*

He turned to look at the town. It was nothing but two streets, one running along the bluff and one below, the latter hardly more than a strip of rutted beach. The buildings of red brick were English in style, including the church and two fine houses; but the rest were of wooden clapboards or shingles. This hamlet was to be their naval base, and a Union Flag now snapped over the courthouse, proof of who commanded here.

The same breeze that unfurled that flag spun the little clacking windmill. Beyond the windmill ran the steeper cut of Yorktown Creek, a natural defensive barrier. The rebels could never take this place by storm, Tom decided. They would have to resort to the slow grinding of a siege.

Behind him, the work resumed, the dull thud of the picks giving way to the scraping of shovel blades as the men took up their spades. Gibb's song had long since finished. Tom turned his attention back to the straining, glistening fellows in the ditch. He stifled a grin as he watched Hassler attack the loosened soil as if it were a platoon of rebel infantry. The private stabbed his spade down with all his might, then slapped its contents against the wall.

"Ah, me," Tom remarked. "Now, if only you will be that energetic in battle, Private Hassler."

Hassler's foot suddenly slid out from under him while his spade was in mid-swing. He fell forward with a cry, burying his face in the loose earth. The men watching exploded with laughter, and even Tom struggled to maintain his composure.

"That serves you right, mate," someone sang out. Hassler pushed himself to his feet, spitting dirt.

"I'll teach y' to laugh at me!" he cried. He retrieved his spade and brandished it like a battle-axe, the red earth caked on his massive chest and arms. With his heavy features contorted in fury, he looked formidable, like some demon from the pit; but that only made the men laugh all the harder.

"Will you take on the whole lot of us?" someone shouted at him.

"Damn you, I will!" Hassler thundered. "One at a time!"

Tom leaned forward to intervene.

"Lay down your spade, Private! I'll have no fighting amongst ourselves. Save your animosity for the enemy."

Hassler peered up at the wall until he could see him through the glinting sun.

"I'll not be made a joke of, Sergeant."

"Private," Tom began, with a note of warning, "you will only make yourself a joke if you persist in this course. If the men laugh at you, it is because you are their comrade. You are either a member of this company, or you are not."

Hassler blinked. He was quivering with rage. It was clear to Tom he did not understand.

"Sergeant!" Lieutenant Nicholson called from his end of the parapet, finally making his presence known.

Tom stiffened to attention, his fusil at his side.

"Sir?"

Nicholson's face was white with outrage.

"Have that man taken into custody at once!"

"Sir!" Tom acknowledged. He had hoped to settle this matter without resorting to army justice, but he would not disobey an officer. "Corporal Gibb?"

That was all Tom had to say. Gibb and three others threw down their spades and advanced on Hassler. Hassler faced them, continuing to hold his spade like a weapon.

"Don't you bloody touch me!"

"Don't make it harder for yourself, then," Gibb said.

Hassler held his position but made no move as Gibb's three companions surrounded him. Two men took his arms and he went limp, as if finally understanding there was no escape. The spade fell.

But suddenly he flailed his arms, bellowing with rage, attempting to shake his captors off. His last-minute resistance surprised them, although not enough to make them lose their grip. A third man snatched the tight queue of hair that hung down Hassler's neck, pulling back his head, but Hassler pitched himself backward. All four men crashed to the ground in a heap of struggling, cursing bodies.

Tom scrambled down from the parapet. He had hoped to find a way to reach Hassler, to bring him into the fold; but the fellow was too stupid, and now it was too late. The rest of the lads saw Hassler as an outsider, a disruptive force. He had to be corrected. Discipline had to be maintained.

Hassler continued to bellow, but his resistance had grown weaker. He lay on top of the man who still gripped his hair. Tom hurried over to him, then swung his musket down until the tip of the fixed bayonet touched Hassler's throat.

"Cease your struggles, man," he growled. "You're under arrest."

⁂

The British camps at York lay snug within the inner line of defense, the rows of tents filling a small space southeast of the town proper. Inside this cramped position was room for a small parade ground. There, in the golden light of an August morning, Tom Martin brought his company into line with his battalion. One by one, the other companies also arrived, until the entire Light Infantry Brigade was present. The brigade formed a hollow square, the men in two ranks, facing inward. They stood easy, relaxing in formation, leaning on their muskets. They were ready to witness punishment.

Tom surveyed the assembled ranks. Every soldier had turned out in his best order of dress, coats as well as waistcoats, breeches and black gaiters in place of overalls, their leather belts white with fresh pipe clay. They all looked very fine, in contrast to the terrible object that stood in the centre of the square.

This was an improvised whipping post, fashioned from four espontoons—a tripod with a crosspiece near the bottom of one face. Arrayed next to this "triangle" were the combined fifes and drums of the brigade. To one side of the musicians waited the brigade commander, Lieutenant-Colonel Robert Abercrombie, resplendent on horseback. The adjutant and surgeon of the 1st Light Infantry were also nearby. The adjutant held a leather bag fastened with a drawstring. It was a familiar scene.

Tom glanced to his left as the prisoner, Private Stephen Hassler, arrived, marching through a gap in the square. A sergeant and three privates formed Hassler's escort. Hassler wore no uniform, just his shirt, breeches and gaiters, but his hair was neat, and white with fresh powder. His hands were free, his mouth a sullen downward crescent.

Hassler halted before the triangle, the sergeant at his right elbow. Two wooden buckets of water sat on the parade near his feet. All was in readiness, Tom thought, for the brutal procedure that was about to take place.

He glanced at the sky, at the faint traces of cloud spiraling against their backdrop of deep blue. A flurry of smells assailed him— the dust and grass of the parade square, the wool of his uniform, wood smoke and cooking from the camp, the sweat of his comrades. He could smell the sea.

"Carry on, Major," Colonel Abercrombie intoned, voice raised for all to hear.

The adjutant stepped forward. He was the very picture of a British officer, his uniform spotless, his gold gorget glinting as he stated the charges.

"Private Stephen Hassler, you have been found guilty by fair tribunal of contravening the Articles of War. Said court-martial has sentenced you to the penalty not to exceed one hundred lashes."

Tom saw no one flinch at the sentence. It did not come as a shock to these fellows, nor to him. If anything, it was lenient. This was army discipline, discipline Tom had witnessed many times. It was not a pleasant thing to watch, but as a sergeant and one sworn to uphold the King's regulations, he could not openly disagree with it.

The men who received such punishment, in his experience, had deserved it, for their crimes usually endangered the lives or welfare of their comrades. He had seen men flogged for stealing, for falling asleep on guard duty, for drunkenness when an alert mind was imperative, and for missing roll call. He had seen men, like Hassler, flogged for disobeying orders and causing a disturbance. He had once seen a man receive a thousand lashes in a single session. Somehow, the man had survived.

It was a terrible thing, but cruelly justifiable. One hundred lashes, Tom thought, seemed a slight punishment in comparison. Perhaps the fact Lord Cornwallis did not care for flogging on principle had influenced the court martial, convinced the members to be merciful.

"Remove your shirt," the sergeant of the guard commanded. Hassler glared at him, but obeyed, pulling the shirt over his head and passing it to one of the guards. His shoulders were sunburned from building the redoubts, but his lower torso was as white as a fish belly, glistening in the sun.

The guards took Hassler's hands and lashed them together, then guided him toward the triangle. They tied his hands to the apex of the crossed pole-arms, above his head near to where the blades met, and his feet against the base of each stave. His knees were braced against the crosspiece.

One guard pushed a leather bit into Hassler's mouth to prevent him from biting through his tongue.

The drum major and two drummers stepped forward. The drummers were hulking lads, both stripped to the waist like the prisoner. The adjutant opened his leather bag and drew forth a pair of leather cat o' nine tails. He gave a cat to each drummer.

"You may proceed," he said to the drum major.

The drum major touched his hat to the officer, then said, "Drummers, do your duty."

The drummers took positions on either side of the prisoner. Without further ceremony, the lad on Hassler's right twirled on his heels to deliver the first blow. The knotted leather ends of the cat struck Hassler's flesh with a sound like a flat stone striking wet sand.

"One," the sergeant of the guard stated.

The next drummer delivered the second blow, and so the two young musicians took turns. With each lick of the cat, the sergeant stated the number.

Hassler's face was turned away, but Tom saw his body jerk. At least Hassler did not cry out. Tom was glad for that, that the man would not add further disgrace to himself or his company.

A man on Tom's left coughed, then retched.

"Quiet in ranks," Tom snapped. He saw several ashen faces in the assembled companies, yet just as many men wore grins.

By the fiftieth lash, Hassler's head was jolting upward with each stroke. A lattice of crimson stripes covered his back. The drummers paused, dipping their cats in one of the water buckets to rinse away the clotted blood.

After a few dozen more lashes, Hassler's body sagged, dangling from its bonds. The surgeon held up his hands, and the drummers paused. They were breathing heavily, their torsos covered in a spattering of red drops.

The surgeon examined the prisoner. Lieutenant-Colonel Abercrombie called, "Surely, he has not expired so soon?"

The surgeon looked up and declared, "He has only fallen into a swoon, sir." He nodded at the sergeant. "You may continue."

The sergeant took the bucket of clean water and poured a measure over Hassler's head. Hassler groaned and lurched back into consciousness. The flogging resumed.

The punishment lasted almost three-quarters of an hour. When it was done, Hassler's back was a red pudding. The August sun beat down, and Tom could smell the sweet fragrance of blood. Several men from his battalion had fainted, dropping onto the grass.

The sergeant poured the remains of one water bucket over Hassler's back, then draped Hassler's shirt over his shoulders. The guards cut him down.

Tom turned to Corporal Gibb and said, "Carry on."

"Escort," Gibb said, "take care!"

Six men snapped to attention. Gibb ordered them to fall out of ranks. As members of Hassler's company, they would escort him to the camp hospital.

Hassler walked. With his ruined back hunched and knees bent, he marched before Corporal Gibb's squad.

Colonel Abercrombie dismissed his brigade to breakfast.

Tom spent the rest of the morning and part of the afternoon at the target range he had established on the beach. There, the saltiness of the sea and cries of the gulls mingled with the stench of burned powder and the crack of his musket. He was angry, angry at the shame and dishonour Hassler had brought to his company, and angry with himself that he had failed to correct Hassler in a less drastic manner.

That evening, as on every evening, Tom reported to Captain Barlow's tent. The air was still warm and alive with the chirping of crickets. He presented the company sick list, and Captain Barlow read it. Three more men were down with fever. It had become epidemic. Now Hassler was added to the list, thanks to military justice.

"Damn this climate and its fevers," Barlow said. "And now we have lost another man. Private Hassler will not be fit for duty for at least a month."

Tom could find little sympathy for the insubordinate private.

"You regret the punishment, sir?"

Barlow did not answer for a moment.

"No, I regret the necessity of it."

"I feel the same way, sir."

Barlow reclined in his chair.

"Well, it is done. A troublesome man has been dealt with, or so we trust. Perhaps in future he will learn to have more respect for his comrades."

"Such is my thinking."

"Well, to other business." Barlow took the able list from his camp desk and held it up to the light of a hanging candle sconce. "Despite our shrinking numbers, we need to address our lack of non-commissioned officers. I have let this deficiency fester for too long. I need your recommendations, Sergeant. I wish to ask the colonel to promote two more sergeants. With yourself as senior man, that will give us three. And two corporals to assist."

Tom did not hesitate.

"I recommend Corporal Gibb at once, sir. And Corporal David Rush, as well. Both men will make fine sergeants. As for the corporals, I am afraid I must consider the matter further."

"By all means, Sergeant." Barlow snatched a pen, dipped it in ink, and scribbled the names of those mentioned on a fresh sheet. "And thank you." He stared at the list of names for another moment, then added, "That will be all for now. I will see you in the morning."

Tom nodded. "Good night, sir. I will have my recommendations ready by then, sir."

"Very good."

Tom put on his cap, then stepped out into the night. From below the bluff came the gentle rushing of surf, from the creek the full-throated croaking of frogs.

Chapter 13

The Loyalist

*C*atherine was in the kitchen preparing dinner when Abigail burst through the door. The younger woman's face was alight with mingled excitement and alarm as she exclaimed, "There are more horsemen coming!"

Catherine paused with her knifeblade halfway through an onion. *Daniel has returned,* she thought, and felt her heart quicken. She threw down her knife and snatched at her apron, pulling its hem up to wipe away the false onion tears. *I must look presentable. I must be composed.*

She had missed him from the moment he had departed. The house felt empty without his presence, just a hollow shell. It was not the refuge it had once been. She knew now that her growing attraction to him had been genuine, but she was not certain she could marry another soldier.

"Has Lieutenant Brattle returned?" she asked, and could hear the eagerness in her own voice. Then she realized what Abigail had said. "There are horsemen approaching? How many?"

"More than a dozen!" Abigail squealed. "They are dressed in green, like the others, but not green and red. They are green and black. They all carry swords!"

"Not Daniel," she breathed, and she leaned with both hands against the edge of the table. She had been foolish, nothing but a foolish girl nurturing false hopes. Daniel would be unable to leave the army again so soon. "A squadron of cavalry. Perhaps in search of forage."

Abigail covered her mouth with both hands.

"Will they rob us?"

Catherine pushed away from the table. Her hands were trembling. She wiped them on her apron.

"We will see. I will go and meet them."

Her legs were like lead as she made the short journey from the kitchen to the main building, her footfalls loud upon the flags. She could hear voices, and paused before the back door, taking a series of deep breaths. The men had already entered the house.

She pulled the door open, and it swung on silent hinges. She could see clear through to the front door, which also stood agape. There was an officer in the hall. He did not see Catherine, but shouted up the stairs, "Adam? Are in you in here, man?"

She wondered how he could know Adam, but there was no malice in his voice. She cleared her throat and managed a faint, "Hello?"

The man looked in her direction, squinting. She knew that he saw her, but he said nothing.

"Who is there?" she added.

The officer removed his helmet. It was black with a black fur crest, a green cockade on the left. The man's dark-green jacket was cut short and decorated with silver lace and black facings. Two other men in similar dress had come into the hall behind him.

"Good afternoon, sir," Catherine tried, managing to force a note of authority into her voice, although her fear had not diminished. She advanced a few steps. Abigail had followed her and was clutching her skirts, hiding behind them. "How may I be of service?"

"Forgive me, ma'am," the officer said at last, his tone polite but wary. He was of middle age, his natural gray hair tied with a black ribbon. Catherine found his square, lined face familiar. "I am seeking the retainer of this property. Are you perhaps his guest?"

"Adam will be in his hut with his family, but they will be coming soon for dinner."

The man's brow furrowed.

"Do I know you, ma'am? How came you to my house, to be giving dinner to my servants?"

"*Your* house?" Catherine repeated. Then she leapt back with a gasp. She had not recognized him in the uniform.

"Cousin John," she stated. "Cousin John, is that you?"

The officer's squinting eyes widened in astonishment.

"Could that be Cousin Catherine? My dear Cousin Catherine?"

"It is!" she cried. Then, for a few seconds, she simply stood in place, not knowing what to do next. It was as if some ancient wish had suddenly come true, a wish that could not possibly be real. "I came to see you, but you were not here."

He shook his head in his incredulity.

"No, of course I wasn't! All loyal men are enemies in this country." Then he exclaimed, "For God's sake, girl, how did you come to be in Virginia?"

"I wrote, but you did not reply," she explained. Warm tears suddenly sprouted from the corners of her eyes. She rushed to him, sobbing, "I had to come! I did not know the danger. It was foolish, but I had to come."

"God's blood," he whispered. He took her in his arms, and she felt how strong he was, and now Abigail was embracing them both, leaping up and down, laughing and crying at once. "Oh, my girls, my girls! This is a shock I never expected. I have not laid eyes on you for some five or six years. I didn't even know you. I thought you still in New York.

"Well, you are safe with us now. You, and little Abigail." He cradled Abigail's head against his shoulder. "There, there, my dear. It seems like I have not seen you since you were knee high. But it will be all right now."

"Have you come back to stay?" Catherine asked. "Has there been a victory?" She dared to hope there had been. Then she realized if there had been a battle, Daniel might have been involved.

"No," her cousin said, releasing them and standing back. "We are not staying. The army has moved up from Portsmouth to York, close by here. Well, some twenty miles or so, this side of the river. I had to make certain the rebels hadn't torched this place. I have not seen it since I was forced to leave."

"Adam kept it safe for you, John. No one has bothered us since our arrival."

"Good for Adam. Well done. But I cannot tarry. Colonel Tarleton expects us back. I must find Adam and charge him to continue his vigilance, but not to resist if the enemy comes, for his own safety. I suspect there will be rebel foraging parties setting upon the place soon." He glanced around, his movements frantic, as if this were his last chance to look upon the walls. "Now I am glad I decided to come back! You must come with me, my dear cousins. You cannot stay here. This is country controlled by the enemy. You must come with me to York."

Catherine held her hands against her cheeks to steady herself. She had prayed for this moment since the crushing discovery that the house was unoccupied, but she hesitated at the thought of leaving. She did not want to.

"Can we not remain here with Adam?" she asked.

"I would not think of it! My house is well known; the enemy would come to know you as my relation. And the war has come to this country in earnest. The rebels will try to attack York, of that I have no doubt. I do not believe they will get the better of my Lord Cornwallis, but this house, this dear old house, may still find itself in ruins. The enemy may burn it simply out of spite if the next engagement does not go their way, and I tell you it will not!"

Further argument died on her lips. A small inner voice insisted that she would still be safe, no one would harm them here, that she had made this house her own. But the words did not come.

"Lord Cornwallis is in York?" she asked.

"Yes, he is," John stated, then added, "You will be safe with the army of Lord Cornwallis."

"I will feel safe with you, dear cousin," she said, and she let herself feel happiness at his return as relief suddenly flooded her. "Oh John, John. It is so good to see you."

She threw her arms around him again, and then Abigail joined her. The three of them wept for joy.

Chapter 14

The General

The French engineers had built an observation tower of logs and sawn planks, and Washington stood on its summit, taking in the view of the Hudson River to the east. He could smell the new wood. The day was bright and still, a few wisps of cloud hanging low on the horizon. He had enjoyed days like this as a boy, and he was reminded of that happy time as he watched the spectacle unfolding below him in the bulge of Haverstraw Bay.

The armies were on the march to the Chesapeake. The river crossing began on August 19 at ten o'clock in the morning, the army moving unencumbered. Washington had issued a general order forbidding camp followers, warning that no provision, whether for food or transport, would be made for them. He knew a train of women and children would slow the progress of the march, and speed was of the essence.

Now, barges laden with French infantry, horses, and wagons were following the diagonal ferry route from Verplanck's Point on the east bank to Stony Point on the west. There, the route linked with one of the main roads going south. Most of the American forces had already crossed, a few at Dobb's Ferry in the south, the rest here at King's Ferry.

It had rained the first day, but not enough to dampen the General's spirits. He had ridden through the downpour here to King's Ferry and had found the observation platform waiting for him, a small gift from the French, and one for which he was thankful. From this vantage point, he had watched his Continentals cross the hissing water; and he had known, at that moment, this could truly be the beginning of something grand and significant.

As each regiment left the barges to form on the near bank, he had raised his hat in salute. The cold rain had soaked his hair and face, but he paid it no heed. The regiments marched past under the platform, the men staring up and cheering, some waving their hats and shaking their muskets. Men who had not received their pay and had not been properly fed for months, if not years, cheered him and cried out for victory. Their enthusiasm had swelled his heart.

He supposed that within a few days the excitement would be a memory, and the complaints would begin anew. But not now. Not now.

Sun glinted from brass band instruments, buttons, and bayonets as the French host flowed from east to west. When the infantry landed on the near bank, they formed in ranks of eight, arrayed in column. Even after the dust and sweat of their march, Washington found their turnout impressive. He had grown accustomed to his shabby and motley Americans, but here every black hat matched, and every man wore a coat and breeches of sparkling white. Each regiment sported a different facing colour on its uniform—yellow, sky-blue, or rose—and their accoutrements were new and in superb condition.

"It is quite a sight," he said to one of his companions, Claude Blanchard, the French Quartermaster-General. "The French army looks very well today."

"They march to a better destiny," Blanchard replied in his perfect English. "They sense that something glorious is in the offing, General Washington."

At Blanchard's words, the third occupant of the platform, Brigadier-General Henry Knox, lifted his hat and held it against his chest.

"I must thank you for allowing me to witness the progress of our allies, General," he said to Washington. "And again, for including me in this great endeavor."

Washington nodded, suppressing a smile. Knox was one of those officers who often complained about his lack of promotion, but he was an unswerving patriot. He wore the uniform of the Continental Artillery—a blue coat with red facings, a buff waistcoat and buff breeches—garments remarkably similar to those of the British Royal Artillery. The coat draped from Knox's heavy frame, and his oval head, with its close-spaced eyes and heavy double chin, seemed to squat on top of the collar.

"There was no question of bringing you and your guns, General Knox," Washington stated, although some did not agree with that decision. The French had supplied all the artillery necessary for the campaign, including the heavy siege guns, which Admiral de Barras would carry in his transports. There was no actual need for Knox's pieces, and they would slow the march.

Washington, however, remembered how the unassuming artilleryman had dragged those guns overland from Fort Ticonderoga in 1776. Those cannon had then forced the British out of Boston, giving the Americans their first success. He appreciated the power of symbols; Knox's artillery would, indeed, go to York, at all costs.

"We could not do this without you, General," he added, feeling a moment of true affection for this man's unwavering loyalty.

Knox seemed to swell, and turned his attention back to the procession on the river. The French columns on the near bank now stretched along the road like a vast white ribbon. It was a great host, a great power.

I must not be swayed too much by visions of grandeur, Washington thought. *When I descend from this platform, there will be work to do.*

He scanned the horizon, searching for signs of the enemy. This was an ideal opportunity for the British to strike the rebels and their French allies, to inflict heavy damage while they were strung out on the road. So far, the cavalry had reported no motion in the British lines, no evidence that General Clinton suspected his adversaries were leaving him and going south. Clinton sat idle in New York, perhaps too preoccupied with his parties and fancy balls.

That was as Washington wanted it. He had done all he could to convince the British the Americans were simply redeploying their forces for the long-awaited attack on New York. He had supplied false information to known spies, sacrificed couriers who carried false documents, and the various ruses seemed to have worked. His first fear—of an attack while the armies were crossing the Hudson—had not come to pass.

"Providence has smiled on us these last days," he said, knowing he would ask for no further help from the higher powers. He would trust in his allies, and in his preparations.

Most of all, he thought, *I will trust in the devotion of those dear fellows who have stayed with me through thick and thin since the war's beginning.*

Chapter 15

The Continental

*J*oshua entered the tent just as Daniel was finishing his long letter to Catherine Seawell. Daniel looked up from his improvised camp desk—an empty biscuit barrel—as the rush of air from the open tent flap made the candles in the iron lanterns flicker. Joshua closed the flap and slowly advanced on a folding camp chair, one arm outstretched as if the chair were fleeing from him.

"You were not gone long," Daniel said.

Joshua sat with a sigh, brushing a lock of hair from his forehead.

"I'm a tad weary tonight," he said.

Daniel studied him. His brother remained on the sick list, and the battalion surgeon had warned him not to tax himself; but he insisted on taking walks through the camp, hoping to build his strength.

"I thought perhaps you might want advice in your letter," he said, finding his lopsided grin. "The advice of an older, more experienced brother."

"I think not," Daniel snapped. "Besides, I have finished."

Joshua slumped in his chair.

"I speak only in jest, little brother. Do you hate my opinions so much now that you find resentment even in my little attempt at humour?"

"No, Joshua," Daniel said, but he knew that to be untrue. He was always angry with Joshua now since they had returned to the camp, to the war.

"I would never even consider showing you disrespect, Daniel," Joshua continued. "You are an officer, but it is the duty of an older brother to help a younger, and that is a habit I find difficult to break."

Daniel kept his eyes on the page before him. From somewhere outside came the mournful music of a single fiddle, then a burst of rough laughter. The sounds of an army camp, sounds he knew so well; but since his return everything seemed changed.

He still believed in the cause of independence, at least in a rational sense. America was not England. England was a country he had never seen, far across the ocean. It was a country that controlled the destiny of America for its own benefit, a country that expected America to serve it. America's interests would always remain secondary in such an arrangement.

He recalled his father saying once, "I was born a Briton, but when the king and his ministers betrayed our trust, when the king dared to speak as if we were simple-minded and unruly children that needed a good switching, I became an American. This is my nation. This is my first loyalty—to my land and my family's future."

A noble cause, Daniel thought, *a just cause, to fight for one's freedom.*

England had not been defeated, and would not be; but Daniel's decision to fight on would not be rescinded. He would fight until the end, until he could fight no more.

"I understand that you no longer hope for success as you once did," Joshua was saying, "but I know you, Daniel. That will pass. You've shown your devotion to our poor company, training them every day, putting them through their drills. They may grumble, but I see the sense in it, and one day, they will as well."

Daniel nodded, but did not explain that he drilled the company to give himself something to do, to take his mind away from thoughts of Catherine.

"The extra drill will increase their steadiness," he said, "and ensure they survive when the next defeat comes."

Joshua grimaced. "There won't be another defeat."

Daniel ignored him.

"Captain Holyoak has agreed to deliver my letter. He will take it to the farm on his next patrol."

"Good, very good. You have something to fight for in Miss Seawell, some tangible thing, even though she comes from a Tory household. But after all she did for me, I would never speak a disparaging word of her. Keep writing your letters, and seek her out when the war is over."

"I wish I did not have to wait."

"And yet, you do. What did you think when you spoke of not coming back to the company? That you could stay with her and pretend the war was won? We still have work to do."

Daniel bit back an angry retort. He did not wish for an argument.

"But I did come back, Joshua." *Though there is nothing but doom awaiting us and our cause,* he added inwardly.

He folded the letter. A future with Catherine seemed the stuff of fantasy, a wish for what might be, but he would continue to hope just as he would continue to fight. He would carry on.

Chapter 16

The Loyalist

Catherine did not want to leave the farmhouse, but John gave her no time for argument or deliberation. She had come to Virginia to find him, so she would go with him.

But there was one thing she insisted on doing before they left. She would write a letter to Daniel Brattle, explaining what had happened, that her cousin had returned and she was leaving for York.

When the letter was finished, she sealed it and gave it to Adam.

"Daniel promised to return," she said. "If he keeps that promise, deliver this to him."

Adam nodded. "I will, Miss Catherine."

Catherine embraced him, then his wife, who stood with him on the step. Fannie did not bother to hold back tears.

"You take care now," she said, her lined face further creased with worry and perhaps, Catherine imagined, regret. "And you, too, Miss Abigail."

"We shall miss you both," Abigail squeaked.

The sisters had already thrown a few articles of clothing—new things they had made themselves from stores of fabric they had found in the house—into a battered old trunk of John's, and a pair of dragoons carried it out to the road where three wagons waited behind yokes of oxen. Catherine and Abigail followed. The wagons were piled high with sacks of oats and other grains, but the dragoons shifted the load in one, making room for the baggage.

"You will be safe in York," John said as he helped them climb to the bench seat of the first wagon.

"You must tell us everything," Catherine said. "Where have you been? Why did you decide to become a soldier?"

John's face contorted with a strange combination of gravity and embarrassment.

"In time, I will, my dear. I will. But it will have to wait."

He mounted his horse and took position at the head of the troop. The remaining dragoons fell in, formed in twos. John raised his right hand, calling out the command, and the march began. The wagon driver, a sullen fellow with crooked, rotten teeth, cracked his whip; and the cumbersome vehicle lurched forward.

Catherine held Abigail's hand. The comforting stone face of the house receded farther and farther. Adam and Fannie still stood near the step, not moving.

I am running once more, Catherine thought, blinking back tears. *I will never see this place again.*

The wagons bumped and lumbered, past the unkempt fields, the rotten and tumbled fences, jarring her this way and that. Then the road took them into the pines, and the house was gone.

John rode back along the column.

"It is no more than fifteen or twenty miles," he told them. "We should reach York by morning tomorrow. Tonight, we will rally with the rest of my regiment, the British Legion, east of Williamsburg. It will be all right. You will see."

"I am used to journeys, cousin," Catherine said. "I have no fear."

He smiled. "That is the cousin I've come to know."

≈⚜≈

Catherine felt every miserable lurching yard. Her wooden seat was as hard as granite, and the driver's breath stank. A few times, John had ridden back to offer encouragement, but for the most part his duty kept him at the front of the column, or to the rear to investigate a rumour of pursuit.

She distracted herself by examining the countryside. Much of it was swamp or woods, although they had passed several wide stretches of cleared land —plantations with fields and manor houses. Most of the houses appeared to be well maintained, evidence of continued occupation by their owners.

They had stopped once to rest and water the horses in a creek, but the respite was all too brief. The journey resumed; and close to an hour later, as the afternoon grew aged and weary, one of John's forward scouts pounded up and halted in a swirl of dust. He reported that the rest of the regiment was nearby, about a mile ahead.

John gave the order to hurry, and soon they came upon a larger body of cavalry, some standing in the road, others bivouacked in an adjacent pasture. Catherine sat in silence as he greeted another mounted officer, a young man with reddish-brown hair, a long handsome face and close-set eyes. When the officer returned John's salute, she noticed he was missing most of the index and middle fingers on his right hand.

He and John exchanged words, then both turned about and approached the wagon.

"Colonel Tarleton," John said, "allow me to introduce my northern cousins, the Misses Seawell."

Tarleton's eyes took in Catherine's shabby dress, and she thought she saw amusement there, perhaps even contempt, although his smile was pleasant as he touched his helmet, nodding.

"I am pleased to make the acquaintance of two such fine specimens of the fairer sex. Allow me to introduce myself. I am Lieutenant-Colonel Banastre Tarleton, of His Majesty's Loyalist corps the British Legion."

"Catherine Seawell, sir," Catherine said, not caring for the colonel's words or his tone. This young man was a rogue, she had no doubt, but she held her tongue to avoid embarrassing her cousin.

"And I am Abigail—Abigail Seawell," her sister chimed.

"Ah, indeed," Tarleton said.

An oily leer, it seemed to Catherine, took hold of his dark eyes, and he flashed a sudden crooked smile. Abigail blushed and looked at her feet. Catherine bristled.

Tarleton turned back to John.

"I have received new orders, Captain. Upon our return to York Town, we are to cross the river to Gloucester Point. I have been given command of the outpost. You will find quarters for your men there."

"Very good, sir." John saluted. Tarleton returned the gesture, glanced again at Catherine and Abigail, then reined about and cantered away, his horse kicking up dust and small stones.

"Well, then," John said, shielding his mouth and nose with one hand. He gave Catherine a dubious look. "He is, in general, a good man, Catherine. To be sure, he has his faults, but he is not as bad as some say."

"I have never heard of the man," she said, "and so do not know of his reputation."

This was a lie, for Daniel and Joshua had spoken the name of Tarleton with disgust and hatred.

John smiled. "Then you may form your own opinion. All will be well. And we will be in Gloucester by tomorrow."

⚜

Gloucester proved to be a tiny hamlet on the north side of the York River. It was surrounded by great heaping earthworks—four redoubts with a connecting wall, with palisades of rough logs extending into the water on either flank. Catherine counted some twenty cannon in three separate batteries, most of the smaller sort on travelling carriages facing inland, while to the north stretched an expanse of ugly pine stumps that had recently been forest.

"I do not like it here," she whispered to Abigail.

Abigail huddled close to her.

"But at least we will have some company."

Within the village, they found more Loyalist troops and a herd of civilians who had followed Cornwallis for months. The fugitives lived in the houses and in the camps—men, women and children of all ages.

"Many of the younger men have joined Tarleton's legion," John explained, "or Colonel Simcoe's Queen's Rangers."

John reported to his regimental adjutant, and soon he was directed to the house that would be his quarters. It was a fine dwelling—large, with three stories. The owners had abandoned it and all its furnishings, fleeing on the first approach of the British ships. John would share the place with three lieutenants and another captain, but he arranged to have one room on the second floor set aside for Catherine and Abigail.

The sisters tried to settle into their new surroundings. Abigail began unpacking their trunk while Catherine returned to the main parlour, looking for John. She found him perched on one end of a fine Queen Anne settee, tugging at his riding boots. He dropped one to the carpet, sighing with relief as he massaged his toes.

"I feel as though I have been in the saddle for days on end."

Catherine sat next to him, folding her hands in her lap.

"This is a very grim place to which you have brought us, Cousin John. All of these forts, these cannon, these poor refugees."

John tugged at his other boot.

"Heavens, my dear! Our situation is grim, and has been for years! You don't find these walls give you some comfort?"

"These walls suggest that we fear the very country that surrounds us."

"My colonel will soon change that, I think."

She leaned forward and touched his arm.

"I am not ungrateful, please don't misunderstand me. You must tell me what has been happening! How did you come to be in this regiment?"

His smile was sheepish. "Absurd, isn't it? Me, a soldier! And yet I assure you, it is true."

"You must have your reasons. I suppose it is another sign that our world has changed."

John slumped against the back of the settee. Dust from their journey covered his breeches.

"Indeed, it has, indeed, it has." Then he added, "Colonel Tarleton is despised by our enemies, Catherine. I'll have you know that. He was blamed for killing rebel troops who attempted to surrender after an engagement in the Carolinas, although he had fallen from his horse and did not have command at the time.

"These rebel complaints are nothing but hypocrisy. The persecution of Loyalists in the Carolinas saw no restraint. No restraint. Entire towns burned by rebels, countless plantations destroyed. The rebels refused to give our troops quarter as well, most notably after the battle at King's Mountain." Again he massaged his toes. "I had no notion of whether my house had been spared. Things have not been as severe here in Virginia, but I did not know."

"So, you decided to fight? Is that what you are telling me?"

"It took me a long time to make up my mind, my dear. A long time. I have been absent from my home, the house you occupied, for nigh on two years, since the spring of seventy-eight."

The admission astonished her. She had never thought it had been that long.

"Two years!"

"Yes, it's true! That was when the friends of Patrick Henry declared all so-called 'Tory property' forfeit to the Virginia government, thus ordering all remaining Loyalists to leave. There were few of us left, mind you. Very few. Most had gone after that fool Governor Dunmore was run out in the summer of seventy-six.

"I learned not to speak my mind after that, but my sympathies had become known. I faced the choice of declaring myself a neutral or remaining true to my conscience. I did the latter, and complied with the order before I could be arrested."

It was a familiar story.

"And you offered your services to the Crown as a soldier."

"That was not my immediate design. I was content to allow others to fight the battle for me." He laughed. "Imagine me, an old sea trader, an alleged farmer, a soldier! Yet circumstances have placed me where I am. That, and my ancestors. Do you recall Grandfather's old sword?"

"The one he carried against the French in the last war?" Catherine remembered him showing it to her when she was a child—a slim blade, so slim it seemed it might break if handled with too much vigour.

"Yes. I have it still. It hung above the mantel in my study, but I took it with me when I abandoned the house. It is with my baggage. Not much good to a dragoon, so I do not use it, but it compelled me into the service. After a time, the sight of it made me feel a coward.

"Opposing the war does not change the reality that the war is here. No, it does not. One must fight for what one believes. Thus, I joined the British Legion, and they made me an officer at once. I am a respected landowner, and a practiced horseman, so they believe I can command.

"Sometimes, it strikes me as quite ridiculous, me in charge of men who have fought in great battles while I have seen nothing but patrols, foraging expeditions, acts of desecration against the countryside, and precious little of the enemy."

He laughed again, but the sound was not one of humour.

"So, that is where you have been. All this time, and I wondered whether you were even alive…"

She saw remorse in his eyes.

"I had no idea my letters would bring you here, my dear! No idea! I am so sorry, so sorry."

She quickly took his hand and squeezed it.

"But now I find you are safe! And though you may think yourself absurd or ridiculous, I do not. You seemed brimming with confidence on our journey here. You need not raise your sword to lead, John."

He stared at his stockinged feet.

"I suppose not."

"And perhaps you never will. Neither side in this war is making progress, that much is clear. Perhaps the time has come for negotiations, for an end to the fighting."

He shook his head.

"There were attempts at discussions after we took New York, but they were bungled by the king's deputies. I swear more than half our troubles have been the result of the king placing power and responsibility in the hands of men with thick heads! Uncommon thick! It is tempting to believe Great Britain has run out of great men. Perhaps too many were killed in the *last* war."

Catherine folded her hands in her lap.

"You do not speak as though you have much hope, cousin."

John began to unbutton his green jacket.

"Hope is something we must create for ourselves. There can be no peace for us without victory, Catherine, else there is no place for us here anymore. We have no alternative." His voice grew very soft. "I sought the life of a farmer, hoping to make my fortune in comfort and security. I built my farm from nothing with my bare hands and the resources of my previous endeavours. Now, that is all gone, stolen from me, and the thieves purport to rule the country. I will fight, but I do not know if I will ever gain it back. Ever."

"We must never give up hope for peace," Catherine insisted.

"Too much has changed. Too much blood has been spilled. One side must win. It is not just property we fight for, dear Catherine.

"You know I never favoured independence. I never could. I call myself British, and the king is my sovereign. I have always been British, though I was born in America. I can think of myself in no other way. I am forced to fight to retain my very identity."

"You can never lose who you are, dear John. Wherever you are, whomever you may be with, you can never lose that. If you were to live in Spain or France, you would still be British."

He gazed on her with fondness.

"Your optimism is refreshing, cousin. Refreshing."

But she could see the war had worn him down. She knew he was a fine horseman, but not with a sword in his hand, even their grandfather's elegant blade. Such were many of the Loyalists she had known in the north. They had not supported the king and his taxes, but they had not wanted war. Some had feared loss of position, but many were of a conservative bent and had simply feared change, feared independence. Thousands had volunteered to fight the rebellion, but as many had refused to take up arms and still huddled in places like New York and Charleston. Like John had, they hoped others would win the war for them.

She sometimes wondered if this last category, held their opposition to a violent rift with the mother country—like hers—as the true basis for their loyalty to the crown, rather than a love for aristocratic institutions.

"You are right, however," John said, pulling off his jacket and draping it over the arm of his the sofa. "The campaign has become somewhat confused. We have changed purposes. We are here in York and Gloucester to build a new naval base. Lord Cornwallis is waiting for the arrival of Admiral Graves with a fleet from New York. Admiral Hood is in the waters off Rhode Island. They will be arriving to supply us and provide a strong naval presence for operations in the Chesapeake."

"Another stronghold," Catherine said, unimpressed. "Another tiny patch of ground against the sea."

"Yes, we sit by the sea." He leaned forward, hands on his knees, and at last he smiled at her in his melancholy. "You look so much like your mother, Catherine. Like her, too, you are as sharp as a knife edge, as compassionate as an angel. She would have wished for peace as well. I was very fond of her when I was young. Though she was my aunt, I thought of her more as a sister. My frail little sister. She was never very strong in body."

Catherine smoothed a wrinkle in her petticoat, a nervous habit.

"You miss her as I do."

"Yes." A great sigh. "I miss her, I miss my home, and many other things." He stared at the ceiling, hands clasped. "I miss the world as it was."

Chapter 17

The Earl

$\mathcal{A}$s was usual this time of day, the study in the house Lord Cornwallis had taken for his headquarters was crammed with officers. In addition to the earl's secretary, who was seated at the Chippendale desk, there was the earl's aide, Major Alexander Ross, and his commander of artillery, Captain Rochfort. Brigadier-General O'Hara was also present, sitting in an armchair beneath the tall front windows, bathed in afternoon sunlight.

Cornwallis kept his subordinates waiting as he dictated a letter, his latest communication to General Clinton.

"The situation in York has changed," he stated. "Though I have followed your orders and established the new post, I find it remains vulnerable without naval support or reinforcement. The French are near. With my own eyes, I have counted the sails of almost forty French vessels lying between Cape Charles and Cape Henry, some of them very large."

He paused as the secretary scribbled the last line. He did not wish to exaggerate his predicament, although he found the sudden appearance of a French fleet alarming.

"The arrival of an English fleet would do much for the security of this post," he continued.

An English fleet would discourage whatever designs the enemy had, of that he was certain. The French usually ran from the British navy rather than risk open battle. The simple presence of Admiral Graves's men of war should be enough to frighten them away.

"An English fleet, and further troops, as we have discussed, are a necessity to make this post practicable." He rubbed his forehead. "That is all. I am yours respectively, et cetera." He waved one hand at the secretary. "Translate into code."

"My lord," the secretary replied, snatching a new sheet from a pile on the table, then reaching for the code book.

Cornwallis moved to the windows.

"The enemy ships would not have come in such force unless they were needed to support a move on land."

General O'Hara's ruddy face split into a wide grin.

"It would be a shame if this fine house, the finest in town, were subjected to a French bombardment."

"I could just as well stay in a tent," Cornwallis grumbled. He had done so throughout the Carolina campaign. To live as his men did kept him close to them, let them know him better. But he could not do so now. Not as long as this fever threatened.

O'Hara turned to Captain Rochfort.

"The old rebel who owns this property, Mister Thomas Nelson, was once the secretary of the Virginian legislature. His nephew is the rebel governor of Virginia, successor to the notorious Thomas Jefferson. The younger Nelson owns the other fine house in town." He chuckled. "He is one of those who signed the Declaration of Independence."

"We are Secretary Nelson's guests," Cornwallis reminded him, for the elder Nelson, aged and infirm, was confined to a bed on the second floor.

"Indeed, my lord. The strangest houseguests I am sure he has ever had the pleasure to entertain."

A low chuckle spread through the room. Cornwallis grimaced, unable to share the fellowship. Despite his efforts to remain calm and reasonable, his unease had been growing these past days.

He folded his hands behind his back. He needed to determine how long they could endure a siege if the French landed troops. To do so was simple prudence.

"How stand our stores, gentlemen?" he asked.

Rochfort spoke first. "We have sufficient ammunition for both small arms and cannon to withstand a siege of about three weeks, if such a siege were forthcoming. For my part, Milord, I do not think it is. The rebels in this province have no large siege guns, only small cannon fit for the field."

"Unless the French supply them, Captain," Cornwallis pointed out. "Although, like you, I do not believe they have done so. Not yet." He turned to O'Hara. "What of our other supplies, General?"

"Good and bad," O'Hara said. "We possess a full stock of new shoes and uniforms, which I suggest we do not issue until absolutely necessary. Ample stores of rum and other rations, though one thing does give me pause. Our food stores are very good, but in this heat, they will not last. The commissary has already complained of rot."

Cornwallis nodded. "The heat and damp of this country have ever been our enemy, with its fevers and mosquitoes. Our cavalry must continue to range the countryside for supplies and forage."

O'Hara shifted in his chair, then stretched out his legs, crossing them at the ankles.

"Upon my word, I can't see how this small American rabble under Lafayette and Wayne could unseat us from this post, even adding the troops of von Steuben. They have proven no match for our British line, unless they receive massive reinforcements. And we are well entrenched."

"The French, my dear Brigadier, lie off our coast! If the French Navy is here, then French troops—professional disciplined troops—are not far behind it. The Americans may receive those reinforcements yet."

O'Hara pressed his thumbs together and stared at them, his brows knitted.

"You have never cared for this post, Milord. Yet we are here, and we must make the best of it."

"The navy will soon add their presence," Ross added.

Cornwallis scowled. It should never have been necessary to compose the letter he had just completed, but Clinton's orders to him had been so addled he did not doubt others were equally at a loss. It would not have surprised him to discover the navy had no knowledge he had just provided them with another base.

"They are late. Do you see any ships, save those few I already have under my cooperation? General Clinton insisted on his base for the navy, and I have given him that base. Now, where is the navy?"

No one spoke, although O'Hara actually chuckled. Cornwallis ignored his subordinate's cheerfulness and gazed through the window. Civilians were passing in the street—two women going about some daily business. Life continued, ordinary life, if somewhat restrained. The citizens of York had greeted his army with an array of attitudes. Some had shown resignation, some hostility, and others indifference. The usual mix.

A sudden wave of heat passed through his body, and he pulled a handkerchief from his waistcoat pocket. He wiped his brow, gasping. The air in the room had suddenly become stifling, almost unbearable.

"Are you quite well, my Lord?" Ross inquired. "Like the French, of late you have given us some cause for concern."

"It is nothing." His breathing was already returning to normal, and the room was not so close as he had thought a moment ago. "An old malady that I am able to master. Have no fear for me, gentlemen."

He fumbled to fold the handkerchief, to return it to his pocket. From outside, he heard the distinctive song of an oriole.

There is a song one cannot hear in England, he thought.

"I admit to suffering some fatigue," he said at length. "We have done so much, and yet achieved nothing conclusive. How many men have tried before us, only to give up in the face of it? How many good officers have refused service in America? I had my doubts, but thought that I had a duty to set them aside."

O'Hara frowned. "Milord, I am not certain I understand your implication."

Cornwallis pursed his lips. He could never admit defeat to a subordinate, even one so high in rank as O'Hara. Had he come so close to doing so, and with Ross and Rochfort here?

Yes, he had almost let slip his true feelings—that this operation was flawed, and that any plan of campaign, however sound, might just come to nothing, as all their colonial campaigns had to this date.

But, no, he told himself. *We have not been defeated. The rebels have maintained an army in Virginia, but it has shrunken. I have worn it down. One more bold push, perhaps from this base, will destroy it altogether.*

"I believe it is best if I rest," he said, sinking into an armchair. "I will see you for supper tonight, gentlemen."

O'Hara gave him a level stare, then stood. The meeting was at an end.

"Very good, sir. I look forward to it."

Chapter 18

The General

When the first French regiments entered the city of Philadelphia, the last were still two miles away in the countryside. The head of the long column snaked toward the State House, passing through crowds of cheering citizens, a roar of enthusiasm that told Washington support for the army was still strong.

He had arranged this parade as a demonstration of power, to prove the allied armies were a force to be reckoned with. Some of his officers had complained the show would take precious time, but the march south had been swift, and the danger of a flank attack was over. The General could allow himself to enjoy this moment, here on the State House balcony in company with Rochambeau and the members of the Congress, as he prepared to salute the soldiers in white.

The thirteen Congressmen doffed their hats as the first French regiment passed beneath the balcony. The brass bands blared, the fifes and drums squealed and rumbled as the Congressmen beamed with pleasure, and Rochambeau called out, "Ah, well done, my beautiful soldiers!" Washington also raised his hat, maintaining a studiously indifferent gaze even though the sight of so much pomp never failed to stir him.

He suspected the French infantry had paused before entering the city to clean their kit, brushing away some of the road dust and whitening their uniforms with talc. Their buttons, buckles, muskets and bayonets all sparkled from fresh polishing, their accoutrements gleamed, the facings of their white coats—violet, green, rose, and sky-blue—standing out in an impressive contrast. Just as impressive were the artillery in their gray coats with red facings, the burnished bronze field guns rolling behind them. Such shining cannon were a rare sight, for in battle they would be left dull with mud and dust so as not to present so obvious a target.

Washington replaced his hat, then raised it again to another white silk flag of royal France. He thought of his Continentals, how they had made such a contrasting picture when they passed through the city yesterday. The fortunate ones had worn the new regulation blue frock coat, some with buff facings, some with white, a few with red or yellow. Most had looked shabby and tired, their grim faces sunken and unshaven. Despite the swift movement south, despite that success, there were still many rumours of mutiny. The men had not received their pay, and most did not realize the importance of this march over so many miles of choking roads in the heat.

The General replaced his hat and glanced at the assembled Congressmen. He fought to control a rise of anger and drew in a deep breath. It was these men, in their expensive wigs and fine broadcloth, who were to blame. They and the state governors. The Articles of Confederation had left the Congress unable to tax the states or command them in any way. The Congress could make recommendations, give advice, but nothing more; and most of the time, the states did not heed that advice, even when it was sound. It was an absurd situation. The politicians cried out for their independence from Britain, but few were willing to fund it even while so many of their sons were paying in blood.

Gold for the troops was on its way, but it was already late. The General again recalled the faces of his men, his sullen, unhappy men. They had no comprehension of how he had fought for them, how he had struggled to find some way to illustrate how much the country still cared for their welfare. How could they know? The average soldier could not see beyond his bayonet, much less beyond the regiment. All he understood was that his belly and his purse were too often empty.

We must achieve some measure of success soon, he thought. *I cannot allow discipline to become lax, not even for a moment. The very nation is at stake.*

He thought of de Grasse, wondered at his progress. The General had received reports the British fleet had already sailed from New York. If British ships reached the great bay before the French fleet, Cornwallis would have an escape route by sea. The campaign would fail before it began.

He would not allow his distress to show, would give no one cause to doubt his confidence. Even Rochambeau did not know of his inner turmoil. The French commander stood on the balcony like a pillar, raising his hat time and again, saluting regiment after regiment with open pleasure.

Finally, the last regiment passed. As the music faded in its wake, the throng of citizens began to disperse. Washington turned to his companions, who were already showering him and Rochambeau with compliments for a fine parade.

"Is not Philadelphia itself named from the Greek?" one remarked. "A reference to the love a soldier has for his comrades?"

The General nodded, and then said, "Shall we proceed to dinner, gentlemen?"

"Indeed," someone replied, "some celebration is in order."

The General thought celebration premature, but he held his tongue.

⁂

When the meal had ended, Washington retired to his Philadelphia headquarters in the house of Robert Morris. There, he dealt with the everyday affairs of the army, discussing matters of logistics with his officers and preparing more letters. The parade and its organization were already a distant memory.

The next day it was more of the same, and the next. While the armies carried on south, the General remained in the city, hoping for news of de Grasse and passing his time in more planning, in finding solutions for a host of petty problems. Why, he wondered, did he bother to deal with these things himself? And yet he did, deciding how to provide shoes and food for the men, how to procure wagons and transports. He decided who deserved promotion, who punishment.

The sun had risen once again before he and Rochambeau at last left the capital, traveling south by sea to Chester. It was the fifth of September. Rochambeau wished to tour the site of the battles fought in 1777, so the two commanders agreed to part ways for a few hours.

"I have already seen those battlefields," Washington explained.

He did not add that those places would only remind him of another year when all had hung in the balance, a year when it had seemed, for a time, that all was lost. His mind flashed back to Valley Forge and the snow—the bitter snow with its fresh trails of blood, the men with no shoes, no coats.

Now what he wanted was action. With Billy Lee, Tilghman and the rest of his staff, his "family," he went on horseback toward the head of the Elk River. He allowed his white charger to gallop, for he no longer had Rochambeau's comfort to consider, and the speed served to mask his continuing anxieties. It was always a pleasure to ride, to lose everything in the moment, to feel the wind in his face and the power of the animal beneath him.

Soon, he had closed the distance to the army, meeting the baggage train and easily passing it, although when he reached the rearmost regiments, he slowed to a more reasonable pace to allow Tilghman and the others to catch up. He paused to study the marching column, and what he saw brought no encouragement. The men seemed to shuffle, muskets canted on their shoulders. Some recognized him, and shouted greetings from the ranks. Others looked away, he feared on purpose, perhaps in protest.

The pay wagons, he thought, *had bloody well better arrive.*

But at once a new concern struck him. Head of Elk was the northernmost inlet of Chesapeake Bay. From there, he expected the armies to continue by sea. He had ordered transports, but whether those would be waiting or not remained to be discovered.

He hurried on, although not so rapidly Tilghman had trouble staying with him. When they reached Head of Elk and saw the congestion of troops, his already grim mood darkened.

Regiment after regiment stood, waiting and idle, clustered about the little collection of houses. Scores of men relaxed under the trees or sat on the ground in their lines. No large vessels rode at the wharves. The transports had not arrived.

"Goddamn those white-livered sons of bitches!" he said, at last losing his temper. Turning to Tilghman, he said, "Establish my headquarters, Colonel. I will wait for General Rochambeau. He is coming down the river by barge and will be joining us within the hour."

He remained in the saddle to wait, not moving, anger smoldering. His jaw began to throb. Time passed, and he watched more regiments arrive. Those that had been here for some time were beginning to lay out camps, apparently anticipating several days of delay.

He noticed a young dragoon officer coming toward him, the man's horse blowing and covered in lather. The fellow was well-appointed in a white coat with dark-blue facings, buff breeches and fine leather boots. The shoulder belt from which his sword hung was black, the silver buckles gleaming.

The young officer reined in, turning his horse and touching his helmet with his right hand. His gaze lighted on the sky-blue ribband that crossed the General's chest within his coat. The man smiled.

"General Washington?" he asked.

The General nodded, touching his cocked hat to return the salute.

"What is it, Lieutenant?"

"Thank God I found you, sir." The dragoon seemed out of breath, but from exasperation rather than exertion. "I have mistaken three other generals for you, sir, despite their pinkish sashes. Begging your pardon, sir."

Washington leaned forward in the saddle, suddenly brightening.

"You bring a message? Is there word of Admiral de Grasse?"

The dragoon's smile broadened.

"Indeed, General Washington. Admiral de Grasse has arrived in the Chesapeake. He has been there for several days, and awaits the coming of your army."

"Several days?" the General cried. "He has been there for several days, you say? How large is his fleet?"

"Twenty-eight ships, and he brings an infantry division of more than three thousand men under General Saint-Simon. They have already disembarked to join General Lafayette."

The General slowly digested this information. He spied Tilghman approaching, returning from his mission, and he called out, "Colonel Tilghman, we must convene a general assembly. I have a message to deliver to the troops!"

Here was his chance, he realized with a rise of excitement. Here was his chance to give them reason to hope.

Soon, the fifes and drums rolled out the Assembly, and the long lines of Continentals formed in a field already designated as the camp parade ground. The General waited, regarding the faces of those closest to him. He feared he would see hostility, but instead he saw simple weariness—and expectation.

When all were silent, watching him, he cried, "Soldiers of the Continental Army, we have come many miles, and many of you do not know the purpose. You are weary and footsore, but you have already achieved success by reaching this place, this great bay of the Chesapeake.

"Our grand object is to link with the army of the Marquis de Lafayette in a campaign to trap General Cornwallis in his base at York Town, on the York River. In this great project, our allies the French have agreed to lend us the support of their fleet.

"That fleet has arrived! The French Navy has sealed off Lord Cornwallis from the sea. All that remains is for us to strike him from the land. Gentlemen, our success is assured, if all but do their duty!"

He paused, and the men stared at him. Then someone cried, "Three cheers for General Washington, hip-hip…"

"Huzzay!" the assembled army shouted. Two more cheers followed. Many of the men tossed their black hats into the air. At last, the General felt his heart warm, and the pain in his jaw subside.

The regiments were dismissed. Washington rode down to the docks and dismounted. Rochambeau still had not arrived from his tour of the old battlefields. The day was advancing; Rochambeau was late, but Washington did not care. A smile tugged at his lips.

He and Tilghman waited while Billy held the horses. His hat in his hands behind his back, Washington paced the thick timbers of the dock. He breathed in the scent of tar and creosote, the salt air. A few gulls cried, or squabbled over bits of flotsam on the shore. He could feel the locket under his waistcoat, the locket containing the portrait of his wife, and for a moment, he thought of home. With every mile, he was getting closer.

"I believe I see a barge," Tilghman declared at last.

Washington squinted along the narrow line of the river. A low brown shape was approaching.

The barge carried no cargo. He could see men standing upon its low deck. He pulled a handkerchief from his pocket and raised it as a signal. He shook it in the air, then raised his hat.

He felt his control dissolving, his restraint giving way to the flood of emotion he had held in check for so long. He started to laugh, waving his hat in circles. His anger at his allies for taking him away from New York was gone, evaporated. It no longer mattered. The march was almost complete, and Cornwallis was cut off.

Finally, as the pleased and astonished features of General Rochambeau drew near, the General began to leap up and down like an excitable boy who has just received the promise of a gift. The barge bumped against the wharf. The French commander did not wait for the crew to secure the vessel. He leapt from the deck to meet his ally, crying in his limited English, "Why, what is wrong my friend? You look so very happy!"

They embraced, both laughing now. Washington explained his joy.

"De Grasse has arrived! Victory is within our grasp!"

"What of the English fleet?" Rochambeau inquired. "There is no news?"

"They are not far behind, I think. But they have lost the race. I only hope that Admiral de Barras does not come upon them, for thus we lose our siege guns and supplies of beef."

"We must not think of such things at this happy time," Rochambeau said. "We must ride south at once."

Washington decided he was too excited to remain in this place, waiting for the stalled transports. He would move on to Baltimore, following the French column, which would march by land.

The long trying day was ending, the September sun low and golden, stretching the shadows. The ocean lay on their left. With their staffs, the generals rode. Washington felt as light and unencumbered as a child. The plan, he realized with something approaching astonishment, was working. Again he let the fine white horse run, and only Billy Lee was able to keep pace, their French companions struggling to keep up.

Suddenly, Washington held up his hand, bringing his mount to a rushing halt. His companions did the same, the dust swirling in the air, catching the sunlight.

They listened.

"Cannon fire," Tilghman said. "There's no mistaking it, sir."

The General nodded. To his left, off the coast, a battle had begun.

He glanced at Rochambeau, and found the Frenchman looking back. In the distance, the guns rumbled like late-summer thunder.

Neither man spoke.

Chapter 19

The Redcoat

𝒜ll along the edge of the bluff southeast of York Town, redcoats and civilian labourers had gathered to stare out to sea. From the distance came the popping of cannon—single guns—as the French and British fleets dueled with bow and stern chasers. Somewhere, a battle had commenced.

"Don't know what we're looking at," Tom Martin said, for a northward curve in the river obscured the entrance of the bay from view. "It's not like they'll be sailing up the river itself."

"They mean to keep us corked up here in York," said Sergeant Gibb. Despite the heat, he was wearing his new sash and silk epaulettes. Bone sat at his feet, gaze following the stares of his human comrades. "Then the rebels will have at our walls, Tom."

"They'll never try it if Admiral Graves breaks through," Tom declared. He plucked a stem of grass and began to chew its end. Around him, the soldiers and civilians chatted and laughed, cracking wise about the French and rebels. Everyone had been anxious about the French fleet for days, and the gunfire could only mean help was near, that Admiral Graves, long looked for, had arrived from New York.

"We'll put the Frenchies to flight," Gibb predicted. "They never stand up when our fleet comes for 'em."

"They'll be off with their sails between their legs," quipped young Sam Webb.

Tom smiled at this last remark, but then he spied Captain Barlow walking along the edge of the bluff toward them.

"Take care, my lads. Here comes the captain."

The soldiers stood to attention at Barlow's approach. Tom was bareheaded, so he simply nodded in greeting.

"Good afternoon, sir."

"Good afternoon, Sergeant." Captain Barlow took in the gathering on the bluff. "So, here is where our idlers have got themselves to."

"Taking our ease before we go back in tonight," Tom explained, for the 1st Light Infantry was to relieve the 76th Regiment, MacDonald's Highlanders, in one of the outer redoubts that evening.

"Nothing to do but watch and listen, eh?" Barlow added.

"The lads are learning to use their imaginations, sir."

Barlow snorted. "A valuable exercise, I am sure." He opened a small leather case he wore suspended from a leather strap, taking out a small brass telescope and extending the interlocking tubes with a snap. He sighted on the horizon. After a few seconds, he said, "Nothing to see, of course."

He lowered the telescope, but at that moment, there came a distant roll of gunfire. Tom recognized the characteristic report of a broadside hammering home.

"French puttin' up a fight," Gibb said, sounding mildly surprised. "They mean to keep our lads out of the bay. Try and trap our army 'twixt land and sea."

"Not like 'em to put up a fuss," Sam Webb complained. "They usually just run away."

Gibb rubbed Bone's side.

"The jack tars always see us through. They never been beat."

"Our tars will give 'em a right tarring," joked Webb.

Tom listened to the comments, but he could not silence an inner voice of warning. The French admiral had sailed into the Chesapeake unopposed, then had disembarked a division of infantry on James Island. Observers had placed the division at three-and-a-half-thousand-men strong.

"We shouldn't have let their infantry land," he muttered. "We had them outnumbered. We could have cut them up without effort."

Neither Gibb nor Webb said anything. Barlow gave him a thoughtful glance then turned back to the water. The rumble of gunfire was increasing, but still there was nothing to see. The disappointed spectators began to wander away from the bluff.

Sergeant Gibb stood and clapped his hands, commanding Bone to follow as he started running along the path to the beach. Webb joined them, shouting and laughing like the boy he was.

Tom was alone with Captain Barlow.

"You are bothered about the military situation, Sergeant," Barlow said. It was not a question.

Tom weighed his words before responding.

"I think we have missed some opportunities, sir, but it's not my position to say so."

"Yes." Barlow nodded. "Not your position. It is the generals who decide when we fight, and when we sit idle. And it is the politicians who decide *whether* we fight. And whether we do not."

Tom hesitated. "I suppose that's correct, sir."

The officer collapsed the telescope and returned it to its case.

"I cannot say these things in the officer's mess. The others call me Whiggish. But the truth is, my father *is* a Whig in the Commons, and he does not support the war. I am a soldier, and I go where I am told. As you state, I do my duty.

"I have no influence. I am a captain of infantry. But the people of England, I can tell you, no longer support our presence here. They may have cried out at the first of it, but since then, it has become increasingly costly, and seemingly pointless. The papers are full of it. The government is on its last legs, its support is crumbling."

"We have to give them a victory, sir," Tom insisted.

Barlow barked a laugh.

"A victory! Yes, if at all possible, though I would prefer if we focused on our old enemies, those in Europe who have taken advantage of our situation for their own selfish ends. The Americans are our kin. I sometimes wonder that we should not make peace with them and direct all our resources against Spain and France."

Tom opened his mouth, then shut it with a snap. Had he heard aright? His captain was talking of abandoning America.

Barlow sighed and looked away.

"I love our company, Sergeant. The light infantry are now the best men in the army, ours the best in the battalion. I would not squander them uselessly. You are an intelligent man, an educated man. You must see the sense in what I say."

"I don't know, sir," Tom said. He could not disagree with an officer. He could not speak his mind, tell Barlow that victory was a matter of will, and officers who spoke as Barlow did demonstrated a lack of it. "I have no opinion on such things."

Barlow gazed at him with narrowed eyes, but he said nothing more. Over the sea, beyond the twin capes guarding the Chesapeake, the broadsides continued to rumble.

Chapter 20

The General

$\mathcal{T}$he courier was the same dragoon officer who had related the news of de Grasse's arrival. The man made his report from the doorway to the little parlour Washington now called his office, a pleasant room on the ground floor of the Fountain Inn in Baltimore. Washington tried to listen, but he had already heard several similar reports, and thoughts of home distracted him, tugging at him like an anchor chain stretched to its limit. The locket under his shirt was warm against his chest, as if the metal itself pleaded with him to grasp this rare opportunity.

Virginia lay only a few miles away, Mount Vernon only a few miles farther. The war had brought him back. The army would pass, he realized, within a stone's throw of his house.

"The battle appeared somewhat inconclusive, but the French still occupy the bay," the dragoon was explaining. "The English have broken off."

"They did not press their attack," Washington said. He sat tall and straight in his chair, feet planted on the broad pine boards. Every description of the naval action off the capes had agreed that neither navy had seemed to get the upper hand, but the General was not yet satisfied the danger was past.

"We saw no indication of ships sunk or captured," the dragoon continued, "but the English were drawn out to sea in the course of the engagement. Only de Grasse has returned. What is more, Admiral de Barras has at last joined de Grasse. Their combined fleet now includes more than thirty ships. They vastly outnumber the enemy."

"So, Admiral de Barras has got through with our siege guns and stores!" Tilghman cried.

Washington raised his eyebrows. This was something the other reports had not mentioned.

"That is, indeed, good news. *Good* news. We are again successful."

He nodded as he spoke, but still he worried about the English fleet. Admiral de Grasse held his position, but the battle had by no means been a fierce contest.

He stood and faced the dragoon.

"Thank you, Lieutenant. You have brought valuable information."

The man smiled. "I am happy to be of service, sir."

"You have been. You have, indeed."

His duty concluded, the courier saluted and turned on his heels. When he had gone, the General turned to Tilghman.

"Time is a luxury we do not possess," he said. "The British fleet will come back, strengthened, to attempt to break our blockade. Admiral Rodney may sail from England, and he is the most talented commander afloat in any navy."

"That will take weeks, if not months, sir," Tilghman suggested from his corner. "We are mere days away from our objective. You should rest, sir. Visit your home. Things are well in hand here."

"They are now, though they were not so a few days ago."

Washington thought again of the missing transports, those that had never arrived at Head of Elk. Again, he had been forced to take it upon himself to find a solution for a basic problem. He had written to every friend he knew in Maryland, asking them to collect fishing boats and other vessels for the army's use. Every reply had contained the same excuse—that the British had gathered up every large vessel on the bay. The General had only managed to locate enough boats to carry about two thousand men. The rest would have to march another fifty-five miles to Baltimore.

He had feared mutiny, that the men would think of their bruised feet and refuse to march; but it was then that money had at last arrived by ship from Boston and Philadelphia. The sight alone of so many kegs filled with silver half-crowns had been enough to cause many to forget their complaints, at least for a few hours.

But a few hours had been enough. Every man in the Continental Army had received one-month's pay in specie; and with their pockets full, they had at last set out, some of their discontent alleviated.

Mere good luck, the General thought. *Mere luck.*

"What else is there for you to do," Tilghman added, "until the army reaches Williamsburg?"

"There may be many things for me to do," the General said. He began to pace the room, from one pleasant yellow wall to the next. "Sometimes I feel that I am indispensable. It is a strange sort of selfishness on my part, a certain conceit."

"All the more reason for you to take some time apart. Trust in your men, sir. Trust your generals. Trust in them as they trust in you."

The General halted and stared at his aide. That was precisely it. It was a matter of trust.

He made his decision, forcing his mind to relax. His fears of disaster had never been realized. Fears for the future, for things he could never control, were pointless. There truly was nothing for him to do until he reached Williamsburg.

"You are right," he declared. "You are right."

"Just a few days, sir."

"Indeed, I will go to Mount Vernon for a few days, and bring General Rochambeau as my guest."

It was what he wished, what he had wished for since the campaign had been conceived that day in his tent.

The General was going home.

Chapter 21

The Subordinate

$\mathcal{T}$he entrance hall to Secretary Nelson's house was crammed with officers, aides and couriers lounging about, waiting for assignments. Brigadier-General Charles O'Hara waded through this small host of colourful uniforms, flashing his usual brilliant smile.

"Good morning, gentlemen. We all look in fine form today."

As usual, there was a chorus of friendly greetings. O'Hara knew he was popular and well liked, a fact that pleased him, although popularity had never been his particular objective. He was a professional soldier, had been lieutenant-colonel of the elite Coldstream Guards, a regiment in which his father had served before him. His family had a tradition of good service, where duty was foremost. To uphold the honour of the British crown and defeat its enemies had always been his stated purpose.

He halted before the door on the left side of the hall. Beyond the door was the study where Cornwallis had made his office. O'Hara knocked, and a voice cried, "Come in."

He opened the door, and at once found several others were already present. Colonel Tarleton had crossed the river from Gloucester, and there was Captain Rochfort, Major Ross, and Symonds of the Navy. *The usual cast of rogues*, O'Hara thought, smiling to himself.

And there was Lord Cornwallis, sitting at his desk facing one wall. Sunlight from the windows made a pattern on the floor, but the desk was in shadow.

"General O'Hara," Cornwallis said, pivoting in his chair. "Please take your ease."

All the others were standing save Tarleton. O'Hara gratefully sank into his favourite upholstered chair in the corner under the windows. He was accustomed to a hard life of campaigning, but he would take comfort whenever it was available.

Cornwallis took a stack of letters from his desk, then moved to a second armchair across from O'Hara. The earl rested the letters in his lap. O'Hara suspected he knew what the letters contained, and a moment later, Cornwallis confirmed his notion.

"Messages from General Clinton have been numerous," the earl said. Taking the first letter from the top of the bundle, he unfolded it. "Here is his message dated the second day of September. General Clinton warns that the Allied army of French and Americans is now clearly marching southward with the intent to attack us here. When they crossed the Hudson, General Clinton made the assumption they were merely repositioning for an assault on New York from the southwest. Thus, he did nothing to hinder them. However, it appears to have been a ruse; the enemy did not assault New York. They are coming here."

O'Hara nodded. This explained the large French naval presence, the landing of troops on James Island. The news was no surprise, merely a confirmation. They would soon have a battle on their hands. His ruddy face split into a wide grin. If they were lucky!

"An opportunity, Milord," Tarleton said in his casual manner, echoing O'Hara's thoughts. "If Mister Washington himself is coming to us, this may be the chance for striking him a fatal blow."

"I would agree, Colonel," Cornwallis said, "if it were merely the Continental Army we should be facing. But now we have the French to contend with. The old enemy is with us again."

"More men and cannon," Captain Rochfort snorted. "That is what we need here."

"General Clinton has promised to reinforce us," Cornwallis explained. He studied the letter in his hand then read, "'You may be assured, I shall either endeavour to reinforce the army under your command by all the means within the compass of my power or make every possible diversion in Your Lordship's favour.'"

O'Hara's eyebrows shot up in surprise.

"I fancy reinforcements, but it's rather late for a diversion, I should think. Not now, when Admiral Graves has failed to break the French blockade."

"Quite my thinking, and that of the commander-in-chief." Cornwallis folded the letter and unfurled the next in the stack. "This second message arrived by express boat, which, I can assure you, encountered no difficulty slipping past the French fleet. It is dated September the sixth. General Clinton states,

'I think the best way to relieve you is to join you as soon as possible with all the Force that can be spared from hence which is about four thousand men.'"

O'Hara shifted his legs, grunting in agreement. This was as it should be. The army here in York was an effective force, but it was small. If the Continentals and French were massing to strike, four thousand fresh men could make the difference between victory and defeat. It might even prove to be the final major campaign of the war, with Clinton and Cornwallis facing Washington himself.

"When will he send these reinforcements?"

Cornwallis raised the letter. "They will leave on October fifth."

For the first time since coming to York, O'Hara felt a spark of disquiet. The French were already here, and the Continentals—at least those under Lafayette—were at their doorstep.

"That is almost a month away, Milord."

The earl stood and returned to his desk. He placed the letters on top of another bundle that had been tied with a length of black ribbon.

"I have written to say that we can last six weeks," he explained. "But I must confide in you that I have my misgivings."

"The enemy will be here in force within two weeks," Tarleton stated.

Cornwallis shook his head.

"Gentlemen, forgive me. Forgive me, but I cannot impress upon you how dire is our situation! Dire! The navy has failed us, for the first time in its noble history. Our food is rotting where it sits, and our men grow sick. The entire French and Continental Army has been on its way here for some weeks, and Clinton has done nothing to stop them!"

The officers stared at him, Ross, Symonds and Rochfort in unfeigned surprise. Tarleton remained a study of indifference save for one raised eyebrow.

O'Hara studied the far wall, suddenly embarrassed. For weeks, he had watched the hopes and optimism of his commander degenerate into this near fatalism. Concern was one thing, but this outburst was completely unwarranted. He thought again of how Cornwallis had not bothered to oppose the French landing on James Island. It was all very strange. The earl had always been one of the most aggressive and resourceful officers in the army, and their situation did not seem quite as dire or hopeless as the earl seemed to think.

O'Hara understood that one duty of a second-in-command was to prevent the commanding officer from losing his grasp on reality. Some subordinates, he was all too aware, would have exploited a weakness in their superior as an opportunity for their own advancement. O'Hara would not. It was his task to help Cornwallis maintain his perspective.

"We must use what resources we have," he stated. "There may be a way to break the French blockade from within, thus allowing Admiral Graves to resupply us."

Cornwallis turned to him, a glimmer of hope in his eyes.

"You have a suggestion?"

"I believe Captain Symonds has been entertaining a design, have you not, Captain?"

Symonds started, as if awakening from a doze. He glanced at O'Hara, then cleared his throat before addressing Cornwallis.

"We have many small vessels, Milord—schooners and such—at our disposal. One is already outfitted as a fire ship. Perhaps we may so outfit two or three more."

"A risk," said Cornwallis. "Fire ships are notoriously unreliable."

"Yet superior to nothing at all," said O'Hara. "It may break the blockade."

Cornwallis paced, hands behind his back. Then he stopped, declaring, "We will make the necessary arrangements."

O'Hara nodded with satisfaction. Here was the old bulldog he remembered.

Chapter 22

The Continental

Daniel hurried west along Duke of Gloucester Street, Williamsburg's main thoroughfare, his slim sword held tight against his left leg. He had done his best to improve his appearance, had brushed his frock coat, donned new stockings and buckled shoes. He was late for his appointment with Major Osborne, late to hear the news he had been expecting.

That command of the company would be his, and the rank to go with it.

He skirted the edge of the street to avoid a crush of vehicles and riders, military carts and wagons. A heavy field gun rumbled past behind its team of eight horses. The city was crawling with soldiers. They had been coming in from the north ever since Lafayette's army moved from Richmond to Williamsburg, and rumour had it Washington himself was not far behind.

Cornwallis had shifted his army to York, and that was the intended target. Cornwallis again, just as it had been these many months. As usual, the Americans were hopeful of victory, although Daniel was not. He refused to allow himself to be seduced by that hope again.

I will do my best for my men, he thought. *I can do no more.*

At last, he reached the Raleigh Tavern, a rambling wooden structure set back from the north side of the street. The tavern had been a favourite meeting place for prominent Virginians before the revolution, a place to debate the policies of King George and to determine how to change or oppose those policies. Now, it was a place where officers met to socialize, and to discuss matters of military importance. Osborne had asked Daniel to meet him there.

Daniel paused before the door to catch his breath. Above him swung a signboard depicting the famous English explorer whose name the tavern bore, and over the doorframe was a bust of the same man. Another reminder, Daniel mused, of the changing nature of the world.

He opened the door and entered the taproom, a spacious chamber with walls of white plaster and unpainted wood paneling. Sweeping off his cap, he squinted into the smoke-filled air, surveying the faces of those who crammed the many small tables. At last he spied Osborne, leaning with his elbows on the long bar. The major called out when he saw Daniel. Daniel crossed the floor to join him.

"I apologize for my lateness, sir," Daniel said. "I fear that I misjudged the distance from camp."

Osborne's long face was beaming.

"Never fear, Daniel, my boy. Never fear. I have a table reserved."

He led the way to a small round table near one of the front windows, where he placed the two filled glasses of madeira he carried.

"General Washington often dined here in his younger days," he said when they were settled in their chairs. "Soon he will be here again, with the northern army. Have you heard? We will be seeing some of our old comrades from Massachusetts."

"I look forward to that day, sir," Daniel said. "With all my heart, I do."

"Indeed. But that is not why I asked you to meet me here. I wish to speak of an order of business, Lieutenant. My design for this interview. You understand that your company was in danger of disbandment."

"I do, sir." Daniel started to tap his foot, a nervous habit. He suddenly feared Osborne had asked him here to place the blame for that near-fate of his company on *his* shoulders. It did not seem likely, but if so, he was prepared to defend himself.

"I did not agree with that proposal," Osborne continued. "It was a foolish suggestion that should never have been given a second glance. All of the states are represented in the Light Infantry, and each company in our battalion represents one of those states. How could they disband old Massachusetts, eh? However, it has not come to pass. Your company is still a sizable body of more than thirty men, though few officers, of course."

"We have some good sergeants, sir. We may raise a few to officer rank, as I was. I wonder that the company did not hold elections."

"The practice of electing officers has not proven practical, as I think we agree. A commander must be strong rather than popular, and your company requires a commander. A man like yourself, Daniel." Osborne leaned his elbows on the table, as he had at the bar. "We have taken note of your recent work—the extra drill, even when morning parade has concluded. Assaulting imaginary positions. It is commendable, Lieutenant."

Daniel gripped his madeira glass. So, he had been right in his assumption. Joshua was senior, but he was still not fit for duty.

"Do I understand, sir, that you are offering me the post?"

Osborne leaned back with a pleased smirk.

"I am."

Daniel studied an eddy of smoke that curled above his head, emanating from the adjacent table.

"I am honoured, sir. Deeply honoured that you place such trust in my abilities. I am happy for this opportunity."

"As you should be. However, there is more. I am not happy with your present rank as lieutenant. You are a reliable officer, Daniel. I would never have approved your extended leave if I did not think I could trust you, if I did not think you and your brother did not deserve it. The truth is, I feared neither of you would return to us, that after all you would submit your resignation in order to tend to your brother. You would have been entitled to do so."

"I am grateful, Major, that you understood my motives. Perhaps they were selfish, but in so many ways, it is my family that I fight for. I would have found it difficult to leave Joshua behind."

It sounded like a thin excuse to his own ears, and unnecessary. He had come back, and whatever had happened before was of no consequence.

"My point is," Osborne continued, "that I have recommended you to the colonel for promotion to captain. He has approved my recommendation."

Daniel stared at his glass. More happy news. Command, rank, and respect. All of those things he had once wished for. And now he was elevated above his brother.

"Thank you, sir. I hope that my...that my subsequent actions demonstrate that I am worthy of your trust."

He faltered, for a sudden curtain of gloom seemed to fall before his eyes. Perhaps he was not right for the post. Perhaps the men needed someone who had not lost faith. Someone like Joshua.

"Is something the matter, Captain Brattle?"

He sipped his wine, forced a smile.

"Of course not, sir. I was simply thinking of my brother, concerned for his welfare. But of course, he will be as pleased as I."

Osborne raised his glass.

"You have climbed the ladder from private to captain of your company. I offer you congratulations."

"Thank you, sir. Thank you."

The wine was warm as Daniel drank.

"The play is about to begin," Osborne continued. "The actors are taking their places. The army from the north is on its way, and the French under our dear Papa Rochambeau. If we are successful, France shall remain a friend of the United States for all time."

"There is an irony there, sir," Daniel said, "considering the nature of the last war."

"Yes, we feared the French then, didn't we?" Osborne chuckled. "You are too young to remember, and I had only just become a man near the end of it. I saw no fighting, though I did see some of its result, when the war was over. With the French defeat, there were idle soldiers in the streets, and wounded with their stumps where limbs should be. Beggars and redcoats everywhere—in the taverns, billeted in the towns with nowhere else to go. Bored warriors with no one left to fight, and so they rubbed the noses of the citizens. Thus we find ourselves amidst another war."

Daniel rubbed his chin. Suddenly, he saw Catherine's face, heard her voice.

"If only they would have been recalled to England, perhaps there would have been no war at all."

"We had to fight for our rights as free men. Every man who could shoulder a musket. Now, at last, with the aid of Papa Rochambeau, we may prevail."

"Then, I presume, we shall all find our peace and happiness."

Osborne chuckled. "Yes, the 'pursuit of happiness,' eh? When the war ends, *if* we can end it. And when they disband all of our glorious regiments."

Daniel rested his chin in his hands.

"I don't know what I will do when I am no longer a soldier. I no longer care to pursue my studies at Harvard."

Major Osborne reclined in his chair, fingering his glass.

"Do you know what my profession was before the war?"

"No, sir. I don't believe you have ever mentioned it."

Osborne grinned. "I was a wig maker. A supplier to the ladies and gentlemen of Boston."

Daniel returned the smile. "You astonish me, sir."

"Indeed. Imagine a wigmaker leading men to battle against the hosts of Britain. These days, everyone may be a soldier."

Daniel surveyed the room. American officers mingled with the French officers of General Saint-Simon's division. Ordinary farmers and merchants of the New World laughed and drank with professional soldiers of the Old.

If nothing else, he thought, *I have seen this.*

"We shall remember these times, won't we, Captain Brattle?"

"Indeed we shall, sir," Daniel said. "Indeed we shall."

⁂

Joshua was sitting on a camp stool polishing his sword with a rag when Daniel pulled back the tent flap. Joshua started, but quickly recovered.

"You're back, I see," he said.

Daniel held the tent flap open but did not enter.

"Yes. There is something I would like to tell you."

"Well, before you say a word, little brother, there's something you need to know." Joshua set his sword down on the unrolled blanket at his feet, then stood. "Captain Holyoak arrived while you were gone. He brought news."

"News from Catherine?" Daniel exclaimed, all thoughts of his promotion banished for the moment. He stepped into the tent. "Did he deliver my letter?"

Joshua's usually cheerful face remained grim.

"It's not the news you were looking for, I'm afraid."

Daniel froze. "What is it? Has something happened?"

"No." Joshua took a folded sheet from the top of their improvised camp desk, the same they had used while in Richmond. "Holyoak tried to deliver your letter, but Catherine and her sister were no longer at the house. The care-taker, Adam, explained that his master had returned. Their cousin. They had gone with him, but Catherine left this letter for you in Adam's care."

He passed the letter to Daniel, who took it with trembling hands, fumbling to unfold it. It was just a few lines, and he read them quickly.

Catherine's cousin John Chester had returned.

"There is little time for me to say all that I would hope to say," the letter explained, "but Abigail and I must leave. Cousin John insists it is not safe here, and I have not the strength to disagree. We are accompanying him to York Town, on the York River, where Lord Cornwallis has his army. From there, I do not know where we will go, but I have not forgotten you, nor have I forgotten your affection for me. I hope that someday soon our paths will cross again."

That was all. A short note, obviously written in haste. He held it, reading it over.

"She has gone to York," he said at length. "With her cousin."

"York?" Joshua echoed. "York Town? Where Cornwallis has dug himself in?"

"She will not be safe there, either."

And it also meant she was with the enemy, and he would never find a way to get word to her. To see her.

"She is lost to me," he murmured, and he sighed. So, she was a fantasy after all, an interlude amidst the madness of war. A dream, a ghost. He could not imagine their paths crossing again, as she hoped, any more than he could see the possibility of an American victory.

He had been made captain, but now the world that should have been bright seemed to have grown pale and gray, its last shred of colour faded.

Chapter 23

The General

With a roll of field drums to announce their arrival, General Washington and his party rode into the French camp at Williamsburg. He had sent word ahead to Lafayette that he was coming, but only a small honour guard stood ready to greet him—chasseurs with green cockades sprouting from their hats. The General sat tall in his saddle as he slowed his mount to a walk then halted. His staff gathered around him, Tilghman at his left side, Rochambeau on his right.

Washington breathed in the fragrance of wood smoke. Beyond the rows of tents, through the haze, he could see the brick buildings of the College of William and Mary. From the kitchen line, stews simmered for dinner, and shouted commands rang from the parade ground as a battalion or company drilled. These were the sights, smells and sounds of a well-ordered army camp, he thought, a camp where all was well. He was glad to be back.

His visit to Mount Vernon had rejuvenated him. His three days there had been three days of freedom, his mind unburdened by the responsibilities of his office. Six years of campaigns, marches, and battle plans melted away, and at times it had felt as if he had never left his home. He had slept well; his dreams, although he did not remember them, left him refreshed and eager to meet the day.

It was right to visit Mount Vernon, the General decided. Why had he ever been so foolish as to hesitate, even for an instant?

He had returned to discover things had not fallen to pieces without him there to hold them together. The allied army had reached Baltimore on the twelfth of September, where they found nine naval transports waiting at the docks with five frigates as an escort, a gift from Admiral de Grasse. The ships carried the army across the bay, landing at Jamestown, the original seat of English America. From there, they marched to Williamsburg.

The honour guard presented arms, and Washington and his companions doffed their hats in response. When the guard had again shouldered their muskets, the General climbed down from his saddle. The others followed, the aides holding the horses. Washington suspected Lafayette would have prepared some kind of formal reception in addition to the honour guard. He was prepared to wait.

A tall man suddenly appeared from beyond the guard, a man in the uniform of an American general officer. With some surprise, Washington recognized Benjamin Lincoln, his second-in-command. Lincoln had led the American contingent of the allied column on the long march from the north. Washington assumed he had ridden ahead to the camps.

Lincoln hurried toward the cluster of officers.

"General Washington, General Rochambeau," he cried, "I am pleased to see you both well." He halted, touching his cocked hat and making a slight bow. Washington returned the gesture, but Rochambeau bowed low, his right foot drawn back, making a leg in the European fashion.

"Well, indeed, General Lincoln," Washington said, advancing and shaking Lincoln's hand. "I see you are the victor in this race! I did not expect to see you. You have found things in order, I trust?"

"The Marquis of Lafayette is ill, General," Lincoln said, "though he is aware of your arrival."

"Lafayette is ill?" the General repeated, concerned although he judged by Lincoln's tone that the malady could not be life-threatening. "I trust it is not serious?"

"A bout of malarial fever. He has confined himself to his bed."

The General clasped his hands behind his back, relieved. The young marquis was very dear to him.

"He should not trouble himself. I will attend him later at his headquarters."

"Perhaps Lafayette will be revived by your arrival, sir," Lincoln remarked, grinning. He was nearing fifty, a man with thickening jowls but hard intelligent eyes. He carried with him an air of determination that belied the recent military defeats under his command—the first the failed attack on Savannah, then the failed defence of Charleston. His confidence, Washington thought, suggested he did not expect a third disaster here in Virginia.

"Perhaps you are right," Washington said. "Our arrival seems to have revived *you*, General. Now the tables have turned in our favour."

"You have guessed my thinking. My one regret is that General Clinton is not here to receive us."

Washington nodded, understanding and identifying with Lincoln's desire to avenge himself for his greatest defeat. Clinton had led the British forces at the siege of Charleston. Lincoln capitulated after a stubborn defence of several weeks, yet Clinton had denied him the honours of war. The British commander had insisted on an unconditional surrender, with parole for the American officers and prison for the men.

"And while Lord Cornwallis did not command at Charleston," Washington mused, "he was present. It is as if you are come full circle."

He stared past Lincoln at three horsemen approaching along the camp street at a quick trot. One was in French uniform, his red waistcoat and breeches bright, his blue coat looped with gold lace across the breast. Another was obese, his bulging frame a misfortune for the mount that carried him. The third was as thin as the second was fat, with a narrow nose and dainty mouth, his spare frame adorned with the Continental blue-and-buff. With a wordless exclamation, he spurred ahead of the others.

Washington stepped forward, his face lighting with joy. For the second time in recent weeks, he allowed his restraint to give way.

"My dear Lafayette!" he cried in astonishment, spreading his arms.

The young marquis halted and at once swung down from the saddle. The General could see that his skin was pale, his thin face glistening with sweat, but there was no mistaking the delight in his eyes. He advanced—he, too, with arms outstretched—and grasped Washington in a firm embrace. The General could not suppress his laughter as Lafayette kissed him on both cheeks.

"I am overjoyed to see you," Lafayette declared as they moved apart. "Now I feel that our deliverance must come."

"I am as glad to see you, my young friend."

The group of officers gathered close together, with expressions of delight.

"With such rapture in the air," General Rochambeau declared, "success must surely be at hand."

Lafayette then introduced his companions. Washington was familiar with the obese man—Governor Thomas Nelson, commander of the Virginian militia. Rochambeau knew the other, who was General Claude Saint-Simon.

"The remainder of our army will be here soon, gentlemen," Washington announced. "There is still much work to do. General Lincoln, I would appreciate your returning to the column to urge its haste. Every day we lose now is comparatively an age."

Lincoln nodded. "I will return at once, General Washington."

They should not be seduced by the success of the campaign so far, the General understood. They were well placed, but the battle for York Town had not yet begun.

Washington soon found himself engaged in a series of introductions. First, he attended a formal reception in General "Mad" Anthony Wayne's camp, where the Pennsylvania Brigade were formed up to deliver him three cheers. The Pennsylvania Line had been troubled by mutinies in the past, but the sincerity of their cheers was unmistakable. When the last echo died away, the General was surprised to find himself fighting back tears. These men still believed in him as their leader.

Afterwards, he met most of the brigade's officers, each saluting and shaking his hand in turn, in the doorway of his new headquarters in Williamsburg, the fine brick house of George Wythe. Wythe, a lawyer, scholar, and signer of the Declaration of Independence, had been overjoyed to have his home serve in such a capacity.

However, Wayne himself was conspicuously absent.

That evening, Washington attended a dinner in the tent of General the Marquis de Saint-Simon. Lafayette was also present, despite his persistent affliction. Washington found the French true to their reputation, for the food, divided into fourteen courses, and the wine were excellent, the conversation entertaining. Lafayette spoke throughout the meal, relating everything that had happened in his command since the battle near Green Spring Farm.

"General Wayne was wounded in the leg," the marquis explained, solving the earlier mystery. "He was coming to visit my division camp, and he failed to give a sentry the proper countersign. The sentry did his duty, I am afraid. Fortunately, the wound is not serious."

When the last course of cheese and nuts and coffee had concluded and the servants had removed the plates, there were toasts to the allies and to the Congress. After that, the gathering moved to seats outside, where a French brass band performed a concert of operatic melodies.

In the middle of this serenade, Washington felt a tap on his shoulder. An aide whispered in his ear, "Sir, a message from Admiral de Grasse."

"Thank you." He took the offered slip of paper and opened it, turning to catch the light of a standing torch.

He felt the blood drain from his face and read the note a second time to make certain he was not mistaken. In his neat hand, the French naval commander had written he could not remain in the Chesapeake past the middle of October. At that time, his duty bound him to return to the West Indies.

"I am annoyed by the delay," the letter proclaimed in its final few lines. "Time is passing, the enemy is profiting by it, and the season is approaching when against my will, I shall be obliged to forsake the allies for whom I have done my best and more than could be expected."

Washington mulled over this last phrase, his teeth clenched, grinding against each other. Goddamn the man, how could he say he had done more than could be expected? As far as Washington was concerned, the admiral had done considerably less.

It was imperative the navy remain for the duration of the campaign, or the entire operation was pointless. Cornwallis would be re-supplied, reinforced, or he would escape. How could de Grasse not understand that?

The General drew in a deep breath. He did not understand the French naval temperament, other than that they were inclined to be overcautious. He suddenly feared that here was what might undo all of his plans.

He would send a message to de Grasse at once. He would request an interview, do his best to change the admiral's mind.

The concert continued, but it no longer held any pleasure for him. When it was over, he thanked his hosts and said his farewells, but the enjoyable evening had been ruined.

He hurried back to the Wythe House. There, he sat at the desk in the study and penned the necessary letter. Only when it was on its way and the matter settled in his mind did he consider retiring for the night. He had done all he could for now, and he cherished his sleep, however brief.

He awoke before dawn. He was impatient for an answer from de Grasse, and it was an irritation to deal with routine matters making arrangements for the distribution of food and ammunition. His aides were just leaving to transcribe the required documents when Tilghman brought the eagerly-awaited reply from the French admiral. Washington forced himself to be calm, opening the letter slowly although his heart was thundering and his blood rushing in his ears.

The note was written in French, so he returned it to Tilghman.

"Translate it, please, Colonel."

"The Admiral will be pleased to meet the Commander in Chief," Tilghman said, "on board his flagship, the *Ville de Paris*, presently stationed off Cape Henry. For your convenience, he has sent with this reply the former English schooner, the *Queen Charlotte*, to serve as tender."

Washington closed his eyes, pressing the lids together.

"We will embark as soon as is practicable. I shall require General Rochambeau and General Knox to accompany me."

"I will make the arrangements, sir."

Less than an hour later, Washington, Rochambeau, and Henry Knox, with their respective staffs, boarded the little *Queen Charlotte* and sailed down the James with the current, heading toward the mouth of the great bay. This time, Knox did not thank the General for including him. As the commander of artillery, he had the air of a man who knew he should be present at such an important affair.

The French flagship lay at anchor, a towering three-decker of black and gold, yards squared and sails furled. The generals and their aides crossed the water in the schooner's longboat, then climbed the ladder to the ship's quarterdeck. Washington recognized de Grasse at once, a tall handsome figure resembling some ancient Roman statue in blue-and-scarlet. A broad red sash, the Order of St. Louis, lay stretched across his massive chest.

The Marines presented arms, and de Grasse advanced to meet his guests. Washington received the admiral's embrace and a kiss for either cheek.

"*Mon cher petit generale!*" de Grasse cried.

Washington found the remark irritating, and suspected it might have been delivered partly in condescension. However, he decided to reserve his judgment. He needed to be at his diplomatic best here.

The party made their way to the great cabin. In the light from the stern windows, they sat on mahogany chairs upholstered in maroon velvet. Tilghman took a place at a small table and produced a pocket writing case, two pen nibs and a vial of ink. He would both translate and record the admiral's replies to Washington's questions.

The ship rolled in the gentle swell to the music of creaking timbers. Tilghman opened a valise and removed a sheaf of papers, which he passed to the General. Washington crossed his legs and ordered the papers against his knee.

Forcing a slight smile, he said, "We thank the admiral for his generous assistance, and ask his indulgence for several matters pertaining to the campaign."

He glanced at the first sheet of paper, where he had written some appropriate opening remarks, then half-read, "The measures we pursue are big with great events. The peace and independence of my country, as well as the general tranquility of Europe, will result from our complete success. Disgrace to ourselves, triumph to the enemy, and probable ruin to the American cause will follow our disappointment."

He glanced up at intervals, now and then adding a word or paraphrasing.

"The first is certain if the powerful fleet now in Chesapeake Bay can remain to the close of the regular operation, which from various unforeseen causes, may be protracted beyond our present expectations. The second is much to be feared, if from concern of losing the aid of the fleet, the land operations are precipitated faster than a necessary prudence and regard for the lives of the men will warrant."

De Grasse seemed to listen with patience and interest as Tilghman translated. He nodded for the General to continue.

"Under this state of matters," Washington said, "I beg that the Count de Grasse will have the goodness to give me a resolution of the following questions. First, it is in the interests of our land forces to know whether the admiral's orders name a fixed date for his departure, and if so could he name the day to which your departure is determined?"

He kept the papers in his hands, but he paused, eyes fixed on the French admiral. De Grasse reclined in his chair, swaying with the ship, seeming to ponder. A servant placed a tray of Madeira on a small table. Like the rest of the furniture, the table was fixed to the deck. The wine tilted in the glasses, first one way, then the other.

"I may answer your concerns, *mon generale*," de Grasse said in heavily accented English. Tilghman leaned forward in his chair, his tiny pen poised above his paper. "My instructions fix my departure to the fifteenth of October. Some engagements which I have made for other operations oblige me to be punctual. However, having already taken much upon myself, I will engage to stay until the end of October."

This was the most important point. Washington felt relief flood him, his muscles relaxing, but the answer also bothered him. De Grasse had seemed to agree too readily, as if he had already decided to remain longer than his letter had suggested. Or perhaps all he had needed was for Washington to make the strength of *his* resolve be known.

The General did not like to be tested, but he vowed he would show no anger or disrespect. He merely nodded before returning to his papers.

"Second, whether the admiral's orders require him to return the regiments of General Saint-Simon by a certain time. And, if General Saint-Simon must depart, whether a naval detachment could serve for their transport while the main body of the fleet remains in the Bay, to form a sufficient cover to our operations, preventing the enemy from receiving supplies by water and any attempt by the British to relieve Lord Cornwallis."

Washington placed the first sheet of paper behind the others. He waited for de Grasse to reply.

"The troops under the orders of the Marquis de Saint-Simon have a particular destination," the admiral confirmed, "and I am not altogether at liberty to dispose of them. But as my vessels will not depart before the first of November, you may count upon these troops to that period. For the reduction of York."

Again, the General nodded. This, also, had been a key point, as was his next.

"Soon our present operations against York will commence," he continued. "The General wonders whether the Count de Grasse, with a portion of his fleet, could force a passage of the upper York River, so as to get above the enemy and complete his encirclement." He again looked up, facing the admiral. "This measure will grant us infinite advantages. It will secure our communications on both sides of the river, and will allow us to draw supplies from all parts of the country."

De Grasse rubbed his chin.

"The thing would not be impossible with a good wind and favourable tide, but those factors are not within my sphere. I am an officer who commands ships and men, not the forces of nature." His smile was warm. "Thus, I can give you no answer save my opinion, and that is that such a measure would not be useful. We may establish good communications on the lower river without having to pass the enemy batteries. However, I will suspend my definite answer until I have observed the situation, the strength of the enemy." He shrugged his massive shoulders. "I shall certainly do everything in my power."

The General hid his disappointment. To not secure the upper York would provide Cornwallis with one possible escape route.

"I am, of course, not well versed in naval affairs," he said. "Land operations are my domain. Would it be possible for Your Excellency to lend us some heavy cannon and other artillery, with shot and powder?"

De Grasse knitted his brows and sighed.

"The action against the English admiral Graves has left my fleet rather lower in ammunition than I find comfortable. I may only spare a small quantity, or be no use to you should Graves return."

General Knox shifted in his chair before interjecting, "I am confident that my artillery, in combination with that delivered by Admiral de Barras, is sufficient. Though I *would* appreciate whatever ammunition you may spare, however small the quantity."

"I shall have the figures for you after some consultation with my captains," de Grasse promised. Then his smile returned. "But we must not engage in half measures, *oui, mon generale*? I understand the dilemma my note may have caused you. It is the policy of the French Navy to be cautious. Storms are common in these waters once autumn is upon us.

"However, I must defer to your wisdom as commander-in-chief of these operations. I will serve no one by departing early, frightened away by a bit of wind. Again, upon my honour, I will remain in the Chesapeake until the end of the month of October. Not one ship of mine will weigh prior to the first of November."

The ship's gentle roll was becoming more pronounced, the song of timbers and rigging increasing in volume. The Madeira in the decanter and glasses heeled farther. De Grasse snatched a glass. Knox took the others from the table and handed them out to his companions.

The General sipped his wine, remembering that day in his tent when the first important letter from de Grasse had arrived to begin this campaign. French sailors were cautious to the point of timidity, he decided.

But de Grasse had given him most of what he wanted; there was no reason to feel vexation at imagined slights. He could allow himself to rest. The pieces were still falling into place.

He felt the warmth of the wine spread through his long limbs, like the warmth of satisfaction.

Chapter 24

The Redcoat

*T*he redoubt was known simply as "Redoubt Number Ten." It was the same little fort Tom's company had helped to build. Now, it and its neighbours were complete, the defences of York Town ready to face the enemy.

The fort was square, with a *fraise* of sharpened wooden stakes ringing its low ramparts, a hindrance to anyone attempting to storm the position. In the defensive ditch stood a wooden palisade, and before the ditch, an abatis of tangled tree branches presented a further obstacle. It was a time-honoured system that had withstood countless sieges for over a century.

Perhaps the rebels and French will soon put that system to a new test, Tom thought. *A test against their own flesh and blood.*

He stood with Sergeant Gibb on the parapet, gazing out over the river, its surface pale blue and unruffled in the morning light. He was tired, and rubbed his eyes with one grimy knuckle. His company had manned the redoubt throughout the previous night, and he had not slept a wink.

Instead, he had perched here with Gibb, watching as four darkened schooners sailed past like silent wraiths below on the water. Rumours had been rampant, and everyone in the army knew the schooners were on their way to break the French blockade, their holds filled with tarred faggots and loose sticks. The intention was to bear down on the French squadron that was watching the mouth of the river. When the schooners were close enough to the enemy, their captains would set them on fire, then escape in boats.

Tom had still not heard whether the scheme had worked, but Captain Barlow had set out about an hour ago to find out.

Otherwise, the morning had dawned like any other here in York, the fifes and drums pounding out reveille, the men rolling out of their dew-soaked blankets. They would have breakfast, then sit in the fort until dinner, when a company from another regiment would come to relieve them. Nothing special, Tom thought. Nothing worth mentioning in a letter home.

He glanced down into the redoubt as Private Hassler entered through the gap that served as its rear gate. Hassler bore two camp kettles—large tin canisters with round lids and wire handles, their bottoms blackened by fire. He swung them as he walked, and one top popped off, the contents of the kettle sloshing over the side and into the dirt.

"Have a care with the gruel, now, Private Hassler," Tom said. "It does not mix well with the Virginian soil."

Hassler gaped at him in bafflement, not having noticed his accident and not understanding.

"It were mixed with water, Sergeant," he said.

"Quite so," Tom replied. There was no sense in trying to explain the joke. "Carry on, but note that you've dropped one of your lids."

"Man's like a hitching post, Tom," murmured Sergeant Gibb.

"At least he's an obedient post."

Hassler had put the two kettles down and was wiping the errant lid on his breeches. Bone snuffled at his feet, licking at the spilled porridge.

"And at long last he has made a friend. The dog has accepted him."

Tom had seen men improve after punishment, and so far, Hassler had made no further trouble. He had been on light duties since returning from the camp hospital, cooking for his mess, fetching and carrying water, filling his comrades' canteens from the spring. He had enough to occupy his time and did not complain.

The stout private at last returned the lid to its proper place and retrieved both kettles. The men of his mess waited to serve out the morning's offer into their empty tin cups or wooden bowls or whatever their preferred container.

Tom frowned in distaste, not relishing the thought of yet another bland meal. He had grown weary of army rations, the same meals every day—plain beef and bread, perhaps mixed in a stew with some peas, carrots, or beans. Maybe they would have some cheese later, if it had not all gone to rot, which seemed likely. At least the colonel had obtained some spruce beer, although Tom did not like it as much as ordinary beer or rum.

He turned to Gibb.

"I wonder where the captain has got to?"

As if the question were a summons, Barlow entered the redoubt through the gate in the rear. Gibb cupped one hand around his mouth and called, "Any news, then, Captain?"

Barlow paused, frowning. Seeing his two sergeants, he mounted the low rampart.

"I have news, indeed, Sergeant," he stated.

Tom felt a rising excitement.

"Was the breakout successful, sir?"

Barlow swept his gaze north and west, toward Gloucester, then toward the courthouse and windmill. The mill fan was turning slowly.

"Sir?" Tom repeated.

"It was not successful," Barlow muttered. "It would be better if we forgot the entire affair."

"Oh, well, that's a shame, sir," Gibb commented.

Tom chewed the inside of his lip, more frustrated than disappointed.

"What happened, sir?"

"One of the ship's masters was a privateer captain, a man who should have known his business. The schooners were advancing toward the French fleet under wind. The privateer set his schooner alight too soon, alerting the enemy. The nearest French ships were able to withdraw. I have heard that several ran afoul of each other in the darkness, but there does not seem to have been any serious damage. The entire thing was a travesty."

"A shame," Gibb repeated.

The stern set of Barlow's features suddenly relaxed.

"It was bad fortune, Sergeant Gibb. Bad fortune. We have had bad fortune since this war began, it seems."

Tom gritted his teeth. This had become Barlow's favourite refrain, that the war had somehow become pointless.

"We must turn bad fortune on its ear, then, sir," he said.

Barlow's smile was half mocking.

"Certainly, we must, Sergeant. Certainly, we may try."

He said nothing more. The three men stood on the rampart, surveying the silent ring of forts and batteries about York while, below, the men ate their porridge and licked their spoons clean.

Chapter 25

The Loyalist

Catherine and Abigail picked their way among the stones on the riverbank, passing under the lee of one of Gloucester's many wharves. They each wore a straw hat against the sun, wide-brimmed and low-crowned, pinned in place and decorated with a bit of ribbon—blue for Catherine and green for her sister. Abigail carried a small basket.

The air still smelled of high summer, the gentle breeze a warm caress; and from somewhere came the whirring of a grasshopper. Overhead, a hawk cried, and Catherine gazed aloft in time to spy an osprey circling in his hunt for food. *How free he looks*, she thought; and for a moment, she longed to be gone from here, to soar like a bird, away from the army and its forts, away even to the western mountains.

"There he is, Cathy," Abigail suddenly cried.

Catherine followed the osprey for a few seconds more, then pushed aside all thoughts of escaping on the wind. The moment passed. A senseless fantasy. She spent too much time longing for something she could not have. It was the present she had to concern herself with. She hurried after Abigail.

Not far from the wharf, she and Abigail met a small boy, the son of one of the Negro labourers. He was barefoot, his shirt threadbare and his worn waistcoat of an older fashion, his wide-brimmed hat frayed at the edges. He had pulled a boat up onto the riverbank and stood next to it, waiting expectantly. Catherine often met him here by the water to purchase crabs or other fish he had taken in the local waters. She thought of him as an innocent, an unfettered soul who led his simple life outside the context of the larger events that surrounded him; and in that way, he seemed free.

In a way, he resembled the osprey, Catherine decided, traversing the river and perhaps even the bay in his boat, plying his modest trade without anyone to bother him. Aside from his customers, no one seemed to pay any attention to him at all. He could come and go as he pleased.

The boy displayed his catch—five sizable crabs he had snatched from a creek that drained into the river.

"They look very fine," Catherine said, and Abigail placed them in the basket and covered them with a handkerchief. Catherine paid the boy, putting five pennies in his outstretched hand. He gave her a wide, toothy grin.

"Many thanks, Missus!" He pocketed the coins and at once began dragging his rowboat back into the water.

"Good-bye, then," Catherine said.

"So long," he replied, leaping into the boat. Taking the oars, he started backing into the river. When he was about fifty yards from shore, he freed one hand to wave. Catherine smiled and waved back.

She realized she had never asked the boy his name.

"We'd best go back," Abigail said. "I'll put the crabs in the covered bucket until we're ready for them."

Catherine sighed. "Yes. It is time to return to our prison."

They began the climb from the shore, hoisting their petticoats to keep them out of the mud. Again they avoided the rounded stones as they passed the wharf with its hanging weeds and heavy scent of tar and creosote.

"I don't know why you don't like it, Cathy," Abigail said. "I think it's all very exciting having all these soldiers about day and night. This isn't like New York. This time we're living within the very camp!"

"Soldiers may be exciting, my dear, but they can also be dangerous."

Abigail rolled her owl eyes in dismissal.

"You did not seem to find the *rebel* soldiers dangerous. And they're our enemies."

"They were but two men we came to know well," Catherine argued. "They were not an army."

Abigail made a sour face.

"You have grown so stodgy lately!" She stuck out her tongue then skipped ahead, the basket of crabs swaying in one hand. Catherine watched her with something close to exasperation.

She is changing. She no longer listens to me as she once did.

Abigail had almost reached the house. A cavalry officer stood in the side yard, tightening the saddle girth on his horse, and he looked up as she approached. Catherine felt a stirring of distaste. The officer was Colonel Tarleton.

Tarleton mounted, then edged his beast away from the wall. Catherine hoped he was preparing for another patrol, that he would leave and not come back for at least a few days.

She detested his visits. Every second or third evening he arrived at the house, smelling of horses and dust from a foraging expedition, intent on spending a few hours at cards. He often brought with him some of his closest comrades, harsh and brutal men. From her upstairs room, she could hear his horrible boasting and cursing, the coarse laughter of his companions, and the clinking of their wine glasses as they polished off one bottle after another.

"The rebels should have been given a firm hand from the first day they complained about their taxes," she had heard him declare one evening. "Hang a few of the principals and the rest would have kept quiet. Strong measures should have been the game once the war began."

Catherine agreed that such a firm hand—burning townships and hanging rebel leaders for their opinions—would have ended the war sooner, although the success, she knew, would have been on the rebel side. There would have been far fewer Loyalists under such circumstances. As it was, harsh British policies had helped lead to the war in the first place. Those policies had played into the rebels' hands, allowing them to respond with calculated outrage. The king's agents had given the revolutionaries an excuse for hoarding powder and ammunition, and for contemplating war.

Tarleton was incapable of understanding a people who had built a society from nothing with their own hands, she decided.

On another evening, she had heard him scoff, "A government without a king? How can such a thing survive? Men need an authority to lord it over them. It is a simple fact. If the Americans were to win their independence, they would elect a king, or pine away for the one they lost."

At other times, he bragged about his prowess with women. Often, he named his conquests, women Catherine knew, women here in Gloucester.

Cousin John was forced to attend these rough parties, to be part of the society of his commanding officer. Catherine would sometimes glimpse him through the parlor door as she passed in the hall, sagging in his chair and seeming very out of place. To her knowledge, he had never invited Tarleton's company. Tarleton invited himself, for he expected to entertain and be entertained by all of his officers. John could not refuse.

But for all her sympathy for her cousin, it was Abigail who had become Catherine's greatest concern. Within the span of a few months, she had begun to leave her girlhood behind. Her shyness was diminishing, and at times, she was even willful, rebellious. She no longer walked with eyes downcast and shoulders slumped. And she enjoyed Tarleton's company. She often found reasons for speaking with him when he was in the house or nearby. Catherine could understand her sister's attraction to the man's good looks and dash, but it filled her with dread. Tarleton was dangerous, the sort who saw women as mere playthings.

Now, Tarleton sat his horse in the yard, watching Abigail. Catherine hurried to catch up.

The younger woman stopped in the muddy street. Tarleton walked his mount toward her. His mouth curled up in a prim smile.

"Miss Seawell. Good morning."

"Good morning, Colonel," Abigail replied, bending in a little curtsey.

Tarleton leaned forward, reins held in a casual grip.

"Now, what have you got in that basket, my pretty girl?"

"Just some crabs, Colonel."

"Ah." The officer snickered. "Not what I had in mind."

Catherine halted next to her sister, pausing to catch her breath. The greencoat dragoon turned his smile on her.

"And the other Miss Seawell—or should I say 'Mrs. Checklee.' Two birds in one bush."

Catherine took Abigail's hand.

"We must be away, Colonel."

"Pity. I would enjoy the company of both of you, I am sure."

Catherine glared at him.

"Good day, sir."

Abigail did not resist as Catherine drew her away, but she turned and waved. Catherine heard Tarleton's laughter follow them as they rounded the side of the house. The sound sent shivers up her spine.

I must protect my sister, she thought. *I must protect her from men such as Tarleton, and I must protect her from herself.*

Chapter 26

The Continental

*T*he morning drill parades, lengthier and more intense now that the northern brigades had arrived at last, were over. The officers of Gimat's regiment gathered in the crowded taproom of the Raleigh Tavern, their table near the front windows. Even Joshua was present, having returned to the active list at last. As Daniel's second-in-command.

"Gentlemen, I have missed your good fellowship," Joshua declared, raising his glass. "And these interludes are to be fewer now that all we seem to do is drill, drill and drill again."

"A glass of wine with you, sir," Major Osborne said, also raising his glass. "I am happy to have you back with us in good health."

They drank, and Daniel said, "All this drill is important if we are to become one army again, and be ready for the coming action, whatever it will be."

"Indeed," Osborne agreed, producing a clay pipe and a small pouch of tobacco from his pocket. "Though I think we're already one army again. Our little army of the south is to be absorbed into the larger formation."

"We are still under Lafayette's command, I trust?" Daniel asked.

"We are, though Monsieur le Marquis de Lafayette's forces will henceforth be known as the Light Division. Our battalion is now part of the First Brigade, under the command of Brigadier-General Muhlenberg. Brigadier Hazen will command the Second Brigade."

The other units in the reconstituted American army included the Second Division under General Lincoln, Osborne explained, with its regiments from New York, New Jersey, and Rhode Island, all of the Continental line. The Third Division came under General von Steuben, and contained regiments from Pennsylvania, Virginia, and Maryland. The Virginia Militia made up a final infantry division under the fat but still energetic Governor Thomas Nelson. Henry Knox brought almost three regiments of artillery and one of sappers, while the American contingent also included two companies of cavalry.

The French army was somewhat larger, with three infantry divisions, an artillery battalion, and a large detachment of cavalry. The French cavalry were an elite unit, the dashing hussars of Lauzun's Legion.

"A sizable force," Daniel admitted.

The combined armies numbered some sixteen thousand men. In contrast, Cornwallis had no more than seven thousand, and spies had reported many of those were ill.

"If we had a few more months of Virginia summer at our disposal," Joshua said, "we might let the fever do our work for us. It will wear Cornwallis down to skin and bone."

"Cornwallis has been suffering casualties since his victory at Camden," Osborne stated, "We have yet to defeat his main force in the field, but we have fatigued him, and the climate has fatigued him still further. He is weakened, and when we get our grips on him, it will be like tightening a noose."

"We'll dangle old Cornwallis over the bay," said Joshua, "by his best wig."

There was laughter, genuine good feeling. It had been like this ever since General Washington had arrived. Hopes were running high again, although Daniel was still unable to share them.

"The British may still escape," he warned. "Their fleet could return. Reinforcements might come from New York. Cornwallis may put up a stalwart defense, fever or no fever. We might have problems securing enough ammunition."

The others stared at him.

"We will overcome those problems if we face them, little brother," Joshua suggested.

Daniel stared back, regretting his words. His pessimism had no place at this table.

"We will not fail here, Captain Brattle," Osborne added. "Can't you feel it in the very air?" He waved his pipe in an arc, taking in the crammed taproom. "Did you know that some of the northern regiments refused to complete the last leg of the journey here until they received their pay? They were one step away from open mutiny! Their officers implored them to continue, appealing to their patriotism, but they did not budge until the ringleaders had been arrested.

"These are the men who have joined us—weary, footsore, and prepared to quit the ranks and make their way home. But have you heard a complaint from them since? No, by God! They boast of dangling Cornwallis over the bay, like Joshua here. They have found their spirit again. Something miraculous is afoot. It is as if God Himself has intervened on our behalf."

"The Lord helps those who help themselves," said Daniel. "Is that not the phrase, sir?"

"Indeed. So, we will never waste our time. General Washington and our Papa Rochambeau will see us through. We will march for York Town in a few days. I am certain all will be ready."

This seemed to be the last word.

"Hear him!" some cried, while others thumped the table.

When the commotion died, Joshua thrust back his chair and stood.

"I fear, gentlemen, that I have a miracle of my own to nurture. By that I refer to my continued existence on this earthly plain. I have enjoyed our conversation, but it's time for me to take my daily constitutional. If I am to join the march, I must continue to build my strength."

"By all means, Lieutenant," said Osborne. "We will see you later for dinner?"

"Of course, sir," Joshua said.

"I'll go with you," Daniel said, also standing. "To look after you in case you should fall on your face or something equally undignified."

The brothers left the table and wended through to the front door. Once outside, they turned north on Duke of Gloucester Street, passing clumps of off-duty soldiers. Daniel noted the many grinning faces and heard frequent snatches of laughter.

"Major Osborne is right, you realize," Joshua said as they strolled toward the old state capitol.

A breeze rustled the leaves in the Dutch elms. The trees had retained their deep green, without a hint of autumn gold.

"About what?"

"Green Spring and all the other defeats are behind us. The army has been rejuvenated. I haven't seen nor felt such excitement since the first year, when we had Gage bottled up in Boston."

"Nor have I," Daniel agreed. "And should we fail after such expectations, we'll never recover."

Joshua shook his head in wonder.

"The brother I once knew would be at the head of the column, damning all caution and challenging Cornwallis himself to a duel with swords."

Daniel remained silent. He suddenly thought of Catherine, remembered the soft glow of her skin in the candlelight. Something he would never see again.

"I will be at the head of the column," he said at length, "when we storm York Town's defences."

"And I will be beside you. Never forget that."

They stopped on the side of the street. Daniel met his brother's eye and saw something there he had never seen before. Or never recognized before. He saw the respect given an equal.

"You don't regret that I have been given command of the company over you?"

Joshua shook his head. "Why should I begrudge you anything? I realize I may seem overbearing at times, but that is the burden of little brothers. But there is no one I trust more, Daniel, than you. I hope that you still trust me."

Daniel reached out and took his brother by the shoulder.

"You will serve with me as your captain?"

Joshua gripped Daniel's arm.

"Of course. I would be honoured to serve under the younger brother who sat by me, day and night, and who would not leave me. Who saw me through fever and sickness. The younger brother who I know better than he knows himself. The one who will never give up, whose spirit never truly flags, even when he fears that it has."

They stood in that way on the side of the street. Joshua did not release his grip. Warmth flowed from his hands.

"We'll see this through together, then," Daniel said, almost choking on the words.

"Aye, that we will." Joshua let his old lopsided grin break loose, twisting his hollow cheeks. Daniel noticed he had lost a tooth. He had been diminished in body, but not in spirit. "To the end."

Part Two

SIEGE

Chapter 27

The General

$\mathcal{W}$ashington rode at the head of the two armies; it was the final leg of the long march. With him rode some of his most trusted companions—Colonel Tilghman, Generals Lincoln, Knox and Lafayette. The road they traveled was a good one, dry-packed earth for most of its length, rough corduroy where it passed through lower country, the bark still clinging to some of the logs that lay crossways to raise the surface above the mire.

The General knew this land well, this land of pine forest, swamps, farms and fields, split-rail fences and hedgerows, sprawling plantations and humble cabins. This was the country of his birth. Perhaps, with luck and the continuance of an already staggering effort, it would also be the country of his greatest military achievement.

Civilians, both black and white, had gathered on the verge to watch the passing of the armies. Most stood in curious silence, while others shouted questions, asking where the army was going. Some simply cheered. No one derided the soldiers, for this was predominantly friendly country. Whenever a voice would demand the whereabouts of General Washington, the General would nod or raise his hand, then receive a shout or cheer for his effort.

The French bands and the fifes and drums blared throughout the march, maintaining the cadence and the spirits of those who did not have the privilege of a horse.

After about five miles, the armies came to a fork in the road. One trail bore left toward the York River, while the other kept a straight course south and east. The General broke away from his companions, taking a position at the point where the roads diverged. The long lines of Continentals marched past, taking the straight course, and he touched his hat to each set of colours, his eyes following the regimental flags and the striped banners of the United States.

When next those proud standards are carried such a distance, the General thought, *I pray that it will in triumph following victory. There is no other option open to us.*

He remembered marches past, this year and the last, and the one before that. It was as if all of those miles—in the rain, the snow, the mud and the heat—had led him to this point. This was the apex. If he was to lose this gamble, he did not think the war would continue. But if all went well...

When the last Virginians had gone by, the head of the French column appeared. There was Rochambeau, riding in the lead. This time, the General raised his hat, and Rochambeau returned the gesture. Their eyes met, and although they exchanged smiles, they did not speak. There was no need for words. They were on their way, marching "to a better destiny" once again.

It was another beginning, and the General realized how the last weeks had been nothing but beginnings, one after the other. Today they marched, and so they forged another link in the chain of events. With the investment of York Town would come another link, another beginning.

The French army wheeled onto the left fork, snaking along, colour after colour. Washington paid the required compliments, as was his duty. When the column had passed, he turned his horse and rode forward along the line of his Continentals. The French would become the left wing, would come upon York by the river road. The Americans, although the smaller contingent in raw numbers, would take the honour of the right.

The General resumed his place at the head of his army.

⁂

The sun was beginning to dip when he emerged from a thick belt of pines, the prickly boughs parting like curtains on a stage. The town of York lay on his left, about four thousand yards away across an expanse of flat fields dotted with copses. There were the even lines of the British fortifications, like red earthen scars; and there rose the masts of a few ships in the river. He could see a little windmill, and could just make out the British Union flag flying over the courthouse.

Behind him, the marching regiments began to stutter to a halt, and he turned to watch the nearest unit pile arms. This was where they would make camp, for they had come far enough for one day. In the morning, they would carry on to outflank the town.

Colonel Tilghman reined in his mount beside him and pointing with his right index finger.

"There is a patch of higher ground yonder, sir. Under that large tree."

The General nodded. "Then let us take a look, and see if the enemy will favour us with an appearance."

They rode to the knoll, dismounting under the tree, a spreading mulberry. Tilghman snapped open a telescope, but Washington shook his head, preferring to gaze toward York Town with his naked eyes. He suspected he would soon grow weary of watching this place through a glass. For now, he wished to take in the broader view.

"Aha!" he exclaimed, and now it was his turn to point. A bright scattering of redcoat dragoons had appeared in the distance, perhaps two thousand yards off. The setting sun glinted from polished accoutrements, or perhaps an officer's gorget. "They have seen us. Will they do anything but watch?"

A moment later, he received an answer. A squad of French Chasseurs advanced to engage the British horsemen, but the dragoons wheeled about to gallop back toward the town. The chasseurs halted in a swirl of dust, not bothering to continue the chase.

"It seems we will not be a witness to excitement tonight," the General said to Tilghman. "So, it is down to business. I will make my headquarters here, on the ground under this tree."

"We can pitch the tent, General," Tilghman suggested.

Washington shook his head. "Never mind. We mean to move on in the morning, and it will be wasted labour. The armies will bivouac under arms tonight. That is, if the men can sleep at all, now that we are so close!"

Tilghman grinned. "These are professional soldiers now, sir. They can sleep anywhere."

The General spent the next half-hour disbursing his aides to deliver the necessary orders to his division commanders, although the camp was already taking shape of its own accord. The men gathered wood, and bivouac fires sprang to life. There was still no sign of the baggage train, which had lagged behind.

At last, the General called for a map of the surrounding region. When he received it, he spread it on the ground; and he and Tilghman studied its features, identifying the most obvious landmarks. He discovered that some confirmed his plans for the army's deployment, while others would force modifications.

"The French," he said, "will command the ground between the York River and the town. They will prevent Cornwallis from escaping along the river road. Our Continentals will carry on along the main road until we are south of the town. These two creeks, of course, dictate our route of approach. We must assault the enemy from the south." He tapped the map with a finger. "Then there is Gloucester Point, across the river. We must make certain the enemy detachments there are hemmed in."

"The Duke of Lauzun's division is on that side of the river," Tilghman reminded him. "A fine set of French cavalry."

"Yes," the General agreed. "They should suffice."

He dictated further orders to Tilghman, details as to the deployment of each division.

"I will deliver these instructions myself," Tilghman promised.

When the aide had left on his errand, the General stared at the map a moment more.

"This is to be our battle ground."

He spread a blanket beneath the mulberry, then stretched his long frame upon it. The night was balmy. He did not bother to remove his coat, for he wished to be ready at once when he rose.

"There is nothing left to do today," he reminded himself. The operation was clear in his mind. It was time to rest his body.

Thick roots of the mulberry tree made a pillow for his head. He folded his hands over his belly and thought no more of plans, no more of the future.

"Perhaps Colonel Tilghman was right," he whispered, "and we may sleep anywhere we choose."

That was his last thought, for a moment later, he had drifted off to sleep.

Chapter 28

The Redcoat

Jt was midday before the enemy struck their temporary bivouac and started moving south. Tom Martin stood with his officers watching the American rebels with growing dismay.

They marched in a long column of fours, strung out in a snaking line about three thousand yards from his position. He counted the flags hanging limp at the head of each battalion, and he listened to their distant music, the squealing of their fifes and rumbling of their drums.

It made no sense. First the French had been allowed to land a division unmolested, and now the enemy was allowed to encircle York. Why had Lord Cornwallis done nothing to stop them?

"We should attack them now," Tom muttered. "We should send out a flying column and move up artillery, strike them while they are still deploying."

But he knew there would be no attack. Cornwallis had simply ordered his army to "stand to" in the outer ring of defences and wait.

The 1st Light Infantry had formed behind a line of breastworks near the redoubt on the north side of the Godley Road. Tom's company occupied the redoubt itself, offering support for two bronze twelve-pounder cannon. His men stood in idle lines along the earthen firing step, flanking the guns. Like Tom, they leaned on their weapons and watched as another opportunity to attack marched past, soon to be lost forever.

"Perhaps the enemy will be good enough to throw themselves on our line," he said. He hoped they would, that they would at least send a probe against the British works. He ran his left hand along the smooth stock of his fusil, caressing the section he had planed away to use as a cheek rest. He was eager to put the musket to good use.

"We must have patience, Sergeant," Lieutenant Nicholson commented, his tone full of condescension, as if he were speaking to a child. "The enemy has us outnumbered."

"They always have, sir," Tom wanted to say, but he held his tongue.

Captain Barlow's sword scraped from his scabbard, and he sloped it against his shoulder.

"Let us hope they attack us. I am ready for them."

Tom detected a tremor in the captain's voice. Perhaps the old soldier, the hard campaigner, had returned now that action was upon them. Or perhaps, Tom realized, Barlow was just putting up a good show. He no longer understood his company commander.

He turned away from the officers, studied the Royal Artillery as they began loading the two twelve-pounders, ramming home powder, wadding, and the heavy iron shot. At least the gunners would see some action. Linstocks wrapped in slow match smoldered in the rear of the batteries, and Tom inhaled the acrid smell. It brought with it memories good and bad, of triumph and fear, horror and exaltation.

The captain in charge of the twelve-pounders laid each gun with ponderous skill, sighting along the bronze barrels and making adjustments with the trail handspike. When he was satisfied, he gave the order to fire. The sergeants in command of each gun relayed the order to their crews, and the proper men took up the linstocks, touching the slow match to the vent of each gun. The powder in the quill ignition tubes flashed, and Tom stuck his fingers in his ears as the guns discharged one after the other. White sulfurous smoke drifted past his line of vision, and he did not see the fall of the shot. When the smoke had cleared, there did not appear to be any damage within the rebel line.

"Out of range," he muttered.

Few twelve-pounder cannon could send a shot much farther than two thousand yards, if that. Tom suspected the artillerymen were simply trying to relieve their frustration, but he realized he was glad for it. Although ineffective, the fire still demonstrated a show of defiance, and one Tom's men appreciated.

Private Hassler had climbed to the top of the parapet, and as the twelve-pounders fired a second salvo, he cried, "Take that, ye damned rebels!" A few of the men chuckled, and others took up the call, hurling insults they knew the enemy could not hear. Tom smiled to himself. These were his men, his comrades. It was good to hear Hassler speaking out again, and even better that the fellow was directing his rage toward a more appropriate target. Perhaps in the simple duties of camp cook he had found belonging. Whatever his motivation, Tom was pleased with his conduct, which had been steady and obedient.

"Come on, ye bloody cowards!" Hassler shouted. Several others cried out in agreement.

"Maybe they will attack," Lieutenant Nicholson said, speaking at a more reasonable volume.

"I hope that is their intention, sir," Tom said, hefting his fusil. *A probe, at least*, he thought again. He had seen no sign of a siege train, no sign of heavy guns, so perhaps the enemy planned to make another foolish assault, like they had at Savannah. If so, it would be to their detriment. "I would dearly love to see the rebels break themselves against this position."

He waited, anticipating action. The British fortifications were strong. He knew they would never be taken by storm. Without siege artillery, the enemy had no chance.

The last of the American column was crossing a bridge over Beaverdam Creek—American engineers had built the bridge during the night. Now, the long white lines of the French were spreading on the opposite flank, in the north. Tom noted the French would be facing the strong star-shaped redoubt near the river road. The 23rd Regiment, the Royal Welch Fusiliers, manned that fort. The Welshmen would never give in to the French.

The sun soared high overhead, and still the enemy marched, a testament to their numbers. Tom told off the men in rotations, allowing half to eat their dinner. It was a sorry affair here in the outer forts, just the bread they carried in their haversacks and some green apples they had foraged a few days ago. Tom ate his share on the firing step, paid a quick visit to the privy in the rear of the redoubt, then scurried back toward his observation perch. It was then he heard the distinct crackle of musketry from the far right.

Heart pounding in sudden excitement, he leapt onto the firing step and shielded his eyes with his hand. The enemy was attacking after all! There, in the distance, a French battalion had advanced against the star redoubt. Smoke rose as the Fusiliers dealt them a bit of punishment.

"That's it, lads!" Tom cried. "Show them the Welsh can do more than sing!"

But the fight lasted no more than ten minutes. The French line withdrew, their white uniforms like the foam on the crest of a receding wave. The noise of musketry began to die away. It had been a probe after all.

Tom waited, perspiring in the afternoon sun, barely speaking to his companions. The men started games of cards or dice upon the rampart or on the ground. Some slept according to Tom's rotation schedule, while others checked and rechecked their weapons. The educated scratched letters to send home. Sergeant Gibb wrestled with Bone. Tom simply folded his hands and leaned on the wall.

Silence settled over the wide landscape. Now and then a British musket would crack or one of the batteries would open to hammer away for a few minutes; but the range was still too great, and the artillerymen knew they had to conserve their ammunition. At one point, a skirmish broke out on the far left. Tom watched it through Captain Barlow's telescope, saw that some *jaegers*—German light troops—had set out on a probe of their own, striking at the American right near a mill pond at the head of Wormley Creek. The exchange of fire lasted about twenty minutes; then the jaegers, like the French, withdrew.

Suppertime came, but it was only more bread, this time with tea the troops brewed over small bivouac fires they started in the fort itself. The long day was drawing to a close, with nothing to show for it. Tom's frustration returned, mingling with a creeping exhaustion. It was too late for the rebels to attack now. Perhaps they would come tomorrow.

"Sergeant Gibb," he called. "Take the watch. Relieve me when you have had enough."

Gibb waved from the other side of the redoubt, where he sat with one arm around his beloved dog.

Tom settled with his back against the redoubt wall and closed his eyes. He would try to sleep for a few minutes. A soldier lacking sleep was not as effective as one well rested.

He awoke with a start to the crash of artillery. The twelve-pounders had opened fire again. The cannon flashed, illuminating the shapes of his men in the redoubt, some standing on the firing step, some squatting, some reclining against the walls. Tom realized it was now twilight, that about two hours must have passed.

He cursed and rubbed his eyes, then lurched to his feet, still groggy. He did not see Captain Barlow or Lieutenant Nicholson. Sergeant Gibb stood a few feet away. Bone sat at Gibb's feet, eyes fixed on the gun crews as they reloaded.

Tom climbed the firing step and gazed past the row of sharpened stakes. The horizon was still visible, the enemy fires already burning in the south like so many fallen stars. He did not understand why the artillery was continuing to fire.

"Sergeant," someone called, and he turned to see Captain Barlow enter the redoubt from the gate in the rear.

"Sir?" Tom said.

Barlow halted below the firing step.

"The company is to fall back on the battalion. We are withdrawing."

Tom stared at him. He knew what Barlow had said, but he could not believe it.

"Withdrawing, sir?"

"We are moving back to the inner defences, Sergeant. Lord Cornwallis means to abandon the outer line. Form the men."

Barlow strode away.

Tom glanced at Gibb, who stared back in astonishment. Tom hoped Barlow was mistaken.

"Has anyone come to relieve us here?" he asked.

"No one," Gibb replied. "Looks like we're giving up this position, though I can't see why."

Tom stood still for a moment, his heart pounding. That they had not attacked the rebel column was bad enough, but to abandon the outer forts...

There was nothing he could do. An order was an order, even one that made so little sense.

"Company, assemble!" he shouted.

Bone wagged his tail, sensing that his people were about to move. The company formed in a ragged line, and Tom soon dressed their two ranks. The twelve-pounders fired once more; then the gun crews wormed and swabbed the barrels.

Tom turned the company into file and marched them out through the gate. Artillery drivers, teams, and gun limbers waited outside to remove the cannon from the redoubt. Next to them was the rest of Tom's battalion, already formed in column. He halted the company in their rear. Gibb stood with him.

"Looks like we'll leaving all this to the rebels," Gibb remarked.

"Aye, falling back," Tom said. He tried to find a reason for such a maneuver, but all that came to mind was "Maybe it will entice the rebels into attacking us."

Gibb barked a laugh. "Or entice them into taking all them empty forts. A ready-made siege line!"

Tom said nothing, but he knew Gibb was right. He glanced at the darkening sky, the stars crisp against a velvet backdrop. There was a gentle breeze, the air still warm, the crickets still loud, but his chest and arms felt numb. He suddenly knew the enemy would not simply attack. They would not make such an obvious mistake, a move that went against all the principles of warfare. Before there was any assault, there would be a siege, a long, dull game of waiting. Maybe the enemy would bring siege guns off the French ships in the bay. Or maybe they would wait and try to draw the British out from behind their walls.

Whatever the case, Tom knew that, by the middle of the next morning, the redoubt his company had just abandoned, leaving it undefended, would be an American fort.

Chapter 29

The Dragoon

The train of wagons stretched along the road toward Gloucester, the teamsters shouting and snapping their whips. Droves of cattle, foraged from the countryside, followed the wagons, snorting and lowing. Behind the cattle, cursing at the ruts, hoofprints and piles of manure, the green-coated infantry of the Queen's Rangers marched with the redcoat light company of the 23rd Foot. The cavalry of Tarleton's British Legion, less concerned with the road surface, brought up the rear.

John Chester rode at the head of his troop. He sat easy in the saddle, but he was nervous as he surveyed the fertile fields that lay on either side of the road, the green-and-brown patchwork enclosed by split-rail fences. Bordering the fields ran belts of forest, mixed pine and hardwood sprinkled with dashes of autumn colour. It was an idyllic scene, yet beneath its beauty lay hidden danger that kept him glancing over his shoulder every few minutes, watching for the Virginian militia and French infantry that had dogged their heels throughout the day.

"You suspect the enemy will close their pursuit, sir?" his covering sergeant asked, also stealing a glance backwards.

"I do, Sergeant," John said. "I do, for Gloucester is an open door. An open door. I suspect the rebels mean to shut it."

He spoke as if it were just a fact, and not a dire threat.

The rebels had tightened their grip on York, seizing the entire outer defensive line Cornwallis had ordered abandoned. John had agreed with those orders, for Cornwallis expected relief or reinforcement from General Clinton in New York, and there were not enough able men to hold the dispersed outer line. However, the withdrawal also meant the British Legion and the Queen's Rangers had no choice but to keep Gloucester open as both a supply route and an escape route.

Thus today, John thought, *I may see battle for the first time. And how will I fare? Will I melt with fear? Will I run and hide, just as I have hidden these last years?*

"We have been successful today," he said, as much to encourage himself as his sergeant. "Better than any other single day that I can remember."

The harvest had been good, and the rumbling wagons bulged with maize, grain, vegetables, bales of hay, even smoked meats and other amenities. This was the necessary fuel for the beleaguered garrison. Much of the food already in storage at York was rotten, so it was crucial that these fresh supplies reach Gloucester.

"The rebels would dearly love to get their hands on these wagons," his sergeant commented.

"Then it is our task to prevent them from doing so," John declared. "It is our duty."

"Of course, sir."

He glanced at the sergeant. Had he detected a hint of mockery in the man's voice? He could not be certain, but he still felt an outsider amongst these men, hard fellows who had seen many campaigns. Most of them were from the Carolinas, while he was a Virginian. All of them had demonstrated their prowess in battle, while he had not. He commanded them purely because he was a landowner, a man of social station among Loyalists. And he knew this country.

He turned to his lieutenant, who rode a few yards to his left.

"You have the troop for a moment," he called. "I can't see well enough from here, and wish to take a closer look. I will rejoin you presently." Then, to his sergeant he added, "I shan't be long."

He turned his horse, falling out of the column and halting on the grassy verge. Tugging a handkerchief from his pocket, he pushed back his leather helmet and mopped his brow. There had been no relief from the heat.

The rear of the column moved past him, and he held the handkerchief over his mouth against the rising dust. The soldiers presented a motley appearance, some still sporting the white cotton frocks they had adopted for the southern climate, the rest wearing their Provincial green jackets. Here and there was a splash of red—a member of the 17th Light Dragoons. The dragoons were on service with the British Legion, but they had refused to assimilate into the Loyalist regiment, retaining their short-tailed red coats. They were a proud unit, having been raised by the officer who had brought the news of General James Wolfe's victory at Quebec to the king in 1759.

Their brass helmets resembled those worn by the ancient Romans, with a metal crest and a wool band in place of the turban. A skull-and-crossbones badge on the front peak commemorated Wolfe's death at the moment of his victory.

This was a good company, John told himself. The foraging party was strong, the equivalent of two full regiments, one of horse and one of foot. The French and Americans had even greater numbers on this side of the river, but the quality of their troops, he supposed, could not be as great.

The final rank in the column approached and passed, and the dust cloud slowly settled. John drew in slow draughts of searing air and gazed along the road toward the north, toward where the danger lay.

As he watched, two horsemen emerged from a sparse stand of woods about three hundred yards distant. There they halted. John could almost feel their menacing eyes upon him, probing.

He returned the handkerchief to his pocket, opened a saddlebag and removed a brass telescope. Extending the tubes, he trained the glass on the distant riders. He saw a glimmer of white-and-gold. Mounted infantry officers.

"Not ours, sir?" his covering sergeant said. The man had followed at a slight distance but would not leave John's side. John supposed the fellow knew his duty.

He slammed the telescope shut. The head of the French infantry column had appeared behind the officers, more men in white coats. He could hear the rattle of their drums, pounding out the cadence like the voice of an approaching serpent.

"The French," he said, stating the obvious. "They are closer this time. The wagons have slowed our progress. We still have four miles to go before we reach Gloucester."

More men and horses were gathering around him—other officers who had fallen out of ranks to watch for their pursuers. John extended the telescope again. The French infantry had crossed the road, moving eastward into a field of goldenrod that had gone to seed. John swept the glass along their line, then turned back to the road. He froze.

Cavalry had moved up behind the infantry. The horsemen wore sky-blue dolmans ablaze with golden looping around their buttons. Their tight breeches were red, and their saddle blankets matched their jackets. Every man wore a shako—a tall cylindrical cap, black with yellow cording. John had never seen them before, but he knew who they were. French hussars, trained professional cavalry.

"The men Colonel Tarleton has been waiting for," he murmured. He struggled to keep his voice steady, but it quavered just the same.

He recalled an incident that had occurred a few hours earlier. They were passing through a village; and as often happened, the people came out onto their steps to see the soldiers, curious as to whether they were friend or foe.

A fetching young woman, a girl with hair like straw, had stood at the edge of a rail fence.

Colonel Tarleton had reined in next to her, gazing down in appreciation. John had heard him ask, "My dear, I wonder if you could possibly tell me the whereabouts of the Duc de Lauzun, the famous French cavalry commander. I long to shake hands with him."

The girl had shrugged and said she had not seen him. Tarleton had shaken his head as if in pity, saying, "Perhaps another time." Then the column had carried on.

John stared at the sky, the drifting wisps of cloud. Even with the heat, it was a remarkably beautiful day. A butterfly danced across the road, fluttering over the rail fence to his left.

Acute fear seemed to strike him from nowhere, rising from the pit of his stomach and spreading through his body, so sudden and intense it made him grunt. There was a difference, he realized, between knowing something was true and actually facing it. He had known battle was possible today, but now it stared him in the face. Tarleton wished to attack the French cavalry, and there they stood.

Still another officer approached and halted, sending up a thick cloud of dust. John turned, slowly, his right hand rising to touch his helmet even before his eyes fell upon the face of his commander. He had known it was Tarleton.

The young colonel's eyes blazed as he edged his horse closer to John's.

"So, there he sits," he said. "Our enemy is upon us. I do not feel much like running from them again, Captain Chester."

"We have to save the cattle and wagons, Colonel," John stated, a small part of him still hoping they would continue to push for Gloucester, although he knew Tarleton had longed to meet de Lauzun in combat, one cavalry officer to another, like the knights of old.

"Precisely," Tarleton said. "We are close enough to Gloucester to allow the wagons to carry on as we establish a rearguard." He smiled, a wicked grin. "We will fight them here."

John's stomach clenched, the fear swelling again. That was it, then. He took another deep breath.

"We seem to be equally matched in numbers, sir," he said, his voice sounding thin to his own ears. "Equally matched."

The distant cavalry had advanced beyond the infantry line in the field. The lead horsemen carried lances in addition to their sabres and pistols.

"They are the Duc de Lauzun's Legion," Tarleton said, gleeful. "His infantry and hussars, at last. We shall give them a charge!"

John looked for the wagons, but he did not see them. Instead, he discovered the Legion had already turned about to face the enemy. It was reforming in the field west of the road, facing north.

"What of the Virginia militia, sir?" he asked, not from fear but genuine concern. "They have been nipping our heels all day. Perhaps we should wait until they show themselves."

"I am not afraid of the Virginia militia," Tarleton sneered. He turned to the man on his right, a mounted infantry officer of the Queen's Rangers. "Form your men in that line of trees." He pointed to a thick belt east of the road, birch mixed with pine. A slender lane ran through the trees from the road, northeast in a diagonal. "Do not place them in the lane. Face them north, along the northern edge of the field. And hurry. There is not a moment to lose!"

The officer reined about and galloped south to bring up his men. John watched as de Lauzun's hussars slowed to a halt and began to dress their lines. They stood well in advance of the French infantry—too far in advance, he realized, for the infantry to give them support if the British charged now. The French horsemen were also disordered, still assembling after their march.

"This is an opportunity," he stated, and knew the advantage lay with Tarleton's forces. They could do this.

His entire body was vibrating, but he was ready. There was no sense in waiting.

He pulled his horse around, wheeling across the road, back to his troop. He found his place in their front, and his covering sergeant pulled in on his left. Their knees almost touched. John hoped the man would not notice his trembling.

Tarleton placed himself square in front of the regiment, then drew his sword. The distant blue cavalry was still forming, still compressing itself into even lines.

"Battalion," Tarleton shouted, "draw...*swords!*"

John gripped the leather-bound hilt of his heavy dragoon sword, pulling the broad, straight blade from its scabbard. He held the weapon in his right hand, his reins in his left. His palms were slick. His horse stamped the turf with eagerness, knowing the order of commands as well as he from the parade ground.

The commands came quickly. First Tarleton cried, "Walk...*march*," and they started forward. Within a few yards, Tarleton added, "Trot!"

The Legion was moving, hooves muffled by the short grass and stubble. Scabbards and harness jingled. It made a powerful machine, John thought with wonder, all of these horses and men advancing like a wall. He tried to tighten his grip on his reins, felt the strength of the animal beneath him, its eagerness to run.

He had always loved a good chase, a day's outing on horseback. It was a joyful thing . . .

The French began to widen their frontage, spreading into the field to meet the charge, to protect their right flank. Their movements were hasty, their alignment becoming ragged. John concentrated on his horsemanship but saw sunlight flash as the lancers brought down the steel-tipped weapons that gave them their name. A few others leveled their long pistols. Puffs of smoke appeared as they opened fire, but John knew the range was too great.

The Legion was moving faster. A gap opened between the ranks in line, the column extending forward like a bellows. Tarleton and the men in the first line pulled away, now moving at a canter. John's troop made up the second line. The first line would strike home first. John would see the fight develop before he was part of it.

They moved faster and faster, the horses increasing the pace without urging from their riders, the men not bothering to check it. John felt the wind in his face, and suddenly, he found himself laughing. Laughing as a strange joy built within him, smothering the fear.

Tarleton dropped his sword, holding it outstretched, straight at the enemy. John did not hear the command to charge over the thundering of hoofs, but the front ranks leapt ahead, widening the gap.

He could not let them leave him behind. He leaned forward, standing in his stirrups, thrusting his sword forward as Tarleton had. The air seemed to burst from his lungs as he cried, "Charge!"

The command was unnecessary. The troop was already moving at a full gallop.

Tarleton's ranks met the hussars with an audible crash. Horses and men screamed. Shapes swirled in the billowing dust, swords glinting as they rose, ringing as they met. Pistols thundered from both sides. Through the confusion, John spied Tarleton about to engage an officer with a tall plume on his cylindrical felt cap. John recognized the officer as the Duc de Lauzun himself. The two commanders were flailing with their blades, trying to reach each other.

The events that followed occurred within seconds, but to John, time seemed to stretch, to elongate. He saw a pair of lancers, perhaps determined to save their leader, put spurs to their mounts and charge toward Tarleton. A redcoat dragoon drove to block their path. Both lances pierced the chest of the dragoon's horse, and the animal screamed, rearing before falling sideways, spilling its rider onto the field.

The collapsing horse tore the lances from the hands of their owners; then the dying beast's heavy body crashed into the legs of Tarleton's mount. Tarleton's horse in turn stumbled as it trampled the fallen dragoon. The Legion commander pitched sideways from his saddle, dropping to roll in the grass, his sword bouncing from his grip.

The Duc de Lauzun kicked his mount's flanks, rushing forward with a small group of his men, shouting in triumph.

At that moment, John's troop and the following ranks smashed into the melee. De Lauzun stopped short as Tarleton crouched, trying to avoid the rushing horses and flailing hooves. John charged for the French colonel, screaming a wordless war cry and reining in so hard his horse nearly threw him. He kept to his saddle, sweeping his heavy blade sideways and down. De Lauzun parried, the steel ringing, the blades scraping together. John raised his sword for a second blow, but the tide of men and horseflesh drew his opponent away. Redcoats of the 17th were on either side of him, leveling their massive dragoon pistols. The pistols flashed and boomed. John saw one hussar pitch from his saddle, another duck.

Then the fight ended; the enemy was gone, and time again unfolded at its normal rate. John realized the French were withdrawing back to the north. A fresh troop of the British Legion, so far unengaged, thundered past in pursuit.

Two dragoons had swung out of their saddles and were helping Tarleton to his feet.

"Sound the withdrawal," the colonel gasped, slapping at his breeches.

John searched the still-milling ranks of Legionnaires, a collage of green-red-and-white. He spied a trumpeter and pointed with his sword.

"Trumpeter! Sound the withdrawal."

The brassy notes peeled out across the fields. Tarleton had caught his breath and was demanding, "Where in hell are my aides? You there, Lieutenant! Take a message to Colonel Simcoe. The Queen's Rangers and other light companies will cover our withdrawal. The Legion will reform for another charge." He spat, wiping a hand across his mouth. "Someone get me a fresh mount!"

The Legion wheeled again, heading south to reform beyond the belt of trees where Tarleton had placed his infantry. John chanced a look back and saw that the hussars had already reformed in the north, were already moving forward. But the infantry of the Queen's Rangers had made a rough line amongst the birches, pines, and elms, and on their left was the redcoat light company of the Royal Welch Fusiliers. They stood at the ready, waiting for the French horseman to come into musketry range.

"Give them hell and brimstone, boys!" John shouted to them; then he was back with his troop and wheeling again, turning to face north before halting. De Lauzun was spurring forward along the road and the field left of it, just as Tarleton's men had done only minutes before.

John swayed in the saddle for a moment then steadied himself. Sweat soaked his shirt under his jacket, and he blew a clod of dust from his nose. He glanced about him at the terrain. Flat ground, good for cavalry. Again he noticed the diagonal lane that ran through the trees behind the British infantry. The lane was a dark tunnel that led to the enemy, a natural covered way.

He suddenly remembered the missing Virginia militia. His mind seemed clearer than it had ever been, sharper; and he realized the militia officers would have knowledge of this country. They might know of the lane.

He turned back to watch de Lauzun's men, a more immediate concern. They were now moving at the canter. Perhaps the French had not seen the redcoats and the Rangers in the trees. Or perhaps they were arrogant enough to think they could rout infantry from so strong a position.

A volley crashed from the Rangers and Fusiliers, a long line of bursting smoke. John imagined he could actually see the hail of lead strike the front and left of the hussar column. Two horsemen went down at once, the others checking their pace, wheeling left and right. A second volley crashed, smoke jetting and swirling. More horses fell, their downed riders rolling and cursing on the trampled earth.

Tarleton, on his fresh horse, raised his sword then brought it down. The Legion spurred forward again.

When the charge struck home, it swept into a cloud of dust and smoke so thick John could not see more than a few yards in either direction. The fight raged on all sides, a chaos of grunts, shouts, and screams, the din of horses and men colliding, the ringing of swords and barking of pistols. He swung his sword at an opponent, but the hussar ducked and dashed past. He laughed involuntarily, then turned his mount about, saw a horse move by with blood streaming from the stump of its right ear. A musket ball hummed past his head.

Then he heard the trumpet, calling for a second withdrawal.

The hussars had broken off, and the Legion retired to its original position. John found himself opposite the little lane again. He checked his ranks, saw that the regiment appeared to be close to full strength. Casualties had been light so far.

He fought a wave of dizziness. His blood was pounding in his ears, and his throat was dry as kindling. He reached for his tin canteen, opened the wooden stopper and took a sip, then a long pull. The Legion had paused for a brief rest. The hussars were also sitting in a fresh line across the road, not moving. The French infantry had not advanced.

The rest lasted about ten minutes. Tarleton placed himself at the head of the column. His sword rose and fell. They advanced for a third charge.

This time the hussars waited to meet them. They stood like a wall, and the clash was brief. John's troop did not engage before the Legion withdrew.

The next charge swept in a wide arc through the field in an attempt to take the French in the flank. Another confused melee ensued, a flurry of sweat and rage. Neither side gained an advantage.

John found himself back near the lane. He was exhausted, his right arm numb from the weight of his sword, his lungs burning. His helmet had become greasy with sweat, and it kept sliding down over his eyes. His horse was soaked and blowing, champing at the bit, but John did not want to stop. He was a warrior. He was fighting for his home, his land, his beliefs, his very identity. Let them try to stop him!

The trumpet sounded the Officers' Call, and he assembled with the others in a semicircle before the colonel. Tarleton appeared as exhausted as the rest.

"We will exhaust our mounts," he said, then pointed north. The hussars also appeared to have had enough. They had taken a new position in the rear of the French infantry. "Another French infantry regiment has appeared. Or perhaps fresh companies. We will wait and rest. Our infantry will deal with them."

John nodded, then prepared to wait, to catch his breath.

The Queen's Rangers advanced from the trees, taking cover behind a half-ruined rail fence. The French infantry also came forward, but not far. The two sides faced each other at a distance of about a hundred yards. Volleys rang out from the French line, but their marksmanship was poor. The Rangers replied, trading volley for volley. John sat with Tarleton, not speaking, now and then glancing over his shoulder to the south. He was glad to see that the wagons were nowhere in sight. They might have been safe in Gloucester by now.

He sheathed his sword and reclined in his saddle. His eyelids drooped, and he fought to keep them open.

"I am too old for all this scurrying about," he said, and tried to chuckle, but all that emerged was a parched, creaking sound.

"We have done well today," Tarleton replied. He continued to observe the ineffectual musketry duel. "The wagons are saved."

There was little triumph in his voice. John looked southward. A reserve troop of the Legion sat there, alone.

He again glanced at the little lane on the right. Then he sat upright, all weariness dispersing.

"Sir!" he cried.

"I see them," Tarleton snapped. "Damn their eyes!" He turned to the trumpeter. "Sound the general withdrawal. Our position, gentlemen, has become untenable."

To the beat of a drum, a narrow column of Virginia militia was advancing along the lane. John knew that soon they would be in a position to strike the Loyalist troops in the right flank and rear.

"Exactly what I feared," he commented. "They must have worked their way around us while we were engaged with the hussars."

"I don't care about them," Tarleton said in disgust. "I will leave Captain Bennet's troop as a rearguard. We have done what we could. We must return to Gloucester."

The trumpet rang out. The battle was over.

John thought of Gloucester, of the trenches, breastworks and redoubts. They would be hemmed in there, just as the main body of the army was hemmed in at York Town. He did not see how their small force would ever be able to break out against the numbers the enemy had at their disposal.

They had not been able to keep Gloucester open, he realized. They were under siege on both sides of the river. This would be his last foraging party.

Yet, strangely, none of that mattered. Not now, at this moment. He had met the enemy at last, and he had stood and fought.

They fell into the road and again made their way south. John stared about him like a newborn child, marveling at the intense green of the fields, the blue of the sky. Then his hands began to shake, and his teeth to chatter. Try as he might, he could not steady them. They shook and chattered all the way back to Gloucester, and did not stop until he was safe inside the breastworks.

Chapter 30

The Loyalist

$\mathcal{T}$hey stood on the beach looking across the water to York Town. Smoke rose beyond the far houses, and the air trembled with the dull thud of distant cannon. John focused his glass, then passed it to Catherine.

"The guns you hear are ours," he said, his voice filled with expansive pride. He had still not changed his clothes since returning from the foraging expedition, and red dust coated his breeches and black boots. "They must be, for the enemy have not yet got their siege artillery in place. They have a few field pieces, but that is all."

Through the glass, Catherine studied the shore, the houses and the docks. She could see little of the fortifications save for the low breastworks that lined the bluff on the seaward side. A few redcoats loitered on the docks.

"Let me see," Abigail demanded. She was sulking, for she had called out to Tarleton when John's regiment had returned, but the colonel had shooed her out of the way as he rode past, cruelly whipping his horse.

"A moment, Abigail," Catherine said, trying to be patient.

She turned the glass to the warships—the *Charon* anchored directly ahead, the *Guadaloupe* far to her right. She could also see three transports, one she knew as the *Bonetta*. Several small boats plied to and fro, following the shore or crossing the channel. One approached from the southeast, along the coast from where Wormley Creek drained into the bay. The boat's path was blocked by the British stockade that extended several yards into the water.

"Since I joined the Legion," John continued, "I have done little else but study the art of war. From books, mind you. Today's action was my first engagement."

"You must be very brave, cousin John," Abigail said.

"I think I was simply too occupied to be frightened. Still, I am no longer in fear of the enemy.

"We all must take heart. You see, my dear girls, the rebels and their French friends must conduct a proper siege if they are to have a hope of succeeding against us. If they assault our works over open ground, they will be cut down by our artillery and musketry. Mown down like grass. Thus, they must dig a system of trenches.

"It is very simple. They will begin with a trench parallel to our works, perhaps three or four hundred yards away." He slashed one finger through the air, as if drawing on an invisible slate. "This will give them cover from our cannon fire. There, they will build sheltered emplacements for their siege batteries. From this first parallel, they will construct diagonal approach trenches—to get close to our walls, they need the cover. Then, they will dig a second parallel. Perhaps that will enable them to get close enough under cover to then attempt to storm our works.

"But that, I do not think, will ever happen, nor would it succeed. Not at all."

Catherine was only half-listening. The boat from Wormley Creek had paddled out into the river around the stockade, having crossed from rebel-held territory to British. It seemed incredible, but no one had paid it the least attention.

Then she recognized the boat and its single occupant. It was the Negro boy who had sold her the crabs and fish. He continued his venture, ignoring the presence of the French and rebels. Perhaps he sold his wares to both sides. Perhaps each considered him harmless, unimportant, so he was free to come and go as he chose.

"These things take time," John said. "The enemy have not yet begun digging their first parallel. Our scouts have reported that their siege guns have just begun landing from the French men-of-war. They will have barely begun their work by the time General Clinton comes to relieve us."

Catherine lowered the telescope and passed it to Abigail, who snatched it from her hands. Catherine did not rebuke her, for a singular thought had taken hold in her mind. She stared at the houses in York, but she did not see them.

Daniel will be there, she thought. *Across the river.*

"The Marquis de Lafayette's men are here?" she asked.

"Yes," John said. "We are completely invested by almost the entire Continental Army." He placed one large hand on her shoulder. "I will not tell you lies, Catherine. Our garrison is small and worn down by its campaigns. Our situation is not a good one. But our men are skilled, and we cannot lose hope of reinforcement."

"I have not lost hope yet, cousin," she told him. "I will keep it for another few weeks."

She watched a large and solitary bird soar high over the river, a bird with a mixture of light and dark feathers, wingtips like fingers. The osprey. Perhaps the same one she had seen before. It was gliding away toward York. Soon, it would be over the American lines. Over their camps. Daniel was in one of those camps.

Her heart began to quicken, and she pressed both hands to her cheeks, felt the blood flooding her skin.

"Are you quite well, Catherine?" John asked, and she felt his gentle touch on her shoulder.

She shook her head.

"I think I must rest. I would like to go back to our room."

His voice was soft, his manner fatherly.

"Come, then. It will be all right."

She let him guide her back to the house, chancing one quick look behind her at the smoke rising above York.

⁂

There was only the three of them for supper that evening. Catherine found herself unable to eat, her stomach humming like a beehive.

"I am only tired," she insisted when John continued to express his concern. "It has been a trying day."

He nodded. "I have been ordered to the breastworks tonight. We will act as dismounted cavalry now for a while, I think. I would stay with you if I could."

"I will be all right. Abigail and I shall amuse ourselves with our sewing."

He kissed the top of her head as he prepared to leave.

"We must have faith in our generals. Lord Cornwallis is undefeated. It will be all right."

When he was gone, Catherine and Abigail retired to their room. Catherine sat with a thimble on her finger, the unfinished bodice of a new short gown draped across her lap. This is what they did—carried on with domestic life sewing, washing, helping prepare meals, as if all was right with the world. *Idle work*, she thought.

The house around them was quiet; there did not seem to be a gathering of officers tonight. She supposed that most of them, like John, were helping to man the breastworks and redoubts now the enemy was at the gates.

It was not yet dark. Now and then, the windows rattled from the concussion of the artillery in York Town—the cannon in Gloucester had been silent for several hours. Catherine could not concentrate on her work.

"So, the war has come back to us," she murmured.

But it had also brought Daniel to her, as if the Fates had conspired. She made up her mind.

"I must fetch something from the parlour," she told Abigail. "I will be back in a few minutes."

Downstairs, the parlour was dim and empty, the clock over the mantel loud in the stillness. Catherine sank onto the settee, folding her arms. She knew what she wished to do. She could not escape Gloucester, could never go to the American camp, not without raising suspicions on both sides. But she could write Daniel a letter. She could tell him she was here, that she was safe. That she remembered him. She could send the message by way of an unobtrusive little boy. A boy who went fishing within the rebel lines.

At once, her stomach began to settle, her agitation easing with the decision made. It was dangerous, she realized. If she was caught, she could be accused of passing information to the enemy. And the boy's ability to deliver a message, to understand the nature of the task, was unknown to her. Yet her need to communicate with Daniel seemed greater than the risk.

There was a writing desk in the study across the hall. There might be writing paper there, quills and sand and ink. If not, she would find what she needed elsewhere.

She moved into the hall, crossing to the study with long, determined strides. Leaving the door ajar behind her, she went to the desk and lifted the lid. The items she wanted were there, quills, a bottle of India ink, and a bar of sealing wax. She folded two pieces of paper, then slipped everything inside her petticoats, into a pocket.

She heard the front door open, then a footfall on the boards. Assuming it was John, she stepped back into the hall. She found herself facing Colonel Tarleton. He stood at the bottom of the stairs, an unopened bottle of wine in his hand.

She froze, her skin prickling.

"Good evening, Mrs. Checklee," he said, bowing from the waist. "I am looking for Captain Chester."

"He is not here, sir." She was unable to keep the coldness from her voice. "He is on duty in the forts, where I presume you ought to be."

"I do make time for myself, ma'am. And my adjutant composed the duty rotation, which I have not read in full. It is a pity Captain Chester has been called away. I was hoping for his charming, rather naive company." He chuckled, a light, malicious sound. "He did well in his first combat. I am indebted to him. But now I have *your* charming company, ma'am. Charming—for you must understand I care nothing for what you think of me. You may hate me all you like. It does me no harm. Much of the American continent shares your opinion."

She started for the stairs, hoping to slip past him.

"If you will excuse me, sir, I have matters to attend."

He caught her arm before she could mount the first step. Despite his two missing fingers, his grip was like iron.

"I am a soldier of His Majesty's forces," he hissed. "This is a cruel world, ma'am, and I did not create it. A soldier must take what he wants if he wishes to survive. This is something you could not possibly understand."

"The world *is* cruel, sir, but there is love, friendship, and beauty here still. And there would be more if some did not insist on adding to the cruelty which you describe. Now..." She took his hand and began to pry it loose. "Unhand me, sir!"

His thumb and remaining fingers sprang open as if mounted on springs.

"You are a sentimentalist, like all of your sex. It is a great weakness. We shall see where your philosophies lie when Mister Washington's cannon begin tearing us to pieces. When the streets of York Town run with blood." He scowled to emphasize his disgust. "You presume to judge me, but you are not a soldier, ma'am, and you have never truly seen war. Nor its effects."

She laughed at him.

"Oh, but I have seen it, sir, and I have felt its effects, whatever you may think. Now, you must excuse me."

She climbed the stairs. She did not look back when Tarleton called after her, "I have no designs on your slip of a sister. She is the cousin of one of my troop commanders. Whatever you may believe, I have my honour as an officer!"

He said nothing more. She reached the landing, and again heard the clamor of his boots on the hall floor. The front door banged shut.

In their room, Abigail said, "Colonel Tarleton was here."

"He was. I believe he was already drunk."

Abigail concentrated on her sewing. She sat in her old familiar stance, shoulders hunched over her work.

"I heard what you both said."

Catherine studied her, then crossed the room and encircled her sister's slight shoulders with her arms. Abigail set her needle down, returning the embrace, resting her head against Catherine's breast.

"What will become of us here?" she murmured, her voice small and muffled.

"We must do as John says," Catherine said. "We must trust in Lord Cornwallis." Yet, even as she spoke, she realized that to trust in Cornwallis was to hope for a rebel defeat, for the destruction of Daniel and his comrades.

Oh, this is intolerable!

She needed to send her message. She did not know whether the boy could help her, or if it was possible for Daniel to reply. At this moment, it did not matter. She needed to act.

She stroked Abigail's cheek once, then released her. Abigail silently retrieved her needle, and Catherine pulled a chair to the dressing table. She took the things from her pocket, unfolded the paper then scratched a few quick sentences with the quill. The letter was brief, the message simple. She folded it in three, sealing it with a glob of wax melted in the flame of the candle.

"What is that?" Abigail asked.

"Something I must deliver tomorrow morning," Catherine replied. "Alone. I'm sorry, Abby."

She slept little that night and rose early, moving in silence to avoid waking Abigail. It was cold, and she wore her new red wool cloak as she hurried to the wharf at the little inlet where the boy usually tied up his boat. He came every morning. She would wait for him.

The British cannon were already thundering in York Town. She wondered how the siege was progressing, whether the rebels had begun to dig the trenches John had described.

About an hour passed before the boy finally appeared, paddling slowly along the coast, this time from the north. When he saw her, he smiled. There were baskets in the bottom of the little boat.

Catherine glanced back toward the houses of Gloucester, but there were few people about. The boy dragged his boat onto the shore.

"Got some good ones this mornin', Missis," he said as she joined him.

"I don't want any fish today, thank you," she told him. "I have something else for you to do."

The boy grinned. "Yes'm?"

"Yes. I want you to deliver something for me." She cringed inside, suddenly not certain what she intended wasn't treason in the midst of a siege.

But her letter was private.

She lowered her voice. "You have been to the enemy."

The boy shook his head. "I don't have no enemy, Missis."

"You took your boat over there." She pointed. "You talked to the rebels. Beyond Wormley Creek."

He nodded. "Yes,'m. I been there, with the other soldiers. They didn't mind."

She pulled the letter from her petticoats and held it out to him.

"I'll give you something special if you go back there and deliver this. It is for Lieutenant Daniel Brattle, of the Light Infantry."

The boy's eyes were wide. For a moment, she wondered if he had strong loyalties after all, if he would report her for harbouring rebel sympathies. Perhaps his father was an escaped slave, promised his freedom by the British, who despised the rebels and had taught his son the same. It *was* possible, although from his words she had assumed he was one of the many who did not care one way or the other. Or that he was too young to understand.

She was not prepared to change her mind. She glanced around again to make certain no one was watching, then pressed an English penny into his hand, one of her last.

"Please. There is a man there who is my friend. I want to tell him I am safe. He is with the rebels. The Light Infantry."

"Light infantry," the boy repeated.

"That's right. Will you take this to him? Give this to one of the soldiers and ask them to deliver it to the Light Infantry? I will give you something else when you return."

The boy's grin had returned upon receipt of the coin.

"Sure will."

He took the letter and stuffed it into a pocket of his long waistcoat, fastening the flap with its wooden button. Catherine grasped his small shoulders and gave them a squeeze. She felt the strength there, astonishing in one so young.

"You are a good boy," she said. "Come to me again when you return."

"I'll come back," he declared. "I come here all the time!"

She nodded, releasing him. He ran to the boat, began dragging it to the water, wading to his knees before leaping in and taking the oars. She remained on the bank, clutching her cloak tight about her. The boy backed the little craft into the river, and within minutes, he had gained the channel. There was a long running swell, and she watched him rise on the wave and disappear in the trough.

This is pointless, she suddenly thought. *Desperate. He does not understand, and will never deliver the letter.*

She turned, intending to return to the house, but the sight of a dragoon in green coming along the shore locked her in place. For a moment, she mistook him for Tarleton, but quickly realized he was a junior officer in John's regiment, a lieutenant she did not know well.

The dragoon touched the bill of his helmet, bowing and clearing his throat.

"My apologies, madam," he said. "I did not intend to startle you. I was merely taking a turn along the riverbank. Perhaps I should have trod more heavily."

"Indeed, sir," she replied, her heart still racing. "However, no offense is taken."

He nodded, then glanced toward the river. The boy had reached the far bank and was now rowing toward the stockade and the rebel lines beyond.

"That young fisher lad," he said, "you are one of his patrons?"

"Yes," she said, fighting rising panic, convinced he had seen her hand over the letter. "He had nothing to interest me this morning."

"Ah, that's unfortunate." He pursed his lips. "I find these Negroes a bit of a nuisance, in general."

"Some would say so, sir," she replied. She did not wish to argue with this fellow, to insist that all loyal subjects had a right to the protection the troops here offered.

"Yes, quite a nuisance," he repeated. "Though I daresay useful as labourers." He chuckled. "At any rate, I must continue on my way. I find a cavalryman needs to walk now and then."

"I should think so, sir."

"Indeed. Good morning, madam!"

He bowed again, and she nodded. When he moved on, continuing along the bank, she watched until he had passed under a stand of willows.

What would he have done, she wondered, *if he had seen me give the boy the letter? Surely, he would not have assumed the worst.* There was nothing obvious to connect the boy to the enemy. The letter could have contained money, a message for the boy's family, anything.

A chill passed through her. What was treasonous and what was not, in this land where a good portion of the population was in rebellion against their rightful king? If she were to throw in her lot with the revolutionaries, John would call her traitor, and Daniel would declare she had come to her senses. Was a Continental soldier who deserted the army to return to his fields a traitor to the revolution? Or was he merely exercising his right to liberty? She considered that most famous of turncoats, the notorious Benedict Arnold, who had first rebelled against King George then reversed his decision to side with the British. Was his second treason merely a correction of his first?

Perhaps Arnold's treachery lay in the nature of his actions, she decided. He had sold information in secret, skulking in the shadows like a thief, a coward. She remembered Daniel saying so once. Perhaps there lay the heart of treachery—in dishonesty, in hypocrisy. Arnold had turned against the cause he had at first so fervently embraced, a cause for which he had risked his life, his livelihood. He had then shown himself false. He could never again be trusted by either side.

I have skulked like a thief, she thought, *here on the riverbank. I passed a message in secret, fearing discovery.*

Yet, her letter contained no information that would bring harm to anyone, nor have an effect on the struggle. Were she not surrounded by the warring armies, she could have sent the letter by ordinary post. It would not help the rebels in any way to know that she, Catherine Seawell, was in Gloucester.

If anyone wished to accuse her of disloyalty to British efforts, they would have to point to her earlier actions, to the time when she had given shelter and aid to two enemy soldiers. In that, her conscience had always been clear. There had been no other option. To turn Daniel and Joshua away would have made her a traitor to humanity.

She started climbing the slope back toward the town. She would worry no more on the implications of what she had done here. She had betrayed nothing and no one. Not the army of Cornwallis, nor the convictions of her soul.

Chapter 31

The Redcoat

*T*om squatted behind a hummock of grass, his musket loaded and primed. He was patient, like a hunter in his blind, waiting for the enemy survey party to wander closer to his position. Here were some prime targets, including what looked like a high-ranking Continental officer and a trio of engineers in French uniform. The rest were Continental soldiers, half-a-dozen armed men in ragged hunting shirts.

Tom stroked his fusil's oiled stock in anticipation. The weapon would see some use today.

"Maybe we can bag us a general," young Sam Webb whispered in his left ear. "Maybe even Washington himself, eh?"

"Who knows, Sam?" Tom muttered. "Maybe we'll nab one of the French engineers, if that Continental fellow gives us the slip."

It was a possibility. Tom had fifteen good men with him, all intent on harassing and delaying the enemy work. As he'd predicted, the Americans had taken the abandoned British redoubts almost at once, raising their striped rebel flags as proof of ownership. Now, they used those redoubts as bases, sending out engineers to survey the ground in preparation for digging their first siege trenches. Tom wanted to stop them.

"It has fallen to us again," he murmured to himself.

It had fallen to him, a mere sergeant, to lead this little attack. Captain Barlow should have been here, or at least Lieutenant Nicholson; but Nicholson had fallen ill, and Barlow had turned the task over to Tom. In truth, Tom preferred it this way. *Let the officers rest*, he told himself. Let them wallow in the camps where almost two thousand men now lay sick in hospital tents, stricken with various forms of fever. He was glad to be on his own, glad for the responsibility.

A few shells roared overhead as the artillery from the British inner defences continued to lob shot at the captured redoubts. Tom's men hugged the ground, pressing into a shallow dip, the grassy hillock providing added cover. Their eager confidence showed in their faces, and Tom felt a surge of pride. The other companies had suffered from desertions to the American and the French lines, but his had not.

"Let's see what we can do here today," he said.

The rebel survey party was now no more than sixty yards away. One engineer held a roll of paper under his arm—a map or set of plans. Another held a tall pole for use in triangulation.

"There ain't many of them, Sergeant," Sam Webb whispered. "We can take 'em all."

"They have a larger covering party somewhere," Tom warned. "Hiding like we're hiding. I'd say just over that hump, lying flat." He pointed to a low rise just beyond the surveyors, and at that moment, he saw a flash of sunlight, a reflection from a badge or buckle. "There are men there, all right," he concluded, staring hard. Now he was even certain he could see the edge of a man's hat.

Turning to his left, he whispered, "Sergeant Gibb!"

Gibb scrambled over to him, trying to remain hidden behind the hillock. Tom wondered if Gibb's cap was also visible to the Americans. He hoped not.

"Same plan, then?" Gibb said.

Tom nodded. Before setting out, they had decided that half of the raiders would stay here to counter the enemy covering party. The other half would go after the surveyors.

"I will lead the attack," he said. "The covering party is yours."

"Aye, Tom," Gibb agreed, nodding. "We won't let 'em get the jump on you."

Keeping their voices low, Tom and Gibb told off the men, deciding who would stay and who would go forward. Each man nodded grimly as the sergeants gave him his assignment.

Tom chose Hassler for his detachment. The fellow had earned a chance to prove himself, one way or the other.

There were no formalities, no drill from the manual of arms. Tom gathered his men on one side of the hillock. They were dressed in their sleeved waistcoats and white linen trousers, and carried nothing but their muskets and bayonets, full cartridge pouches, and tin canteens. Gibb's men waited, crouching in line a few feet away. Tom raised his hand, but kept his eyes on the surveyors. The engineers were not looking in his direction.

"Forward," he cried, leaping to his feet.

His men were with him, reassuring supports to his right and left. They ran toward the surveyors, calling a loud, drawn-out, "Huzzay!" The Americans gaped at them in astonishment.

Suddenly, a white blur raced past Tom on his left, baying like a hound on the hunt. It was Bone. Tom had thought the bulldog was in camp, but he must have followed them. He ran with tail bobbing, perhaps thinking this was all a game.

The engineers ignored the armed redcoats. They saw the bulldog, turned, and ran.

Tom halted and brought his fusil up to his cheek, sighting on the backs of the enemy. He did not fire. There seemed to be no point now that the rebels were running.

A few members of his detachment continued to charge after the engineers, hoping to catch them. Hassler was out in front, bellowing. One rebel straggler was within his grasp.

Tom lowered his fusil. A few muskets cracked from behind the rising ground in his front—the rebel covering party, showing themselves, kneeling and firing. Tom's comrades under Gibb returned fire. Tom saw one rebel throw out his hands and fall backward.

Hassler was the only redcoat not to have given up the pursuit. He had almost reached the edge of the rebel lines when he suddenly threw down his musket and dove for the legs of the straggler, catching the fellow around the knees. The man fell, hands outstretched, his musket clattering to the ground.

The American kicked at Hassler. Hassler let him go and retrieved the fallen musket. The man rolled onto his back.

"Damn ye, ye lobster!" Tom heard the man cry, his voice a nasal shriek.

The rebel scrambled to his feet, but Hassler swung the musket like a club. The butt struck the American in the side of the head, and he crumpled to the dirt a second time. This time, he lay still.

Hassler stood over the body, prodding it with his foot. Muskets cracked from the rebel covering party, but Hassler was oblivious.

Tom decided they had done enough for now.

"Private Hassler," he shouted, "we are withdrawing!"

Hassler glanced at him, then back toward the rebel lines. The surveyors were gone, and their covering party had begun to withdraw, one man at a time. Bone dashed back and forth, nose to the ground. Now and then, the dog lifted his head and let out a sharp bark. No one had fired at him.

The man at Hassler's feet did not move.

"Private Hassler!" Tom repeated. Despite the enemy's withdrawal, he felt exposed on this open ground.

Hassler hefted both his own musket and the one the American had dropped, then started jogging back. Bone ceased his aimless scurrying and followed.

"Back to the Hornwork," Tom shouted. "We'll find a new location, wait for 'em to come out again."

They rejoined the rest of their party, then started for their lines. Tom walked with Sergeant Gibb, Bone snuffling along beside them.

"Bone chased them off," Tom said, trying to control his anger. He could not admonish a fellow sergeant in the same way he would a private, but Gibb needed to understand his mistake. "We might have taken some prisoners, and Bone might have become a target if their covering party had been inclined to shoot at a dog. You should have chained him."

Gibb stared at him in dismay.

"I could never do that, Tom!"

"Well, then, you may lose him some day!" Tom snapped. He was unhappy with the attack, had hoped to bag a precious engineer. The two American casualties almost seemed pointless. And something disturbed him about Hassler's drive. It had been desperate, obsessive, unthinking, as if his punishment was showing effects other than improved discipline.

"It's all a ruddy mess," he muttered. His commanders had let the enemy come, encircle them, and now did nothing.

"We'll find another hiding place," he repeated to Gibb, softening his tone. "Try again."

Chapter 32

The Continental

"*J* expect them to show at any moment," Daniel said to Joshua. "They won't let us simply finish our work."

He gazed across the moonlit fields toward York Town. With other detachments from the light infantry, his company was manning one of the captured British redoubts, providing protection for the sappers who would begin digging the first parallel. The great siege guns had arrived from the French ships, having landing seven miles up the James; and the French engineers had at last managed to map the location for the first trenches and the siege batteries. When completed, the works would link the old British outer redoubts in a wide arc. Tonight the construction would commence.

"They did nothing to bother us last night," Joshua reminded him.

"The rain deterred them as much as it deterred us," Daniel insisted.

The previous evening had brought the first foul weather of the season, fog and rain that had thwarted the first American attempt to begin the works. All they had managed to accomplish was to lay down pine boards end to end to mark the line of the trench.

"The clear sky is now our enemy," he added.

The British will see us working, he thought, *and they will sortie.*

He gripped his sword hilt, his stomach churning. The enemy had already made some effort to hamper them, lobbing shot and shells day and night. For those who laboured to convert the captured redoubts, the only defence had been to post sentries to watch for muzzle flashes. The rapid flight of solid shot made it almost impossible to detect, but howitzer and mortar shells arced through the air with a high-pitched whine, trailing smoke like a comet, allowing for the warning cry of "Shell!" There was often time for the men to find cover, although sometimes not.

Tonight, the enemy guns were silent, but that made Daniel no less uneasy. The British, he reasoned, would hear the noise of pick and spade and come out in force.

Joshua seemed unconcerned.

"The lobsters are in for a surprise tomorrow morning," he whispered to the nearest kneeling soldiers. "They'll find us on their doorstep. In a few days, we'll be banging the knocker!"

There were chuckles, and Daniel cursed his churning guts, cursed his fears and doubts. He did not want them, and had no use for them.

He moved along the low firing step. The line of pine boards the sappers had placed last night was clearly visible a few yards in front of the redoubt, a vivid streak against the dark ground, like a borderline drawn on a map. A little to his left, almost on the bright line, stood a small collection of men—Continental officers, by the look of them.

"Those must be our engineers," he whispered. "Some last-minute survey work, do you think?"

The tallest of the officers turned, and now Daniel discerned some of his features—the long nose, the firm mouth.

"That's General Washington," Joshua said, with some surprise. "And his staff."

Daniel stared, wondering if Joshua was correct. He recognized the General's stance, the confident bearing, the way he held his head. It was the Commander-in-Chief himself standing on the trench line.

From behind the General, a line of sappers advanced, armed with their picks and spades. They halted along the edge of the planks. There was no shelter, and ample light from the moon.

The enemy will strike now, Daniel thought. *Just when our commander is most vulnerable…*

One of General Washington's aides passed him an object; Daniel realized it was a pick. The General took it and raised it over his head. It hovered there, suspended, for an instant then fell, striking the sandy earth.

The first blow.

The line of sappers set to work, their picks rising and falling. When they had loosened enough earth, they piled it in front of them, fashioning the beginnings of a rampart. Washington and his staff remained for a moment, as if to admire the sappers' efforts.

"Go, sir," Daniel murmured. "Go."

Washington said something more; then he and his companions turned and began to stroll away, as if on an afternoon outing. Daniel breathed a sigh of relief.

He still could not understand how the noise, the digging and grunting of the sappers, did not alert the enemy sentries.

The night passed slowly, but the redcoats did not stir. Daniel did not sleep. By dawn, a shallow trench made a curve that enveloped York from the edge of the bluff above the river to the head of Yorktown Creek. In front of the trench lay a low but stout parapet.

Daniel examined the work in the pale morning light with mild astonishment, and a strange irritation that he had been wrong. They had dug the first parallel. The enemy had made no move.

"No rest for the weary, brother," Joshua said at his side. He was pointing at the British walls opposite. "They've seen it at last."

Daniel followed the gesture. The shapes of gunners were moving in a battery opposite. One man withdrew the rammer from the black muzzle of a cannon. Smoke burst from the muzzle. A dark iron ball slapped into the new parapet, and the report followed seconds later. The ball bounced high, hurtling toward the rear. The tired sappers cheered.

"The redcoats seem a mite angry with us," said Joshua.

⚜

The company was relieved after breakfast, but by mid-morning Daniel and Joshua, now off-duty, decided to return to the redoubt. The completed trench now had to be defended, and for that, it needed to be occupied around the clock. The first troops scheduled to do so were men from Lafayette's Second Brigade, the battalions of Lieutenant-Colonels Alexander Scammell and Alexander Hamilton.

When the brothers reached the redoubt, they found it crowded with dozens of curious off-duty soldiers. Some even stood in the open behind the new trench; others crouched in natural depressions in the ground.

"It seems everyone is familiar with Article Twenty-five," Daniel commented, referring to a clause in General Washington's siege regulations. Under that clause, all reliefs would be performed with drums beating and colours uncased. Under Article 26, each Continental and state colour would be planted to fly on top of the parapet. As a result, the formal occupation of the trenches would prove a grand sight, something akin to a ceremonial parade.

The British now kept up a steady fire. Daniel and Joshua sought a sheltered position beneath the ramparts of the redoubt. Daniel knelt on the firing step, peering over the parapet to discover that the works had progressed since the morning. Fresh waves of sappers had dug the trench deeper and wider and begun constructing zigzag approach trenches. They had also strengthened the parapet with gabions and fashioned embrasures for the field guns that would be employed to discourage British sorties. Army carpenters had built gun platforms of pine boards, and the guns already sat in place, although at present they were silent, the ammunition having not yet come forward.

He settled with his back to the wall. Joshua remained standing, oblivious to the cannon fire as if his one brush with death had made him immune.

"For God's sake," Daniel warned, "keep your head down! It wouldn't do to get killed while sightseeing."

Joshua grinned at him. "On the contrary, there is something here I think you ought to take in yourself."

He pointed toward the enemy lines and laughed. Daniel pushed to his feet. "What is it?"

Joshua indicated the large Hornwork—two triangular projections that dominated the British defence line. It housed the battery that had fired the first shot earlier that morning. Its guns were now throwing solid shot at the new American rampart, but the sandy earth was absorbing much of the force of each blow.

"There he goes again!" Joshua cried, and now Daniel saw a large white bulldog crawl out of the British ditch and scramble through the abatis of tangled tree branches. The dog dashed after one of the spent British shot as it rolled backward from the American works.

"The poor thing thinks it's all a game!" Joshua cried.

The battery fired another salvo, three cannon in succession. Daniel flinched as the black iron projectiles slammed into the trench parapet to his left, spraying fountains of earth before bouncing toward the American rear. Spectators scurried out of the way, but to Daniel's amazement, the bulldog chased after the balls, bounding across the open ground between the combatants, leaping down into the American trench and up the other side.

"He's within our lines!" he shouted.

One of the shot continued to thump along the ground, at last outrunning its pursuer. The dog halted, staring after its quarry with ears pricked.

"Maybe one of us should capture him," Joshua suggested. "We could tie a message around his neck and send it back to his masters."

"And who will dare?" Daniel asked, laughing. "Not I, Joshua. He looks somewhat too ferocious."

The dog chased another shot, which also outran him. Men laughed and leapt out of the creature's way, and Daniel wondered how soldiers brave enough to stand here under fire could not summon the nerve to confront the stocky little animal, which was, after all, simply someone's pet or mascot.

At length, the dog grew tired of the fruitless game and scampered back to his own lines. Daniel waited for him to reappear, but he did not. The sun climbed the sky, its rays stabbing down through drifting batches of powder smoke. Perhaps the bulldog's owner had chained it, he thought, to keep it out of danger.

A solid shot skipped over the parapet, spraying earth and a few broken wooden stakes. Daniel ducked, and a second later, someone cried out in shock and pain. A man was writhing on the ground in the redoubt, blood pumping from the stump of his right leg.

The fellow's nearest comrades ran to his aid, doing their best to staunch the flow of blood with a scrap of rag. As they lifted him and began carrying him to the rear, Daniel turned away.

"A game, indeed," he muttered, again settling against the parapet. It was so easy to become complacent. His stomach gave a twinge. "Maybe a game to a dumb beast."

The cannon continued to roar. It was past noon. Now, over the din of the artillery, there rose another sound—the piercing music of fifes. A moment later, Daniel could also hear the drums. The troops were coming at last.

The first battalion marched in fours along the lane from the camp. The colour party strode along just behind the musicians, their two huge square banners snapping in the wind—the white-and-gold regimental colour displaying the motto *Manus Haec Inimica Tyrannis*. Lieutenant-Colonel Alexander Hamilton was at the head of the regiment. He was a notorious figure, well known for having forced General Washington to free him from the General's staff so he could take a command in the field. A glory-seeker, many said, for all his short stature, his body like a stout barrel.

Hamilton's regiment changed from fours into twos and entered one of the approaches. The fifes and drums ceased, and a minute later, the long file of soldiers wheeled into the right flank of the parallel. Behind the first regiment came another, then another, until the first parallel was filled. As per General Washington's orders, the colour parties of the three regiments planted their flags on the earthen parapet, thrusting the poles deep into the dirt. The flags stood as a calculated challenge to the enemy, a dare.

"A fine sight, indeed," Joshua commented.

Shouted commands rang in the trench, the caps of the men bobbing back-and-forth. The ceremony was over, having taken scarcely a quarter of an hour, but Hamilton's battalion was still milling about. As Daniel and Joshua watched, a few of them began climbing the parapet.

Daniel frowned in confusion. Now, the entire regiment was leaving the shelter of the trench, forming ranks on the rampart. The sergeants began dressing the line while Hamilton faced his assembled companies with his sword sloped on his shoulder. His back was to the enemy.

"What is he doing?" Daniel cried. "His men will be slaughtered!"

Hamilton's battalion stood at attention, the soldiers elbow-to-elbow, muskets at the order. If the British gunners wished to, they could blow those close-packed ranks away in an instant.

But the batteries fell silent. Smoke drifted in small clouds like airy bales of cotton, as all at once, the cannonade ceased. There was silence. Somewhere, a cricket began to chirp.

Daniel stared in amazement as the enemy gunners clustered in their embrasures, handspikes and rammers in their hands. All eyes were focused on the strange drama about to unfold.

Colonel Hamilton suddenly shouted, "Battalion, shoulder...firelocks!"

The order came out sharp and clear, and the battalion obeyed, bringing their muskets up in unison. Then Hamilton proceeded to shout a series of commands, and his men responded as if on the parade ground.

"Order...firelocks! Ground...firelocks! Take up...firelocks!"

"He's taking them through a drill," Joshua said in disgust. "He's giving them von Steuben's manual of arms."

Daniel made no comment. Hamilton's men fixed their bayonets, shouldered their muskets, faced to the right, to the right again, then to the right about to come back to their front. Throughout the entire display, not one British gun fired.

"It seems there is still glory in war," Joshua remarked. "For some."

"I would never endanger my men for such a display," Daniel scoffed. There was something arrogant and pompous about it—a display for the colonel's fellow officers as much as for the enemy. And yet, there was something grand in it as well, a show of defiance and discipline that even the British seemed to respect.

When the exercise had concluded, the battalion turned their backs and stepped back into the trench. Hamilton alone remained, facing the enemy, as if expecting applause.

What he received was a blast of smoke and flame from a cannon. The ball struck the parapet next to his position. The bombardment had resumed.

"What other strange and bizarre sights shall we see today, brother?" Daniel wondered, ducking behind the wall.

When he managed to peer over the parapet again, Hamilton had returned to the relative safety of the trench.

Chapter 33

The General

General Washington dismounted in the rear of the completed battery. A junior aide took his reins, and the General joined Colonel Tilghman to enter the battery. It was cold, the breath of men and horses steaming in the morning air, a reminder of the advancing forces of winter. It was already well into October, with scant weeks before the French fleet departed. The General hoped the silent cannon before him would do their work well, and quickly.

The battery was an earthen crescent perched almost on the edge of the bluff, high above the river. General Knox had styled it the "grand battery," and it *was* grand with its row of powerful guns—three eighteen-pounders, three twenty-four-pounders, two eight-inch howitzers, and two ten-and-a-half-inch mortars. The mortars sat on peculiar platforms that could be raised in the back, allowing them to hurl their shells straight into the enemy walls. It was another of Knox's innovations, proof that Washington's faith in him was not misplaced.

Knox was already present. He advanced to meet the General and his party, saluting, grinning behind his spectacles.

"All is in readiness, Your Excellency!" he cried.

"Well done, General Knox," Washington said, his pleasure genuine. The work had been difficult but rapidly completed. Men, horses, and oxen had been pulling the great guns into their emplacements since the completion of the parallel; and now six American batteries faced the British walls. In all, the batteries held forty-one siege guns, and more were on the way.

"Nothing remains but to begin," he added, pausing to admire the scene —the iron shot stacked in their garlands; the artillery stores arrayed beside each piece; rammers, worms, and handspikes within easy reach. The striped Continental standard flew from the center of the parapet, and the ready matrosses were at their posts.

Knox directed him toward the rightmost gun, a long eighteen-pounder. As they approached a gathering of men—off-duty soldiers—quickly stood aside. Some stiffened to attention, recognizing their commander-in-chief, but others simply gawked.

"More curious idlers, sir," Tilghman grumbled. "Despite your orders."

"Apparently, there is no other pressing business in camp," Washington remarked. "However, I do not think these fellows are making a hindrance of themselves."

It had been the same yesterday, with scores of off-duty soldiers coming out to watch the opening of the trenches. Many had stood in plain view of the enemy guns—in the redoubts, on the ramparts, and even in the open without so much as a tree stump for cover. Several had been injured by British artillery, some mortally.

As a result, the General had issued a proclamation ordering all those not on duty to remain in the rear of the trenches. The order had stopped short of forbidding them to sightsee altogether, for although he did not care for the risks they took, the danger they exposed themselves to, he had worked long and hard to improve morale, and judged it unwise to do anything that might counter the excitement building among the troops.

Today, he trusted he would add to that excitement when he completed his ceremonial duty here, in Knox's grand battery.

He took a position on the parapet, climbing with three quick, nimble purchases. Tilghman and Knox followed.

"It is a splendid view, sir," Knox was saying, puffing from the exertion of mounting the firing step. "And a clear shot!"

"Splendid, indeed," Washington agreed. "It certainly affords the best vantage for our purposes, gentlemen."

Tilghman extended a telescope and passed it to him. The General took it, but waited a moment before raising it to his eye. Below, the artillerymen were loading, preparing for their moment. Another symbolic act, he mused. He had broken the first ground two nights ago, and now he would fire the first American gun. The stuff of myth, like Knox's field guns, although the field guns had since found a practical use in defending the trenches against potential enemy sorties.

So far, there had been no such sorties. Washington thought that strange, for Cornwallis had a reputation for aggressiveness, for exploiting opportunity. He had not done that here. His men had not been sparing with their artillery—and even now their guns pounded and rumbled, targeting the allied center; but for the most part, the British infantry had remained passive inside their protecting wall.

"All the better," he murmured. The mistakes of the enemy were sometimes the key to success, if they could be used to advantage.

He raised his glass, training it on the nearest enemy works. These were a pair of redoubts that stood out a few yards from the main British wall. The smaller squatted on the edge of the bluff directly opposite the battery, while the larger was several yards inland. Washington knew them, for the Americans had learned the names of some of the British forts from deserters. The larger outlying redoubt was known as Redoubt Number Nine, the smaller Redoubt Number Ten. The large projection in the center of the British main line was their "Hornwork," the usual designation for a central defensive structure. This one had the appearance of strength, and would have to be reduced. The two redoubts seemed isolated. All would make fine targets.

The General shifted the glass to better see the Hornwork, its walls bristling with gun ports spouting fire. In its rear stood a large brick house with a gabled roof, the home of Secretary Thomas Nelson. The house was the most prominent feature of the town, the finest in York. Cornwallis himself was probably there now, about to have his late breakfast interrupted.

The sergeant in command of the first gun cried, "Ready!" Washington collapsed the telescope.

"We are ready, sir," Knox stated. "The honour is yours."

Without another word, the General handed the closed telescope to Tilghman, then descended the firing step. The long cast-iron eighteen-pounder had been loaded and run up, its muzzle thrust through the embrasure, the crew standing at their positions in echelon, facing the rear.

He mounted the wooden gun platform. The captain in charge of the battery held a linstock wrapped in smoldering slowmatch. He passed it to General Washington.

Washington studied the end of the smoking match. The tip flared for a second, as if in eagerness. The British guns continued to rumble, but silence seemed to descend on the world. He stepped closer to the gun and slowly brought the linstock down to the ignition tube in the vent.

The vent flashed, jetting smoke skyward, and the long gun recoiled on its trails. The ball was clear against the sky, a black speck hurtling toward the town, rising over the British parapet, then descending. It struck the clapboard wall of a house, tearing a large hole. A second later there came a splintering crash, then several lesser crashes as it ripped through the other buildings along the street.

The artillerymen in the battery let out a sharp "Huzzay!" Some snatched off their cocked hats and waved them in the air.

Washington returned the linstock to the battery commander.

"You may commence firing, General Knox," he said.

Chapter 34

The Continental

$\mathcal{D}$aniel stood transfixed. With the opening gun as the signal, batteries all along the allied line had begun to speak. Shot after shot roared toward the town and the enemy forts. Shells rose high in the air to plunge, shrieking, behind their comet-tails of fire. Smoke trails hung in the air for up to a minute after the shells struck their targets, and soon the American and British lines appeared to be connected by parabolic tendrils of vapour.

"I would not have missed this for all the riches of the Orient," he said to Joshua, shouting over the din.

They had found a perch to the right of the grand battery, affording them a fine view of the British works and the houses of York Town. They could even see the large French battery in the north, beyond Yorktown Creek, that had been pounding the British star-shaped redoubt for days.

"No one wants to miss it," Joshua shouted back, waving at the crowd of off-duty soldiers that had gathered, in compliance with the spirit of General Washington's orders, in the rear of the trenches. They stood in bunches, talking, laughing, pointing, and cheering as the great guns pounded York.

The enemy could not withstand many days of this, Daniel realized. Jets of red earth sprang from the British earthworks; and bits of wood, shattered gabions, and broken gun carriages were hurled into the air. In the rear of the great Hornwork, the prominent brick house of Secretary Nelson was already scarred, its windows broken.

The smaller enemy guns only managed one shot every few minutes, and at the sight of their feeble attempt to reply, Daniel felt something stir within him. For the first time, he felt a new doubt. Doubt in his conviction the war would be lost.

Perhaps there is a chance after all, he thought. *Just a chance, unless Cornwallis escapes…or drives us away with a powerful sortie.*

"Here are some of *our* fellows," Joshua was saying, pointing to a pair of men strolling along the trench line, grinning like boys at a country fair. Daniel recognized a sergeant from his company named Williams and a private named Blaire.

"Good morning, Sergeant," Joshua said when they were close enough.

"A fine mornin', sirs!" Williams declared. "This is the day we've been waitin' for. Soon, every man'll be free to pursue his own devices, without needin' to bow, scrape, or pay tax or tribute to anyone!"

Daniel hesitated, not fully understanding the man's meaning.

"Well, you shall pay taxes to Congress, I imagine."

"No, sir!" Williams declared. "Not after all this fightin' I done. If Congress stoops to that, I'll fight 'em, too. Fight 'em with as many or more cannon than we got here, sirs. You mark my words."

Three mortars on the left of the grand battery discharged almost as one, abruptly ending the conversation. The big shells rose like fat skyrockets. Williams laughed.

The shells shrieked as they fell, but crossing their path was a pair of trails heading in the other direction. Daniel's jaw worked as the hostile shells descended toward a group of onlookers. The men scattered, shouting in alarm an instant before the shells struck the turf. Bouncing and smoking, they burst. Two men fell.

Daniel looked away, his brief optimism instantly fled.

"We must not be too confident," he muttered. "The enemy is not simply going to give in."

⚜

The sun set orange and dull behind a screen of blowing smoke. By dark, the exchange of fire slackened, but it did not cease. Despite the difficulty of locating targets without light, there was to be no respite.

That night, Daniel's battalion went on duty in the first parallel, a duty that would last a full twenty-four hours. They went in at midnight, advancing along the covered approaches, drums beating and Colours flying, although Daniel could barely hear the fifes over the roar of cannon.

Once in the trench, the troops kept under cover, but Daniel and the other officers could not help staring over the parapet toward York. Here and there, fires burned in the town, and he thought he could detect the outlines of damage—gaping holes and shattered glass. No candles or lights of any kind showed in the windows of the houses.

"We fired almost four thousand rounds today," Joshua said. "I am heartily glad I am no lobster!"

Daniel settled into as comfortable a position as he could, leaning against the parapet. The air was chill and permeated with the sulfurous stench of burned gunpowder.

"We have a long night ahead of us, and a long day tomorrow. I'm sure we'll witness the effect of four thousand further rounds."

The sappers arrived, filing along the covered ways, this time causing as little disturbance as possible. Their work continued—additional batteries had been completed, and now more than fifty guns were in position. Tonight, the sappers would continue work on the approach trenches that extended from the parallel. Within a day or two, they would begin the second parallel.

The roar of guns and shells, the rhythm of the picks and spades filled the hours. The men slept in rotations. It was still dark when Daniel heard the music of reveille rise from the British camp. It seemed an unbelievable sound in the circumstances, a mundane military routine as if this day were the same as any other. A minute later, similar music peeled out from the American and French camps. The combatants were so close to each other the different melodies conflicted, resulting in a cacophony of random notes and drumbeats.

"A war of the fifes and drums," Joshua commented. "A more civil form of combat."

Dawn broke as a gray smudge, then a burst of orange and gold over the hovering stain of burnt powder. In the fresh light, a new approach trench was visible. It stretched forward almost in a straight line, running for about two hundred yards toward the British redoubts Number Nine and Number Ten.

"See those redoubts, little brother?" Joshua murmured. "They lie across our path. We won't be able to dig a second parallel unless we take them."

Daniel examined the two grim little forts, each like some vast porcupine with its protective abatis and fraise of stakes. Joshua was right. There would be real fighting here soon, not just this slow grinding of guns.

"It's time to call the roll," he said.

His sergeants were rousing the men, pushing them into line along the bottom of the trench. Daniel accompanied the orderly sergeant, telling off the names, making certain no one had deserted during the night, running off for home right under his nose.

All were present.

They settled down to eat their breakfasts—the bland contents of their haversacks, more jerked beef and bread. With the growing daylight, the rate of artillery fire again increased, beginning with the French Grand Battery. Soon, a new American battery of four eighteen-pounders joined the fray, then another. By mid-morning, the conflagration had grown.

"I'd venture to say the storm is even greater than yesterday!" Daniel shouted.

The sappers kept at their work digging the approaches, but today the British guns did not hinder them at all. Daniel assumed the opposing gunners were hiding within their walls, that after yesterday they had come to realize their small cannon could not compete with the massive siege guns.

The bombardment went on. Only once did it pause, when a white flag rose above the Hornwork. Daniel's entire battalion mounted the parapet to watch as an elderly civilian hobbled toward the American lines under a British escort. Once there, the redcoats turned and went back to York while the old gentleman remained with the allies. The white flag disappeared, and the guns resumed their deadly symphony.

Late that afternoon, orderlies arrived, bringing extra rations—fresh bread —for Daniel's men. Daniel asked one fellow if he knew who the old gentleman had been.

"That was old Secretary Nelson," the orderly explained. "Cornwallis let 'im go, it seems, in fear for his safety." He flashed a toothless grin. "Old Nelson says the redcoats are suffering somethin' bad under our bombardment! Cornwallis 'imself is livin' in a cave below the bluff, trapped like a rabbit in a hole!"

"If he's a rabbit," Joshua said, "let's send in some hounds. They might compel his surrender."

The orderly chuckled. "Aye! We're sendin' hounds in, all right—made of iron and filled with powder!"

The day stretched on and passed, the sun sinking —a lurid crimson ball. Just as on the previous night, the bombardment did not halt with darkness. The British works were visible in silhouette, enough to guide the mortars and howitzers as they lobbed their bursting projectiles. Fires again started in the town, and on the river, three of the anchored ships began to burn.

"One is a man-of-war," Joshua stated as he and Daniel enjoyed an unobstructed view of the burning vessels. "What will happen when the flames reach its powder magazine?"

The other two vessels were transports. Flames rushed up the masts and along the tarred rigging, the sails shriveling like paper. The crews abandoned ship, their longboats pulling for the Gloucester shore. They escaped just in time, for within minutes the loaded guns of the man-of-war began to go off one-by-one as the fire heated the cartridges. A moment later, as Joshua had predicted, the powder magazine exploded, sending up one vast pillar of boiling flame and splintered wooden fragments.

"The sight warms my heart!" he cried.

Daniel held up one hand to block out the glare. He could feel the heat even at this distance.

"It *is* a sight, gentlemen," said a voice from his left. Major Osborne was approaching along the trench, the light from the burning ships playing across his solemn features. "And bright enough to read by, I'd warrant."

Daniel said, "Good evening, sir."

"Your company is well? Not too fatigued, I hope?"

"Not in the least, sir."

"Good, then, good." Osborne nodded, then reached into his coat. He pulled out a rumpled and folded piece of paper. "I come on a peculiar errand. I have a letter here for you, Captain Brattle. It did not come by way of the post, but was passed to one of our pickets by a local boy. The sentry thought it suspicious, for evidently the boy is known to come and go as he pleases. It was passed to our headquarters, thence to me, though it is addressed to you. That is, your name is written on it. As Lieutenant Brattle."

Daniel took the letter and held it in the flickering light. The seal was an unmarked blob of wax, but there was his name, written in a fine, graceful hand that was somehow familiar.

"You say a boy passed it to a sentry?"

The major nodded. "A small Negro boy. He was certainly acting as a courier. I received the letter from a member of Colonel Gimat's staff—the people who deal with such things, with matters of intelligence. They thought nothing of it, but I deemed it prudent to also read it myself." He paused. "I bring it to you in person by way of apology, for I have judged it harmless."

Daniel could see now where an earlier seal had been removed.

"I understand, sir."

"You may read it, then."

Daniel turned the letter to catch as much light from the blazing ships as possible. He broke the repaired seal as Joshua and Major Osborne looked on.

"I do not know if you received my first letter," the message began.

> If not, know that my cousin returned and insisted that we abandon the plantation, as he feared the approach of the rebel army. I think now that we were hasty, that perhaps we should have remained there, since now we are besieged. It is difficult to be certain of anything, save that I wish for nothing more than this madness to end.
>
> I am at this moment in Gloucester Point, across the river from York Town. I wish for you to know that we are safe here, and that you are often in my thoughts. I hope that God keeps you safe as well, and that these cruel times will bring no further injury upon you or your brother."

"It is from Catherine," Daniel whispered. "She is across the river, on Gloucester Point."

"Catherine?" Joshua echoed. "She sent you a letter?"

"Yes." Daniel stared past the ships toward Gloucester. Perhaps a few lights burned there tonight, but he could not tell for certain in the glare from the river.

Joshua shook his head. "It is fortunate that she is not in York Town, as you feared, eh?"

"This is the woman who took you in?" Osborne questioned.

"Yes," Joshua explained. "That was a risk, sending a letter into enemy lines."

"She is trapped there," Daniel stated.

Joshua put his hand on his brother's arm.

"She must think well of you to make such an effort."

But Daniel felt no happiness, only a rising anger touched with despair. He had cherished Catherine's memory but had abandoned all notions of a reunion. Now, here was the tiniest shred of hope, so very small, just enough to tantalize, to suggest the fantasy might again be reality.

Yet she was still beyond his reach.

He looked at the dark humps of redoubts Number Nine and Number Ten, and the glare of the burning ships beyond. All at once, the forts seemed like mountains ringed with fire.

Chapter 35

The Loyalist

*T*he burning ships lit the parlour, their amber brilliance flickering and dancing through the southern windows. There was no other illumination in the room. None was needed.

Catherine sat across from John, hands folded in her lap. John slumped in his customary armchair.

"I have told you often that we have ample food supplies," he said, "and that was so, but they have long since become putrid. Putrid meat and wormholed biscuits. Lord Cornwallis was forced to issue an order compelling the Negro labourers to leave. They are an unfortunate strain on our supplies and, as noncombatants, not necessary."

"So, that is what happened to them," Catherine said, for she had not seen the boy for days, had waited on the shore for him, had fretted and worried at his absence. She had feared for his safety, and feared she would never learn whether he had delivered her letter.

"Yes. Many have already been driven out. Driven out, mind you! Lieutenant Cameron insists that some wandered into the country between our breastworks and the enemy's and were cut down by the crossfire. Slaughtered!" He wrung his hands. "I know that soldiers can sometimes be cruel, that they are not always recruited from the best calibre of citizen. Some are saying those poor people were driven out to their deaths. On purpose. Some even say that, since they are suffering worse from the smallpox than we, the Negroes were sent to infect the rebel camps."

Catherine refused to believe such terrible nonsense.

"Surely not, cousin!"

"The soldiers are frustrated, you see," John continued, as if trying to justify these speculations, should they prove true. "The infantry, that is. The infantry. Things do not sit well with us. You told me to be truthful with you, Catherine, and I will. The enemy's cannon are much more powerful than ours. When they first arrived we thought they had no siege guns at all, but they soon began landing them from the French ships. They possess mortar shells weighing upwards of one hundred pounds, and now they are knocking our works down as fast as—or faster than—we can repair them. The camps are in ruins, the men forced to live under the parapet. Even when off-duty that is where they stay."

"And we in Gloucester are not subject to this torture."

John's voice was heavy with sadness.

"We do not matter much, I think."

Catherine sighed. "That is precisely how I feel."

"I am certain the people in York wish they did not matter, either. The remaining citizens have also been forced to shelter in caves under the bluff. Close to one hundred people have perished from the bombardment. Not soldiers, mind you, my dear Catherine. Most are neutrals or professed patriots, rebels themselves." He shook his head, and his voice almost broke as he added, "Such is war, I suppose."

"War is cruel," she said, as she had said many times before. "Those who have the power to do so must work against it."

John's long hair had come loose from its ribbon, and it hung about his shoulders. He ran a hand back across his scalp.

"What is the use? The war is here, it is upon us. Yet less than half our men are fit for duty. The numbers of sick and wounded rise daily. And General Clinton has not appeared with our reinforcements."

"There must be something we can do," Catherine insisted.

John said nothing for a moment, then added, almost in a whimper, "I fear all is lost." He grasped his head with both hands and leaned forward.

Catherine felt a sick horror, although not for herself or their situation. It was for him, for dear cousin John. His optimism, which she had always suspected was partly a façade, seemed to have evaporated overnight. Now, he had the appearance of a man utterly defeated.

She rose and went to him, crouching to cradle his head on her shoulder. The act made her think of Daniel, how she had done the same for him; and she wondered, as she had wondered a thousand times in the last days, if he had received her message. Seeing the boy again to confirm the delivery had been her obsession, but now she would likely never know.

"All is not yet lost, John," she said, but her voice sounded pessimistic to her own ears. She realized that, now, she *did* feel lost, her last shred of purpose gone, taken from her.

She would have to move beyond this moment. She could not dwell on that which she could not change. She would find a new purpose. People were suffering in York Town. She was still healthy and strong. She could help ease that suffering.

"All is not yet lost," she repeated, and now there was strength behind her words. "The reinforcements will arrive, bringing ships to break this blockade. They may arrive at any moment. And we still have the strength of our hands until our food is gone, or we are killed or wounded. Until that time, we are not defeated. Listen!" She pulled his head up and fixed her gaze on his startled eyes. "I wish to go over to York Town. I am not sick. I do not require much food. I can help with the wounded, with those in need."

He pulled away and sat up.

"Nonsense, Catherine! You would leave this safe haven for that hell?"

"I would. I believe I must."

"But you may be killed! I cannot let you abandon this protected place and go there!"

She kept her voice soft.

"Dear cousin, you know me better than most. You know that I cannot sit idle while others suffer. The very thought seems criminal."

He stared at her.

"I do know you, Catherine. I know you have always been stubborn, have always been hasty, and have always given to others before you think of your own welfare. But that is not always the wisest course, and most certainly not in times such as these."

The light from the ships was dying, the dancing shadows deepening. She ignored his objection, her mind turning to the details of advancing her decision. Abigail could not come with her—John was correct that York was a place of mortal danger. She would not subject her sister to that, not after having forced her to come to Virginia.

No, Abigail must stay here, where she would be safe. Even Tarleton was no longer a threat, if he had ever truly been. The dragoon commander showed no interest in Abigail, and she no longer went in awe of him. She would be safe here in Gloucester with John.

But if Abigail knew Catherine was going, she would insist on accompanying her. She had developed her own stubbornness of late. Catherine would have to leave without her knowledge.

"I will need a boat," she said. "Some supplies—anything that might be spared. Clothing, my sewing things."

John lurched to his feet, then shuffled to the window. He looked much older than his age.

"You will never listen to me, will you? You will always do the most impulsive things. Your coming to Virginia in the first place was one such act. Now here is another!"

She joined him, took his elbow. She knew he would do nothing to stop her, that he would voice his concern but nothing more.

"It is not an impulse. I refuse to be useless, John."

He sighed, as if accepting he could not win this battle any more than he could defeat the rebels single-handed.

"I will order one of the Rangers to take you across. Or perhaps the sailors. But only when night is about to fall, as then the shelling is not as severe. Perhaps tomorrow evening. But you must return come daylight. You must promise me you will at least obey me in this."

She could have told him he had no right to insist on her obedience, but that would be to ignore his kindness.

"I promise to return," she said, but she would not say when. That would be contingent on what she found in York.

He did not catch the omission.

"Then I will aid you in this matter, God help me."

She gripped the sleeve of his coat.

"You must promise me something else as well. Look after Abigail, and do not tell her where I have gone until I have already departed. She will want to follow. I may choose to risk my life, but I will not risk hers again. Keep her safe. She has become...energetic."

He nodded. "I would do so even if you did not ask it."

"And I must go tonight." She did not want to spend another minute in this house. "She is sleeping. If I delay, I won't be able to keep my intentions from her, and every hour lost brings more misery."

John sighed, nodding. "I knew I could not keep you here another day once you had made up your mind."

<hr />

Catherine hunched in the bottom of a longboat, wrapped in her cloak and clutching a blanket bundle filled with things she had gathered from her room —a small sewing bundle of the sort known as a "housewife," scraps of linen and cotton, wool yarn. A midshipman and a detachment of seamen from the burned and sunken man-of-war, the *Charon*, sat poised to take her across. They had not left the shore since abandoning the vessel and were eager for action of some kind. They had agreed at once to transport her when John made the request.

The boat shoved off and moved into the wide, sluggish current. They were close to where river met sea, but the water was calm. John stood on the dock, right hand raised. Catherine watched his figure recede into the darkness, then turned to face the approaching shore. The burning ships were now nothing but embers smoldering on the waterline, but a few random shells still fell on York Town, flashing like lightning when they exploded.

The passage was swift, the men at the oars seeming to propel the boat with the force of their anger, their outrage, at having lost their ship. York Town loomed ahead, dark houses with broken windows like the eye sockets of skulls.

The boat landed on the beach, and the men dragged it onto the sand before helping her out. A fife-and-drum corps was assembled on the shore, playing, she presumed, to keep up the spirits of the people gathered there. She quickly surveyed her new surroundings and saw it was true what John had said. The entire town seemed to have moved below the bluff. Here were a few army tents and ramshackle lean-tos, some crude shelters fashioned from blankets and scraps of wood. Campfires burned in the mouths of the few cramped caves.

She turned to the young midshipman, a boy not much older than Abigail, perhaps younger.

"Thank you, and thank your men. You may return to Gloucester now. I will be staying here."

John had given the midshipman instructions to fetch her back in the morning, but the boy did not insist on obeying them. He glanced in distaste at the people on the beach.

"Very well, ma'am," he said, touching his cocked hat. "And may I wish you good luck?"

"You may."

She did not watch the boat pull away. She wanted to see the upper town but knew it would not be wise to go there in daylight. Now seemed safe enough. The few incoming shells were falling far away, perhaps targeting the fortifications alone.

She passed the fifes and drums—boys in tall bearskin hats, their coats bright, possibly white, in the gloom, their arms covered in lace chevrons. They played now a soft mournful tune with the fifes alone.

She moved along the street, although "street" seemed rather too grand a name for the strip of beach lined with warehouses and docks. The warehouses were now home to both redcoats and dispossessed citizens. Between two of the buildings, a wide lane or path led up toward Main Street, its surface uneven and eroded like a dry stream bed that had cut through the edge of the bluff. Catherine followed it. The sky before her blazed crimson and orange.

Something blocked her path, and she stooped to investigate. It was a man's body, lying across the lane. A dead redcoat. The corpse had no head.

She straightened quickly, staggering backward. She put a hand to her mouth, afraid she might be sick, but the nausea passed. She reminded herself she had known it would be like this.

Keeping a tight grasp on her bundle, she ran the rest of the way to Main Street. There, she paused again, breathing heavily and staring about. The street was covered in bodies and bits of debris, broken wagons and dead horses. The bodies lay within dark patches in the dust, many lacking arms, legs, or heads. She kept her eyes raised, pressing on, making her way south toward the enemy lines.

She heard a terrible screaming, and wondered what new horror lay in store for her. In front of a house, she came upon two men in the act of slaughtering horses, slitting their throats. The horses were nothing but skin and hair stretched over bones. The men wore black coats. One glanced at her, bloody knife in hand.

"Get under cover, woman!" he shouted. "What are you doing out in the open?"

A mortar bomb burst behind him. Catherine watched as a lurid cloud rose, its light revealing the shells of ruined houses and remains of blasted trees.

That was enough. She turned and ran back toward the beach. Scrambling down the lane, she made for the place where she had landed. She leapt over several large craters she had not noticed before. The bombs had fallen here, as well. It seemed nowhere was safe.

Resting against a warehouse wall, she struggled to catch her breath. It was more terrible than she had imagined, but she would never admit to having made a mistake. She would dig herself a shelter in the soft bank, or ask one of the soldiers to help her. She knew it was in her power to do so.

She surveyed the people, some still in fine clothes, others in rags. She would help them, somehow. She would find the field hospitals and ask the surgeons if she could be of assistance. If they would not have a woman getting in their way, she would find someone else who would not refuse her.

She *would* stay here, despite the danger. Whatever happened, she would stay. She would hide in safety no longer.

Chapter 36

The Redcoat

$\mathcal{D}$awn spread across the Hornwork, revealing the makeshift camp that had risen within its walls. Tom Martin had passed another uneasy night under the rampart, a bit of canvas propped over his head for shelter. Two hogshead barrels filled with sand, one on either side, served as barriers against flying shell fragments. Now that it was no longer safe in the camps, this was home. The forts were the only place where one could find a semblance of security.

He lay in his shelter, savouring a state of half-sleep, grateful that his company had not drawn picket again last night. For two evenings in a row they had stood sentry on the churned glacis outside the fortifications. It had been a miserable experience—cold, exposed, without even the warm companionship of a pipe or fire lest they reveal their positions to the enemy. Tom had ordered the lads to sit or lie down to decrease their visibility against the sky and the glow from shell bursts. The enemy was so close he had been able to hear their sentry changes during lulls in the firing. In contrast, the British pickets had not dared to make any noise at all.

He sighed and rubbed his eyes. He was reluctant to crawl out, to face another day of this monotony. A memory came flooding back to him, from his schooling days, of his warm bed in the parsonage. At times, he had found it difficult to leave that bed as well, especially on winter mornings when the ice had rimed the inside of the window frames. However, his lessons had been waiting.

I have even less choice in the matter now, he thought.

He steeled himself. There was no use in further daydreaming. Rising was like swimming in a cold pond—one had to leap in all at once.

He pushed himself to his feet, shoving past one of the heavy hogsheads, then stretched his legs and lower back. The bombardment had already begun to escalate, the pauses between each round growing shorter. The French Grand Battery beyond Yorktown Creek was particularly active, doing its best, Tom supposed, to awaken the Royal Welch Fusiliers in the star redoubt. The French had made several unsuccessful attempts to capture the fort, but the Welsh-men had not given up yet, nor, Tom suspected, would they. As a result of their brave defiance, everyone had started referring to their little stronghold as the "fusilier redoubt."

The filled water bucket sat against the wall. The water was fresh, a sign someone had braved the fire to venture to the well last night. Tom stooped to splash water over his face, gasping at the cold, then scrubbed his hands. He stared at his black and cracked nails, the dark skin of his palms stretched thin across the small bones. He wondered what his face looked like. He wondered if his poor mother would recognize him, and realized he had not written to her in some time.

"I doubt I shall have the opportunity today, either," he murmured. He sought Sergeant Gibb and, when he found him, said, "We'll take the roll right here."

There would be no battalion assembly this morning—the cannon fire had made it too dangerous.

He formed the company under the rampart. Once again, he was pleased to discover all able men were present and ready for duty. With this bit of military routine satisfied, he dismissed the company to breakfast, and they did their best to behave as if the growing artillery fire did not exist, that random death would not strike at any moment. They were still soldiers, Tom noted with pride, still men of discipline.

They sat in half-circles around their little bivouac fires, which were poor substitutes for the earthen fireplaces back in camp; the flames burned bright in the new dawn. Bubbling kettles hung from sticks or sat on piled rocks. Plain rice gruel, of course, which was all they had eaten for days. A few times, they had dined on the stringy meat of slaughtered horses, but only in small quantities.

Private Hassler was nibbling on a ship's biscuit. Between bites, he grimaced in distaste. Bone sat before him, staring expectantly. The bulldog looked healthy enough, having survived on rats and field mice.

"Don't beg, my fine fellow," Sergeant Gibb said to the dog. "It's unseemly."

Hassler passed the biscuit to the bulldog; Bone crunched the morsel in his strong jaws. Hassler then scooped the dog into his arms and rose to his feet. He looked at Tom, who saw something reflected in his eyes. A question, or perhaps a demand.

Then he knew. The other members of the company were also on their feet, their weary, sunken eyes fixed on the two sergeants. The youngest man, Sam Webb, stepped forward. Sam held his cap in his hands, like a schoolboy come before the headmaster. He glanced once at his comrades, then turned to Tom and said, "Sergeant, the boys have been thinking. We're running out of food, Sergeant. It won't be long before—"

"Oh, no, you bloody buggers!" Gibb suddenly screamed. "Don't you even think of it for one moment!"

He leapt upon Hassler, grabbing hold of Bone. Perhaps recalling the lash across his back, the private let the dog go. Gibb jumped back out of harm's reach, Bone struggling in his arms.

"But in a few days we'll have naught to eat!" Hassler cried, more astonished than angry.

"The boys are tired of horseflesh and rice and rotten biscuit," Private O'Malley insisted.

"Curse you for a lot of cannibals!" Gibb shouted. "You would never eat our dog!"

Bone continued to struggle while Gibb tried to calm him with soothing words. At last, the creature settled with his head on Gibb's shoulder. The sergeant stroked the mascot's smooth flank.

Tom faced the assembled company. It was evident they had discussed this matter in secret. He felt a hard knot forming in the pit of his stomach. For a fleeting second, he realized none of them would escape if a shell were to land amongst them now.

"You said it yourself, lads," he stated, struggling to control his anger, his disgust. "In a few days, we'll have nothing to eat. Then what will we do? Perhaps we'll consider the unspeakable act of making a stew of our company mascot. But that will be our last resort, the last resort of wretched men!" He paused, then added, "Is that what we have become? Is this cannon fire so bad it has shaken away your senses? Are we desperate, at the end of our tether, or are we still the light infantry?"

"Not so desperate," someone muttered, but the rest kept silent. There were a few nods, and Tom began to relax. They at least understood the logic in his argument, if not his attempt to salvage some of their pride.

"That's my word on it," he declared. That was enough.

Gibb was clasping the bulldog tight to his chest. Bone's long pink tongue lashed out at his ear, knocking his cap askew.

"That's it, my fine fellow," Gibb whispered. "I won't let 'em touch you. No better than the blasted rebels."

"There's still plenty of rice," Tom added. "We're the light infantry. The best there is."

The men did not disperse, just stood in awkward silence, some with eyes downcast. Tom hoped they were feeling at least a flicker of shame.

He did not hear the three hissing rebel shells until they landed a few yards behind the assembled company, rolling in through one of the gun embrasures. The gunners jumped for cover behind their hogshead blinds, but Tom froze, waiting for the shells to explode.

All three fuses went out, sputtering and dying. The shells sat motionless, useless.

"More fine Yankee work," he said in relief, but knew here was uncanny luck. He remembered his thoughts of a few minutes ago, of how one well-placed shell would kill them all.

A solid shot struck the outside wall of the fort. It seemed the Hornwork had just become a favored target. Tom's men began to scurry back to their hovels under the rampart. He joined them, barely dodging a ball that rushed through one of the embrasures in the left battery. A second ball followed it, striking the muzzle of a bronze eighteen-pounder. The gun rang like a cathedral bell, and the end of the muzzle spun away, shorn clean off.

More shells whistled and shrieked overhead. Tom ducked and scurried for his dugout as mortar bombs burst in the battery, obliterating the carriage of a twelve-pounder. A young gunner fell, screaming with a long wooden splinter in his leg. His comrades braved the fire to pull him behind the blinds.

"It's going to be a hot morning," Tom said to himself.

He squeezed between the hogsheads as earth showered over him. The wounded artilleryman's anguished wailing persisted, loud even over the roar of the bombs.

Chapter 37

The Earl

Lord Cornwallis strolled amongst the trenches and redoubts, ignoring danger and exhorting his men to remain brave. A few of them turned away in disgust, which saddened him, for they could not understand his strategy. They were angry at what they saw as his inaction.

The truth was that he saw little point in risking their lives if reinforcements were coming. They only had to be patient. And the majority of his soldiers seemed to grasp this truth, for they offered him hearty cheers. They knew he had their best interests at heart. He had always prided himself on sharing their hardships. Now, he braved the same storm of fire, and the waiting for Clinton to do as he had promised.

When he came to the Hornwork he found things in a sad state. The prominent fort made rather too obvious a target for the enemy siege guns. The left battery had been destroyed, the embrasures knocked in; two guns had their muzzles shorn, another was dismounted. Nine men had been killed and almost thirty wounded.

"There, now, it will be all right," he told an injured gunner, a pale young man with a dark-stained bandage bound tightly around one leg. "You have all been very brave to endure this fire. It won't be long now, I assure you!"

"My Lord," an aide said from behind him, "there is an officer here who wishes to speak to you."

"What officer is that?" the earl said, turning. "I am not finished making the rounds of the garrison."

He faced the newcomer, intending to tell the fellow to wait. The man wore a plain travel-worn uniform without adornment. A broad grin lit his rugged, handsome face.

"Major Cochrane!" Cornwallis cried. "I do declare, this is a surprise! What brings you back to us after all this time?"

"I am serving as a courier. arrived from New York by whaleboat just now, with twelve seamen and two swivel guns as my escort. I bring a letter from General Clinton."

"Ah!" This was altogether too important. The rounds could wait. "When did you leave New York?"

"The third of the month, my lord. The journey was uneventful, the French blockade no barrier for my tiny vessel."

"Well, I am pleased to see you, Major." Cornwallis was glad for the return of this sturdy Scotsman, a former Marine who had served since the beginning of the war, who had stood on Lexington Green when the first unfortunate shots had been fired. "But we can't speak here. Let us seek better shelter in Secretary Nelson's house." He smiled to himself, for he knew of the rumours, those that said he had abandoned his headquarters for a dingy cave. "It has taken something of a beating, but its brick walls, I find, are as strong as any redoubt."

They made for the house, and as they walked, Cochrane said, "I am happy to have rejoined my comrades at last. I was too long away." He reached into the flat leather pouch that hung at his side. "I should give you this, my lord—General Clinton's dispatch. I am dearly sorry not to bring brighter news."

Cornwallis halted and gave his companion a level stare. He had expected good news, not more excuses, not another broken promise.

"Let me see it."

He took the letter and broke the seal. Behind him, shells crashed and exploded along the walls he had built here.

"Your Lordship may be assured that I am doing everything in my power to relieve you by a direct move," was Clinton's reassuring first line. However, the note went on to say, "I have reason to hope from the assurances given me this day by Admiral Graves that we may pass the bar by the twelfth of October, if the winds permit, and no unforeseen accident happens."

Today was the twelfth. Cornwallis read on. The letter recommended he should hold out until as long as the middle of November, at which point Clinton would attempt a diversionary attack on Philadelphia.

The paper crumpled in the earl's clenched fingers. He could not hold until the middle of November!

I must not despair, he told himself, breathing deeply to calm his temper. In his mind, he began composing the reply he would send at once. He would explain the situation, repeat what he had already written in his letter of the third. He would insist that nothing but a direct move to the York River, including a successful naval action, could save his garrison. He would explain the ferocity of the enemy bombardment, that he had lost some seventy men, that his works had been badly damaged. The ground here offered so few advantages he could not hope to resist a determined attack for long.

He cleared his throat, smoothing the crumpled letter.

"It is regrettable that the commander-in-chief does not understand our state of affairs."

Cochrane removed his hat and scratched his head.

"There is something else, my lord. Upon my arrival, I inquired as to your whereabouts. I came upon a gathering of your officers in the dugout shelter below your headquarters. They requested I bring you a message that they wish to have a meeting with you."

"They wish to have a meeting with me?" the earl repeated. His temper threatened to boil over again. Subordinates did not call their commanders to meetings!

"They are waiting for you now, sir."

Cornwallis sighed in exasperation, but the dugout was only yards from where they stood now.

"Come along, then, Major. Let us see what they want."

The shelter had been constructed beneath Secretary Nelson's house—a hollow space lined with planks and reinforced with wooden beams—and was perhaps the source of the rumours that he was living in a rabbit hole. Cornwallis stooped to enter its low portal, blinking in the dim candlelight. The assembled officers stood at his approach, and he took in their faces. Tarleton had come from Gloucester; O'Hara, Captain Rochfort, Captain Symonds and a few others of lesser stature were also present. They faced him, their eyes reflecting the candles, each one prepared to offer him advice. Advice he had never sought.

Whatever their effrontery, the earl was ready to listen to them with at least an outward appearance of patience. He had always considered himself a fair commander, willing to entertain suggestions. But he would take control of this gathering at once.

"Gentlemen," he began, "our meeting here is opportune. You have met Major Cochrane. He has brought dispatches from New York which I must present to you."

He read Clinton's letter out loud, thus setting an agenda. When he was done, he said, "I mean to reply at once. I feel the commander-in-chief does not comprehend what we face. I will urge his haste, all the while trusting that he has already departed, as he states."

"That is what we wish to discuss, my lord," O'Hara announced, his ruddy face grave.

"We should evacuate these miserable works here in York." Tarleton took the lead, his tone one of open disdain. "Every hour here is an hour of watching and of danger to both soldiers and officers. Every gun is dismounted the moment it shows."

"Strange, for so brave a man as yourself, Colonel Tarleton," Cornwallis said, "to suggest abandoning our post."

"There is honour in abandoning fortifications which are not tenable, sir," Tarleton insisted. "Abandon them now, but adopt a design which at this juncture has every probability of success."

"We have discussed the matter, my lord," O'Hara agreed. "What you present to us confirms our feelings. Every line of the letter Major Cochrane has delivered points to the possibility of General Clinton's delay. We cannot tarry here, waiting for him."

Cornwallis folded his hands behind his back. Outside, the air was filled with the rumble of guns, the shriek of shells. Now and then, earth fell in dusty rivulets from the dugout ceiling.

"And what is this new design you wish me to adopt?"

Tarleton took a step forward, his ruined right hand balled in a fist.

"Under cover of darkness, retreat from this side of the river to Gloucester. Shift the entire garrison, save perhaps a detachment to mind the sick and wounded. Such a transfer would swell our numbers in Gloucester enough to allow us to break out. The Duc de Lauzun's forces are not so large. I assure you, my lord, we would gain a head start of a hundred miles, by rapid marches, before Mister Washington would be able to react."

Cornwallis studied his officers. By their expressions, he knew they agreed on the matter. Even O'Hara, who had done everything to encourage him, wished to give up on York.

He pretended to weigh the plan, but he had already made his choice. Tarleton was forever proposing these schemes, had even wanted to assault Williamsburg when Washington's army was encamped there. Tactically sound plans, but impractical. Cornwallis could even see the sense in what he proposed today, could even agree with it; they should escape now, while they could.

Yet every direction from the commanding general so far had told him to maintain his position, and he had long since given up on waging his own campaign. He had never liked this place, never agreed with the rationale of coming here; but the promised reinforcements might have left New York this very day. It was too soon to justify running.

"General Clinton has mentioned several factors which may lead to his delay," he said, "but his instructions are clear. He means to reinforce us when he is able. Until that plan is abandoned, and until I receive explicit instructions as to its abandonment, I must remain here. In York Town."

"My Lord—" Tarleton began.

Cornwallis raised his hand.

"I will keep your design in mind, gentlemen. It is sound. But the time is not now."

They regarded him in silence, but he had said all he would. He had made his decision. He would wait for Clinton as long as he thought prudent.

Chapter 38

The Loyalist

*C*atherine had finally found what passed for a field hospital in a dingy to-bacco warehouse near the Town Wharf. The curve of the bluff sheltered the building from the French battery in the north, but that was its only favourable quality. There was no ventilation save the main doors, two small windows, and a few holes in its rotting roof. The wounded exceeded a hundred in number, but only one surgeon and a small group of surgeon's mates were available to tend them. The patients lay in their own blood and filth, some on straw pallets, most on the bare floor.

Catherine had expected to be welcomed, for the need was great. But when she offered her services, the surgeon stared at her as if she were mad.

"I'll have no woman in my way," he declared. He was a shabby man with strands of lank brown hair dangling from beneath a worn periwig. His flesh was pallid, his eyes rimmed with red. Worse, he stank of rum.

"But you have so little help with all these poor men," she pleaded. "And more wounded arrive daily. You cannot possibly manage."

"Damn you, woman!" the surgeon whined. He tugged a filthy handkerchief from his sleeve and wiped a dripping nose. "I said go away. Go and pester one of the other surgeons. I am overworked enough without having to deal with you as well."

He moved off and began examining a row of patients, reaching into their waistcoats to feel for a heartbeat, checking to see who still lived. Catherine retreated, but she did not leave the hospital. She hovered inside one of the great double doors that opened onto a small jetty. She would not give up so easily. She would make the fellow change his mind.

It was one of the surgeon's mates who approached her, a young private with crooked, protruding teeth.

"I could use your help, ma'am," he said softly. "I believe there are many lads here who could. Never mind the sawbones. He spends most of his time in the bottle. He won't even notice you."

"Thank you," she said, relieved. "Tell me what I can do."

He led her to the row nearest the double doors.

"I put these lads here, near the door. Some of 'em have a chance, if they get the care they need."

She nodded, gazing down at the clutch of pathetic figures. Some slept, while others stared back with pleading eyes. One was babbling to himself in unintelligible whispers.

"Thank you," she again told the mate, then turned back to the patients. "Gentlemen, I am here to help." She dropped her blanket bundle against the wall, then stooped over the nearest wounded soldier. The surgeon's mate shuffled away behind her. "What is your name, Private?"

"John, Miss," the wounded man replied, shocking her with the voice of child. Upon closer inspection, he appeared to be no more than thirteen or fourteen years old.

"I have a cousin John," she told him, kneeling. "He is in the army, too. In the cavalry."

The boy shrank back against the wall. Catherine realized his left arm was gone, leaving only a bloody bandaged stump. It had been hidden in the folds of his coat, which lay in a heap at his side.

"I'm a drummer, Miss," he said, his face contorting. Silent sobs shook his small frame. "Now, how will I ever play again? What will I do?"

She fixed her eyes on the wall, blinking back sudden tears.

"It will be all right," she said, knowing the words sounding empty, foolish.

She gazed out over the expanse of the warehouse, at the rows of wounded and sick, the surgeon's mates moving amongst them. The stench in the place was almost overwhelming—the air close, the floor a filthy disgrace, here and there the boards stained with blood. There was so much to do here, too much for a dozen attendants; and she was only one. She turned back to the boy, who still wept silently.

This is what war does, she thought. *It destroys.*

"There, now, it will be all right," she repeated, and as she spoke she took the boy's right hand. His fingers locked on hers, squeezing until she felt pain, but she did not let go. Instead, she stroked his forehead. He was just a child, probably the son of a veteran soldier, as were many drummer boys. She wondered where that father was now.

Within a few minutes his weeping stopped, and he said, "Bless you, Miss. Please don't leave me."

"I will be here every day from now on," she said. "Here with you by the doors. But right now, I have to see to your friends as well." She managed to free her hand, and when he protested she added, softly, "Hush! I will be right here. You are a brave young soldier. Never fear."

He nodded. "All right. All right."

She moved to the next in line, then the next, until she had examined every man in the row. To her dismay, three were dead. Two others had been left in the hospital by their comrades. The surgeon's mate had looked them over, they claimed, but the surgeon had never seen to them at all.

Catherine offered what she hoped were reassuring remarks. Only the poor fellow who muttered to himself did not respond. He did not seem to notice her presence.

She sat back against the wall, already exhausted, at a loss for what to do next. The first order of business, she supposed, was to have the three bodies removed. Then she could help tend the neglected men—clean their wounds, replace their crude bandages, bring fresh water from the creek, and simply talk to them. Perhaps that last was the best thing she could do. She could provide sympathy and companionship.

She stood. It was time to begin her work.

She was outside carrying water when Cousin John found her. He had landed at the Town Wharf with a group of Legion officers, and had just set foot on Water Street. She had been about to enter the hospital by a side door when he called her name.

"Cousin John!"

"I had not expected to find you so quickly!" he cried, rushing to her and taking one of the buckets. His brows knit. "I had believed it was your intention to return come morning!"

She could not take his attempt at lecturing her seriously. It was not in his nature to be demanding.

"I had intended to send word, but I have not found the opportunity. There is too much to do here. I apologize for my lack of consideration."

He winced as a mortar bomb exploded on the edge of the bluff, spraying leaves and bits of blasted tree limbs.

"The danger here is too great!"

"The danger is greater for those poor men lying neglected in the hospital," she insisted. "For me to leave them now, or even tomorrow, would be a tremendous sin. John, I have to stay as long as I am able. If I show you the hospital you will understand."

He gazed past her shoulder at the warehouse, and she saw something in his face fall.

"Yes, conditions are very poor," he at last admitted. "I have no need to see it with my own eyes."

"The hospital is sheltered by the bluff. It has escaped the bombardment. You need not fear for me."

"Though you do not wish for Abigail to join you."

She thought of the wounded, how they had already responded to her presence.

"I have since found reason to doubt that decision. She would be useful here, if she were to come of her own choice."

"She does wish to come, now that she knows what you have done, but I have refused her." He held up his hands at her protest. "You may think me heavy-handed, but this much I insist on. If you are to stay here, she must stay with me!"

He was trembling, sweat beading on his forehead; and she realized his agitation was nothing less than mortal fear of losing something else to the war. His two living cousins were all he had left of his former existence.

"You are right about Abigail," she agreed, kindly, and with remorse. Her selfless actions here were, in a sense, just her selfish need to feel useful. "Forgive me, John. I do not mean to cause you undue worry. You really should come to the hospital and see why I must remain here."

He hefted the water bucket. "Well, I will help you with this chore, but then I will return to Gloucester as soon as I can procure another boat. My only business this side of the river was to locate you, and I have succeeded in that."

She took his arm.

"Thank you for understanding. You have done a great deal more for me than you know simply by caring for us. I don't mean to be cruel."

He sighed, and his voice was very soft as he said, "Cruelty is a trait that I do not associate with your name, dear cousin. You are the very definition of the opposite."

Chapter 39

The Continental

"*T*onight we go on duty in the trenches," Daniel said, standing before his assembled company. They were dirty, their caped hunting shirts a uniform gray save where the Virginia soil had stained them red. They listened with mild boredom, slouching, leaning on their muskets, their little caps worn at a variety of angles, seeming to want only to return to their tents and some well-earned rest.

But Daniel was not finished.

"However, this night will be unlike any other," he continued, "for tonight, there will be an assault."

He paused, almost relishing the sudden change. At the word *assault*, every eye had brightened, every stooped shoulder had straightened. They still retained their fighting spirit. They had never lost it.

"I cannot tell you the nature of the attack, but I have volunteered our company. We are the best-trained men in the battalion. I expect every man will do his duty."

"We shall, sir!" cried Sergeant Williams, and the rest roared their agreement, tearing off their caps and breaking into three cheers. Daniel let the sound wash over him, wishing he could tell them more; but the camps were full of civilians who had flocked to the army, seeking a market for their goods, and there was no way to tell friend from foe. Tongues would wag, and information would doubtless make its way to the enemy.

Major Osborne had explained the situation to Daniel the previous evening, although Daniel had already understood it well enough. The sappers could not complete the second parallel, for Redoubts Number Nine and Number Ten stood directly in line with its right flank, blocking passage to the bluff and river. The redoubts needed to be taken, and there was no time to slowly grind them down with cannon. It was already the fourteenth of October, and in two weeks, the French naval squadron would depart for the West Indies. The redoubts had to be taken now.

The last cheer slowly faded. Daniel took in every excited face. They were a motley assortment. Here were aged farmers, hunters, fishermen, eager boys, immigrants who had come to America seeking a better life, free blacks and slaves hoping to win their freedom. They were light troops, they were his, and tonight he would take them into the fire again.

The attack would be carried out by two detachments, one French and one American. The French detachment would be composed of the elite flank companies of the Soissonois regiment, the best troops the French possessed. The other detachment, as Osborne had explained it, would come from the elite of the Continental Army. The Light Division. These boys.

And so the long-contemplated battle is to begin, the action I have so dreaded since Green Spring Farm. But there is to be no turning back. We will stand or fall.

"Sergeant Williams," he said, "you may dismiss the company."

Williams fell out of his position on the right of the rear rank, behind Joshua.

"Sir!"

"And, Sergeant, make sure every man's weapon is spotless and in proper working order. I will inspect them before we go in, as usual."

"Of course, Cap'n Brattle."

That was it, then. Now there was just the waiting.

<hr/>

In the golden light and long shadows just before sunset, the troops filed into the first parallel. The French wing was on the left, the American on the right. Daniel's company crammed the trench close to the grand battery where Washington had fired the first shot of the bombardment. An approach trench led away from here, making a beeline to the objective—Redoubt Number Ten.

"They're taking quite a pounding," Daniel remarked, for the siege guns had battered the redoubts all day to the exclusion of all other targets. Shells continued to burst all along the enemy parapet.

"It will soften them up," Joshua said. "Though I suspect it has also let them know we're coming. They will be prepared."

"Yes," Daniel agreed, and a burst of raw nerves flared up from his guts. He struggled for calm, as always, taking deep breaths, reminding himself the

British were worn down from the blockade and the bombardment. There would be no trap, no reinforcements waiting in hiding. The attackers held the advantage of numbers.

The French, who would take the larger Redoubt Number Nine, had almost a thousand men at their disposal, although they planned to use only four hundred if all went well. The American wing also involved some four hundred infantry and sappers, the troops detached from Gimat's and Hamilton's light battalions, with Hamilton in overall command. Henry Laurens, Washington's former envoy to France, would add two more companies. In contrast, the British had only seventy men to defend the redoubt.

Daniel gripped the wire hilt of his sheathed sword, the cold metal biting into his skin. Soon, he would put the weapon to use; his company would be in the first assault wave, behind the sappers. Soon, he would find himself in the midst of the screams, shouts, pain, terror and strange elation of battle. He had thought he could take no more, but here he was all the same.

An image of his father came to him, unbidden. He saw him sitting in his study, reading by candlelight. Then, he thought of his brother Benjamin— poor Benjamin, hiding in New York; and that in turn reminded him of Catherine, somewhere in Gloucester. All of them safe, away from the storm. Or perhaps they only seemed safe.

He remembered the words of General Washington, delivered less than an hour ago to the assembled Continentals before they had entered the trenches.

"I urge you to be firm and brave," the General had said. "The success of the attack on both redoubts depends on you. The French cannot hold the center if their flank is open."

Victory depended on their actions here tonight.

He yawned, and an involuntary shudder shook his body. Fatigue suddenly crushed down on him, his eyes drooping shut of their own will, and he shook himself awake. He had not slept well last night, knowing what the day would bring, but he could not afford to doze off on the verge of battle.

He started to pace, struggling to keep himself alert. Darkness was gathering, and the blazing artillery lit the expectant faces on either side of him. Each burst also outlined the stout figure of Colonel Hamilton where he stood on the firing step, one leg forward, a hand on his hip.

"There's a proud fellow," Joshua commented. "Though I daresay he'll see us through right enough."

"He will," Daniel agreed, ceasing his pacing.

He saw the flash of Joshua's teeth.

"So, there, you believe again, I see. Just a little bit, maybe? Or is it that now you have something to fight for besides your country?"

Daniel hesitated before replying.

"If you mean Catherine, then she *is* my country. Isn't that what we're fighting for? To settle in peace and prosperity, to build our homes and families without interference?" He shrugged. "That's what I tell myself, at any rate. At least since receiving Catherine's letter. It's Lord Cornwallis who stands between us."

"And some seventy of his men."

The stars gathered above them in a clear sky, although a smudge of cloud was thickening over the river. Daniel welcomed the prospect of rain. It would only aid them, would provide cover. It did not matter if it ruined their powder, for it was too dark for effective musketry. This was a night for cold steel, for swords and bayonets. Many of the officers had already prepared themselves, having fixed bayonets to poles. Joshua had brought a tall pike stave. Daniel would trust in his sword.

He drew it from its scabbard, hefted it in his right hand, testing its exquisite balance.

It's time to prepare for action.

Sloping the sword on his shoulder, he called out, "Sergeant Williams?"

The sergeant scrambled toward him.

"Lot more men here than I expected, Cap'n. There going to be a general assault? Are we going to storm York Town itself?"

Daniel shook his head, smiling at the sergeant's enthusiasm.

"Assemble the other corporals and sergeants, and I'll explain the details of the operation."

Williams turned to a nearby corporal and said, "Fetch the boys."

A moment later, Daniel was addressing seven men, his surviving noncommissioned officers.

"We are not to assault all of their works at once," he explained. "There will be no general assault." He then discussed the need for the attack on the redoubts, which most of the men already understood. "The French and American attacks will be simultaneous. The signal is six mortar shells fired from the French grand battery. At that, our sappers will go forward and cut a path through the enemy abatis. After them will proceed our forlorn hope—twenty men. They have already been chosen. The rest of us will follow."

"And follow close, won't we, Cap'n?" Williams asked, his eyes shining.

"As close as I deem practical, Sergeant. Colonel Gimat's and Colonel Hamilton's columns will carry out the frontal assault. Colonel Laurens and his two companies will circle around in the darkness and take the redoubt from the rear. There is a gate there, and a covered way leading back to the main British line. Our boys can get in that way." Then he added, hoping it did not sound forced, "There'll be no escape for the enemy tonight!"

The men grunted, unable to cheer for fear of giving away their position. They exchanged glances and nods.

"We will fix bayonets," Daniel said. "Muskets will remain empty. Any man who has loaded his musket already, have him draw the charge at once. We are not to risk a premature or accidental firing that will alert the redcoats."

"I'll relay the orders now, sir," Williams said.

As the sergeant moved off, Daniel gazed at the sky and said to Joshua, "It's as dark as it will get. We'll be advancing soon. It can't be long now."

"Rush on, boys," Joshua said, quoting the watchword for the night. The word was, in fact, "Rochambeau," but the other pronunciation was a clever aid to nervous men.

A metallic rattling filled the trench as the assault companies fixed bayonets in unison. Despite the thunder of the cannon, the men still tried to stifle the noise, the sergeants whispering their commands. Daniel stared at Colonel Hamilton, waiting for his sign to move forward, for the companies to take their ready positions.

Almost as if on cue, Hamilton raised his arm. The advance party—the sappers and forlorn hope—began to file into the approach trench. A moment later, Daniel followed, leading Joshua and the company.

It was like moving through a tunnel, the walls of the trench towering over him. He could not see the redoubt ahead, only the back of the man in front of him, a private in a ragged hunting shirt, his black leather cartridge box hanging behind his right hip. Then the artillery flashed, several shells rushing overhead. Daniel started, thinking these were the signal shells already, but he realized it was too early.

The floor of the trench began to slope upward, the walls shrinking; and then Daniel emerged onto open ground. He turned and faced the files behind him, pointing toward the river with his sword. His company wheeled to the right. He followed them and, when he was certain they had reached their assigned ground, called for them to halt, keeping his voice low. It took some time for the sergeants to relay the command, but when everyone had shuffled to a stop, Daniel ordered them to turn into line, then to lie down. The men faced front, faced the enemy, before dropping onto the grass and into the dirty craters made by shells falling short.

"We will wait here for the signal," Daniel whispered, crouching as he moved along in front of the line. He passed several dark spheres—spent shot littering the ground. "Be brave, boys. Stay down. We wait here until the signal. The bloodybacks have good reason to fear us tonight."

When he was certain every private had heard him, he located the center of the line and lay on his side, propped on his right elbow. Joshua crouched a few yards away on his left. Beyond Joshua was the flank of the next company in line.

Daniel stifled another yawn. A few yards in front of him loomed the shadowy figures of Colonel Hamilton, Colonel Gimat, the sappers, and the forlorn hope. By now, the French had assembled somewhere even farther away, opposite Redoubt Number Nine. He could not see them, which was a comfort. That meant the British could not see them, either.

Time seemed to stand still. The artillery continuing to rage, the shells whining and bursting along the edges of the redoubts. Daniel fought his growing fatigue, but his eyes grew heavier. He closed them, planning to rest, just for a moment.

They sprang open when the artillery barrage suddenly ceased. The last shot echoed away, followed by a heavy, eerie silence without even the chirp of a single cricket. The night had grown darker, the stars now obscured by thickening mist off the water. The redoubt was a black hump in front, not more than fifty or sixty yards away; he had not realized how close they had come. He could even hear the voices of the enemy, caught a snatch of conversation within, although he could not make out the words.

Light flashed far to his left and front—once, then twice, then a third time—pursued closely by a series of loud reports. The signal!

The first three shells were already falling, shrieking, when the last three arced toward the sky. The first burst on target, illuminating the ground and the lines of men, revealing their faces—men with wide, staring eyes, mouths set in determination, knuckles white where they gripped their weapons.

Daniel was on his feet, waving his arms, shouting, "Up! Up!" Others took up the call, the word running along the line. This was it! The last three shells burst, and in their flare, Daniel saw Hamilton, Gimat, and the sappers already charging forward.

It was an effort to wait here, wait for them to clear the way, his legs tight like coiled springs. He watched as the sappers attacked the abatis of tree branches, pulling it apart. The forlorn hope crowded behind them, not pausing for the sappers to finish their task, their uncontrolled eagerness carrying them forward. They pushed through the still-intact abatis like men picking their way through heavy brush; then they were moving toward the ditch in silence. Daniel was not surprised when the sappers ran after them, although they had orders not to charge the fort.

A voice cried out from the darkened redoubt, "Who's there?" The attackers said nothing, and the voice cried out again, "What's the password?"

Daniel could wait no longer.

"Forward!" he hissed, and as he did, there came the deafening roar of a musket volley. A line of smoke and flame erupted along the redoubt wall. The British had opened fire.

The attackers cheered, unable to hold back their excitement any longer. Daniel started to run, advancing with his sword over his head, his breath loud in his ears. His fatigue had been banished by a desperate energy. Tips of bayonets glinted as his company surged forward on either side of him, and now he was at the abatis.

A second volley crashed in front of him, and men fell, grunting. Too many seemed to drop, at least a dozen. The volley could never have been so accurate in the dark. For a second, he feared the attack would be repulsed, that the redoubt was home to a larger garrison than they had thought. They had been tricked again!

Then, he was falling himself, dropping into an enormous shell crater. Men scrambled out the other side; they were not wounded, had not been shot. The ground was simply uneven.

He tripped over some loose stones, regained his balance and crawled up the far slope and into the abatis. He had lost sight of Joshua. Debris lay everywhere—bits of wood, even parts of uniforms. He stepped around a fallen Continental who lay on his back, making little yelping noises between breaths.

Now he was at the ditch, the soft earth dropping under him again. There were shouts and cries ahead. The sappers and forlorn hope had climbed the wall, were at the fraise, stabbing downward with their bayonets. Colonel Hamilton urged them on, but his small stature made it difficult for him to climb the parapet. Two men gave him a push from behind, and he was finally able to scramble to the top.

"Rush on, boys!" Hamilton shouted. "Rush on! The fort is ours!"

Muskets cracked, spitting fire in all directions. Daniel let loose a long, wordless war cry. His men were with him, crawling up out of the ditch. He swallowed, his mouth full of dust, his chest burning as he climbed using feet and hands, his sword blade ringing faintly as it slapped the wall. His pulse was loud in his ears, his fear strong but not acknowledged.

There were Americans already in the redoubt, struggling with its defenders. Daniel reached the top of the rampart. In the brief illumination of a musket shot, he saw Joshua, Sergeant Williams and others. Then, he was facing the enemy.

A bayonet lunged for him, and he twisted to one side. The bayonet slid past, and he made a darting thrust with his sword. He did not feel the blade bite, but the redcoat stumbled backward, disappearing as he toppled from the firing step. Another redcoat raised his musket and fired, blowing back a man on Daniel's right. Daniel brought up his sword to strike the fellow; but his company sprang forward on both sides, and the redcoat fell with a bayonet through his ribs.

The other defenders were dropping back, and Daniel at last mounted the parapet, slid down to the firing step, and leapt into the fort. He found himself facing a soldier in a wide-brimmed hat and short red jacket. Daniel swung his slim, straight sword, letting his momentum carry him. The redcoat parried the blow with his musket, and the blade slid along the stock, shaving a strip from the wood.

Daniel readied another blow but never got a chance to deliver it. Two more attackers charged at his opponent silently, stabbing with bayonets. The redcoat screamed in pain and outrage as one triangular blade pierced his side; then, he fell, choking, as the second blade found his throat.

Daniel glanced left and right, saw nothing but a confused melee. A British uniform caught his eye, and he stabbed at its wearer's legs, felt the blade bite flesh. The man cried out and fell, and Daniel was upon him. It was an officer in a frock coat and gold gorget. The officer gripped his leg, face contorted in pain.

"Surrender!" Daniel shouted.

The officer shook his head, then managed to say, "The fort is already yours!"

It was true. Everywhere lay the bodies of men in red—ragged and bloody men, some of them groaning, some of them still.

The fort was full of Americans, gaping about them, looking for someone else to fight. It was over.

⁂

Daniel's company remained to garrison the captured redoubt through the night, prepared to resist a counterattack. Other members of the attacking forces herded prisoners to the rear, while still others stacked their muskets and took up duty as sappers. News had traveled quickly that the French assault had also been successful, and it was an opportune time to finish the second parallel. A fatigue party brought picks and shovels and set to work at once. Daniel's company provided cover, lining the firing step and watching the main British wall.

The enemy did not appear, but after about an hour, the clouds opened and, at last, the threatened rain spilled down. The churned soil turned to mud, but work did not stop. The parallel had to be finished, and all other tasks were secondary. Not even the wounded had received attention, with the exception of the officers. Daniel had heard Colonel Gimat had been shot in the foot and taken to the rear, but soldiers of both sides still lay in blood and mud, groaning and calling for help, the rain pelting their pale, upturned faces.

One wounded redcoat sprawled at the base of the firing step, weeping and calling for his mother. Daniel realized he was only a boy, a lad far from his home. The pathetic cries were too much for him to bear, and he shouted, "Somebody see to him, for God's sake!"

A young private scrambled down from the firing step and moved to the wounded boy's side. He spoke to him in a low voice, offering his canteen. Daniel could see the boy had a great rent in his stomach. He would not last long, and Daniel turned away to stare into the rain toward York.

The stench of blood, mud, and sulfur, the rain and the pitiful moaning of all those who lay helpless all served to dampen any triumph he might have felt. Here was victory, a complete and savage victory, but he knew only fatigue and a vague nausea.

"I surely hope this will soon be over," he said to Joshua.

"They're bringing up guns," was Joshua's response. He pointed to the rear. Troops of the Continental Artillery were manhandling two howitzers forward through the muck, tugging on drag ropes. The cannon would be in a position to bombard the British wall by morning.

Under the direction of Colonel Hamilton, the digging went on through the last short hours of the night. Daniel somehow stayed awake, and with dawn, he was greeted by the sight of the completed second parallel. The sappers had also converted the captured redoubt, filling in the gate in its rear and cutting a new one into what had been its front wall. The howitzers sat grinning in newly cut embrasures.

With the fortifications finished, the work parties at last began dragging the wounded to the rear. The cries of pain began to fade. The rain stopped, and the sky cleared within minutes, the clouds drifting west like ragged fire balloons. The air smelled clean, the stench of war diminished by the freshness of an autumn morning.

Daniel surveyed the redoubt in the full light of day. A few bodies still lay between the mud puddles, bodies with red coats and jackets, twisted hands like wax. The British had also left several hogsheads filled with sand; he assumed they had used these for cover against mortar shells. Metal shell fragments littered the ground, evidence of the terrible pounding the fort had taken.

"Our attack was carried out to perfection," Joshua stated. "We did it, little brother. We did it."

Guns roared behind them from a British battery, and almost at the same instant, a solid shot struck the parapet, sending up gouts of earth. Mud splattered Daniel's cap, face and collar. He crouched behind the parapet, heart thudding in his chest.

"The enemy is voicing his displeasure!" he cried.

He kept under cover, not wishing to give the British an obvious target. Regular incoming fire began to rain down on the captured fort, yet it did not discourage a fatigue party from finally removing the bodies.

Daniel wondered what would happen next. The second parallel was complete. Would the Allies have to take all of York Town by storm?

Or perhaps I have been wrong, he thought. *Perhaps our enemy is on the verge of collapse, and one more push will send them over the brink.*

"Give up," he whispered. "It's time for you to give up."

Dimly, through the blowing powder smoke, he could see Gloucester Point.

Chapter 40

The Earl

*L*ord Cornwallis had shifted his headquarters, finally abandoning the shot-riddled house of Secretary Thomas Nelson for that of his nephew Governor Thomas Nelson Jr., the obese Virginia militia commander. The house was in the center of town, and so less exposed. An occasional shot still struck its red brick walls, and the garden had been reduced to a ruin of craters; but the structure remained sound. Cornwallis was not worried about his personal safety, however. The safety of his army was his primary concern.

He sat in the study at the governor's desk, in conference with his officers. Planks covered the windows as a precaution against flying glass. It was nearing midnight, but only a single candle burned.

O'Hara sat in a darkened corner, leaning forward in his chair. Symonds occupied another seat, while Captain Rochfort stood near the door. Tarleton was still at Gloucester and would not be coming.

The earl faced his senior naval officer.

"Captain Symonds, I trust my message has been delivered?"

Symonds nodded. "I sent it in a whaleboat with a suitably daring crew, sir. We know they had little trouble giving the French the slip. The letter is on its way."

"Well done. I am happy I can rely on the skills of those who remain with us. Swift communications are vital at this juncture."

He spoke with as much enthusiasm as he could muster; but the letter, written in cipher lest it fall into enemy hands, was one he had never imagined being required to write.

"The enemy carried two advanced redoubts by storm," one section began. "During the night they included them in the second parallel, which they are at present busy perfecting. My situation now becomes very critical; we dare not show a gun to their old batteries for long, and I expect that their new ones will open tomorrow morning. The safety of the place is therefore so precarious that I cannot recommend that the fleet and army should run great risk in endeavouring to save us."

The plan he had endorsed for so long was at an end. If Clinton received the message, the long-awaited reinforcements would not be coming. The earl had decided he would have to save himself with the resources at his disposal, with the people he knew he could trust.

He surveyed the faces of his companions. They all showed signs of exhaustion, their eyes dark and swollen, their foreheads creased from the strain; but they were still with him, had not broken faith. These were the same men he had been meeting with for months, if not years, the same players who had accompanied him throughout this long, absurd drama. Nothing had changed in this room. It was as if time had not passed here, although it marched swiftly in the world outside, racing toward some inexorable conclusion.

The earl pressed his thumbs together.

This is truly a dark time, he thought, *a dark time, indeed.*

He would never allow these men, these faithful, to know the extent of his shock when he had learned of the captured redoubts. He had expected the little forts to hold for at least a few days, for their garrisons to fight as hard as the Royal Welch Fusiliers, that gallant regiment that had repulsed repeated assaults on their tiny stronghold. But the enemy had overwhelmed the forts with their numbers, and the defenders had been weakened by hunger and sickness.

His artillery had managed to bring fire on the redoubts for a little while, but within thirty minutes, it had again been silenced by the larger rebel siege guns. In a day, new rebel guns would glare at York from a range of less than four hundred yards.

In one action, this post had become untenable.

He thought about the meeting his officers had forced upon him, urging escape to Gloucester, remembered his anger at their impertinence. He thought of poor Major Cochrane, who had brought him the message. Yesterday, Cochrane had accompanied him to the ramparts to observe the rebel lines, and now the major was dead, his head carried away by an enemy ball. Drops of his blood had stained the earl's coat.

His officers had been right, their suggestion a wise one. He should have moved the garrison to Gloucester. He had known it, but he had been bound to obey that fool Clinton. Now, evacuating York was the only course open to him.

"It is now up to us, gentlemen," he said. "We must decide our next course of action."

"Hear, hear," Symonds agreed, but the others did not join him. O'Hara sighed and slapped his thighs.

"You have something to propose, General?" the earl prompted.

O'Hara seemed to be struggling to contain some passion. He had done his best from the start to place their situation in the best light, but tonight his demeanor suggested the opposite viewpoint.

"Sir. my lord, you know my thinking on this." He kept his voice low and measured. "The letter you have dispatched advises against the one thing we have based all of our actions on, and that is the arrival of reinforcements. Suddenly, we have rejected the central notion of our plan of resistance. The letter as much as concedes defeat. Is that your estimate of the forces we face —that there is little we may do to oppose them?"

Cornwallis considered the question; O'Hara was, as usual, direct. Yet the earl had always known the answer. Part of him had judged their campaign lost from the moment they set foot in York Town. It was as if he had been going through the motions of mounting a defence. A performance as on a stage, albeit one, he supposed, that would win no applause.

Some, in fact, would say his conduct had been shameful. He saw that opinion in O'Hara's eyes—the disappointment. And O'Hara was correct.

He stood, clasping his hands behind his back. A shell burst outside, rattling what remained of the windows, and the candle flickered. He stared at the flame, its hard, cruel light.

Deep within his breast, something stirred, something hard and defiant. The old soldier was still there, preparing to deliver a blow to the part of his soul that had given up long ago. The soldier in him would still search for options.

"I will never concede that all is lost," he announced. "I have determined what we shall do, although suggestions are, of course, welcome. First, honour decrees that we make a sortie against the enemy works. I have already sent Major Ross with orders for Lieutenant-Colonel Abercrombie of the Light Infantry."

O'Hara remained silent, his jaw working. The earl felt a sudden, unexpected spark of irritation.

"I know what you are thinking, General O'Hara," he snapped, failing for once to keep the edge from his voice. "That it is too late for that, that we should have disrupted their works from the first. I remind you that General Clinton promised reinforcements would sail by the fifth of the month. What would have been the use to attack, to risk the loss of life, when we were outnumbered? It would have been unnecessary, had our superior held to his promise."

His bitter words hung in the air. What was the use in hiding his anger? Clinton had brought him to this. Clinton—through his foolish strategy, through his complacency, his blindness, his sitting idle in New York waiting for the rebels to go home to their farms and leave government to those who were born to it.

"Regardless of that, sir," O'Hara replied, "although I do not dispute the usefulness of a sortie at this time, it can only be a diversion. Our one option is that proposed by Colonel Tarleton."

"That is precisely what I mean to do, sir! I mean to break out." The earl channeled his anger, forcing it into becoming determination. "You are right that we cannot do it this side of the river, so we will cross to Gloucester Point. The enemy is weak there. I will give orders to transfer what remains of our forces to Tarleton's command. I will write him his orders at once."

"What of the guns, my lord?" Rochfort asked. His face was bleak.

Cornwallis weighed his answer only briefly.

"We must abandon them to the enemy. There will be no time to transport them."

Rochfort breathed a long sigh.

O'Hara leapt to his feet.

"We must leave a small detachment here, to care for the wounded and see that the enemy treats them well."

Cornwallis nodded once. "Of course."

"We will need boats," Symonds added. "As many as we can find that have not been damaged. The fewer trips we make across the water, the better."

"I am certain you will provide us with the necessary transport, Captain."

Now O'Hara gave the earl a sly grin, his usual enthusiasm having returned at the promise of action.

"I look forward to this venture, sir! With all my heart. I am growing tired of this place."

Cornwallis was heartened by his second-in-command's energy, but he discovered he could not completely silence the voice of his own doubts.

"This will be our final hope, General O'Hara. There will be none other if it fails."

O'Hara's grin faded. "I am in agreement with you on that point, my lord."

The officers faced each other in silence. The windows continued to shake, the candle guttering as, outside, the guns rumbled. The sound was like that of a distant storm drawing closer, borne on an ill wind.

Chapter 41

The Redcoat

*T*om Martin's company of light infantry formed in the defensive ditch outside the Hornwork. The night air was sharp, the wind as keen as a sword's edge, the half-moon pale and cheerless. Tom shivered in his threadbare waistcoat, thrusting his icy hands under his arms. He thought it must be close to three o'clock in the morning, an ungodly hour.

He had not truly slept since moving to his shelter of canvas and hogsheads inside the Hornwork, and he had eaten nothing that day save a few scraps of weevil-infested bread. His joints and limbs ached from fatigue and bad food, although he so far remained healthy, avoiding the fevers and other illnesses that had struck down so many others. His only sickness was the one in his heart, the disgust he felt for what he and his men were about to do.

After all this time, after all the lost opportunities, the 1st Light Infantry had received orders to sortie against the enemy.

So, why do we go now, he wondered, *when I've begged to be allowed to go since the bombardment started? Why now, when it's almost useless?*

"The attack tonight will be straightforward," Captain Barlow was saying. He had just returned from an officers' conference with Colonel Abercrombie. "We make for the juncture where the French and rebel lines meet. We take that new rebel battery we have been so fond of watching since it was erected last night. We spike the guns. We carry on until we reach their next trench. Once there, we may operate with as much independence as we see fit." He laughed, a cruel and humourless sound. "Kill the enemy and spoil his works. That is all."

"We can do that, sir," Tom almost snarled. His nearest comrades growled their agreement; and in the light from a bursting shell, he saw their faces, their grim determination, even though they must all realize they could not accomplish much.

But they were good men, all that remained of the elite forces of the army of Lord Cornwallis, and they would give a few licks.

They had begun assembling at midnight, about three hundred and fifty of them, some from the two Light Infantry battalions, some from the Foot Guards, some from the grenadiers of the 80th Foot. They were ragged and filthy, worn down, more like an assembly of scarecrows than the heroes of the siege of York Town. These were the fellows who had managed to avoid wounds and disease, and this was their bitter reward—this final, feeble chance to prove their worth.

Tom's company was reduced to a mere dozen members. Captain Barlow still remained fit, but Lieutenant Nicholson had died from wounds received during the cannonade—the lieutenant had survived his fever only to lose his foot to a round shot and had never recovered from the shock and loss of blood. Tom did not regret his absence, although he missed many of the others.

A fresh gust of cruel wind curled through the ditch, and Tom stifled a curse. Barlow glanced toward the shadowy form of Colonel Abercrombie, then said, "Place the men in fours, Sergeant. We will advance in good order."

Speaking in an undertone, Tom brought the company to attention. The ditch filled with whispers and mutterings as the other sergeants did the same, ordering fixed bayonets and shouldered arms. Tom changed the company formation from two short ranks to three groups of fours, facing to the right. Since they had stood on the left of the line, they were now situated in the rear of the column. The detachments from the Guards and the Grenadiers were in the lead.

With a faint shuffling of feet, the leading units began the advance. Tom whispered, "Quick, march," and his men also started forward, struggling to keep in step with those in front.

The column followed the contours of the ditch then wheeled left, climbing through a gap in the abatis to cross the blasted ground between the combatants. The gloomy hills of two small redoubts loomed on either side of them, unfinished works Cornwallis had ordered abandoned. The enemy had never made use of them.

The dark shape of their first objective came into view, a new American battery in the second parallel. It was a wide breastwork of wicker gabions and earth, its face notched with gun embrasures, the cannon beyond invisible. The column marched straight for it behind Colonel Abercrombie, maintaining a steady cadence. Even over the sporadic nighttime bombardment, the crunch of their shoes and clink of tin canteens was audible.

Tom knew the battery would be guarded, that the pickets would hear and see them coming, but the column would not slow its pace.

"We'll roll over you," he murmured, and from deep within came a stirring of the old pride. Although shrunken, his company—his men—were still together. They were light infantrymen, moving to the attack! Tonight they would strike the enemy. They would rely on no fancy maneuvers, but upon their simple skills as soldiers.

The vague outline of a sentry appeared above the breastwork.

"What troops?"

"French," came the reply, the voice Abercrombie's.

The sentry said nothing more, his shadowy form unmoving. The breastwork grew closer.

A glint of metal flashed above the head of the column, catching the moonlight. Abercrombie's sword, raised in a clenched fist. Then his voice rose as well, crying in a voice that split the night like a cannon blast.

"Push on, my brave boys, and skin the buggers!"

The column surged forward. No one shouted or cheered. There was only the sound of rasping breath, running feet, the rattle of accoutrements. Then, the foremost men began dropping out of Tom's sight into the ditch in front of the battery.

The battery held several heavy guns—French forty-eight pounders. Now he could see the gaping mouths of their muzzles within the gabion embrasures. He ran, cursing that his company had been placed in the rear. The Guards and Grenadiers, in silence, were already crawling over the wall.

"Forward, boys," he said, "but stay together. We're still one company!"

They kept to their files as they ran. Tom jumped down into the ditch, landing on both feet with his fusil held across his body. The ditch was not deep, but the fall jarred him, and he needed a few moments to catch his breath. The Guards and Grenadiers had already taken the battery, were swarming over the guns. They were pounding spikes into the vents to make the guns useless, their little hammers ringing.

Tom crawled into the nearest embrasure. A few bodies sprawled in the dust—American militia, by the look of them, dressed in ordinary clothes. A few pale, dead hands clutched spades and picks.

Redcoats milled about, and Tom soon had Captain Barlow facing him from within the battery. Barlow grasped Tom's coat sleeves and heaved him inside.

"Reform the men in line," he said.

Tom's men had maintained their order, and he placed them in line in the rear of the battery; some of the other companies now formed on their left. Stray soldiers moved here and there, upsetting shot garlands, breaking handspikes and other stores.

Barlow ran along the rear of the line.

"Right face! Do it now, man! Company, right face!"

There was scuffling as each man turned to the right; then, they were moving again, faster now. Barlow and Abercrombie led them toward the head of a communication trench, Tom's company in the front, behind the colonel. The trench led off to the left, made a sharp turn right, then left again. The sole of Tom's left shoe had partially torn away, and it flapped as he ran.

Abercrombie held up his left hand. Barlow turned to Tom and hissed, "Halt!"

The long file stuttered to a stop, some of the men crashing into those in front and cursing. Tom could see that they had come all the way to the first parallel. There was a battery forward and just to their right. On its parapet perched the dark outlines of men in cocked hats.

"*Qui vive?*" came the cry this time. This was the French battery.

Abercrombie sloped his sword on his right shoulder and shouted toward the battery, "*Français.*" Then he turned as before, raising the sword and shouting, "At them, boys!"

The British at last cheered, a sharp, "Huzzay!" They dashed forward across the ditch and up the face of the battery. Tom's cheer became a wordless cry that bubbled into laughter. A malicious joy took hold of him at last, a release from all of his fear and frustration. He would make sure the damned Froggies tasted his cold steel!

His feet slipped in the loose earth as he climbed the breastwork. He almost fell, but recovered his balance. The survivors of his company were with him—Gibb and Hassler, young Sam Webb.

When he reached the short parapet, he teetered for a few seconds, staring down at a French cannoneer in gray and red, his musket held at his waist like a spear. He let his weight carry him, leaping down onto the firing step, thrusting with his bayonet. The Frenchman tried to parry the blow with a handspike, but over-swung, losing his balance. Tom's bayonet struck home, sliding between the man's ribs.

The man sucked in a sharp breath, dropping the handspike and clawing at Tom's fusil. Tom pulled with all his might to withdraw the bayonet. When it scraped free, the Frenchman sprawled on the ground, groaning, and Tom fell backward against the earthen wall.

Redcoats swarmed over the parapet, stabbing with bayonets, striking with musket stocks. A few Frenchmen held up their hands to surrender, and a detachment of Guards herded them as prisoners to the rear of the battery.

Tom threw his fusil over his shoulder by its sling. Some of the men were attempting to spike the guns with the tips of bayonets, but the three-sided blades did not make a tight fit in the round touch-holes. He dug in his haversack for some forged nails he'd brought with him. He had also brought his hatchet. With this, he beat a nail into the vent of one gun, then did the same to another.

He had just finished pounding in the second nail when Colonel Abercrombie called, "Back to the trench. Back! We have done all we can."

Tom would rather have pushed on, carried the fight further, but his reaction to the order was automatic. He searched for his comrades, finding that they had scattered after all. Some of the other units were already disappearing over the parapet into the parallel.

Tom called out, managing to gather ten men, although Hassler and Sam Webb were not among them.

"It's time to go back, lads," he said.

As he spoke, he heard the deep rolling of a field drum. A gray blur was approaching from the north. He recognized the blur at once as French reinforcements, a company advancing along the open ground behind the battery. The troops marched in three ranks, and those three ranks would be able to deliver devastating musket volleys in the confined space of the battery.

A squad of Guards formed a hasty line to meet the new threat and began loading their muskets. Abercrombie stood on the battery parapet, sword raised.

"Back to the Hornwork!" he ordered. "We have done all we can."

The French company did not pause to fire. There was a collective shout of *"Vive le Roi!"* and they charged, bayonets glinting dully. The Guards had time to fire one sputtering volley. A few Frenchman fell; then the rest struck the redcoat line.

Captain Barlow was at Tom's shoulder.

"We must go," he said, tugging at Tom's sleeve. "We've done our bit. Now it's up to the generals."

Tom kicked at the carriage wheel of a heavy gun. To hell with the generals! The Guards were struggling twenty paces away, outnumbered. With them, he saw Webb and Hassler, still engaged, still fighting.

A Frenchman lunged for Webb with his bayonet, catching the young private in the right leg. Webb did not cry out, did not fall, just staggered backward, the bayonet tearing free. Tom stared at him for a split second, wondering how badly he was hurt; but then Hassler grabbed the younger man by the arm and started dragging him clear of the fight. Others had broken away and were scrambling over the parapet. A few French muskets flashed.

Tom knew there was no point in staying. He had to get his men out. Crossing the remaining few yards to where Hassler struggled, he took Webb's free arm, threw it over his shoulder. Together, they carried the wounded private to the nearest gun embrasure.

"Don't you worry, Sam," Tom said.

They were through the breastwork and back in the approach trench. The rest of the company ran ahead of them, all sense of order lost. The fight still raged in the battery, but they did not look back as they made their way toward the Hornwork and York Town, moving as fast as their burden would allow.

By the time they reached the second parallel and then the no-man's land beyond, Tom had decided the sortie had been useless. Men had died, Sam had been wounded. They had spiked a few guns, but there had not been time to file the heads from the spikes. The French would pry them loose and have the guns back in operation in a few hours.

"Bloody hell," he hissed. The battle fever had left him, leaving him drained, empty. They had done too little. They had done too little, and far too late.

His lungs burned, and he coughed. Sam had started to moan, and hung a dead weight. Tom's mouth tasted full of ashes.

Chapter 42

The Loyalist

Catherine had been at the hospital for six days, and in that time, she had not slept more than a few hours. The surgeon made no more efforts to remove her, and the orderlies seemed grateful for her presence.

Fresh wounded continued to arrive almost as fast as the dead were carried away. John the drummer boy had been among the latter, never having recovered from his amputation, and for him Catherine felt a particular sorrow. Although his death was one among so many, the boy had been her first patient, and his face and name would remain forever etched in her memory.

Most of the new arrivals had been the victims of shot or shell fire, but on the sixth day three arrived with bayonet wounds. The men who brought them explained there had been a sortie against the enemy works, and a sharp skirmish. It had happened in the wee hours of the morning, they said, just hours before.

Catherine examined the newcomers. One had an ugly wound in his lower belly. She knew all she could do was make him as comfortable as possible until the end. The second had been stabbed twice in the chest, and his breath produced an ominous bubbling rattle. He would likely not live, either.

The third was a young man with a round face, and blond hair in a tight queue. There was a wound in his right thigh. Someone had tied a dirty rag around it.

"What is your name, Private?" she asked, crouching beside him.

"Sam," the soldier croaked, his lips dry and cracked. "Sam Webb."

"Well, Sam Webb, let me look at your wound." She reached for the bandage, and the boy stiffened and rolled his head from side to side.

"It hurts, ma'am," he whimpered. "Me whole leg hurts."

"It's all right," she reassured him, gently cutting away the blood-encrusted rag with her scissors. Underneath, she found a rent in the boy's breeches, another mass of dark dried blood, and some scabbing. She cut away the bits of soiled garment, then bathed the wound with river water, sponging away the brown mess. Sam moaned, but did not move. At last, Catherine found the wound, a small triangular puncture.

She stared at it. It was identical to Daniel's brother's wound. The boy had lost some blood, but his case seemed hopeful.

"It's just a wound in the flesh," she said, silently thankful the surgeon had not seen the boy first. He would likely have amputated the limb without bothering to examine the degree of the injury.

"Don't let them take me leg, ma'am," the boy cried, as if reading her thoughts. "Don't let them!"

Catherine leaned forward and sniffed. The skin around the wound was reddened, but the inflammation was slight, and she could detect no sign of corruption. The filth of the hospital could change that if she wasn't careful.

She probed the wound, looking for foreign debris such as bits of cloth. Sam stiffened, drawing in breath, but he didn't cry out. She could find nothing, but the bleeding started afresh, a crimson ooze.

After cleaning the wound a second time, she bound it with one of the strips of linen she had prepared for just such a situation, pulling it tight.

"You are not hurt badly," she said as she worked. "You will soon recover, if you are strong. Perhaps you need not even be in the hospital, though it's safer here than in the forts. I will keep this place for you, near the door."

"Thank you," he whispered, gasping. "I think it feels better. I think it really does."

The surgeon came then. He ignored Catherine and did his own examination, removing the careful bandage and frowning.

"He should be bled," he remarked, addressing her at last, "but I have too many more serious cases. Replace the dressing and leave him in the Lord's hands."

He gave her a curt nod and moved on. Catherine did as commanded. The warehouse creaked and groaned around her, as if the building itself were in pain, the swelling autumn wind pushing and pulling at its ramshackle walls. When she was finished with Sam, she examined the other wounded, discovering that two more men had died. She called for the mates to remove the bodies.

Throughout the remainder of the day, she made frequent visits to Sam's side. Of all the men who had recently arrived at the hospital, he was one of the few she could imagine surviving, one she could save to redeem the death of unfortunates like the drummer boy. She brought him his meagre supper of rice gruel and sat with him, asking him about his home in England.

"It's very green there, ma'am," he said. "Not as hot as it is here, and no mosquitoes. But it rains more."

"I think it may rain here soon enough," she said, listening to the wind.

"I'll stay here, then," Sam said. The strength was draining from his voice. "I'm tired, and it's sheltered here."

The rice bowl slid from his hands. Within moments, he was asleep.

The depth of his exhaustion must be very great, Catherine thought. She watched his chest rise and fall, his breathing slow and even. She reached out and placed her palm against his smooth forehead. There was no sign of fever, no sign of putrefaction around the wound. She hoped he would make a full recovery.

Rain spattered against the wooden wall to her left. She found her cloak and wrapped it around her shoulders. From outside came the distant rattle of drums, accompaniment for the rain and a reminder this was still a post with hale, living soldiers. The wounded in the warehouse shifted, coughed, muttered. It had grown darker inside, and she searched the huge open room for the surgeon; but he seemed to have gone. Perhaps he had fallen asleep himself, full of rum.

She glared upward at the rafters, at the lowering sky visible through one of the larger holes in the roof. Water was already dripping from the broken shingles. If the rain grew heavier, driven by this wind, the roof *and* walls would leak. These poor men would be forced to endure further misery.

The rattle of drums outside grew louder, and with it came the tramping of many feet, marching in step on the sand outside. It seemed an entire regiment had come down to the shore. The sound changed to a deeper percussion as the marchers left the beach, moving onto the wharf. There they halted. Men shouted, and there was the scraping of boats being pulled up onto the sand. A moment later, drums beat again, playing another march, growing closer. Yet another regiment had arrived.

Catherine moved toward the doors, curious; but after a few steps, a wave of dizziness passed over her. She had eaten nothing but some rice porridge and a few worm-infested ship's biscuits all day. Her lips curled in distaste at the memory, but that was all the wounded men had. She should expect no better.

She steadied herself against the wall, and the dizziness passed. Summoning her strength, she pulled open the side door.

She found Water Street crowded. Not just two regiments had arrived, but several, most of them now formed on the beach. They stood in long lines—redcoats, Highlanders, and blue-coated Germans. The townspeople had gathered as well, watching, oblivious to the rain that kept falling in fits.

Catherine stepped outside, sliding the door closed, then stepped a few paces into the open. She recognized Lord Cornwallis, standing on the Town

Wharf surrounded by aides. He wore a fine new coat with glittering gold lace. There was another officer with him, a man with a wide red face, drooping eyes and a narrow nose. Catherine wondered if he might be General O'Hara.

At the wharf, the smaller docks, and along the shore in front of the regiments, boats and crews of sailors waited. The boats rocked and ground against each other, the sailors cursing as they tried to keep the little vessels steady in the growing surf. The river was choppy and covered with whitecaps that shimmered in the darkness.

A regiment began to board the boats from the beach and the docks. Catherine approached an officer and demanded, "What is happening?"

The officer was a young man with a pointed chin. He narrowed his eyes and looked at her with open contempt.

"We are leaving for Gloucester. You and your rebel kin should be most grateful."

"I am no rebel," Catherine stated, offended by his rudeness. "I am Captain John Chester's cousin. He is with the British Legion. I am here to help the sick and wounded."

The officer straightened, stammering, "My apologies, ma'am. Then, we must save a position in one of the boats for you. Lord Cornwallis aims to shift the entire garrison to Gloucester. We will force our way through the rebel lines."

The boats were filling. Catherine glanced back at the warehouse, the hospital.

"I cannot leave the wounded," she said.

"They shall be looked after," said the officer. "We do not have time to move them, so Lord Cornwallis has prepared a letter asking that Mister Washington care for our sick and injured. A detachment will be left behind to capitulate. A sacrifice, ma'am."

She stared at him.

"A sacrifice," she repeated. It seemed unfathomable. They were all to leave York, and she had heard nothing, had no forewarning.

"Yes," the officer said. "The first contingent is about to depart."

A flurry of rain pelted down, and the officer pulled his neck within his stock. A moment later, the shower passed as suddenly as it had appeared.

"Lord Cornwallis estimates it will take three trips with the number of boats we have at our disposal," the officer continued. "You may come with my regiment on the second."

For a moment, she told herself she would stay, be part of the sacrifice. The wounded needed her. Then she remembered John and Abigail. She could never abandon her family.

Her work here was done. She had no choice. She nodded.

"Thank you, sir."

She thought of Sam Webb. He was not strong enough to walk, and if he tried, the wound might break open. He could not afford to lose any more blood. He would have to stay here. He would become a prisoner.

She gripped the front of her cloak as a gust of wind buffeted her. She considered returning to the hospital for her things, but she had given away the extra blanket and clothing already. If she left, she might miss her chance to board the boats.

She sighed in frustration. This was too sudden.

The fierce anger that rose in her was unexpected.

Damn the rebellion, she thought, *and damn the rebels for bringing it!* She could hate them—hate them for making her flee, again and again, an exile in her own country.

Then an image of Daniel surfaced, and her fury ebbed. It was not just the rebels, she told herself. The times held sway, and every man and woman was forced to decide, one way or the other, for good or ill.

I will be leaving you now, she thought, *and I will never know if you received my letter. You were like one shining spark of good amongst so much evil.*

The boats were launching into the waves, one after the other. They rose and dipped in the heavy swell, then disappeared into the darkness. Cornwallis remained on the wharf; an aide held aloft a covered lantern, as if its tiny light could somehow penetrate to the middle of the river.

They waited—Catherine, Cornwallis, the regiments, and the people of York. A few shells fell in the town behind them.

Catherine found a barrel and sat on it. The weather was worsening, the rain coming in blowing flurries. She wondered about the safety of the men on the water. The soldiers on the beach huddled in their worn coats for warmth, some breaking ranks and forming little circles.

Weariness overcame her, and she fell into a light doze. She woke with the rain stinging her face. She gaped about her, blinking, saw that the boats had returned empty, ready to take the next contingent of troops. Waves crashed against the beach and beat on the sides of the docks, tossing them about like corks. Some were having trouble landing. Others appeared to be drifting ever farther from shore, despite the efforts of the men at the oars. Those crews who managed to land pulled their boats far up on the sand.

Catherine hopped down from her perch and searched for the officer she had spoken with earlier. She found him in the same place. He had not moved for hours.

"Are we preparing to embark?" she asked.

He looked at her with a dull expression.

"We are not. My colonel has informed me the crossing is cancelled due to the poor weather. The boats were scattered, and some are still missing. There is no time now for the others to cross. When the weather moderates, the first division that crossed will return here."

Catherine glanced at the wharf, but Cornwallis and his party were gone.

"Return here?" she said. "Then we are not going to Gloucester?"

The officer sighed. "No, ma'am. I am afraid not."

She understood the significance of that at once.

"We shall not be escaping, then."

"No," he muttered. "We shall not." He swayed on his feet. "God help us."

"Perhaps we can try again tomorrow," she suggested.

The officer said nothing. The rain continued to slash down.

Catherine adjusted the hood of her cloak, then made her way back to the hospital. A strange emotion filled her breast. It took a long moment to identify it, and then she realized it was relief.

Chapter 43

The Redcoat

*T*om was seasick on the crossing to Gloucester Point, tossed about in the little boat as it rose on the huge waves and plunged into the troughs. He was soaked, frozen, and terrified he would be cast into the river to drown. Upon finally reaching their destination, he was filled with relief and joy to have survived, and to have seen the last of that damned hovel inside the Hornwork.

Then the order had come to return to York—the weather was causing delays, the first crossing had taken too long, and Cornwallis had cancelled the operation. It was feared that, when dawn broke, the enemy would see the British works largely abandoned. They might be enticed to attack while the last contingent was still on the beach, waiting for the boats.

Tom understood Cornwallis had no choice save to recall the first evacuees, but could not help griping, "So, we are endangered twice?"

So, he had been tossed about again, terrified again. He returned to that damned hovel inside the Hornwork. Now, all he wanted was sleep, but that proved elusive.

Dawn and reveille arrived much too early. With them came the usual increase in American and French shelling, with bombs bursting along the works and in the town. There was something monotonous about it all.

He climbed out of his shelter, shouting for the boys to emerge long enough for him to call the roll. When he was done, satisfied that all eleven able men were present, he hid behind the hogsheads. Artillery suddenly blasted their position, and he covered his ears, coughing from the dust. He did not want to come out again.

After a moment, the fire moved on, the rebels choosing new targets; and in the lull, he heard a voice.

"We would never have been able to break out at any rate. The enemy forces at Gloucester would have cut us to pieces in our weakened state."

"At least we would have gone out fighting!" he shouted from his hiding place. He shoved at the hogshead, struggling to rise. "At least we would have gone out like soldiers!"

When he had at last gained his feet, he saw the speaker had been Captain Barlow. Barlow glared at him. Tom stiffened to attention.

"Sir!"

The captain turned his back, walking to a position farther along the wall. Tom relaxed.

"There's a bit of gruel, Tom," Sergeant Gibb told him. Hassler had a kettle boiling outside his shelter. "If you'd be wanting some."

"I would." He did not really want gruel, but he was hungry enough to eat his ruined shoes. "Thank you."

They sat outside Tom's shelter, spooning the tasteless mush into their mouths. The guns now pounded them from the second parallel, and Tom kept his ears pricked for the warning cries of the sentries. Every few minutes, a shell seemed to whine toward them, and they would freeze. The sound was deceptive. Most of the incoming rounds were falling far to the rear, among the houses.

"We should raise those new tents today," Gibb suggested. The quartermaster had issued the tents just days ago, before the sortie. He chuckled and added, "See if they're bombproof."

"An insult," Tom grumbled, "giving us tents now. Though I suppose we could use them."

He gazed toward the open space where their camp had been before the bombardment. Two men were crossing the pocked ground, approaching the Hornwork—officers, by the look of their fine uniforms.

They stepped over piles of fragmented brick from the Nelson house, smoke and dust swirling around them. When it had cleared, Tom realized one of the men was Lord Cornwallis himself. The other was Brigadier-General O'Hara. They walked erect, heedless of the cannon fire.

He stared at them, his feelings conflicted. For a long time, he had respected Cornwallis. The earl had given the Army of the South many victories, had shared the hardships of soldiering with his men. Tom had considered him one of the few true fighters the British possessed in America.

But Cornwallis had not bothered to fight here in York, had not allowed his troops to strike at their tormentors. He wondered what had happened, what had changed. Why had they sat idle, waiting for reinforcements, wasting opportunities, when all of the earl's previous campaigns had been conducted with such fierce drive and determination?

Cornwallis was alongside Tom's shelter; Tom and Gibb stood. The earl nodded, then climbed the firing step in the rightmost salient of the Hornwork, where a ragged and torn Union flag still fluttered from its slim pole. O'Hara lingered below for a moment before joining his commander.

The earl said nothing. As Tom and Gibb watched, he turned and climbed down from the firing step. His face was the colour of faded ashes.

The generals left the Hornwork, returning to the town. O'Hara glanced back once. He met Tom's eye and held it for a few seconds. Then he disappeared behind the ruined Nelson house.

"What now?" Gibb muttered. "What were they looking at, d'you think?"

Tom tossed his tin cup of porridge to the dust.

"You know 'what now.' Our attempt to break out has failed, and time is against us. How many men will be left to resist the enemy tomorrow? The general will not allow the rebels to storm our works." He scowled. "We will make no grand last stand, fighting to the last man."

Gibb's face contorted in anger, and he drove his fist into the side of the earthen wall.

"Then to hell with the new tents! We'll rip them to shreds. We'll give the enemy nothing if we are forced to surrender!"

"Yes, we must destroy everything the rebels could put to use," Tom said, but the words caught in his throat. He slumped against the edge of the rampart, staring at the Nelson house, at the cratered ground that had been their camp. His mind and body felt numb and empty.

"Maybe I'm mistaken," he said, but his words had no force. In his heart, he knew he was right.

Chapter 44

The Earl

"How does our ammunition stand, Captain Rochfort?" Cornwallis faced his artillery commander. He had gathered most of his officers in the darkened study, although once again Tarleton remained across the river. The room had been reduced to a dismal state, the windows broken, the plaster walls cracked. Grimmer still were the faces of the men assembled, their features made grotesque by the flickering shadows from the candlelight.

Rochfort cleared his throat.

"We have one hundred mortar shells left, my lord, but no round shot. None at all, unless we gather those thrown at us by the enemy."

The house shook, surviving glasses or plates rattling somewhere; but no one gave the disturbance any heed. Cornwallis nodded, then turned to his first lieutenant.

"General O'Hara?"

"The hospitals are bursting, sir," O'Hara said. "Bursting. We are at less than half our original strength, and our surgeons are few."

"Half our original strength," the earl repeated. He clasped his hands behind his back, gripping his fingers hard. He squinted through a crack in the boards that covered the broken windows toward the river, but the intervening trees and shattered rooftops blocked the water from view. "And what should the other half do, gentlemen? Should we fight to the death?"

Rochfort grunted, but O'Hara spoke at once.

"Such an order would doom us all. Doom brave men who have done more than you asked of them, endured this helplessness, this waiting for reinforcement. Within a few hours, they will be exposed to an assault. The enemy outnumbers us at least four-to-one. I must remind my lord that the enemy is required to give no quarter when successfully storming a fortified post such as this. There are Loyalist civilians with the army, as well, here and in Gloucester."

Cornwallis met his eye.

"Then are we to surrender?"

No one spoke. Cornwallis suspected no one wished to. No one wanted to admit the truth, to be the first to speak the unspeakable.

"At least, we may purchase time," Rochfort said at length. His voice quavered. "General Clinton may still arrive."

"Yes, he may." The earl turned back toward the river. "Maybe General Clinton will come."

I might ask for a parley, he thought. *See what terms the enemy proposes.* There was no dishonour in such a course of action. As Rochfort suggested, it would buy them some time. Then, if Clinton were to arrive, the earl would resume his defence. In such a light, surrender did not seem inevitable.

"A parley, then," he stated. "We will see what Mister Washington has to say to us."

Chapter 45

The Redcoat

$\mathcal{A}$s the day progressed, the bombardment became more powerful, the rebels once again concentrating their fire on the Hornwork. Mortar shells shrieked and wailed as they fell like oversized hail, and at times, the noise made it impossible to speak or hear.

Of all the light infantrymen who huddled in their holes under the wall, only Sergeant Gibb was brave—or foolish—enough to risk crossing open ground, venturing toward the town and disappearing behind the Nelson house. He returned some ten minutes later with Bone scampering and barking at his heels. Gibb was laughing as he dashed for Tom's shelter, even as the shells tore apart the sky over his head.

"Where had you hidden him?" Tom demanded once Gibb and the bulldog were relatively safe under the parapet.

"That is my secret," Gibb declared. Then, he shouted to Hassler, "Wouldn't you all like to know?"

"They won't touch him," Tom said, scratching the dog behind the ears. "They would never do such a thing without sanction. They are our boys, under our command."

He thumped the bulldog's sturdy rib cage, wondering what sheltered spot Gibb had found for Bone's refuge. Any number of places would have served, he supposed.

"The haze is lying thick today," Gibb commented, gesturing toward the town. Tom looked and saw that the smoke had settled in a dense cloud over the rooftops. The high wind of the previous few days had died, and now the air was heavy with the stench of burned powder.

The scream of a shell made him wince and cover his ears. He saw the tiny comet fall toward the Nelson house, where it struck one broken wall, exploding and spraying brick fragments in all directions. The smoke and dust from the burst hung in the air, resembling some strange variety of palm.

From the depths of the smoke stepped an officer, waving his hands and coughing. He picked his way through the rubble and shell fragments.

"Narrow miss, that," Tom remarked. He recognized the officer as Lord Cornwallis's aide-de-camp, Major Alexander Ross. With the major was a drummer boy, a little lad in a bearskin hat and a shabby red coat trimmed in dirty white lace.

They entered the Hornwork and mounted the step where Cornwallis had observed the enemy earlier. Tom expected them to halt on the step, but the drummer climbed onto the top of the parapet. There, he brought his drumsticks up level with his nose, paused a heartbeat, then drove them down to sound a roll. Tom recognized the signal for parley.

Ross climbed the parapet and stood tall beside the boy. He held a white handkerchief, which he waved in the air.

The drummer repeated the signal three times. After he had completed the third call and as he prepared to play a fourth, the rebel cannon abruptly fell silent. Ross and the drummer advanced down the slope and out of sight. The drummer continued to play, his call loud in the sudden stillness.

Tom glanced at Gibb; then, the two of them struggled to mount the firing step. Bone went with them, as did scores of other soldiers, all along the wall and in the silent batteries.

The little procession of man and drummer boy had crossed the ditch and abatis, and there they halted, on the open space between the opposing lines. An American officer scrambled down from the second parallel, from what had been Redoubt Number Nine. The man wore the blue-and-buff coat, a crimson sash about his waist. He halted before Ross.

Ross doffed his cocked hat and bowed low. The American returned the gesture. The two men spoke; then, the American took the handkerchief from Ross's hand. Folding it, he tied it around the British officer's eyes as a blindfold. Ross stood patiently throughout the procedure.

As the drummer returned to the British lines, the American led Ross away, toward the redoubt.

"So, now we have a parley," Tom said. "From there, I can see only one outcome."

Gibb was not listening to him. He was laughing as he wrestled with his dog on the firing step.

Chapter 46

The General

*W*ashington sat at his camp desk, far from the siege lines, sifting through a stack of letters. Here were requests for payment from local farmers, complaints about army conduct, the ubiquitous demands for promotion, communications from other theatres of the war. So absorbed was he in reading, analyzing each document, that he did not notice the guns had fallen silent until Tilghman entered the tent and spoke his name.

"Why has the bombardment ceased?" the General asked. He did not speculate, for there could be many reasons; but everything about Tilghman's manner, from the excitement in his eyes to the way he held his shoulders, suggested urgency.

"Your Excellency," Tilghman said, "the enemy requests a parley. Lord Cornwallis has sent one of his aides to speak to you. To ask for your...terms."

Washington sat in silence, trying to absorb what Tilghman had just said. He set down the letter he had been reading.

So soon, he thought. *I had not expected this so soon.*

He stood. He would not rejoice. Only a fool would behave that way at such a delicate moment, when everything hung in the balance. A request for terms was simply that, and a common tactic for gaining time.

"I will see this agent of Lord Cornwallis," he said. "You may have him brought to me here. It is a fine day. We will place some camp stools outside the tent."

He waited in the autumn air, standing beneath two shading oak trees, their leaves a fiery canopy of orange and yellow. From here he enjoyed an unobstructed view of York. The stain of powder smoke still hung over the town.

At length, a little procession approached—Tilghman, some officers from General Lincoln's division, and an officer in a fresh, unsoiled British uniform. When they halted in the shade of the trees, Tilghman removed the British officer's blindfold.

"Sir," he said, "may I present to you Major Alexander Ross, aide-de-camp to Lord Charles Cornwallis. Major Ross, His Excellency, General George Washington."

"I am at your service, Major," the General said. He gestured to one of the camp stools. "Will you sit? We only await the arrival of my colleague, General Rochambeau."

"Thank you, sir," Ross said, bowing slightly from the waist. Washington was pleased to see the Scotsman displayed no outward signs of arrogance, only humility. "I am at *your* service. I will wait as long as necessary."

Rochambeau arrived on horseback a few minutes later, in company with John Laurens and a few aides. When the Frenchman dismounted and his eyes met those of Washington, he smiled.

The officers gathered under the trees, outside the tent, some sitting, some standing. A faint breeze stirred, and the headquarters flag with its square blue field and thirteen stars stood out from its staff.

"Now, Major Ross," the General asked, "what do you request?"

Ross solemnly rose to his feet and faced the American commander.

"My Lord Cornwallis sends a message to Generals Washington and Rochambeau. He requests a cessation of offensive operations for twenty-four hours, and suggests that both sides appoint two commissioners each. Sir, he wishes to discuss terms for surrender."

Washington had expected to hear these words and displayed no reaction. "You have his message in writing?"

"I do, sir." Ross held out the folded and sealed letter. "It is here."

Washington took the letter and opened it. It was a brief note written in a shaky hand.

Sir,

I propose a cessation of hostilities for twenty four hours and that two officers may be appointed by each side to meet at Mr. Moore's house to settle terms for the surrender of the posts at York and Gloucester.

I have the honour to be, &c.
Cornwallis

The General paused, stared at the paper. He struggled to maintain his composure, but he had never found that task so difficult as at this moment. To hear that the enemy wished to capitulate was one thing, but to see it in writing was another. It was no longer simply an idea, one he had nurtured for so many months. Now, it was a tangible, concrete object, a letter in his hand.

"He suggests the Moore house," he said. His voice sounded tight and reedy to his own ears, although he had attempted to speak in a casual manner. "It may suffice."

The Moore house was the home of the miller, Augustine Moore. Washington could see it from here, an attractive two-storey home of whitewashed clapboards, built in the Dutch style. It stood behind the right of his line, facing York Town from a grove of brilliant hardwoods.

"I will consult with my officers," he added. "I will consider the offer of Lord Cornwallis. In the meantime, you are our guest, Major Ross."

The brief initial meeting was over. Washington withdrew to his marquee, in company with Rochambeau, Laurens, Tilghman and a few others. Ross waited outside. The General heard the voices of several younger officers, engaging the British aide in friendly conversation.

Washington went to his camp desk and immediately wrote an order authorizing a resumption of the bombardment. As an aide scurried off to deliver the order to Henry Knox, the General scrawled a draft of the reply he would send to Cornwallis. When he had finished, he read it aloud to his companions.

"'An ardent desire to spare a further effusion of blood,'" he said, "'will readily incline me to listen to such terms for the surrender of your posts and garrisons of York and Gloucester as are admissible.'"

He would also ask Cornwallis to submit a formal written proposal for surrender prior to the meeting of commissioners. He wanted no ambiguity. He meant to control this moment, to allow no loopholes for the enemy to slip through.

"'I will grant a cessation of hostilities for no more than two hours,'" he concluded.

"I have one suggestion on that point, sir," Laurens said. "That is that the word *cessation* be changed to *suspension*. There is no reason to have them believe we are finished with them. We still have plenty of powder and shot for the guns."

"Agreed." Laurens was something of a militant, but Washington valued his advice. He snatched his pen and made the correction before finally handing the draft note to Tilghman. "Copy this four times. If Cornwallis agrees to our terms, I will suggest a 'suspension' of hostilities for the night."

There were murmurs and grunts of approval. Tilghman copied the letter as instructed, then took one copy to Major Ross. Ross left the camp and returned to his lines.

Washington consulted his watch. It was two o'clock in the afternoon.

Impatiently, pacing outside the tent, he waited for Ross to return. The guns had resumed their fire, although now the breeze had thinned the smoke that hung over York Town.

Ross reappeared within the hour. He passed another letter to Washington. The General read it and could not suppress a smile of intense satisfaction. Cornwallis had agreed to every term.

For the second time that day, the guns fell silent.

Chapter 47

The Earl

Charles, Earl Cornwallis, sat alone in the study of Governor Nelson's house. The protective planks had been taken down, and the shattered windows stood open. It was a clear, crisp night, as fine as the previous night had been foul.

Nature itself was against me, he thought.

He rubbed his eyes. From the direction of the fortifications drifted the mournful keening of a lone bagpiper, perhaps a member of the 76th Regiment, MacDonald's Highlanders. The earl slumped in his chair and listened. The player had skill, the pipes perfectly tuned, the notes clear and unwavering.

When the piper had played through his lament, there was a brief silence. Then, the soft harmony of a brass band rose from the French lines.

Just hours ago we exchanged round shot, the earl thought. *Now we exchange music.*

Such was the madness of war.

He reached for his quill, snatched it from the desktop. He held it poised, considering his words. It was a time for truth. He had told himself and his subordinates that the parley would be a method for gaining time, but even as he spoke, he had known his words to be fiction. A relief force had not, of course, appeared at the last minute, and there would be no reprieve. He was not fool enough to harbour even a shred of hope that this process he had begun could be reversed.

He dipped the quill in ink and began his latest and perhaps last letter to Sir Henry Clinton.

Sir,

I have the mortification to inform Your Excellency that I have been forced to give up the posts of York and Gloucester and to surrender the troops under my command by capitulation on the 19th inst. as prisoners of war to the combined forces of America and France...

A chill gripped him, and he shuddered. He waited for it to pass, but in its wake came a wave of heat. He wiped sweat from his forehead, gasping, rubbed his hands through his thinning hair. The old malady. He had kept it at bay throughout this crisis. Now, of all times, it returned with a vengeance.

It was the ignominy of his position that had provoked the attack, he reasoned, the harshness of Washington's terms. Even this insistence on a written statement of his intention to surrender was an effrontery. A spoken agreement should have been enough between gentlemen, but Washington apparently wished to have documented proof of his triumph.

The earl had done his best to achieve something fair for his garrison before the commissioners met to set down the formal articles, but he was unhappy with the results. He had requested that all Loyalists in York and all American deserters who had supported the British not be punished. Washington had denied that request where the Loyalists were concerned, explaining that it was beyond the bounds of his authority. As for American deserters, they would be hanged. Washington had also denied leave for the surrendering troops to depart for Europe. They would be held until the end of the war.

Cornwallis had gained only two small concessions. Washington agreed to grant his officers parole, and the American general would allow the earl to send his personal possessions to New York on board the transport vessel *Bonetta*. The ship would not be searched.

It was all a most bitter fruit to swallow. Cornwallis shuddered again, but in the wake of the chill came a wave of anger that momentarily gave him strength. He resumed the letter, and now its aspect was no longer one of humiliation, but of accusation.

I never saw this post in a favourable light, and nothing but the hopes of relief would have induced me to attempt its defence; for I would either have endeavoured to escape to New York by rapid marches from the Gloucester side immediately on the arrival of General Washington's troops at Williamsburg or I would have attacked them in the open field, but being assured by Your Excellency's letters that every possible means would be tried by the navy and army to relieve us I could not think myself at liberty to venture on either of these desperate attempts.

That was it. He could have escaped, could have struck the enemy a blow, just as Tarleton had wished, but he had waited for Clinton, and Clinton had not come. That was why he had ceased to fight after the battle at Green Spring Farm.

That and no other reason.

Chapter 48

The Continental

*T*he Light Division passed what Daniel could only think of as a peaceful night in the second parallel, the first quiet night in a week of continuous cannon fire. Gone was the overpowering stench of powder, the blowing smoke, the deafening, jarring detonations. The sky was a soft veil of stars. From the British lines, the clear sound of bagpipes emanated, a soul-rending lament that brought him an acute and unexpected pang of homesickness.

When the piping at last ceased and the French bands answered, the strange yearning passed.

"Well," he said, his voice emerging as a hoarse croak, "the storm has blown itself out at last."

"Will it start up again is the question," Joshua replied. "Will the enemy come to terms, or force us to push them into the river?"

"I think they will come to terms." The French band had fallen silent, and now there rose a third music, a more basic rhythm. The crickets had returned.

"I would never have believed this day possible," Daniel continued, rubbing his forehead. "I...I was done, finished, and now I'm astonished and ashamed at my own despair, my weakness. I was wrong, so wrong, Joshua. You forced me to stick with it, and for that I am grateful."

Even in the dark, Joshua's lopsided grin was obvious.

"That's what elder brothers are for."

"Perhaps so, perhaps so." Daniel took off his cap, drew a hand over his hair. "When this is done, I intend to cross the river to Gloucester. I must find Catherine."

Joshua nodded. "She'll be waiting for an answer to her letter."

The rest of the night passed as in a garrison—the sentries changing, the troops in the trench dozing in rotations. Then came reveille, roll call, and breakfast. The guns did not resume their grim work. The suspension of hostilities held, at least for now.

Daniel sipped from a tin cup of steaming tea and examined the closest battery. Some of the idle gunners had straddled the cold gun barrels, faces turned toward what had been their target. Others had climbed onto the top of the parapet, confident of their safety.

"What's stopping us?" he heard Sergeant Williams cry, addressing the company at large. "I want a good look at 'em!"

Using his musket as a crutch, the sergeant hoisted himself up to stand on top of the wall of earth and bundled sticks. The regimental colour of Gimat's battalion hung slack on his left. Two other men joined him around the flag.

What followed seemed the result of some great communal decision, as if a single mind had taken control of the division. In pairs or singly, in small groups, men began to climb to the top of the walls and breastworks, gathering like spectators at a sporting event. There they leaned on their muskets, relaxed, knowing they took no risk.

Daniel gave Joshua one pointed look; then he, too, began to climb, finding easy purchase in the gabions and fascines. When he gained the little summit, he offered Joshua his hand, helped hoist him onto the parapet. The brothers stood together and turned toward York.

Opposite their works, a scattering of British officers stared back at them, so close Daniel could make out individual faces. The officers had likewise climbed the walls of the Hornwork and connecting breastworks.

The two sides in the long conflict faced each other without firing even a volley of words.

Now Daniel noticed more men joining Lafayette's division on the walls, off-duty men venturing out from the American camps, just as they had done during the opening of the trenches, and when the bombardment had begun. He heard laughter and lighthearted conversation, ease and confidence. No longer did they have to worry about paying the ultimate price for their curiosity.

"It appears that our entire army is assembling without orders," he commented.

"And there is the enemy," Joshua said.

Behind the British works, even lines of redcoats had formed for morning parade, using the old drill ground denied to them by the cannonade. Military routine, the practice of the ages, had resumed.

The laughter faded, and a stillness settled, like the hour before sunrise. Few spoke above a whisper. All watched, waiting. The Continental Army held its collective breath, waiting for its foe to accept the truth.

Chapter 49

The Loyalist

C atherine escorted Sam Webb along the sloping street, climbing the bluff from the warehouse hospital. Sam had explained that his wound was still painful, but it was healing without trouble and his strength was returning. One of the surgeon's mates had fashioned him a crutch, and with it he could walk, his steps slow and deliberate. Now that the cannonade had ceased, he had expressed his desire to see the American forts. Catherine had agreed to take him there.

"I'll march out with the rest if we surrender," he said as he hobbled along beside her. "But if not, I'll die here when they storm our lines. If that's the general's choice."

"You are very brave," Catherine told him, "but I don't think you need die yet."

They came to what had been the British camps, and she was surprised to see the regiments drawn up in perfect ranks, arrayed on a new line of camp colours. In appearance, it was like any other morning, with the adjutants and orderly sergeants calling the roll in each shrunken battalion. Nearby stood a line of wagons heaped with what appeared to be fresh uniforms—folded piles of bright-red coats.

"My cousin John mentioned there was a store of new military clothing in York," she said, pausing to watch.

An officer stood with each wagon, presumably the regimental quarter-master. The troops seemed poised to receive replacements for their pinkish and worn-out coats, their gray and filthy breeches and torn gaiter trousers.

Sam was staring forlornly at the parade, and a sudden sparkle of tears came to his eyes.

"Ma'am…Ma'am, I want to join my company. That's them there." He pointed with one slender, almost girlish finger. "That's the First Light Battalion. I don't want to see the forts. I want to go back to my friends and comrades, ma'am."

"Go, then," she told him. "They will be pleased to see you. And you will get a new coat."

He wiped at his face with the palm of his hand.

"Thank you for all you done for me. You saved my life, I'd warrant. You saved me from that stinkin' hole, beggin' your pardon, ma'am."

"I take no offence, Sam. You are welcome."

"Goodbye, then," he said, nodding, his eyes fixed on the waiting ranks. He lurched on his crutch toward the parade ground. He glanced back once, and she waved. Then she watched him approach his adjutant and raise his hand to his cap. Within a few minutes, he had fallen in on the left of his company.

Her chest seemed to swell with satisfaction. She had accomplished something useful after all. If Cornwallis surrendered, the boy would be a prisoner, but he would live, and perhaps in part that was thanks to her.

For a moment, she lingered on the edge of the parade. Her original purpose for leaving the hospital this morning was gone, but she found she did not wish to return at once. She realized she had never seen the forts, either.

She carried on through the ruined camp, passing shell craters, spent shot and metal fragments. She remembered her first night here after crossing the river from Gloucester, when she had seen corpses in the street, men slaughtering the horses for food. It was difficult for her to imagine what the soldiers here had been forced to endure.

She skirted the ruins of the Nelson house, its roof splintered, its windows empty, its walls so pierced through that it was a miracle the building still stood.

Beyond the house, she came to the Hornwork. A few officers perched on top of the wall, chatting in low voices. Below them, the interior of the fort was a chaotic jumble of sagging tents, splintered hogsheads, broken gun carriages, dismounted gunbarrels, pieces of discarded uniforms and accoutrements. She could see where the soldiers had hollowed out sections of the ramparts for shelter, with scraps of tent canvas for protection against the sun and rain.

Picking her way through the debris, she came to the base of the wall. Above her on the parapet, the Union flag drooped on its staff. She did not think it would be difficult to climb the firing step, then to the top of the wall. From there, she would see the enemy trenches and batteries, the beasts that had harried this place for more than two weeks.

She placed a foot on a broken gabion, then took another step, using her hands to help her climb. When she stepped out onto the top of the parapet, the wide landscape opened before her. She drew in a sharp breath.

Arrayed below were not just the enemy trenches, but the enemy itself.

"Quite a sight, is it not?" remarked one of the British officers from a few yards to her right.

For a moment, Catherine couldn't speak. All along the allied lines, along the parapet of the second parallel and in the two captured redoubts, stood rebel soldiers, as if formed up for a charge. The entire Continental Army might have been there, every division, brigade, regiment, and company, although for now they were not preparing for battle. They were simply watching, watching York Town and waiting for an answer.

Heads turned in her direction. She wanted to look away, to cower under the scrutiny, even to flee. These were the men responsible for the pain and suffering in the hospital, the men who had brought the war, who had killed her husband and so many others. There stood their cannon, those greatest instruments of destruction, the blackened muzzles seeming so close, so malevolent, like the mouths of dragons.

She gripped the flag staff to steady herself. She refused to look away. She would face the rebels and their guns. She had run from them for so long, and now that they had caught her, she would run no more. They were just men, soldiers like the British soldiers here. They were not fiends or monsters. Daniel Brattle had taught her as much, he and his brother. They were just men, tired men in ragged hunting shirts, a few with blue Continental uniforms. Many did not wear hats, but little caps. She wondered who they were, where they had come from, how far they had marched. She wondered if any of them knew Daniel, and whether there were men as good as he among their ranks.

Daniel would be with them, she realized. Here was the entire Continental army. Lafayette's men had to be here.

She could go to him, find him. There was a truce. Surely a noncombatant like herself could visit the rebel lines. All she need do was walk a few hundred yards and call out his name, although that would bring her amongst the enemy. She could think of Washington's army in no other way now, after the siege and all she had seen in the hospital.

I will send a letter instead, she thought.

She turned to the British officer who had spoken to her, saw that he was chatting with a companion. Perhaps he carried a pocket writing case, some paper...

But why send a letter when she could speak to Daniel face-to-face? Why wait, squander this opportunity, if Daniel was here, somewhere in that line opposite? Unless he *wasn't* here, had not survived the fighting.

She released her grip on the flagpole and stepped down from the parapet into the blasted ground of the glacis.

"Here, now, miss," the British officer called, "what are you about? You mustn't go over there."

She glanced back, but said nothing. She heard the officer's companion grumble, "Must be a rebel from the town, off to join her fellows."

It didn't matter what they thought. She walked on, southward, the dark cannon muzzles growing closer. A rebel soldier pointed at her, and a few raised their hands. She could make out individual faces, could see the light infantry caps clearly. The closest troops had to be those of General Lafayette.

"That's it, ma'am!" someone shouted. "Come on over to our side!"

"Cornwallis is finished," cried another, "and we have washing that needs doing!"

There were other comments, the men cracking wise. She did her best to ignore them, although her ears burned with rising anger. She paused in confusion, wondering if this was a mistake, but she was more than halfway across already. She resumed her pace, and the line drew closer.

When she was little more than ten yards away, two men scrambled down from the parapet and advanced to meet her. She halted. One of them wore the uniform of an officer, the other a gray hunting shirt. The officer's face was rough and square, his eyes suspicious. Still, he saluted and said, "It is dangerous for you to be out here, Miss. Hostilities may resume at any moment."

"Sir," she told him, "I am looking for an officer of the light infantry. He is with Lafayette."

The officer swept his arm toward the men behind him.

"This is the Marquis de Lafayette's division. Do you know this man's regiment?"

Heartened by the officer's good manners, she struggled to recall the name. "It was a French name, that of his colonel."

"Gimat?" the officer suggested.

"Yes! That is it. Gimat's battalion. The man I seek is Lieutenant Daniel Brattle. He has a brother Joshua."

He nodded. "I know the name. I have had the pleasure of dining with the officers of Gimat's battalion. Captain Brattle's company took part in the assault on the redoubts."

Catherine involuntarily grasped the man's arm.

"He has not been killed in the fighting? He is all right?"

He laughed. "Yes, yes, he is, as far as I know. His battalion is part of our brigade. I'll take you to him, if possible. May I ask your name?"

"Catherine Seawell," she said, and her heart fluttered within her chest.

The officer bowed. "Captain Anthony Scallion, of Portsmouth, New Hampshire. I'm at your service, ma'am. If you'll follow me?" He turned to his companion. "Sergeant, please assist our guest in mounting the parapet."

It seemed as if she walked in a dream. She took the sergeant's hand, felt skin as rough as shoe leather. Together, they climbed the parapet, the soldiers making way. From there, Scallion led her down into the trench where the going was easier, and she followed him toward the right of the rebel line. She heard muttered speculation about who she might be, one man commenting, "Someone from the town. They're all good patriots here in York Town, God bless 'em for what they've had to bear."

Captain Scallion turned to her and pointed.

"These are Gimat's men. Now we must find the proper company."

She scanned the backs of the troops on the parapet, paying particular attention to those in full uniform. She did not see Daniel. She wondered if she would even recognize him after all this time.

"Is Captain Brattle here?" Scallion called. "I have a citizen from the town come to see Captain Brattle."

A few hands pointed, and a voice called, farther to the right.

"Ah, yes," Scallion said, and Catherine followed him a few more yards before she halted, staring upwards. There, on the wall, stood two figures she recognized at once.

Daniel had not changed, but Joshua looked more hale than she remembered.

"A Miss Catherine Seawell to see you, sir," Scallion declared. "I watched her come from York Town, crossing between the lines at some risk to her person."

⚜

"Catherine?" Daniel said. "My God, is that you, Catherine?"

He hesitated a moment, time standing still. Then he leapt, almost tripping and tumbling from the firing step in his rush to reach her. She thought he would sweep her into his arms, but at the last second, he stopped short and, instead, took her hands. She offered no resistance, swaying in place.

"How did you come here?" he cried. "How did you come from Gloucester?"

"Did you receive my letter?" It was the first thing she could think to say.

"I did! I did, and I should have replied, found some way to get word to you. But I knew of no way...none that I could conceive..."

He glanced behind him, then took her arm.

"Come this way." He guided her away from the trench toward the squat form of a redoubt. Over his shoulder, she saw that Captain Scallion was speaking with Joshua, the two men grinning.

When they paused under the shadow of the little fort, farther away from prying eyes, she did not know what to do or say. She clasped her hands, let them fall to her sides, then clasped them again. Daniel was no less awkward and did not even meet her eye, his expression one of anguish rather than joy.

Then he reached out, and he took her hands and drew her close—just close enough—and for a few fleeting seconds there was just the two of them. The contending armies faded, withdrew, grew pale. She held his eyes, could not

245

look away, could feel the warmth of his body and scent the wood smoke on his clothes and hair.

When he released her, he began fumbling in his coat pocket, a look of desperation in his eyes.

"I kept your letter. I must have read it four dozen times." He found it at last, held it for her to examine. "I could hardly believe it was real."

"I could only hope it would find you," she said, thinking of her young courier, the nameless boy who had succeeded in his mission after all. "I had no way of knowing."

"I cannot believe you're here!" he cried, and he again pulled her toward him. His rough hands were warm, and she briefly forgot the horror of the last weeks, as if she had never come to York, had never left the farm. As if Daniel had never left.

After a few minutes, she pulled back, grinning from ear to ear, suddenly blushing and out of breath.

"I thank God that you are safe, and that soon this will be over."

His face clouded. "Yes, I suppose it will. Where is your sister?"

"She is in Gloucester still. I have been on this side of the river, tending the wounded."

"Tending the wounded? Yes, of course you would be."

"I will have to return to her. She is with my cousin now. He is an officer in the British Legion. I fear for him." She brushed a strand of hair that had escaped from her cap away from her face. "I crossed the lines on an impulse. Perhaps it was foolish."

"Foolish? How happy—overjoyed—I am that you did! I had meant to cross myself. There's no danger as long as the truce holds. And you mustn't fear for your cousin. If he is an officer, he will come to no harm, I'm sure."

"Oh, how I hope that will be so."

He took her shoulders in a firm grasp.

"Listen, Catherine. You must listen to me. I will not let you simply vanish on me a second time. Cornwallis will surrender. I want you to come with me when his garrison marches out. Go and fetch your sister, then meet me tomorrow afternoon." He paused, considering. "At half-past three o'clock on the grounds of the Moore house. Do you know it?"

She shook her head. "The opportunity for becoming familiar with the town has never presented itself."

"It's behind our lines, on the right, near the north bank of Wormley Creek." He pointed. "It's the only house of any consequence, and stands near the mill. You will recognize it. Meet me there after you have prepared yourself. When Lord Cornwallis surrenders, I'll take you with me."

She did not understand what he was saying.

"You will take me with you?"

He was growing frantic.

"There will be no protection for Tories, Catherine. They will be made prisoners with the rest. But you and your sister will be safe with me. No one shall ever dare denounce you as a Tory as long as I live."

She studied a button on his coat. She found herself back in the yard at the farmhouse, faced with the same question. To follow her wish—the desire of her heart—or accept cold reality.

"Don't tell me that after all that's happened you're still undecided!" he cried. "You didn't cross between the trenches simply to bring greetings, Catherine. Tell me if your regard for me is true. Tell me if that is so!"

"It is," she admitted.

He threw back his head and laughed.

"It is! And my feelings for you are the same. I thought you were some ghost, some manifestation of my wishes for peace, but with this victory, now I know anything is possible. My proposal of marriage was made with sincerity, and still stands. Come with me. And don't fear for your sister. She will be safe with me as well."

She could not answer. Here was a crossroads, perhaps the crossroads of her life, and she did not know why she hesitated. Why *not* go with him, and take Abigail?

But the war was not ended, and nothing had been decided. He was still a soldier, and she did not believe she could enter into the rebel army, become a part of it. She could never have done so before the siege, and certainly could not now, after what she had seen, whatever her heart demanded.

"Daniel," she whispered, "my admiration for you is unchanged, as strong as ever." She held his hands, felt his strong fingers, for a long time. This could be hers forever. "Go to the Moore house," she said, at last pulling away. "Go there, at the appointed time. Half-past three o'clock tomorrow."

"You will be there, then?" he demanded.

She reached up and touched his face. The pain of his expression eased.

"I will be there, and I will bring my answer."

Chapter 50

The Commissioner

*M*ajor Alexander Ross paused within sight of the Moore house, studying the men who waited on the front steps. There stood the American commissioners, one in Continental uniform, the other in the French blue, scarlet, and white. He at once recognized the astute John Laurens as the Continental. The other he did not know.

He turned to his companion and fellow commissioner, Colonel Thomas Dundas. They had both donned their best uniforms, both powdered their hair afresh. This would prove a long, arduous, and likely humiliating process, Ross suspected; and they were determined to retain at least the appearance of dignity.

It was important he and Dundas do all they could to put the most favourable face on the situation, and so save some fragment of honour for the southern army of Lord Charles Cornwallis.

"Little sense in delaying further," he said.

Dundas nodded.

They advanced, halting at the foot of the steps and raising their hats to the opposing officers. The American returned the salute in the same manner, the Frenchman with more flare, bowing low. Ross then introduced Dundas; Laurens, his face like stone, then indicated his companion.

"Allow me to present the Viscount de Noailles, brother-in-law to the Marquis de Lafayette."

"I am honoured, sir," Dundas replied, and Ross added, "As am I."

The introductions concluded, the allied officers led the way into the house. Ross found himself in a spacious parlour, its walls a pleasant yellow, the trim gray. A small case clock tick-tocked in its place on the mantel. Flanking the clock were fresh candles in silver sticks. Ross knew that, when the hour required those candles to be lit, he might still be here.

Laurens pointed to a single round table, very like a games table, surrounded by four chairs. The men sat facing each other. Laurens opened a wooden dispatch box and produced the proposed terms, passing a copy to each British commissioner.

The document had been written in a clear, fair hand. Ross started to read, sifting through those points already familiar to him. The troops would be interned, not exchanged. There would be no protection for Tories. These clauses were unfortunate but no longer shocking. Ross had reconciled himself to their inclusion.

Then he came to a clause he had not heard mentioned or discussed before. He swallowed, struggling to maintain his composure, but he could feel the blood draining from his face. The clock on the mantel sounded very loud.

"This is a harsh article," he said.

"Which?" said Colonel Laurens, his eyes like hard black beads.

"'The troops shall march out with colors cased,'" Ross quoted, "'and drums beating a British or a German march.'"

"Yes, sir," Laurens said without expression. "It *is* a harsh article."

Ross rested one hand on the paper. According to the usual custom, surrendering troops were permitted to march with colours flying, and to play a march or tune of the victorious nation. It was an odd practice, a mocking salute from the vanquished to the victor, but to deny it was to deny the honours of war.

To deny it was to show contempt.

"A harsh article, indeed," Ross repeated. "Then, Colonel Laurens, if that is your opinion, why is it here?"

Laurens sat back in his chair, his mouth a firm line.

"Your question, Major Ross, compels an observation which I would have gladly suppressed. You seem to forget, sir, that I was present at the capitulation of Charlestown. General Lincoln had maintained a brave defence of six weeks, in open trenches with a very inconsiderable garrison, against the British army and fleet. When your lines of approach were within pistol shot of our field works, he was forced at last to surrender. Yet he was refused any other terms for his gallant garrison than marching out with colours cased and drums not beating a German or British march."

Ross knew this was true. The garrison at Charlestown had been at Clinton's mercy, in no position to ask for conditions, so he had granted none.

But that had been Clinton.

"My Lord Cornwallis did not command at Charlestown."

Laurens smiled at last. "There, sir, you extort another declaration. It is not the individual that is here considered. It is the nation. This remains an article, or I cease to be a commissioner."

The American folded his arms as if that were the final word. Ross hesitated, not ready to give in to what was clearly retaliation for the earlier insult. To punish a nation for the actions of one man was, to him, unreasonable and unacceptable.

"Our army fought a long and desperate campaign through the Carolinas and Virginia," he stated. "York Town is simply its culmination."

"The campaign may have been brave, sir," Laurens allowed, "but its culmination, as you so state, has been a demonstration of passivity in war I think unequalled."

Ross drew in a deep breath. For that, he had no rebuttal. He had heard the whispering, the complaints about Cornwallis, that the earl had lost his drive. The defence of York Town, Ross had even noted himself, had been far from vigorous.

"What of the garrison at Gloucester?" he tried. "Scarcely a shot was fired at them, which seems a demonstration of like passivity on the part of your allied forces."

"Both garrisons, Gloucester and York, are the same," Laurens insisted. "Steady contact was maintained between the two points throughout the siege."

"There is something to be said for the cavalry, however," interjected de Noailles in accented English. "Their defence of Gloucester was a fair display of gallantry, until the situation rendered them ineffectual."

"Indeed," Ross agreed, nodding. The Frenchman had tossed him just a scrap, but a nourishing scrap, nonetheless. He had forgotten about the battle between Tarleton's Legion and de Lauzun's hussars, but had heard it was the largest cavalry clash of the war.

"The cavalry was not involved in the defence of York," Laurens continued, although less forcefully. "A siege is not a place where they may easily operate. However, I concede that their resistance to the initial investment was carried out with some enthusiasm. In the spirit of compromise, I may add a stipulation that they may ride out with sabres drawn." He paused, brows knit. "That is the cavalry. The infantry must adhere to the original proposal."

Ross nodded again, but he smiled. He felt as if he had just won a victory. A small one, but a victory all the same, a welcome concession at a time when British triumphs were few.

Chapter 51

The General

*W*ashington was sharing a breakfast of *pain perdu* and sweet sauce with Rochambeau when Colonel Tilghman arrived at the headquarters tent. Tilghman bore two copies of the document the commissioners had negotiated in the Moore house.

"General Rochambeau and I will review them at once," Washington said, then gestured to the breakfast table. "Have you eaten, Colonel? If not, take your ease while we attend to business."

Tilghman accepted the invitation, and Washington gave up his chair, moving instead to his camp desk. There, he unfolded the document and began to read.

He half-feared his commissioners had made concessions, changes from the original proposal. The meeting in the Moore house had carried on into the night, the lights glowing from the parlour windows almost until dawn. It seemed to him the commissioners must have debated every article at great length.

A dull pain began to pulse in his jaw, the old toothache returning. The offending molar had not plagued him in many weeks. Not until this moment.

"To not grant the honours of war, my friend," Rochambeau said from his place at the table, "this is a very grave decision. Though I, of course, defer to your judgment on all matters."

"A grave matter, indeed," the General replied. He pressed two fingers to his jaw, waiting for the pain to subside. He thought of the anger some of his officers had expressed at the lax resistance Cornwallis had shown, how complacent had been the earl's defence. On this point, he agreed. The enemy had seemed to collapse into listlessness, save perhaps for the Royal Welch Fusiliers in their redoubt and the cavalry in Gloucester.

And there was also the matter of the siege of Charlestown. Honour decreed that a formal protest be made, and the best protest was retaliation. The British would not receive the honours of war.

"I find the article satisfactory," he stated.

"And you agree that the cavalry may ride with drawn sabres?" Rochambeau inquired.

"To that, I have no objection. Tarleton shall have his day." The cavalry commander may have been reviled by the American troops, but his bravery and resourcefulness were not in question.

He read the remaining articles, discovering that one change had been made, and that was to extend the truce. But that seemed entirely reasonable. In a few hours, that truce would be permanent.

Article Ten was troubling, for it promised immunity to all Loyalists taken in the siege. Washington drew a line through this provision with his pen. He would offer no protection to those misguided people; they would have to face the consequences of their decisions. Cornwallis might object, but the General did not think so. The earl had no fight left in him.

The pain in his jaw began to subside. The rest of the document was in order. There was no need for him to wait any longer to conclude the formal surrender.

"We will send both copies of these articles to Lord Cornwallis at once," he declared. "I will enclose a final letter with them, asking that he return them to me by eleven o'clock this morning, signed by himself and his senior naval officer. In addition, I will ask that his garrison march out and lay down their arms at two o'clock."

A soft smile played about Rochambeau's features, although Tilghman's expression remained somber.

"This thing will end today, gentlemen," the General said.

He composed the final letter to Cornwallis, and when it was ready, he sent it along with the articles of capitulation. That done, there was little to do but await the appointed hour.

Wait he did, but not at his headquarters. There was still the power of symbol to consider, so he removed to Redoubt Number Nine. There, he gathered around a little camp desk with Rochambeau, Admiral de Barras, and their aides. De Grasse alone was not there as a witness, having remained on his flagship.

At precisely eleven o'clock, a courier entered the redoubt bearing the returned articles. Washington sat on a camp stool and reread the document in its entirety. As suspected, there were no changes save the clear signatures of Lord Charles Cornwallis and a Captain Thomas Symonds.

The General set the papers on the camp desk and gazed at the sun. It rode high in a deep blue autumn sky. It was almost noon. He stood and folded his hands behind his back.

"Add this line to the bottom," he said after a moment's thought. "'Done in the trenches before Yorktown, in Virginia, October nineteenth, seventeen-eighty-one.'"

The aide who had occupied his general's seat took up a quill and scratched the new line across the first copy, then the second. When he finished, Washington took the pen and added his signature, then asked Rochambeau and de Barras to do likewise.

The General turned to Tilghman.

"It is done. Our armies may take possession of the enemy forts."

Tilghman departed on his mission. By mid-afternoon, the Union Flag that had fluttered for so long over the Hornwork was gone, and the American and French colours flew from the shattered ramparts at York Town.

Chapter 52

The Loyalist

Catherine made her way back to the hospital; but now her most pressing concern was not for the wounded, but for how she would return to Abigail and John. It was not that her sympathy or compassion for the injured troops had diminished, but that the fate of her family took precedence. That fate had never been so uncertain as it was now.

When she descended the bluff toward the Town Wharf, she discovered that part of her troubling question had been answered. Some twenty-five horses stood on the beach, formed in an orderly line. With them were as many riders, men in the green-and-black uniforms that had become so familiar. Out on the river, more horses and riders were arriving on boats and barges, traversing a plane of water as smooth as it had been rough three days ago.

She spied John standing on the wharf, conferring with his covering sergeant. She recognized him by his stance, by the way he moved his arm as he pointed to a barge that had just landed. She began to run, hoisting her petticoats and calling his name. He turned his head, his eyes meeting hers as she reached the wharf and slowed to a walk.

"Catherine!"

She was dizzy from her exertion, her throat burning with every breath, her head seeming about to split. His boots were loud on the planks, his hands strong as he took her shoulders, steadying her.

"My dear Catherine, are you quite well?"

"It is fatigue only," she said, and now her vision was clearing. She saw that John's uniform was new, the silver lace bright in the sunlight. "Has your regiment come from Gloucester?"

"It is making the journey now," he explained, his voice soft but heavy with resignation. "We are abandoning Gloucester. Leaving it. My troop was the first to cross."

"Is Abigail with you?" she asked.

"She is with Jane Bennet, wife of the captain of C Troop. She's safe."

"But where is she, John? I must speak with both of you."

"Speak with me now, but then to her you must go." He leaned forward and whispered close to her ear. "Once the horses had landed safely, I meant to seek you out, but now fortune has intervened so I find you here. You must go, Catherine. All Loyalists who did not fight are to escape on the transport vessel *Bonetta*. Abigail is there now with Mrs. Bennet, and there is room for you. The transport holds Lord Cornwallis's personal baggage. Under the surrender terms, it will not be searched."

"Escape?" The thought had never occurred to her. She still had a promise to fulfill, to meet with Daniel and give him her answer. "Abigail is on board this ship?"

"Yes." John glanced around as if fearing rebel spies here on the wharf. "All of the Loyalists shall go. All of 'em. If they do not, Catherine, they face prison or any imaginable form of persecution. There is no protection for them in the surrender proposal."

"But what of you, John? You are a Loyalist—a Tory to the rebels. They will surely punish those who fought them. You must go, too!"

His eyes were gray with melancholy as he shook his head.

"That would be tantamount to desertion, my dear. I was reluctant to take a commission, but I did it. I have fought the king's enemies. I shall ride out in my best uniform, with my head held high. I trust there is nothing worse waiting for me than parole." He paused, then added, "And, I think, eventual exile."

"You think the British cause lost then? That this defeat will bring an end to the war itself?"

John drew in a deep breath, then let it out in a long sigh.

"I do not know for certain, but it will have dire consequences. It's a shame. You know, my dear, we might have succeeded here. We could have broken out that night, if the storm had not descended on our heads. Colonel Tarleton had discovered a path by which we could have fallen on the enemy from the rear. Our cause would not have been lost. But the opportunity passed us by. It was not meant to be."

Catherine swiped at sudden tears with her fingertips.

"Oh, dear Cousin John."

He thrust a hand inside his jacket, took out a clean handkerchief.

"Do not fear for me. My destiny seems somewhat ordained, my dear cousin. In God's hands. I will face it as a soldier should."

Catherine dabbed her eyes. So, John would surrender, march out with the garrison to present his sword to his enemies. Abigail would escape, waited for her now.

And what would she do?

She remained on the wharf as the horses came ashore. Her heart and her legs felt made of stone.

Chapter 53

The Continental

The hour was nearing half-past one o'clock. Daniel had brushed his coat, polished his sword and blackened his tall boots. He stood on the right flank of his company, waiting on the edge of the Hampton Road south of York Town. Joshua stood on the left flank. They had formed with Gimat's Battalion in full marching order, with arms, knapsacks and blankets, ready to march out from the camps to take their place with Lafayette's division. Just over thirty minutes from now, they would see their enemy humbled at last.

He adjusted his cap, his sword belt. He wanted everything to be perfect, everything in its right place. He glanced toward York, hoping to catch a glimpse of the enemy as they also prepared to march out, but the assembling American battalions obscured his view. Even the captured British works were invisible, so he was forced to imagine the Continental flag, the flag of the Thirteen United States, flying over the Hornwork.

He smiled, thinking of a story that had flashed through the camps in the last hour. The placement of the Continental banner had been the object of one final battle for mastery of the British ramparts. The combatants had been a Lieutenant Ebenezer Denny, of Butler's regiment, and General von Steuben. Denny had been granted the honour of raising the colours, but when he was about to carry out this task, von Steuben had snatched the staff from his hands and driven it into the earth on the British parapet. An outraged Colonel Butler had then faced the general, hurling insults, accusing the Prussian of trying to steal glory from his regiment.

There should have been glory enough for all of them here, Daniel thought, although at least tales of such buffoonery would provide a source of entertainment at the mess fires tonight.

The field drums began to rumble, signaling it was time to move. Commands rang out, and the regiment changed formation from two ranks to a column of fours. The maneuver was performed with an unusual degree of sharpness and drive, pride having lent the drill rare precision. Next came the command to march, and the battalion headed north along the Hampton Road in perfect step, arms shouldered and bayonets fixed. The camps receded behind them.

Daniel stole a glance at the battalion colours where they hung from their tall pikes. He remembered that moment before Green Spring Farm, a memory so vivid he could smell the pines and the swamp grass, could almost hear the popping of muskets in the distance. It seemed like it had happened only days ago.

I will never lose heart again, he thought. *Not after this. Victory burns all the brighter, when in comes at the moment of greatest darkness.*

The column neared a junction with another road, a lane from the southwest. Along this route, the French column advanced on a convergent course with the Americans. The columns met, the French wheeling left along the western edge of the road, the Americans wheeling right. When each column reached its designated position, it halted, then turned inward, back into line. The result was the creation of a cordon of infantry—half French, half American.

The sergeants immediately began correcting the alignment, shouting and prodding with their spontoon staves, perfecting the intervals between the companies. Civilians from the town and surrounding country, their ordeal over, gathered behind the troops to watch; and the sergeants barked at them, warning them not to get in the way.

Daniel studied the French regiment opposite, and again he was struck by their contrast with the Continentals. The American troops had made an effort to improve their appearance, but there was little they could do with their motley assortment of blue, brown, and gray. The French seemed to shine in the sunlight, the gold fleur-de-lis glistening on their white silk flags, their uniforms freshly powdered with talc, their worn and mud-spattered gaiters discarded in favour of fresh replacements. They made a formidable sight.

But he felt no shame, no sense of being superior to his own men, his steadfast comrades. The Continentals were farmers and shopkeepers, ordinary folk who had proven they could fight as well or better than these shining professionals, and with fewer resources. For the two armies to stand together as one body was a remarkable thing in itself.

More units arrived, joining those already formed. Daniel knew he should remain steady, but his curiosity was such that he chanced a look around. The truly shabby Virginian militia took their place behind the regulars so they would not mar the spectacle. General Knox's field artillery then formed on the American right, closest to York, the field guns all in a row, bronze barrels polished and gleaming. On the opposite flank, west of the road, the cavalry took up position in a field bordered by brilliant oaks, hickories, and hemlocks. This was where the British would lay down their arms.

Last to arrive were the commanding generals, entering from the south, their respective staffs trailing behind them. Washington rode his white charger, with Rochambeau at his right hand and General Lincoln on his left. At Washington's approach, Daniel at last turned his eyes to the front. It could not be long now.

The day was warm for October, the crickets singing; and sweat prickled the skin under his coat and stock. Images came to him—of comrades lost, of his estranged brother, of the recent quarrels with Joshua, and of the long road of suffering that had brought him to this point. Now, the future held real promise, real, tangible hope. For the first time.

When the surrender parade was over, he would go to the Moore house, and there he would meet Catherine.

He sucked in a deep breath to counter his sudden impatience. He listened to the crickets, to the men in the ranks shifting and coughing. The commanding generals were speaking to each other in a low murmur. A horse snorted.

Then, from far in the distance, came a mournful wailing of fifes, a slow dirge of drums. The sound came from York Town, from beyond the trenches. It gradually grew louder.

The generals abruptly curtailed their conversation. The ceremony was about to begin.

The British were coming.

Chapter 54

The Redcoat

$\mathcal{T}$he battalion had formed in column of fours. Tom walked on the right, his fusil held at the advance. The march was ponderous, the performance of the fifes and drums sloppy. He found it difficult to stay in step, but he kept his head up, refusing to look at his feet.

The 1st Light Infantry was a composite battalion and bore no colours, but he could see the colours of the other battalions ahead. Sight of their tight black leather cases filled him with outrage and humiliation. There was no justice in this parade. Those cases were the result of conduct to which he had not been a party.

He glanced at Captain Barlow. The officer strode in front of the company, leading as if he had earned the right. And perhaps he had. It was officers like Barlow, those who no longer cared for victory, who had brought them to this, so it was only fitting they stand in the fore.

He sighed and hefted his musket, its weight seeming to have grown. His men made a sorry sight despite their clean new uniforms, new coats as red as fresh-spilled blood. It was obvious that everyone was having difficulty with the march, and it was no wonder. After morning parade and breakfast, the quartermasters had broken out the last of the rum and brandy stores.

It was bloody ridiculous, but Tom supposed it could not have been avoided. They had not wanted the liquor to fall into enemy hands, so the men had drained it to the last drop. It was that or pour it on the ground. So, now they were drunk and staggering, sweating in the heat, their collars soaked.

Some of them wept. Tom saw tears of mortification rolling down Private Hassler's cheeks, pooling in the scrubby growth at his chin. The only cheerful creature in the company was Bone. Having survived the threat of being eaten, the dog walked proudly beside his master, oblivious as to the nature of this outing.

Tom put his foot down in another lump of fresh horse manure and cursed loudly, not caring who heard. The infantry column followed the cavalry, and so had to deal with the mess. It was always that way. The cavalry rode their bony, underfed horses, swords gleaming in their hands, their honour not in question. Meanwhile, Tom's men had not been allowed to fix their bayonets. Another insult to brave men, men who had done their duty.

He wiped stinging sweat from his eye, trying to ignore the nausea building in his stomach. He could see the head of the enemy cordon drawing nearer.

"Right, lads," he said, "we're almost there. Show them what you think of this charade."

There had been a general agreement within the army, passed along during morning parade that day, that the men would turn their eyes to the right, toward the French. They would not acknowledge the shabby Americans, those rebels who could never have won their battle without French help.

The last few yards to the cordon stretched like miles. The fifes and drums of the 1st Light Infantry paused for a rest, but those of the other regiments carried on playing, the slurred music mingling, discordant. Every march was a slow-step, the quick-step no longer appropriate for so solemn an occasion. Tom heard the fifes of the 76th Regiment strike up "The King Enjoys His Own Again," an old Jacobite tune. Perhaps the Highlanders meant some irony by it. Some of the older Highlanders probably had been Scottish rebels just a few decades earlier.

Now they were within the cordon, and his men were looking to their right. He saw the faces of the French soldiers—white coats, black gaiters, black cocked hats. As usual, they were not steady in ranks, but rubbed their noses and scratched themselves without a single sergeant telling them to remain at attention. He wished he could have fought them in the open. They could never have withstood British discipline. They never had before!

A new fife tune began, and Tom drew in a sharp breath. The tune was "Yankee Doodle." It came from his left, from the American lines.

"The vainglorious bastards!" he spat. It was a deliberate act of scorn. The rebels were gloating.

He turned to face the front. Around him, the others followed suit.

"That's it, lads," he heard Sergeant Gibb mutter from within the ranks. "Don't look at either side. Don't give them the satisfaction."

Chapter 55

The Subordinate

Brigadier-General Charles O'Hara rode at the head of the column, chuckling to himself at the irony. He had always wished for an army to command, and now he had it. Cornwallis had not left his headquarters, had not come out to surrender his sword to the enemy. His fever, he had claimed, was flaring again, and he was too ill. Thus, the command had passed to O'Hara.

The second-in-command suspected the earl's attack had been the result of overwhelming passions—of shame in surrendering his garrison, of resentment toward General Clinton. And yet he did not judge Cornwallis too harshly. This was a hard day for all concerned. He knew many would say the earl was hiding from the result of what he had wrought, and that was not how a general should behave, but O'Hara was not one of those people. He was finished with questioning his troubled commander. He would leave that to others, and to history.

He winced as the fifes nearest him struck a series of foul notes, the result of some confusion over the next phrase in the melody, and he chuckled again. Onlookers would think him mad, but everything about this day seemed absurd. The improbable, the unthinkable, had come to pass. Comedy was his only defence against this tragedy.

With some effort, he composed himself as he approached the cordon, affecting a stoic expression as he entered the lane of white and blue ranks. The enemy colours snapped and waved in a sudden breath of wind, but his feelings were strangely neutral. He could find no malice within his heart for either the French or the rebels, although he had assumed he would. Perhaps this was because the responsibility for the defeat was not his.

Halfway along the cordon, just past the gleaming rebel field artillery, the opposing generals sat on their horses waiting for him. He slowed his horse to a halt, and the long column of redcoats behind him did the same, commands ringing dully in the warm air. He sighed, suddenly apprehensive. The harsh, tangible reality of what he was about to do began to take shape before his eyes.

A young man in French uniform approached on the back of a fine chestnut stallion. This could only be an aide to General Rochambeau. The Frenchman halted and swept off his hat, bowing in the saddle.

"*Bonjour, Monsieur*," he said. "I am le Comte Mathieu Dumas, of the army of His Most Christian Majesty Louis the Sixteenth."

O'Hara touched his hat. "Brigadier-General Charles O'Hara, His Majesty's Foot Guards. I have the honour to command in the place of Lieutenant-General Charles Cornwallis, who is unfortunately too ill to attend."

Dumas nodded. "Unfortunately."

"Will you kindly show me the location of General Rochambeau?" O'Hara asked next. Here was his moment, the bit of satire he had mulled over that morning while the troops were assembling.

"On my left, Monsieur. At the head of the French line."

O'Hara urged his horse forward.

"Thank you, Monsieur."

He saw Rochambeau now, a small man in a fine gold-laced coat sitting on a horse similar to Dumas'. The bigger fellow with him was Washington. O'Hara recognized the stern-faced American at once.

He was almost upon the French general when Dumas reined in next to him, his horse kicking up dust from the road. O'Hara stared at him. Then he noticed Rochambeau pointing to the man on his right. To Washington.

"You are mistaken, Monsieur," Dumas said, "for the commander-in-chief of our army is on the right."

O'Hara nodded, a slight smile on his lips. He had expected such a reaction, and it was just as well. He had simply wished to send a message to the rebels. Most of all, he wished to remind the American commander this was a victory he could never have achieved without French aid. The French had supplied the naval support, the siege guns, and had brought more troops than the Americans. Rochambeau was the senior officer, with more experience. Even the aide, Dumas, was a Frenchman.

O'Hara trusted his point had been made and now drew his sword. Turning to Washington, he said, "General Washington, I am Brigadier-General Charles O'Hara. I have the honour to be second-in-command to Lieutenant-General Charles, Earl Cornwallis, commander of the garrisons of York and Gloucester. My Lord Cornwallis sends his regrets, but he is unable to attend the parade due to illness. Thus, I present my sword to you, sir."

He held the sword out hilt-first. Washington looked at it; then he, too, faintly smiled.

"Never from such a good hand, General O'Hara," he said. "You may, however, present your sword to my own second-in-command, Major-General Benjamin Lincoln."

Washington indicated the man on his right. It was all O'Hara could do to prevent himself from exploding with laughter. The rebel could take it and send it back in kind!

He turned to face Lincoln, only to be struck with still a further irony. Lincoln was the man who had surrendered to Clinton at Charlestown.

With a shrug, he offered his sword again. Lincoln took it, then deftly reversed it, presenting the hilt.

"You may keep your sword, sir, as agreed in the terms of the surrender."

O'Hara bowed in his saddle.

"I am obliged to you, sir."

"General O'Hara," Lincoln now said, "you may direct your army to the field on your right, where sit the French hussars in a circle. Your army should enter the circle one regiment at a time, and there they should lay down their arms..."

Chapter 56

The Redcoat

$\mathcal{T}$he column was moving again, marching to the discordant screech of the fifes. Tom realized even the drummer boys were intoxicated. The column reached the end of the cordon, where it wheeled to the right, off the road and into the field where the French hussars waited. There, it halted.

He rocked on unsteady feet. It seemed they would lay down their arms one regiment at a time. He swallowed a rush of spittle, watching as Colonel Tarleton and his green-clad Loyalist cavalry entered the circle of enemy horseman. They tossed their sabres in a clattering heap. Their duty done, they wheeled into an adjacent road that would take them back to York Town.

Next, an infantry regiment entered the field. Tom heard growling, weeping, men shouting insults at the victors, the term "rebel scum" a popular refrain. They threw their muskets next to the swords, cast off their leather accoutrements, letting them fall wherever they might. When they followed the cavalry out of the field, all sense of order in their ranks was gone.

Tom watched a German regiment enter the circle. In contrast to the redcoats, their ranks were steady. They grounded their arms in neat rows and placed their belts and cartridge boxes next to them. With calm precision they reformed fours, then marched back to the road to await their imprisonment. He recognized the superiority of their conduct but knew he would not see its like reflected in the British units. Not this army in its present state. He could feel everything he had believed in since his enlistment begin to crumble, decaying, disintegrating before his eyes.

His regiment drew closer to the circle in fits and starts, marching a few paces then halting. There were officers weeping on the side of the field, having abandoned their men. Tom sneered at them in disgust. At least Captain Barlow had kept his place in front of the company, his back rigid. At least he had the courage not to run.

They marched a few more paces, and now the vanguard of the 1st Light Infantry had entered the field. The circle of hussars drew closer. Tom watched the troops in front of him throw down their weapons on the growing pile. Some men appeared to be trying to break their musket locks, to deny the arms to the enemy.

At last Tom walked into the circle. His legs felt heavy, as if he were wading through water. He gripped his musket in his hand—his polished fusil, his beloved companion of some six years.

"There, now, my fine fellows," a French cavalry officer called, "it is all so bad? You did your best, did you not?"

Tom agreed with the hussar, knew the fellow was right. He *had* done his best, had not failed. His comrades had not failed. Gibb and even Hassler had not failed. Their commanders had failed. The generals and politicians in London had failed them.

"Carry on, Sergeant Martin," Captain Barlow said. "We must present a brave face."

Tom turned on his heels, facing across the front of his shrunken company, the company he had trained and nurtured. His voice cracked only once as he gave the appropriate commands.

"Company, order your...firelocks! Company, ground your...firelocks!"

The men responded, not according to the manual but by dropping their muskets on the pile. Gibb threw his aside before stepping back, breaking ranks and moving away on his own. Bone trailed at his feet. Hassler continued to weep, and cast his musket down with such force the flint splintered and flew in all directions.

Finally, it was Tom's turn to approach the heap of weapons. He raised his beloved fusil above his head and brought it down hard against the ground, determined no one should ever make a prize of it. A sob of frustration broke from deep within his throat. He raised the fusil and brought it down a second time, then once more, until he finally heard the stock splinter.

It was the finest friend he had ever known. He tossed it on the pile like so much refuse, and then walked away with his head up and tears streaming.

Chapter 57

The Loyalist

*C*atherine watched the surrender parade from a hillock near the edge of the Hampton Road. She wept softly when she saw John pass at the head of his troop, his sword gleaming proudly in his hand; but the tears came in a rush when the greencoat cavalry entered the field to lay down their arms. As an officer, John would keep his sword, but he had surrendered to the rebels at last. The world he had known and loved had disappeared forever.

She thought of his last words to her, his last act of kindness. He had explained that the *Bonetta* would likely remain at anchor for a few more days. It was a small vessel and capable of carrying only a very few to safety, and a berth aboard was much in demand. He was still a man of means and had secured passage for the sisters, and had arranged for a boat to meet Catherine at the docks tomorrow morning. The boat would take her to the transport and to Abigail.

It was a simple plan, but Catherine knew there was a second option. She could ask the boatmen to return both her and Abigail to shore, giving up their precious berths to others. From there, they would join Daniel and the Continentals.

She wandered into the road, stood in the dust. The parade was nearing its conclusion, the infantry now throwing down their muskets. She realized it was already three o'clock. When the parade dismissed, when the rebels returned to their camps, it would be close to half-past the hour. Daniel would be waiting for her at the Moore house. She would have to give him her answer.

She had kept John's handkerchief, and with it, she dried her remaining tears. Her love for Daniel was true, but she knew now she had underestimated her lurking resentment against his cause. Witnessing John's surrender had brought it bubbling to the surface, like some foul black oil from the depths of her soul. To rush into the arms of her dear cousin's enemies now, at the moment of his defeat, seemed traitorous.

The resentment might fade in time—Daniel's simple decency could smother it. Or it could poison her love for him.

She turned her back on the parade, making her way along the dusty track. Her answer was ready, her decision made, and she knew nothing would change her mind.

Chapter 58

The Redcoat

*T*hey had marched back to the camps, back to the Hornwork, as if nothing had changed. There, they sat in a circle just as they had after Tom's musketry sessions, when they had cleaned the musket locks and Tom had done his inspection. But now their muskets were gone along with their freedom, and rebel guards stood on what had been their rampart.

Tom rested his head in his hands, trying in vain to shut out Hassler's choking sobs. The sound was too terrible to bear. He had struggled to help Hassler find a proper home here in the army; but it had all come to naught, just like everything else he had struggled for these past six years. His days as a soldier had gained him nothing, and now he faced a future that was only a black, empty, bottomless pit.

He glanced at Gibb, but the other sergeant had retreated into a world all his own. He sat with one arm around Bone, his eyes wide and staring, murmuring, "We'll still have each other's company, then, shan't we? That's my boy."

Yes, Tom thought, *we will all have each other's company for a while yet.*

He looked away, strangely unmoved by Gibb's particular affliction. He turned instead to Private Webb, who sat favouring his injured leg.

"How's the leg, then, Sam?" Tom asked.

"It aches a bit, Sarge. I marched better than most out there today, I'd warrant. It don't trouble me much, thanks to my angel."

Tom nodded. Webb had told them all about the woman who had sat by him day and night.

"I only wish your angel could have delivered us from what our future now holds."

He regretted his words at once, for he saw the fear reflected in Sam's trembling lips.

"Think they'll keep us in an old hulk, Sergeant? I wouldn't like that, not one bit."

"I don't know, Sam. Perhaps it won't be quite so disagreeable." But he knew the prisons on both sides were notorious for their overcrowding, their poor food, the filth and disease that were a more certain path to the grave than the battlefield. "I'll look after you lads, don't worry."

And as he said it, he knew that he would. That would be his final task, his final call to duty, his final objective. They were still his company, still his responsibility. He rubbed angrily at sudden tears, and for a moment hid his face, stifling a growing swell of emotion. His world would not end here. He would not give up on these men yet. He would see them through, as a good sergeant should.

So, it falls to me again.

At last, he raised his head and found himself facing a small gathering of officers in the rear of the Hornwork. Barlow and Abercrombie were among them. Tom wondered how long the officers would remain in York Town before they took ship to New York or home to England.

The sooner the better.

Barlow met his eye. For a second, he hesitated; then, he detached himself from the group and approached the company. Tom fought a sudden wave of nausea. Perhaps it was the effect of the rum, but also, he did not wish to speak to the captain, although he knew he had no choice.

He pushed to his feet. Barlow halted in front of him. Tom kept his hands at his sides, unwilling to salute. The men watched from the ground.

"Well, Sergeant Martin," Barlow said, "this may be the last time we meet."

Tom nodded. "Indeed it may, sir."

Barlow shifted from foot to foot, one hand resting on his sword hilt.

"You know that I will do all that I can for you."

Tom shook his head. "You can do nothing for us, sir."

He did not mean it as an insult. It was the simple truth. Barlow was utterly powerless, and the stricken look on the captain's face confirmed that he knew it. He turned away, his gaze taking in the rest of the men. His neck bulged as he swallowed.

"Well, lads," he said, and his voice cracked. He cleared his throat. "This is to be our final assembly."

The men looked at him, but only Sam Webb climbed to his feet, using his crutch. Perhaps shamed by his example, the rest slowly followed, one by one, assembling on either side of Tom.

"You were a good company," Barlow continued. "You always did your duty and more. You have been brave, but you must muster all of your courage for the days ahead. Britain will not allow her sons to languish for long, forgotten. You will be rewarded for your service. I will see to it."

No one spoke. They regarded him with open mouths, tears streaking through the grime on their sunken cheeks.

"If the government will do nothing, I will use whatever influence I have, whatever power at my disposal. I will bequeath the remainder of my days to that goal. You have my word on it."

"Thank you, sir," Gibb said, at last coming out of his reverie. "Me and Bone both thank you. You were always good to us."

"Yes, thank you, sir," said Sam, and now the rest joined in, a chorus of thanks. Barlow seemed to expand with pride—and sorrow.

Only Tom did not join in. With all his heart, he wanted to believe the captain's words were sincerely meant, but here Barlow was, going home on parole, in most respects a free man, while the company would fritter away the rest of the war in prison. It was easy for the captain to voice these grand sentiments, but he had spoken grand words all along—words of defiance against the rebels—and Tom suspected those words had meant nothing.

You should have used your influence before, he wanted to say. Or even *Very fine for you, who can go home on parole and stand up in parliament with your Whiggish friends and proclaim, "We told you so."*

But he held his tongue. He would not spoil this for the lads.

"Farewell, then," Barlow said at last. He raised his hand, and the men replied, crying, "Farewell, sir! Farewell, Captain!"

"Farewell," Barlow repeated, and he met Tom's eye one last time. Tom saw the hurt there, and something else. Remorse, perhaps. Or guilt.

"Well, then," Barlow muttered. Then he turned on his heels.

Tom stared after him, and something welled up from within his breast—a need to make things right. He thought of the conduct of the army that afternoon, the way they had behaved during the surrender parade. Later, he had been ashamed of himself and of his comrades, yet here he was again, acting with open insubordination, displaying a lack of even basic courtesy. In front of the lads.

The soldier in him remembered his duty, and his anger, his bitterness, seemed to wither. He wanted nothing more than to believe in some bright moment somewhere in his future, whatever its source.

"Sir!" he called.

Barlow halted, then looked back.

Tom brought his hand up in a salute.

"Farewell, sir!"

Barlow did nothing for a few seconds; then, he raised his hand to his cap. His face broke into a smile, but a moment later, that dissolved into a sob.

"Oh, my good men!" he cried. "I will not forget you!"

He turned again, moving quickly away, head bowed. The men called after him just as they had done before. Barlow passed the gathering of officers, who watched him stride away from the Hornwork, disappearing behind the Nelson house.

"That's that, then," Sergeant Gibb declared. He glanced at Bone. "Eh, my fine little fellow?"

"I don't want to go back to jail," Hassler suddenly groaned. The big man was weeping again, rubbing at his eyes with a dirty fist.

Tom would listen to him no more.

"Don't worry, lads," he said, trying to sound cheerful, to take command of the situation. "Our internment will be brief. The war won't last much longer."

The rebels could absorb their defeats, but Britain could not. The war was already unpopular with the British public, and the opposition in Parliament was complaining that it had become too expensive. Support for continuing the long struggle would collapse now. Then Tom and his men would be free.

Chapter 59

The Continental

"The colonel wishes for the company of all of his officers this evening," Major Osborne announced when they returned to camp. "There will be a small affair in his tent in celebration of our big affair."

The major smiled at his weak jest, and Joshua chuckled.

"We would be most honoured to join in, sir. Won't we, little brother?"

"Indeed," Daniel agreed, but he was watching the light infantry as they milled about the camp's streets, laughing, dancing. Someone had produced a fiddle and was sawing away at a New England hornpipe. They were overjoyed at their triumph, at taking more than seven thousand British soldiers prisoner. The prisoners would not be exchanged but would remain interned until the conclusion of the war. The officers could go where they wished on parole, but they could never again take up arms against the thirteen United States.

"I will be happy to attend," he added, giving Major Osborne his full attention. "Though I'm afraid I have another pressing engagement at this moment. One for which I am already late."

Joshua nodded, a sly glint in his eyes.

"You'll be bringing a guest tonight, then?"

"A pair of guests. If all goes well."

Joshua reached out and took his brother's hand, holding it in a firm grip.

"I trust it will."

"Thank you," Daniel said, "big brother."

He gave Joshua a wink. Then, after touching his cap to Major Osborne, he started for the edge of camp, making for the head of Wormley Creek. The cheerful noises of celebration receded behind him, although they did not fade completely. Instead, they mingled with the comforting music of the crickets, and of the long grass as it brushed against his legs.

He passed the silent batteries, the unmanned trenches—vestiges of their struggle here. A little farther on was a grove of brilliant hardwoods, and as he entered the trees he whistled to himself. He quickened his pace, a sense of giddiness rising. Catherine would be there. He did not want to make her wait.

The Moore house came into sight, and he slowed his pace, looking left and right. There seemed to be no one here. He halted in front of the house, near the bottom of the steps.

"Catherine!" he called. "Catherine!"

"I'm here!" She emerged from behind the house, and he breathed a sigh of relief. He saw her clearly now, more clearly than he had in the trenches. She wore a new rust-coloured short gown, her petticoat a bright blue. Her face was shaded by her straw hat, but her neck, her beautiful long neck, seemed to glow in the sunshine.

Crossing the last few yards to her side, he threw his arms around her, knocking her hat askew. Her slender ones encircled his waist.

"I was early," she gasped. "I was wandering the grounds. I didn't mean to frighten you."

"You haven't frightened me," he said, letting her go then clasping her hands and standing back to gaze at her, to take in the glorious sight of her. Her return of his embrace seemed to confirm his hopes. She would come with him! He knew it!

Then, he realized she was alone.

"You have not brought Abigail?"

"No, Daniel."

She released his hands and turned away, gazing out over the river. He stared at her, swallowing. Sudden dread was a cold hand squeezing his heart.

Surely, this is nothing but last-minute doubts, he told himself. *Surely, I could not have been so wrong.*

"You have your answer for me?" he asked. "I can't wait any longer, Catherine."

"I will not make you wait." Yet she paused; and he saw the sorrow, the conflict. "I've come to say goodbye."

He could not speak. He refused to believe what she was saying. He shoved his hands into his coat pockets. He had not prepared himself to be rejected.

"You must understand," she continued. "My feelings for you are unchanged, but I have decided to return to New York with Abigail, and with John. We will remain together until the war ends."

"Returning to New York?" he repeated. "You said you despised it there!"

"I did. Most likely, I still will, but it is the only place for me now."

He would not accept her answer, and searched for a way to change it.

"I don't understand your decision, Catherine. I don't want you to leave. I want you to come with me."

He took her by the arm, and she turned to face him. He pulled her closer. She did not draw away immediately, and he held her.

"It's difficult for me to explain," she murmured, stepping back at last and returning her gaze to the distance.

"I will give you everything you need," he tried. "We would be happy together."

"We were happy, if but for a short time. We will never lose that. But you still have your duty as a soldier, Daniel. That hasn't changed. Nor has my duty to my family."

He placed one finger under her chin, turned her face toward his, and kissed her. She yielded, responding, and he felt a surge of triumph as he drew her into his arms again. He would convince her!

The kiss was long, and then he kissed her cheeks, her ears. Her hat dropped to the ground, but he did not care. She *would* change her mind!

But at length she backed away, shaking her head.

"No, Daniel," she whispered. "No."

Her voice made a somber echo in his ears. He clenched his jaw, and the crushing sense of loss returned.

"Why did you even send me the letter? Why come to find me yesterday, only to reject me now? It makes no sense!"

"Oh, please don't be angry!" She buried her face in her hands. "I didn't know for certain what I would do until the surrender parade today. I didn't know. I have to find a way to make you understand. I have to make you see…" She paused and looked at him, as though she had just made a decision. "Come with me, and I'll show you. Please, Daniel."

He sighed. "Of course I will."

"Then take my hand."

He retrieved her hat, then stared at her slender outstretched fingers for a long moment. He obeyed her demand, and without another word, she drew him away from the house. He followed willingly, eager for even a few more minutes of her company, a few more minutes to state his case.

They crossed open fields toward the edge of the bluff, moving in silence. Before them loomed the American first parallel, abandoned now. When they reached it, she started to climb the parapet. He helped her, then scrambled up in turn.

"There," she said. "Look."

She pointed to the siege works and the British forts, the Hornwork and Redoubt Number Ten, all flying the Continental flag. Silent sentries lined the second parallel, guarding the British prisoners. Beyond squatted the ruined houses of the town, and in the river, the *Bonetta* lay at anchor.

"The significance of this escapes me," he admitted. "I see only what I've been staring at for weeks."

"And it will be here for many more weeks," she said, "and for years after that. We have made wounds in the land, wounds that will not heal for generations. These earthworks will remain for centuries, a reminder of what happened here."

"What happened here was a victory for the cause of independence."

"A victory for some, a defeat for others. You know my opinions where this war is concerned, Daniel." She spoke softly. "These earthworks, these scars on the land, are for me a reminder of homes, families, and lives torn asunder, and of the dead and the maimed. With this siege, my anger has only grown, and it, too, will not pass away quickly."

"We all have such wounds, Catherine." From the camps came a rising din of celebration, laughter and music. He listened, but it brought him no joy. "When this ends, we all must learn to live together as we did before, in peace."

"When this ends, maybe. For now, I would not have the anger in my heart corrupt what I also carry there—my regard...my love...for you. I must work to heal myself, to help my family in these hard times and the harder times to come."

He grasped at what he hoped was her implication.

"Then in time, you will change your mind!"

She touched his arm.

"There is nothing to change. My heart is yours. Perhaps, when the war ends, you may seek me in New York. But not before that, Daniel. Not before."

Her voice broke. A great tear rolled down each cheek, hung for an instant, and fell. Daniel heard them strike the earth at his feet, like solitary raindrops.

"Why wait. Why not now?"

Her voice was full of anguish.

"I have told you why. I don't expect you to wait for me. That's not what I ask. I merely state the facts."

"The fact is that I love you, that I want to live my life with you."

"Please, don't try further to sway me. Abigail is waiting, and I won't leave her. It's too late. The longer I remain here with you, the more difficult this becomes!"

She embraced him again, kissed him again, and he considered trying to hold on to her, not to let her go.

But he could not force her. She was free to do as she wished.

Her lips brushed his cheek a last time, and he felt her warm tears on his skin. At last, she drew away.

"I will seek you out," he promised, "when this is done."

She met his gaze. He saw her love reflected in her eyes, and mingled sorrow and resignation.

"Goodbye, Daniel."

She started down from the parapet to the open ground between the parallels.

"I won't say goodbye," he called. "I *will* see you again!"

She paused, turning to look back.

"I will never forget you, Daniel Brattle."

Then she resumed her course back across the siege lines. He watched her climb the second parallel, move through the standing pickets. Then she was gone, swallowed in the ruins of York Town.

Chapter 60

The General

*W*ashington took in the view from the head of the table, marveling at the change the last months had wrought. In the spring, the war for independence had been on its last legs, and now this. This laughter, this merriment. Hope renewed. A splendid dinner in celebration of victory, the mess tent filled with cheer, the candles warm, silverware gleaming on spotless linen, dishes of fish and fowl, eggs and beef, fresh vegetables. The courses were laid out on the table in their proper places, according to the fashion; and the guests were arrayed on either side, resplendent in their best uniforms. There was the blue-and-buff of the Continentals, the white of royal France, and perhaps most significantly, the scarlet of Great Britain. For a short while, at least, hostilities had capitulated, civilization returning for a brief interlude.

Perhaps it would soon return for longer. The General could not be certain. For now, he would enjoy this respite, and enjoy this banquet, the best his commissaries had been able to provide. He did not even need to fret over aching teeth, for the offensive molar remained quiet, although it was best he avoid chewing on his left side.

Rochambeau sat on his left hand, and the Frenchman raised his glass.

"A glass of wine with you, *mon generale*! This is most excellent fare. I will be—how would you say?—hard-pressed to challenge it."

Washington returned the personal toast. Rochambeau would host a dinner tomorrow, and would try to outdo his ally.

"I thank you, sir, and anticipate the challenge."

The Frenchman sipped his wine then turned to respond to something his neighbor had said. The neighbour was Henry Knox, beaming behind his spectacles. Many of the key players in the drama were here. There was the stoic General Wayne, making a contrast to the open gaiety of his companion, the Marquis de Lafayette. On Washington's immediate right sat the cheerful figure of Brigadier Charles O'Hara, and next to him Major Alexander Ross. This dinner was in O'Hara's honour, and his company had so far proven most agreeable, his manner full of charm and wit. He had managed to provoke a smile or open laughter with almost every comment.

"I may declare with certainty," he was saying, "that Irish horses are superior to any one may find in England. They are the backbone of our cavalry!"

A grinning Knox then asked, "And what of Virginia horses, General?"

O'Hara seemed to ponder.

"On that subject, sir, I confess to knowing very little. Perhaps I will make a study of it!"

Knox chuckled. "I know very little of it myself, being from New England."

Washington listened with increasing pleasure. Such was the nature of the conversation—talk of horses and hounds, amusing anecdotes, shared stories of traditions from the disparate armies. Unfortunately, the French guests were at something of a disadvantage where language was concerned, especially the junior officers near the foot of the table. It was a pity Colonel Tilghman was not here to help with translation, but he had already departed for Philadelphia.

"I have here the dispatch announcing our victory," Washington had said to him just a few hours earlier. "Will you deliver it to Congress?"

"With honour, sir," Tilghman replied. "And with pleasure."

And so he had gone north on his errand while, here at this table, the victory had become a forbidden topic. There had been little or no mention of the war or politics, as was proper in any officer's mess. Even so, Washington, as he thought of Tilghman's historic ride, could not help casting his mind ahead, thinking, planning his next move.

He recalled something he had said to Rochambeau earlier in the day.

"This victory has taught me a few lessons. I believe we may have underestimated the importance of the naval campaign. *I* have underestimated it. I should have given the matter more weight from the beginning."

He had brought overwhelming force against a vulnerable enemy, and so had succeeded; but he could not have done it without the French Navy. Politics, he realized, had also done much for them here. The alliance, the strategy of diplomacy, had led to the removal of Britain's great advantage—her naval superiority.

So have I achieved what I wished to, he thought.

His chief aim had been to keep the cause of independence from dying, to sustain the morale of the country, and to throw Britain off-balance. That had been done, but there was a danger in allowing the light of a single triumph to blind him to the grand scheme, a danger in becoming complacent. Britain still possessed sizable garrisons in Savannah, Charlestown, Canada, and in New York; and together, those troops still outnumbered his Continentals. King George and Parliament had the power to continue the war, if they so chose.

It may be worth considering a secondary strike, now while we hold the initiative. Before winter set in, and the campaign season ended.

Such an operation would be possible if he could convince Admiral de Grasse to remain a few more weeks. Perhaps they could launch an attack on Savannah, or Charlestown.

It was an intriguing notion. At the very least, they would have to discuss further cooperation in the spring, for the war would not grind to a halt. He would continue to push, and push hard.

"Will Lord North resign, d'ye think?" he heard Knox say, and he started out of his introspection, wondering how such a question could have arisen. Surely, the comment was inappropriate, the subject political, and a direct reference to Britain's defeat.

Lord North was the much-vexed prime minister, a man struggling to maintain his government through an increasingly unpopular war. His resignation, as a result of the events here at York, would mean certain victory for the Whig party, who would form the next government. The Whigs favoured peace with the colonies, and recognition of their independence. For the Americans, there could be no better result.

A hush had fallen over the table. The General imagined he saw Knox turning a deeper shade of red than the facings on his artillery uniform.

"I am afraid it may be true," Major Ross said at length. "Poor Lord North was at the end of his rope *before* the siege began. He has few friends left, and now they will be fewer. Your success here at York may mean it is all over for him."

The silence continued, but behind the embarrassment the General detected something else. Ross's words confirmed what they all had hoped to be true.

He met Lafayette's eye. The young marquis smiled.

"Gentlemen!" O'Hara suddenly cried, "I believe I speak for most when I say that myself and my fellow officers have been truly touched by the civility displayed by you, our adversaries." He nodded. "Regardless of the nature or whims of kings and governments, we are like-minded fellows here. I, for one, wish only to dwell on aspects of friendship."

"Indeed," Washington agreed. "We must not speak of adversity, a subject we all know well enough, I am certain. We must take care of our guests, and speak in positives. It was never our desire to make a lasting enemy of England."

As he spoke, his thoughts of the future returned—not of the immediate, of campaigns and marches, but of the long road he could see now stretching before them.

"We shall see what happens," he found himself saying, and he was no longer referring to Lord North and his troubles. "We shall see what comes of this. What our country may achieve from here, that is the question before us."

The possibilities were endless.

Chapter 61

The Commander-in-Chief

Sir Henry Clinton paced the quarterdeck of the *Ramillies*, the flagship of Admiral Thomas Graves. He was angry and confused. He had finally arrived in the Chesapeake, bringing the promised reinforcements, but the situation no longer seemed to require his presence.

The fleet had encountered His Majesty's Ship *Nymphe* off Cape Charles, and aboard the vessel had been a dispatch from Lord Cornwallis speaking of imminent defeat. To make matters worse, among the passengers had been a few ragged soldiers who claimed to have escaped from York Town. Cornwallis, they said, had surrendered.

Clinton held the earl's dispatch in his hand. It was dated the fifteenth, and it was now the twenty-fourth. He unfolded it and scanned its first few lines for what must have been the tenth time.

"The enemy carried two advanced redoubts by storm," Cornwallis stated, explaining that the redoubts had now become part of a second parallel. That was troubling news, but not half so troubling as a line near the bottom that read, "The safety of the place is therefore so precarious that I cannot recommend that the fleet and army should run great risk in endeavouring to save us."

A few gulls circled and cried overhead. Clinton folded the letter and thrust it into his pocket. He vowed not to read it again.

"These people who escaped from the beleaguered post," he began, addressing Admiral Graves. "They tell us Cornwallis has capitulated, but I find that completely incredible! Lord Cornwallis is the most energetic soldier in the service."

Graves shrugged. "We have since picked up other escapees who have related the same sad tale, Sir Henry."

"Preposterous. Are we certain these 'escapees' are not simply deserters, attempting to justify themselves?"

Graves expression was benign, unworried.

"They did not flee at our approach, as deserters would inevitably do. Indeed, they sought us out."

Clinton shook his head in disgust. If such a calamity had occurred, he knew that he, as commander-in-chief, would take the blame, even though it was not his fault. He could not have departed New York earlier than he did. He could never have endangered that post to relieve another. He had been uncertain of Mister Washington's movements and intentions, and there had been the requirements of the navy to consider, the readiness of their ships, the finicky nature of wind and tide.

"We must have further information," he stated. "I am not satisfied with what we have learned today."

Admiral Graves pursed his lips. "You wish to wait, then?"

"Yes. Wait." Clinton was a patient man. He could afford to tarry here a few days more.

He turned to stare at the wide green horizon. He could smell pines on the offshore breeze.

"We have thirty-six men-of-war in our fleet," he said, affecting a note of confidence, "and more are scheduled to join us. Our transports carry seven thousand troops. If Lord Cornwallis can hold the enemy for even a single day more, we will relieve him."

"The French fleet is still in the bay, Sir Henry," Graves pointed out. "We would be obliged to deal with them before landing our troops."

"I have every confidence in your abilities, Admiral," Clinton stated, adding, "despite recent setbacks." He clenched his hands into fists. "If only we knew for sure what has happened!"

The green shore loomed near, but its secrets were closed to him. He strained to catch some echo of distant cannon fire, some evidence that defiance continued; but the only sounds that met his ears were the wind in the rigging, the creaking of timbers, and the lonely cries of the gulls.

Chapter 62

The Continental

Jt was November, and it was cold. Daniel's breath steamed, and when his shoes sank into the wet sand, a trickle of frigid water seared his feet. Another morning parade had come and gone, and he and Joshua had decided to take a turn on the beach below the bluff east of the ruined town to escape the camps for an hour now that dull military routine had resumed.

York Town had become a garrison outpost like any other. The British prisoners had been marched off to their confinement in Winchester and Fort Frederick, and the French Navy had also departed. Rumours of a surprise attack on Savannah had persisted for a few days, but Daniel had never given them much weight. The season was too advanced. It was almost time for the army to enter winter quarters.

He cursed his leaking shoes. The sky was overcast, and the sluggish river resembled molten lead. The crickets had at last ceased their symphony, and the wind had begun its autumn work, stripping the tallest trees bare. The section of beach seemed secluded and lonely.

"I wonder if General Washington was much vexed at the departure of our seaborne allies," Joshua commented. "Though I suppose the navy had never agreed to remain with us beyond the end of last month. They did as they promised."

"We all did as we promised," Daniel said. "Now I suppose a rest is in order, for us and for the French."

Joshua sighed. "Some of us would have fancied a trip to Georgia this time of year. I would much rather winter there or here in Virginia than in the Hudson highlands."

The French, it had been decided, would stay in York, but the Continentals, including those under Lafayette, would return to New York.

"At least we'll be back in country we know. So, our long adventure here in the south is over at last."

They rounded a projection in the bluff, and now the shattered houses of York Town came into view. They paused. Water Street was still covered in debris and the remains of the makeshift shelters the inhabitants had employed during the siege. The shelters were abandoned now, the citizens having returned to what was left of their homes.

Daniel studied the flotsam on the sand. Momentous events had transpired here, and although he had shared the army's joy, the country's elation, that joy had been tainted with loss. Not a lost life, although those had been many; but a lost dream, a fantasy that had slipped through his fingers.

Still, I did not believe in victory here, he chided himself, *and yet it came. Now the army will return to the Hudson valley, and the city of New York is so close...*

Joshua tapped him on the arm.

"In the spring, maybe there will be a new campaign. The last, I expect. Perhaps we'll take New York now, eh?"

"I'm heartily sick of campaigns," Daniel stated. "As you well know. But there is no place I would rather go, I think, than New York."

Joshua rolled his eyes skyward.

"Daniel the mooncalf! I once had a younger brother who was a jolly and agreeable companion. Now, where has he got himself off to?"

"Well, I apologize if I have not been the best of company," Daniel sulked.

Joshua scowled. "Don't brood on her any longer, Daniel. She made her decision, and you must accept it. What one expects is not always what one gets."

Daniel was not impressed.

"So, that is your sage advice? Shouldn't you urge me not to give up the fight?"

"She's a woman!" Joshua scoffed. "She's not independence, she's not the personification of happiness."

"She is for me," Daniel insisted, but as he said it he realized how foolish it must sound.

"You were always so stubborn," Joshua continued. "Well, little brother—"

"I do wish you would not always refer to me as—"

"Well, then, my dear fellow, my dear captain, you have been moping for weeks, and the company is suffering for it. Catherine Seawell is one battle. And as you must have learned by now, there will always be other battles."

Daniel kicked at the sand. Had the company observed these sullen moods? *Had* he allowed them to affect his duty?

But he was unable to ponder these questions, for Joshua was not finished.

"You've occupied yourself for so long looking in one direction that you've blinded yourself to the true significance of our victory here. In Europe, they call America the New World, and that, I submit, is an accurate description. A new world lies waiting for us. This is victory! Your life, like the country, is a blank slate from now on. Make of it what you will, with no one to tell you otherwise. If you fail at one thing, try another. Seize the opportunity, brother."

"Yes, yes," Daniel said. Now, he was irritated, but he controlled the urge to quarrel.

"Come along—this struggle isn't over, but with God's blessing and continued vigilance on our part, it soon will be. Your men need you in good spirits." Joshua pulled his coat lapels close as a breath of cold wind rose, rippling the surface of the river. "You're still a captain of light infantry in the Continental Army of the United States."

"I am ever so glad that we saved your hide after Green Spring so you could remind me of these things."

Joshua laughed and clapped him on the shoulder.

"So am I, Captain Brattle. As I believe I am fond of observing, that's what elder brothers are for. Now, we have our dinners waiting for us, and after that, a long march north, a war to conclude, and a nation to build."

Daniel nodded. Joshua's words rang true. Some of them.

He felt himself rallying.

"You're right," he said. "In part."

He had fought, and he had won, and now no one, not his brother, not his commanding officer, not even General Washington, would tell him what he could or could not do with the remainder of his life. He had almost given up on the cause of independence, but he would never give up on the cause of his own happiness.

He would make a new life in this new world, and he would do so with Catherine at his side. He would find her.

He took a few paces along the sand.

"Come on, brother. Let's get back to camp. I'm hungry, and mean to eat my fill."

END

About the Author

HAROLD R. THOMPSON is the author of the For Empire and Honour series of military historical novels, which includes *Dudley's Fusiliers*, *Guns of Sevastopol*, and *Sword of the Mogul*. He is also an amateur filmmaker and writes short science fiction in addition to historical fiction. He works for Parks Canada and lives with his family in Nova Scotia.

About the Artist

APRIL MARTINEZ was born in the Philippines and raised in San Diego, California, daughter to a US Navy chef and a US postal worker. Dissatisfied that she couldn't make use of her creative tendencies, she started working as an imaging specialist for a big book and magazine publishing house in Irvine learned the trade of graphic design. From that point on, she worked as a graphic designer and webmaster while doing freelance art and illustration at night. April lives with her cat in Orange County, California.

www.ingramcontent.com/pod-product-compliance
Lightning Source LLC
Chambersburg PA
CBHW021956010726
47494CB00003B/762